Tabini smiled.

"Time is ours now; perhaps not, if these remote aliens begin to dictate the schedule. Therefore, paidhi-ji, I'm sending you to the station."

My God, Bren thought.

And: No. I can't.

It was the dream of his life, that the space program should have just gotten off the ground with him to witness it. That *Shai-shan* should turn out to be his creation . . . he'd stood on the side of the runway and watched its first flight half a year ago, watched the shuttle become a gleam in the sky, and a dot, and a memory and a hope. When, two weeks later, he had stood on that same runway and watched *Shai-shan* land as easily as any airliner—God, he'd wept.

But go *up* there? That wasn't for *him*.

His face, he discovered, didn't react, hadn't reacted. Like his predecessor, Wilson, who'd forgotten how to deal with human emotion, he'd stopped reacting.

"Aiji-ma," he said quietly, accepting that this would happen, "on this flight?"

"On this flight," Tabini said.

DAW TITLES BY C.J. CHERRYH

THE ALLIANCE-UNION UNIVERSE

The Company Wars
DOWNBELOW STATION

The Era of Rapprochement
SERPENT'S REACH
FORTY THOUSAND IN GEHENNA
MERCHANTER'S LUCK

The Chanur Novels
THE PRIDE OF CHANUR
CHANUR'S VENTURE
THE KIF STRIKE BACK
CHANUR'S HOMECOMING
CHANUR'S LEGACY

The Mri Wars
THE FADED SUN OMNIBUS

Merovingen Nights (Mri Wars Period)
ANGEL WITH THE SWORD

The Age of Exploration
CUCKOO'S EGG
VOYAGER IN NIGHT
PORT ETERNITY

The Hanan Rebellion
BROTHERS OF EARTH
HUNTER OF WORLDS

THE MORGAINE CYCLE
THE MORGAINE SAGA OMNIBUS
EXILE'S GATE

EALDWOOD
THE DREAMING TREE

THE FOREIGNER UNIVERSE
FOREIGNER
INVADER
INHERITOR

PRECURSOR
DEFENDER*
EXPLORER*

OTHER NOVELS
PORT ETERNITY
HESTIA
WAVE WITHOUT A SHORE

*Forthcoming from DAW Books

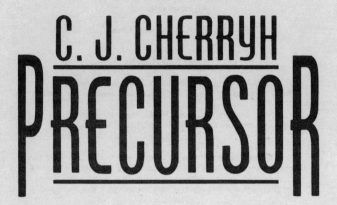

C. J. CHERRYH
PRECURSOR

DAW BOOKS, INC.

DONALD A. WOLLHEIM, FOUNDER

375 Hudson Street, New York, NY 10014

ELIZABETH R. WOLLHEIM
SHEILA E. GILBERT
PUBLISHERS

www.dawbooks.com

First Paperback Printing, October 2000
1   2   3   4   5   6   7   8   9   10

To Kira and Kasi

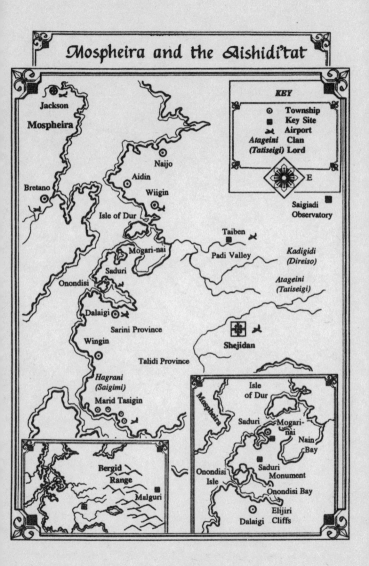

Mospheira and the Aishidi'tat

KEY

⊙ Township
■ Key Site
✈ Airport
Atageini
(Tatiseigi) Clan Lord

E

Jackson
Mospheira
Naijo
Aidin
Bretano
Wiigin
Isle of Dur
Saigiadi
Observatory
Taiben ✈
Mogari-nai
Kadigidi
(Direiso)
Padi Valley
Saduri
Onondisi
Atageini
(Tatiseigi)
Dalaigi ⊙ ✈
Sarini Province
Shejidan
Wingin ⊙
Talidi Province
Hagrani
(Saigimi)
Marid Tasigin

Bergid Range
Malguri

Isle of Dur
Mospheira
Saduri
Mogari-nai
Nain Bay
Onondisi Isle
Saduri Monument
Onondisi Bay
Dalaigi ⊙
Elijiri Cliffs

1

The jet that waited these days was passenger-only, carrying no baggage but that which pertained to the paidhi and whatever diplomats happened to be traveling under his seal.

More, since a certain infelicitous crossing three years ago, the plane itself bore the colors, the house seal, and the personal seal of Tabini-aiji, which served as an advisement to any small craft that, anyone else's personal numbers be damned, the paidhi's jet had absolute right of way.

Diplomatic status on the island enclave of Mospheira, however, did not mean a luxurious lounge. It didn't even mean access in the public terminal, where the island traffic came and went and delivered more or less happy families to holiday venues. No, diplomatic passengers embarked from the freight area. Security preferred that defensible seclusion. The State Department arranged a red carpet across the bare concrete, a small concession to appearances on a tight budget.

Bren preferred the seclusion, carpet or no carpet. A mission from Mospheira was already aboard, so security informed him, about five minutes ago . . . they'd not been waiting long, but they were all the same waiting, now, safe, their baggage aboard.

He carried his own computer, that was all, a machine with information certain agencies would kill for, and set it down to say his good-byes. Seclusion might mean family partings in a dingy, spartan warehouse, but it also meant he could indulge those partings in private: maternal tears, brotherly hugs, on a hasty Independence Day visit that had nothing to do with family obligations, rather four days occupied with official duties, then an overnight stay with his mother that ended one day before the official holiday.

On his way out of the human enclave, arriving by private car and not having to run the gauntlet of news cameras, he'd already changed his island casual knits for the calf-high boots and many-buttoned frock coat of atevi court style. He'd braided his hair unaided into a respectable single, tight plait, precisely—he hoped—between the shoulder blades, with his best effort at including the proper white ribbon of the paidhi's rank. He had lost one cufflink into the heating duct of his mother's guest room, or somewhere, this morning; he was relatively sure it was the heating duct, but he hadn't had time to dismount the grate and retrieve it. His mother had regaled him with an elaborate, home-style mother-cooked breakfast—her substitute for the holi-day—and what could he do but sit down and spend the little time he could with her?

He'd borrowed a straight pin to hold the cuff, which he now tried to avoid sticking into his brother's shoulder as they embraced.

It was: "Take care," from his brother. And predictably, from his mother: "You could stay another day or two."

"I can't, Mom."

"I wish you'd arrange another job." This, straightening his collar. He was thirty years old, and probably the collar needed straightening. "I wish you'd talk to Tabini. At *least* get a decent phone line."

Tabini-aiji was only the leader of the civilized world, the most powerful leader on the planet and probably above it. A decent phone line in his mother's reckoning meant one that would take calls in Mosphei' instead of Ragi and let his mother through the atevi security system at any hour, day or night; that would suffice. The fact that there were four diplomats and a situation waiting aboard the plane was not in her diagram of the universe. Next it would be: Get a haircut.

"You have the pager, Mother." It had been a birthday gift, last visit. "I showed you—"

"It's not the same. What if I had an attack and couldn't use the pager? I'm not getting any younger."

"If you couldn't use the pager, you couldn't use the

phone. Just talk to the thing. It's all automatic, state of the art."

"State of whose art, I'd like to know."

"It's Mospheiran. Bought right here on the island."

"You don't know where it goes. You don't know who's listening. And atevi made it. They make everything."

"I know who's listening," he said, and attempted conciliation with a hug. She was stiff and resisting to his embrace.

"Shots in the night," she muttered, not without justification. "Paint on my building." That was years ago, but he couldn't blame her for blaming him.

His brother moved in—a diversionary tactic. Toby put his hand on their mother's shoulder, simultaneously offered Bren his right hand in a handshake, and gave him a clear passage to the red carpet.

"See you," Toby said. "Go."

It was smooth. It almost worked.

But a wild cry of: "Bren!" came from beyond the security station, and a woman in fluttering white came running across the concrete, in fragile yellow shoes not designed for athletic effort.

Barb—the ex-girlfriend he'd successfully evaded for the last four days, who'd sent him voicemails he'd deleted.

Barb—whom he'd almost married.

She'd not put in a personal appearance during this visit or the last or the one before that, though his mother on all his visits had talked of Barb—Barb did this, Barb did that; Barb did her shopping, ran her errands.

Barb, married, had all but adopted herself into his mother's apartment, and yet didn't manage to show up while he was there . . . not that he'd advertised his visit, or even given his mother advance notice of last night's visit. Barb had tried to meet him, he was sure. He'd "just missed her" twice, this trip. He didn't know what the sudden insistence was. He wondered if he should have deleted those voicemails.

And now she'd gotten into this departure area on her husband's high-clearance security card, he'd damned well bet.

"Barbie," his mother said lovingly.

"Go," his brother urged him under his breath. Whatever was going on, Toby knew.

"Security window," Bren said with a frozen smile. "Have to go. People waiting on the plane. Mom. Toby. —Barb." He offered his hand. "Nice to see you. Glad you're seeing to Mother. Kind of you to come."

"Bren, dammit!" Barb flung herself into a hug. Bren could find no civil choice but to return it, however distantly. "I know," she murmured against his shirt, "I know you're angry with me."

"Not angry, Barb." He did the most deliberately hateful thing he could think of, tipping up her tearful face and kissing her . . . on the cheek. "I'm glad for you. Glad you're happy. Stay that way."

"I'm not happy!" She seized his lapel, flung a hand behind his neck, and kissed him fiercely on the lips. Passive resistance didn't do enough to resist it . . . at first: and then he found to his dim distress that he didn't respond at all. Barb's kisses were nothing foreign to him—longed-for, for years of his life. Her mouth wanted, tried, to warm his . . . but nothing happened.

He was disturbed. He turned from anger to feeling sorry for Barb and a little distressed about himself. For old times' sake he tried to heal her embarrassment by returning the kiss, even passionately, tenderly . . . as much as he remembered how.

But still nothing happened between them—or, at least, nothing from his side.

Barb drew back with a stricken, troubled gaze. He gazed at her, wondering what she knew, or why his human body didn't respond to another human being, why warmth didn't flow, why reactions didn't react. Pheromones were there; it was the old perfume, the very familiar smell of Barb and all Mospheira, to a nose acclimated to the mainland.

Interest wasn't there. Couldn't be resurrected. Too much water under the bridge. Too many "I'm sorrys."

And for that one frozen moment he stood there staring into the face of the human woman he'd meant to marry just before the fracture . . . the human woman who, when the going had been rough, had fought his battles and risked her life—then married a quiet, high-clearance tech named Paul, opting to protect herself behind his security shield.

Could he blame her for that?

He didn't, particularly, in cold blood. But from dismayed at himself, he transited to angry at her. It wasn't about the marriage; the anger was all for her campaign to get him back, and doing it by attending on his mother, running her errands.

What in *hell* did Barb think she was doing? was the first subsurface question. Why did she come now? Why did she court his *mother,* for God's sake?

And looking into her face as he did, he didn't truly know. One lonely woman befriending another? One woman who hadn't been lucky in love, crossing generations to find a kindred soul, as close to love as possible?

In Barb's paralysis, in that long, stricken stare . . . he disengaged, and with his face burning, he hugged Toby, hugged his mother, whispered a farewell, grabbed up his computer case, and followed the carpet to the waiting plane, head down, eyes on the carpet underfoot.

"Bren!" Barb shouted after him. Angry. Oh, damn, yes. Now she was angry. His nerves knew that voice, and for both their sakes, he hoped Barb *was* angry . . . angry enough to get on with her life. Angry enough to divorce her new husband, or settle down and live with the choice she'd made three years ago—angry enough just to do something toward a future of her own. Whatever that choice eventually was, it wouldn't be his choice, not any longer. It wasn't his mother's responsibility, either.

They couldn't take up again where they'd left off. It wasn't just the fact she'd married. It was the fact that he himself was no longer the Bren Cameron she knew. Then, he'd been a maker of dictionaries and a translator . . . until his life had exploded and put her in danger she'd been lucky to escape. He couldn't go back to that safe anonymity now. Couldn't join his mother's fantasy, or Barb's, that that anonymity would ever exist again. There was a reason for this concrete isolation.

And a great deal that was human wasn't within his power to choose anymore. He'd already lost everyone on the island; he was about to lose his only human companion on the mainland. He wasn't happy about it, but that was the choice far higher powers made.

He climbed the metal steps to the hatch of the airliner and still didn't look back, refusing to give Barb a shred of encouragement, even if it meant he didn't look back for his brother and his mother, either. His mother's health *was* fragile. He had reason to worry about her. Toby had had threats on his life and his family's lives, because of him. And Barb had been a target . . . and knew it. Now she wasn't, and she couldn't let well enough alone.

His mother and his brother would come to the mainland for visits. Barb, on the other hand, couldn't get the requisite pass—no matter how powerful her husband's influence—because the visa depended on the atevi government, not her husband's security clearance in the human one.

And doubtless she was upset about that, too. Barb wasn't used to *no*. She really hated that word. *It's over* was another thing she'd made up her mind not to hear. *I regularly sleep with someone else* was damned sure outside her comprehension. If she knew, and knew that individual wasn't human, that might figure in her determination.

But he hoped to hell not even his brother knew . . . certainly not Barb, because the next step was his mother knowing and the third was the whole island continent knowing.

"Mr. Cameron." A human steward welcomed him aboard and took his formal coat as he shed it.

In that process he scanned the narrow confines of a jet configured for luxury. The passenger shell he'd used in the plane that had previously run this route had always sat as a removable inclusion in the hull just ahead of dried peas and fresh flowers; but this sleek Patanadi Aerospace number, the aiji's plane, had tapestry for a carpet runner and seat upholstery of ornate atevi needlework. When it wasn't ferrying the paidhi across the straits, it did transcontinental courtesy service for the aiji's staff and guests . . . and the seats and furnishings were all to atevi scale.

Consequently, four Mospheiran diplomats sat like ten-year-old children in large-scale chairs, grouped around what was, relative to the chairs, a low table . . . sipping Mospheiran alcoholic beverages from atevi-scale glassware.

They'd be oblivious before they landed, if they didn't watch themselves.

He knew who was who in the group, having been briefed; knew two of the four in the mission prior to this meeting, at least remotely: Ben Feldman was a spare, unathletic young man thinning at the temples, Kate Shugart, a woman with close-cut, dull brown hair drawn back in a clip—she'd trained to have his job, but the job had ceased to exist, and she'd never made the grade. Those two of the four were Shawn Tyers' people, old hands in the Foreign Office. He trusted Shawn, or he had trusted Shawn—with his life, while he'd been an official working for the Foreign Office.

The other two . . . however . . .

He walked to the group, still with the taste of Barb's lips on his mouth and a large breakfast queasy in his stomach. Shawn hadn't briefed him about this more than to remind him Mospheira had applied to go to space, and to say that the aiji in Shejidan had cleared their mission most unexpectedly. They'd felt no choice but to go, immediately.

More, Shawn had said, the station in orbit had just called its second and *last* representative home, on this impending flight. A decision that would affect his work . . . profoundly.

And Tabini-aiji had cleared it.

It was one huge, upsetting mess, and Shawn couldn't brief him fully, not any longer. They served different governments. He could only say the Mospheiran government wasn't disposed to say no when the aiji approved a chance they'd looked to take, oh, a year to clear . . .

Mospheirans never had understood how fast the aiji could move when he wanted to.

The question was why the aiji wanted to.

The shuttle was still in testing; the payload for said test had been set and calculated to a fare-thee-well . . . one had to be atevi to fully comprehend just what manner of disruption such a change posed. Inconvenient, yes, but more to the point, profoundly disturbing to a people whose culture revolved around *felicitous* numerical associations. Change one kilo of payload, and the entire mission might need to be redesigned.

It was more than Barb's maneuver that had his stomach in a knot.

He could imagine Lord Brominandi making his speech in the legislature: Let the fool humans risk their necks in a shuttle that had only made four prior flights. Mospheirans suddenly declared they wanted seats, just seats, nothing major in the way of baggage, Shawn had told him, no great additional mass . . . oh, let the shuttle just carry enough fuel. No great problem. No recalculation at all, oh, no, nothing of the kind.

He was appalled. Infuriated. It was *his* shuttle, dammit, and even the possibility of a glitch-up and the loss of the shuttle turned his blood cold. God, the whole program set at incalculable risk. For what?

And Tabini cleared it to fly?

But the humans in orbit had called their interpreters home, first the one on Mospheira, which hadn't alarmed anyone on the mainland. It was expected, though early.

And they'd thought nothing of it when, on the next turn-around with the only space shuttle in existence, *this* turn-around, this last flight . . . they'd sent down a senior staffer from the station to replace, so he and Tabini had assumed, Yolanda Mercheson as the human-to-human paidhi.

But when Shawn so innocently announced that the station had called home the only other human being on the mainland, the only human being he had regular contact with, to go back to the ship that had sent him down . . . , a fait accompli. No negotiation, no request, no concession to protocols or his plans . . .

That had been cause for alarm.

And had he only found out about that change in plans when the shuttle had landed and deposited said senior staffer unannounced on mainland soil, he might have been able to address those alarms. Instead, he'd been shipped off to Mospheira, delivering that same senior staffer from the station, one Trent Cope, to Shawn's *superiors,* and now he had to learn of Jase's imminent departure from a former colleague who had no idea what a bombshell he'd been dropping.

Yolanda recalled to the station. Now Jase leaving without notice . . .

Now Tabini-aiji cleared a human mission to go into orbit

and deal with the situation on the station before Tabini's own representatives could go aloft?

He was more than appalled. He was furious. And having walked onto the plane with the matter with Barb simmering, an unreasoning fury boiled up in him at the sight of human smiles. The friendly greetings of former junior staffers in the Foreign Office grated on his nerves, and two senior staffers from Science and Commerce whose provenance he more than doubted were just the topping on the affair.

He knew damned well what the thinking on the island was: Mercheson had gone up with what *she* could report after her sojourn on the planet, and now the island government grew nervous about what she *would* report about them . . . justifiably, counting that certain injudicious fools on Mospheira had started shooting at each other in her witness.

The human government had changed three years ago, dumped out George Barrulin and his cronies, put in Hampton Durant as president . . . cleaned house, so to speak. Mercheson had fled the island briefly for the atevi-ruled mainland, feeling her life in danger among the human population. When the political dust had settled, then she'd gone back to her job . . . and as of a month ago was up in orbit spilling all the island's sins to the Pilots' Guild.

Which was the reason a shuttle existed: the ship that had brought his ancestors to this planet had left again, lost itself for a couple of centuries and then come back to find the space station mothballed, the labor force become colonists on the planet, and the species that owned the planet more or less in charge, despite the delusions of the island that they were the superior species. The humans on the planet had lost a war, agreed to turn over their technology step by step so as not to disrupt the world economy, and never quite grasped the fact that turning over computer science to the mathematically gifted atevi had let the genie loose. Humans on Mospheira weren't the most technologically advanced beings on the planet . . . not any longer.

And that technological transfer, two hundred years of it, was at an end, as regarded Mospheira passing technology to the atevi government in Shejidan. Right now the only humans with anything to teach the atevi were in orbit, the crew of the returning starship . . . the Pilots' Guild; and the atevi government had turned its attention in that direction. As a consequence, the paidhi, the human interpreter to the atevi, currently one Bren Cameron, as an officer of the Mospheiran Foreign Office, was out of a job; the paidhiin, Bren Cameron, Yolanda Mercheson and Jase Graham, as officers of the atevi government and the Pilots' Guild respectively, were the interpreters of the new order of business.

Now the ship, as if oblivious to the highly specialized nature of that post, called back both their experienced paidhiin, sent a new man down who couldn't keep his meals down, and he . . . he shared a plane with an unexpected human delegation, on their way to orbit, on *his* space shuttle.

Shawn Tyers, always trustable, had not quite answered why they scrambled to this sudden order from Mospheira, when he'd asked the blunt question. *People are nervous,* had been Shawn's answer. *Average people are nervous. They called Mercheson back.*

One could damned well bet they were nervous.

"Mr. Cameron." Ben Feldman, his own age, courteously rose out of his chair to welcome him with a handshake. "We've met."

He wanted to choke the life out of all of them. But diplomats didn't have that luxury. He smiled, instead. "Bren, if you will. Ben, Katherine . . ."

"Kate." Kate got up, offered a hand, and the portly grayhaired man rose. "Tom Lund."

And the gray-haired, long-nosed woman: "Ginny Kroger, Science. Dr. Ginny Kroger. Pleased to meet you."

Virginia Kroger. Out of Science. He knew that name, put a face with it, one of the old guard. And Tom Lund, from Commerce . . . that was a department of the government just a little too close to Gaylord Hanks and George Barrulin, whose influence had damned near taken the world to war three years ago. Their brilliant management was *why* Mospheira was renting seats on an atevi shuttle . . . that and the fact that a few billion years of geologic time hadn't put titanium, aluminum, iron, and a dozen other needful substances in reach of the islanders, where the current aiji's predecessors had settled human colonists.

"You're certainly a surprise," Bren said. "What prompted this sudden hurry?"

"The aiji," Lund said as they sat down. "Cleared the visas, like that. No warning. We've learned . . . we were ready, even if we didn't expect it."

"What—pardon my bluntness—" He suffered a moment of desperation, seeing a thoroughly unpleasant situation shaping up in what had been the world's clear course to the future. "What do you expect to get, up there?"

He, at thirty, was the veteran diplomat. The people he faced, with gray hair in the mix, were utter newcomers to the trade. No one on Mospheira but him had actually negotiated with a foreign power in two hundred years. The Mospheirans from their origins had not been models of good sense in international relations . . . and now they were rushing to insert themselves and their lack of expertise between two armed powers which had had a diplomatic contact proceeding fairly well and without incident.

And they were doing it at the very moment that other armed power pulled its diplomats back without explanation.

He kept a pleasant expression on his face, knowing he was rattled by the whole situation. He certainly didn't intend to blow up the interface, not with people he knew were going to go do their best to double-deal the atevi *and* the Pilots' Guild. He knew it wasn't the friendliest question, but he asked it. "Is this a test run, or is there something specific you intend to do up there?"

"I beg your pardon," Lund said in distress.

"Serious and sober question. I'm worried. *Is* there a reason for rushing up there?"

He saw the flicker of thoughts through various eyes . . . their remembrance, doubtless, that though they were talking to a human being, and though they were on a first name basis, he didn't work for the Foreign Office anymore . . . they were talking, in effect, to the aiji's representative. The aiji had just cleared them to go, but the aiji could unclear it.

"It's your government's decision," Ginny Kroger said, leaning forward. "We filed the request. We had word last night it was cleared. On your own advice, we cooperate, Mr. Cameron. I believe that is your advice."

He couldn't deny that, and he gathered up his self-control, such as still existed. "I don't deny that." So it *was* Tabini-aiji's doing, more than theirs. The ruler of the major civilization in the world had just reacted to the move the Pilots' Guild had made, serially recalling *their* ambassadors for consultation, in effect, and sent up, not his own people, but a complete wild card . . . a handful of Mospheiran experts, two from the ivory towers of University and State, and two old hands in island intrigue.

God, he said to himself, uneasy at the possibilities, and belted in.

"Then I understand what he's doing," he said.

"Do you?" Lund questioned. "That's ahead of anyone in the State Department."

"Atevi occasionally grant audacious requests when they're made . . . just to observe the outcome, even in serious matters. A roll of the dice, you might say. Watching where they fall."

He shot a small glance at the two translators, looking for any sign of comprehension, and it troubled him that only one, Feldman, seemed to twig to the suggestion it was a test of human intentions; but maybe Shugart was practicing that other atevi habit: inscrutability.

"You sent a mission request through." He let the implied accusation enter his voice. "I didn't get it."

The reply and confirmation of the mission had almost certainly come out of Mospheira in the Ragi language, translated by some junior functionary, which was against Foreign Office policy, and he knew Sonja Podesta, an old friend, head of the Foreign Office these days, had to have authorized that message . . . or had it slipped past her?

But past Shawn, her superior in the State Department? Shawn, who had just briefed him?

It was not a pleasant thought that Shawn might deliberately have tried to put one past him, and lied about it face-to-face.

"The transmission missed you, sir." Lund seemed quite anxious to avert his suspicion. "We had no idea you were already on the way to the island."

"Indeed it did miss me. *How* it got cleared without my knowing is another matter."

"If there's any irregularity," Lund said, "it certainly wasn't intended."

"On your part, I well believe."

"At higher level," Kroger said. "We meticulously respect the agreements. We had no idea the request was going through your office in your absence. We did not expect this."

It had been intercepted by someone on the mainland with access to his messages, which could only be the atevi Messengers' Guild, or his own staff—

Or Tabini's security.

And, routed to Tabini-aiji, the unseasonable, foolhardy request had been *granted*.

He wished he'd skipped the hearty breakfast. The search of the grate . . . the missing cufflink was evident, as he sat. The aiji's representative was not at his best, in any sense. He'd been sandbagged by his former friends in the State Department, by the President of Mospheira, who was supposed to be sane, and now he learned possibly there was a leak in the Messengers' Guild . . . an organization which had not been his best friends on the mainland, which had not been loyal to Tabini. *That* could be a scary problem.

But leaks in that Guild certainly didn't get their results approved by the aiji, not unless the message had come in such a public fashion that there was no face-saving alternative but to grant the request. He didn't know what he might be flying into. A government crisis, very likely.

Distrusting the Messengers' Guild didn't encourage him to try a phone call.

The hatch had shut some moments ago, unremarked in the exchange. The plane began its taxi out and away from the building. The alcohol-fed cheerfulness was not quite what it had been, and they weren't even on the runway yet.

"Well," Bren said, deciding to be mollified, at least for their benefit, "well, I understand. My apologies for my anxiousness. But I can't stress enough how delicate the situation is. The aiji didn't get any advance word from the Pilots' Guild when they recalled Mercheson and now Jase Graham. He may have felt sending you was tit for tat, with them.''

That provoked a little thought among the experienced seniors.

"The atevi have been pushed pretty hard," Kate Shugart said very quietly, in her junior, mere-translator status. Three of the five people present knew at gut level how wrong it was to shove badly-done messages through the system. "A great deal of change, when just a few years ago we were debating advanced computers."

. . . Carefully examining the social fabric in the process, to be sure what they released into atevi hands didn't end up starting a war or breaking down atevi society. Atevi had invented the railroad for themselves; humans had lately contributed the culturally dangerous concepts of fast food and entertainment on television, trying not to bring on a second atevi-human war.

Now it was rocket science. And a reported contact with some species outside the solar system, technologically advanced and hostile. The Pilots' Guild had come running home with trouble just over the horizon . . . and the world had found itself no longer in a space race for orbit and the old, deteriorating station, but in a climb simultaneously for dominance in decision-making and for survival . . . against a species the Pilots' Guild had somehow provoked.

Not a pleasant packet of news for the world, that had been, three years ago.

Atevi, who didn't universally favor technological imports, suddenly had to take command of their own planet or abdicate in favor of the human Mospheirans *and* the human Pilots' Guild, who historically didn't like each other and who weren't compatible with atevi.

And in order for atevi to take command, they had to build a ground-to-space vehicle from a design the Pilots' Guild handed them, and haul their whole economy, their materials science, and all their industry into line with the effort.

It wasn't *humanly* possible. If atevi hadn't been a continent-spanning civilization and a constitutional monarchy to boot, with rocketry already in progress, they couldn't possibly have done it . . . certainly not in his lifetime. Witness the efforts of the Mospheirans, who'd complained about the tax subsidy for their only aircraft manufacturer, and who'd let the company go. Now they were buying their planes from an atevi manufacturer, and had no recourse but to pay for seats on the atevi shuttle to orbit.

He knew what Tabini was charging them, and the citizens hadn't yet felt the tax bite.

"If the shuttle should fail," Bren remarked, likewise quietly, as the plane turned onto the runway and gathered speed, "if the shuttle has *any* significant problem, there would be another War of the Landing. Not could. Would. That's what we constantly risk. Forgive me for the interrogation; I'm supposed to have translated that request, and somehow it catapulted past me. It's always dangerous in atevi society when things don't follow routine channels."

"We're not in danger *now,* are we?" This from Ben Feldman, who did understand the risk, as the plane left the ground.

"I have some concern," Bren said. "I want to be absolutely sure you don't walk into something. You're sure that visa really came from Tabini's office."

"It came with verification," Lund said. "You want to see the papers?"

"*That* wouldn't tell me," Bren said. He didn't intend to reveal any of his doubts of the Messengers' Guild, or of instabilities he knew of, not to adversarial negotiators. "What specifically are your arrangements? Who's meeting you?"

"Straight to the space center," Kroger said, looking worried. "Officials of that center."

"That's good. That's the arrangement as it should be," Bren said. "Probably it did come from the aiji's office." He'd disturbed his seatmates, he saw. He wasn't in the least sorry to have done it. Nobody in the world as it was—or above it—should be as naive as Mospheirans tended to be about anything outside their own politics. "Which means he wants this to happen. What's your job up there?"

"We aren't empowered to tell you," Kroger said.

"You're empowered to negotiate."

"With the station."

"With the crew of the ship," Bren said in a low voice. *"We* were the station, weren't we, before the Landing?"

There was the old hot button, the privileges of the Guild, the lack of basic rights of the colonists, once in-flight emergency put the crew in total charge of the mission . . . once a ship went far, far off-course and the crew couldn't get them to any recognizable navigation point, a long, long time ago. The colonists weren't supposed to land. They had. The Guild had argued for respect of the natives and no landing, and had wanted to stay in space.

They certainly had. There was no Guild craft that could land and no Guild pilot that could fly in atmosphere. All that was lost.

The Guild right now didn't want to fly in atmosphere. They wanted the station manned, their ship refurbished. They wanted labor, the same as they'd always wanted.

Mospheirans were fit to be that labor . . . speaking the same language, having the same biology. Mospheirans, however, were of two minds: those whose ancestors had been high-status techs on the station were inclined to be pro-space; those whose ancestors had done the brute-force mining and died in droves were inclined not to.

What do you want? was a loaded question, regarding any delegation of Mospheirans going to talk to the Pilots' Guild.

"We're basically fact-finding," Lund said.

"Find out what they're up to?"

Kroger shrugged.

"Not hostile to the aiji's position," Bren said. "Fact-finding. The big question is . . . are the aliens real? Did they really find something out there? I've worked with Jase Graham very closely for three years . . . and I believe him."

They'd reached altitude. He felt the plane level out.

"And does the aiji hold that attitude?" Lund asked.

"Good question. Because I do, he tends to. He pushed for the space program, over some objection, as you may remember. He's the one who's enabled this whole program to work. The Guild up there has to understand . . . do *anything* to jeopardize Tabini's position and there is no shuttle, no program, no resources, no ticket. Alpha Base, gentleman, ladies. Alpha Base all over again."

Every paidhi-candidate visited that island site, where the clock stood perpetually at 9:18.

Humans floating down to freedom on their petal sails had settled wholeheartedly into atevi culture and offered their technology, blithely crossed associational lines with no idea in the world of the danger they were in. Humans hadn't . . . generally couldn't . . . learn the language to any great fluency, and because humans had never twigged to the damage they were doing, because atevi themselves hadn't comprehended completely what the cost of the gifts was . . . it all had blown up suddenly, and that clock on the island had stopped, precisely at 9:18, on the morning the illusion had gone up in flames.

After that, the aiji who won had settled the human survivors on Mospheira, and appointed the first of the paidhiin, the rare human who could tiptoe through the language.

"We've read your paper," Ben said earnestly.

Yes, they'd read it, and done what they'd done, and gotten permission from the aiji for this flight, nudging the aiji's precedence for the shuttle he'd built.

Considering Mospheiran history, why was he not amazed that even the linguists had missed the point?

"Well," he said, seeing there was nowhere to go with the discussion, "well, you're on your way, and likely it will work. I just ask . . . in all frankness . . . that future conversations with the atevi come by channels."

"I'll be frank, too," Lund said, "relying on your discretion . . . the Secretary of State insists you can be trusted."

He gave a nod. "In good will, at least. I *do* report to the aiji."

"We aren't interested in establishing another human government in orbit. They say they've found hostile aliens out there. They need work crews to fuel their ship and bring the station back into operation, and if your aiji is willing to supply those crews, and if some humans want to go up there and do it, fine. But does the aiji understand the fatality rate?"

"The aiji does understand that," Bren said. "I explained it very throughly. And neither human nor atevi workers are going to work without protection."

"And he takes that position. Absolutely. —Or can we say *he cares?*"

That, from a Mospheiran of Lund's background, was a sensitive, intelligent question. "Yes and no. The short version: atevi reproductive and survival sense are wound together in man'chi. It's a grouping instinct as solid as the mating urge, not gender specific. If a person isn't in your man'chi, no, you don't *care.* If they're inside your man'chi, you all have the same goal anyway, give or take the generational quarrels. But that's the average atevi. An aiji has no man'chi upward, and doesn't give a damn; but he holds together the man'chi of his entire association. If he wastes that devotion, the association will take offense, pull apart, fragment violently, and kill him. They care. Passionately, at gut level, in emotions we don't feel, the way they don't feel ours. The aiji doesn't throw away lives. Biologically, he's driven to protect them, they have a drive to protect him, everybody *cares.* Passionately. There's no chance he'll tolerate conditions such as our ancestors tolerated. On the question of workers in orbit, you can depend on a united front. Protection, or no workers. He won't put up with any Guild notion of high-risk operations that don't benefit the atevi. Second . . . he'll constantly be asking what benefit an action is to his association. As will you, I'm well sure, on Mospheira's behalf. The aiji has everything the Guild's come to extract from this planet; you have human understanding of how the Guild thinks. It wouldn't serve either of us to give away the keys to those resources. The atevi halfway understand Mospheirans, as far as they understand any humans. They *know* they don't understand the Guild."

"We can't speak to each other," Kroger said. "We and the atevi, we and the Pilots' Guild. We had you to interpret, and you left . . . pardon me, but left is the word. Then we had Yolanda Mercheson, and *she* was called back. We don't know what this new man represents. We're rather well without resources. Our mission is to reestablish that understanding."

"Certainly I agree with that. If you figure out the Guild . . . tell *me.* I'll be interested."

That raised a small amusement. Small and short.

"What do you think the Guild wants, sending this new man . . ."

"Cope. Trent Cope."

"What's he like?"

Bren shrugged. "Senior to Graham and Mercheson. Probably higher rank. Sicker than seasick, looking at a horizon. Hard to get to know a man when he's heaving his guts up and drugged half insensible."

"I hope it doesn't work the other way," Lund said.

He'd opted to travel with Cope, having shepherded Jase through his initiation to planetary phenomena. He'd not known then that Jase would get a recall order; not a clue of it. He hadn't emotionally reckoned with that hard hit, which he'd only found out about this morning.

He didn't want to think of it, just wanted to get back to his own apartment in the capital, where he and Jase could have a day . . . at least a day before the scheduled launch . . . to sort out what they did think. He was in an informational blackout, trying to get back to deal with Jase . . . and Tabini-aiji's orders packed him in with the Mospheiran delegation that was part and parcel of the same crossed signals.

"The atevi report a little nausea," he said. It was only atevi pilots who'd been in space, testing the shuttle. Docking. There was a scary operation. "I won't bias you toward it, I hope."

"I hope not," Lund said.

Kroger had fallen silent. Thinking, perhaps. Or keeping her own counsel. The two juniors were very quiet.

Then Kroger asked: "What kind of report do you think Yolanda Mercheson's given?"

Mercheson had fled to the mainland, lived in his household for half a year of her tenure here; but once the government looked stable on Mospheira, she'd gone back. She'd spent most of her time afterward on Mospheira, alone in the culture, miserably unhappy: he knew that. She didn't love Jase passionately, but they'd made love; they weren't working partners, but they were friends of a desperate sort, just the only available recourse for a woman otherwise on the ragged edge of tolerating her exile. Mercheson's early recall to the ship had seemed a solution, not a problem.

What she and Jase had had . . . he wanted no part of, but understood.

That part wasn't the Mospheirans' business.

"A fair report," he said. "She was homesick for the ship. But she bore no ill will to Mospheira, none at all."

"But she will have given a report to the Guild," Lund said.

"Definitely. As Jase will of us."

"A good report?"

"I think so. I think both of them will. There's no percentage in creating any rift . . . any negative report, whatever. They've sent Cope down, as I trust we'll get someone for Jase's spot on the next flight down." He wasn't looking forward to it, not at all. Losing Jase still hit him hard . . . harder than he'd ever anticipated. It might be why he'd reacted as he had to Barb; it might be why he'd gone into this conversation armed and angry. "I don't have to say this to the two from the FO; but listen to your two advisors. You speak the Guild's language; but don't assume that the words mean the same things after two hundred years' separation. Most of the differences will be stupid, small things; a few could be really significant." He glanced at Feldman and Shugart. "They know."

"We trust they know," Kroger cautioned.

"I know these two," Bren said. "They're good." The blushes were irrelevant to him. He meant what he said. "We've only the length of this flight for me to brief you on what we know about the Guild, as I gather the aiji would intend. Expect the aiji to support the agreement between our associations . . . and to oppose any independent agreements with the Pilots' Guild. The aiji won't undermine you. You work with him, I'll work with you, and that's far, far better assurance than you'll ever have out of the Pilots' Guild, even if they hand you the keys to the starship. We both know the history, better than the aiji does. We know it in the gut."

"We do," Kroger said. "And that's exactly right. A looksee into the workings of the Guild. Anything you know is welcome."

"I trust Mercheson's motives; but given the Guild's history, yes, I'm cautious. They'll want speed. We want a minimum of funerals. But we do take seriously the fear that sent them running back here. Jase Graham believes it. I'd stake my life on it being true. And if it is, either a band of angry aliens offended by the Guild's choice of real estate will come here to press their quarrel, or they won't. And if we equip that ship to fly again . . . we equip the *Guild* to deal with the situation that's going to affect the whole planet for good or for ill. We on the mainland aren't sure about the *good* part of it. We want to find out what the Guild knows, bottom line, and then apply our own experience to it, for what good that can do. If we have to fight, and if whatever's out there is that advanced, we've got a problem in dealing with the Guild that's far beyond Mospheira's old quarrels with them. A very mutual problem. Neither of our species wants to provide labor for fools, and neither of our species wants to take for granted that a Guild war is our war."

"We're in agreement on that," Lund said.

The mood improved. The steward came by and wondered what they would drink with their brunch.

It was small talk then, on recent history, Jase's two-parachute landing, the aiji's relations with the island, the building of a second and third shuttle . . . the governments were no longer at odds, both of them looking anxiously at the sky.

Atevi mutating everything they'd learned about computers and playing games with mathematics . . . he didn't mention that—didn't understand it, for one thing. The ateva who was working on the most abstruse part of it was likely a genius . . . a mathematical genius, in a species that did math as naturally as they breathed; damned right he didn't understand it, but he suspected a truth he couldn't prove, that atevi had sailed right past the University on Mospheira and maybe past anything in the lost library, the one they'd lost in the War . . . no way to prove it. But the Astronomer Emeritus scribbled away, and wise atevi heads nodded; his students thought him brilliant, and the occasional number counters and philosophical fanatics who traditionally made aijiin nervous had focused their energies on the Astronomer's ongoing work, too stunned, apparently, or too outclassed to take their sectarian battles onto *his* chalkboard.

A lovable, slightly otherworldly fellow . . . there was the
devil in the design, sweetly philosophical, thinking away,
building a cosmos theory that didn't battle the traditional
atevi philosophies, just lapped away at the sand beneath
them.

The two from the Foreign Office, queried by the steward
regarding refills, shot over curiously shy glances, as if they
feared to open their mouths even to order drinks: advisors
in private, no rank. Bren figured that . . . terrified of the
possibilities, because they were the ones who really knew
how dangerous the atevi-human interface was . . . how ex-
plosive and how treacherous.

Lund jovially ordered another martini, Kroger the same.
The two translators wanted beers, and Bren asked for
vodka and fruit juice.

The steward went about his business.

Lund said, when the man was out of hearing in the general roar of the engines, "How long do you figure this new
man will stay down here?"

Cope: deposited on atevi soil some four weeks ago, a
man tamely landed via the shuttle instead of flung at the
planet the way his predecessors had had to come down . . .
a clerical-looking fellow who'd moved by night and avoided
the open sky. They'd learned with Jason. He'd been too
sick to go on duty for several weeks . . . lodged in the
space center, since atevi security, sensing irregularity and
possibly espionage in his refusal to budge to go to the island, had not let him out of the facility. Jase had gone
there for meetings; Cope remained sickened by everything,
the smells, the irregularity of lights, the flickering of
fluorescent.

And now Cope was on Mospheira, his senses being assaulted by an entire new set of sights and smells. He'd
been, when Bren left him, lying on his new bed, not daring
to venture far from his new, completely enclosed, apartments. How long would he stay?

"I have no idea," Bren said. "To judge by Jase's situation, he may not know, himself. Mostly, he was sick for
four weeks. Possibly younger systems adjust better. We
don't know." Jase had said . . . watch him. *Watch him.* "I'd
be damned careful of his opinion. I said that to Shawn

Tyers when I met with him, and I'll say it to you, since you're going into direct contact with the Guild. He's definitely senior to Mercheson and to Graham. He's very sharp, possibly malingering, very much on his own agenda, probably intends to check up on everything Mercheson reported when she went back up."

"Alarming."

"Since Mercheson didn't lie, I doubt it's a problem. That's what I know. He'll be looking for resources. He'll be testing whether the island's resources exist. Observing the geology from space will tell them some things. Not all. Not whether Mospheirans will work with them, either. Now that there's a space shuttle and safer access, the ship can risk higher-level personnel down on the planetary surface. And that's exactly what Cope is." He had a suspicion the elder members of this group might have friends in the old regime and said it anyway: "The Heritage Party is an embarrassment I hope he doesn't encounter, but he may try to investigate that, too."

The drinks arrived, a small break, a welcome small confusion in the sorting-out of orders and napkins.

"To your mission," Bren proposed then, having shot his small dart at the Heritage Party, the pro-spacers who thought humankind had a natural right to everything in sight. "Here's to tolerance."

"To the aiji and his court," Lund said, "and an alliance of purpose."

Bren sipped his drink, with, at a slight bump, a glance out the window. Billowing cumulus, slate gray in spots. "Ah, spring over the straits. We're in for a little chop for an hour."

"Of course," Kroger said. "They just served the drinks."

Old joke, old as mankind, in the general goings-on of Mospheiran air travel, most of it in smaller, slower planes. General relaxation. This was, by default, the longest flight any Mospheiran who wasn't the paidhi had ever made, except a handful of the paidhi's friends and family; and those generally came with Toby, on the boat, and to the seaside estate. Mospheiran jet service was limited to the island, not flying so high, nor so long between landings.

"So . . ." Kroger asked, then, "will we *meet* atevi when we land?"

The interspecies interface was so meticulously ordered, so bound in regulations, it was a real possibility they would not meet atevi. They weren't to speak to atevi; that was the law. Atevi . . . well, atevi would do as they thought they could, and thank God one species of the two adored the law . . . atevi had a very fuzzy, constantly shifting concept of right and wrong, man'chi-guided and solid as a rock if one knew where man'chi lay.

But written orders and nonspeaking attendants would get them from one place to the other . . . granted the Messengers' Guild hadn't run amok and seized power in the four days he'd been gone, granted Jase was still mediating the paidhi's office, amid his sudden packing . . .

God, he was going to miss Jase. He'd be alone . . . he'd been alone, but he'd gotten used to Jase being there . . .

"I'm reasonably sure there'll be an official escort," Bren said, "Don't expect them to speak Mosphei'. Don't correct their pronunciation of your names. They'll pick what they can pronounce." Ben and Kate knew how their names would turn out. Atevi would likely adjust Ginny to Gin, in uniformity with her companions, for reasons of felicity . . . which would take an hour in themselves to explain to the uninitiated in number theory. Fortunately and by chance, none of the names carried particularly funny or infelicitous meanings in Ragi. "Bow. Don't smile. Don't expect them to."

"But you converse," Ben said quietly, as if saying he could fly.

"Practice," Bren said with irony. Atevi counted items in sets faster than the eye could blink and either took offense or made linguistic accommodations on the fly. "Long practice." Not counting hours and hours of math, until he breathed it; not counting becoming so sensitive to atevi expectation that he had analyzed what was wrong with Kroger's lapel-pin the moment they met, and thought as they entered atevi air space about offering the woman a flower to stick in it . . . but she was going straight to the space center, and the atevi dealing with strangers expected strangeness: it was all right. "Just use the children's language. Nothing more. They'll understand."

"No turning back now," Kate said, out of a long silence.

Well, there was. There was a chance of landing and riding the plane back to the island, mission forgotten. But diplomats hated like hell to meet an absolute and public rebuke, or to run in terror.

Brunch arrived, in some haste. The plane met increasing chop, on a direct flight into a security window opened by coastal defenses, and it wouldn't dare deviate in altitude without a great deal of to-ing and fro-ing on the radio. Possibly they were trying that.

The plane hit a pocket. Bren adjusted his glass of ice melt on his way to his lips, waited, then took a sip.

Human crews.

Human crews flew atevi-made planes; atevi still didn't often land in or take off from the capital of Mospheira. Mospheiran pilots were fiercely jealous of their few long routes, particularly in this day of space shuttles, nationalistically arguing that atevi pilots had a continent to fly in. These days, too, after doing in the aircraft industry, the legislature protected the handful of highly skilled Mospheiran pilots as a major national defense asset.

The human pilots *ached* for a shot at the shuttle. He'd heard that. He'd talked to them, saw the hope they had, but that honor Tabini wouldn't cede to humans, not yet, and for more than national pride. Tabini's pilots, experienced in long transcontinental flights, were an asset in the negotiations for atevi rights in space, on the station . . . to the solar system.

Politics, politics, politics. Everything, even that, was politics, depressing thought . . . it was the one matter in which he meant to make a change in favor of humans if there came a chance. Atevi had taken to the skies, but the same fluidity that they applied to the law they tended to apply to flight rules . . . hence the very conspicuous insignia and paint job on the aiji's plane. The flight crew they had was superb. The backup was, too. When they got down into the ranks of the bush pilots, the prospect was less favorable.

"Comfortable seats," Tom said. "Over all. Chop's not too bad."

"Not bad," Shugart agreed, about the time the plane hit a pocket.

The talk was like that, serious subjects exhausted. The rhythms and sounds of Mosphei' hit his ears with idle chatter, good-bad, either-or, black-white, infelicitous two without a mitigating gesture.

Mosphei' was like that. His mind had been like that, before he acculturated.

Fluent, but not instinctive. The spot-on atevi ability to see numerical sets was more than trained into children: it seemed to him atevi numeric perception might be co-equal with color perception, one of those things that just developed in infancy. It might be emotionally linked to recognition of parents, or safety, if atevi infants developed in any way like humans, and after centuries of sharing a planet without real contact, they just didn't know. Whatever provoked aggression . . . maybe sexual response—that might be involved with pattern recognition in atevi. If it was sexual in any sense, it might be why, though children perceived the numbers, they were immune from responsibility, and spoke a number-neutral language. Again . . . no basis in research. His own observations were the leading edge of what humans did know; and atevi themselves hadn't a clear notion of their linguistic past, by all he knew . . . archaeology was the province of hobbyists, not a well-defined science. Linguistics was something practiced by counters. Comparative biology was mostly practiced on the current paidhi, when an atevi physician had to patch him back together . . . and comparative psychology was what he and his bodyguard did on late winter evenings. He could only imagine what atevi did see, or what disagreeable visceral reaction certain nasty patterns evoked, as atevi had to imagine for themselves that humans somehow saw comfortable felicity and stability in pairs and twos . . .

Twos in marriage; twos in yes-no; twos in left hand and right hand.

The shuttle had had two hatches when they acquired the design. Atevi had changed very few things in the design they'd been handed, and the mathematicians had gone over it and over it trying to justify two hatches, even come to him in agonized inquiry whether he understood the logic of it . . . he didn't. And with trepidations on all sides, there'd been a third hatch, with resultant structural changes. There had to be one exit, or three.

And, God, the other questions they'd come asking . . . the changes in materials science over the last three years . . .

He himself—with wise and capable advisors—had had to pass on how much of that technology ought to go sliding off into the general economy. Was it wise to turn industry immediately to ceramics, bypassing much of the development of exotic plastics? What were the economic costs, environmental costs, social costs . . . costs to tradition and stability, and dared they put a road through to a mine in one subassociation without granting a benefit to another?

Shejidan manufactured certain things. What did it do to the balance of power within the Western Association when Shejidan developed another, and unique, industry?

What did it mean emotionally to the relationship among atevi associations when that shuttle lifted from the runway at Shejidan, heart of the Ragi association, the *aishidi'tat*?

The decisions were all made, now . . . an incredible three short years after the shuttle began to take shape and form. Whatever mistakes he had made or avoided, atevi were in space now. The shuttle had made its first flight six months ago, proving the vessel, a disappointment to the aiji's enemies, vindication for the aiji's program of technological advancement.

The world hadn't blown up. There hadn't been a war. It had been a close call, on that one . . . but the Heritage Party on Mospheira had been turned back in the elections, the new administration had passed the last election with knowledgeable people still in office, still with public approval. There were still stupid moves, one of the most egregious in recent memory being the message that had launched this half-thought delegation and destined them for space before there was any atevi mission . . . but he would get to the bottom of it, quickly so, once he landed. He trusted he could smooth over whatever was going on. If it *was* Tabini's retaliation against Jase's recall, he understood it.

If Tabini was mad as hell and if some misdirected request

from the Mospheiran State Department had brought this
about, Shawn Tyers would owe him for straightening this
out. But he rather inclined to the former theory: they want
humans. . . . let's give them humans.

Let them ask again, what they will, and let us see where
they temper their demands.

It was, certainly, a way of probing the other side's intention. It was damned, bullheaded atevi mindset.

And it certainly wasn't out of line with the way Tabini
had dealt with his own species.

To be first at something . . . wasn't in and of itself either
good or felicitous in the numbers.

He thought about that point, idly conversing with his
fellow passengers while the plane crossed the coast, maneuvering through bumpy skies and a rainstorm.

As they descended through the cloud base, he pointed
out places of interest in the countryside, a river, a small
town, and had an appreciative audience.

They were taking a fairly direct approach, not being
routed to the south, as sometimes happened.

And within a shorter time than usual they were over
Shejidan.

They'd cut three quarters of an hour off the usual time.
By the time the plane was maneuvering for a landing, run-
nels of rain were tracking back over the windows, roofs
occasionally appearing out of the gray.

"We're awfully low," Ben announced, peering downward, and then a sharp bank gave them a view down into
the hillside residence-circles that, with their connecting
walks, served somewhat as neighborhoods and streets.

The leveling of the wings gave them a grand view of the
Bu-javid, the hill palace rising above the tiled, rain-grayed
roofs of the common neighborhoods . . . footed with a pink
neon glow in the general fading of the light.

"Is that the Bu-javid?" Kate asked.

"Yes," Bren replied. "That's the aiji's residence, centermost." So was his, but his wasn't a tourist attraction,
not, at least, to Mospheirans.

"Hotels below?" Ben asked, peering down.

The palace was a vast sprawl of a building with interior

gardens and pools, skirted, these days, by a proliferation of businesses at the foot of the hill.

"Hotels. Neon lights and hotels." It wasn't his favorite change.

"Petitioners to the aiji," Kroger said.

"That's right." Over changes atevi themselves chose, the paidhi had no veto, and Tabini hadn't stopped it, though conservative atevi complained. Three years had seen a neon growth all through the city. The atevi thought it curious. It looked like downtown in the capital of Mospheira, and it afflicted his soul. "Anyone has the right to see the aiji, if he comes here, and the aiji will see he can come here, if he can't afford it."

The plane's next bank brought a view of other neighborhoods past the window now, tiled roofs in varying shades of red. "There's your *ashii* pattern," he said for Ben and Kate. "See the geometry laid out. The unified walkways. Associations. Apparent to the eye once you know you're not looking at our kind of boundaries. That's what the first settlers ran afoul of. Never saw it."

"Not a straight street in the place."

"People walk a great deal more."

"Well, thank God it won't be for us to figure out." Ginny's face, a thin face with a multitude of faint freckles, caught the white light of the window as she looked out on the foreignness of an atevi city. "We've got enough problems."

She hadn't said a thing in a quarter hour. At this precise moment—maybe it was his imagination—she looked scared as hell.

The plane leveled out.

Stewards wordlessly collected the glasses, and they stayed belted in while the familiar signs glided past the window. They were on final approach to the airport.

"Can we see the shuttle from here?" Kate asked, craning forward.

"Not on this approach," Bren said, and drew a deep breath, hoping he might find a stable, peaceful city . . . hoping his security would meet him. Hoping nothing had blown up . . . besides Jase's unexpected orders.

He'd gotten far too used to company . . . psychological

weak spot, he told himself Shouldn't have done it . . . shouldn't have associations he couldn't keep up. Gotten himself attached to someone he damned well knew would leave.

Unwise, in a man who'd made the professional choices he'd made.

Wheels touched down, squealed on wet pavement. The airport buildings rushed past, went slower.

Slower still.

2

The plane braked to an easy turn on a rain-puddled taxiway and rolled toward the security zone while the stewards reunited passengers and coats.

They reached a sedate stop, and there followed the immediate, familiar growl of the ladder-truck.

All four of Bren's seatmates, putting on their coats, simultaneously developed the same angle of furtive small stares toward the windows, dignified, not wishing to be seen staring as the ladder-truck moved up. But at the approach of the first atevi personnel, the first atevi they would ever have seen in the flesh, they stared. Ben and Kate had spent years studying and translating the language, but they had never seen the species who owned the planet they lived on; Ginny and Tom had no association whatever with atevi but trade and scientific exchange.

Bren himself fully expected the ladder-shaking rush of giants up the aluminum steps to meet the opening hatch. He didn't stare, rather composed himself to court standards, as the two atevi he hoped would have come to meet him arrived in the hatchway . . . Banichi and Jago, senior pair of the four who guarded him: black skinned, black-haired, golden-eyed, in the black leather and silver of the Assassins' Guild, against whose size they all looked like children.

His bodyguard, appointed by Tabini-aiji: his dearest friends, humanly speaking . . . and not friends: he was their duty, their association, as atevi felt things.

Human friends, even family, might desert you for very valid emotional reasons, even leave you for hire; and when he was on Mospheira, the human ways crept into his bloodstream and gave nesting room for doubts. But this pair, not being insane, wouldn't leave him except when duty took him overseas, where the law wouldn't let them go . . . and the moment they could rejoin him, sure as sunset, here they were.

They found themselves facing strangers, probably no surprise to them, but their polite impassivity gave no clue even to him. In front of dignitaries from Mospheira they stood, armed, solemn—very, very tall.

"Banichi and Jago," he introduced his bodyguard, then in Ragi, revised the island names to a form the language could accommodate. "Ben Feldman, Kate Shugart, Tom Lund, Ginny Kroger. One believes Tabini-aiji has granted their request to go up on the shuttle."

"Honored," Banichi replied in Mosphei', in a voice that would rattle china. He even gave a nod of the head, signal honor to the paidhi's guests if they knew enough to recognize the fact.

"Honored," Ben said. It was his very first chance to speak a word of Ragi to an ateva face-to-face, and the atevi in question disappointingly spoke Mosphei' to him first. But it was still a life-defining moment for the two linguists. Bren heard the quaver, saw two pairs of eyes wide as saucers, unabashedly staring at what they'd devoted their lives to understand.

Tom and Ginny remained more reserved, staying more to the rear . . . he knew that reaction, too. One felt smaller than usual. Even the scents atevi brought with them were mildly different. All of a sudden and for the first time, Mospheirans found themselves not in the majority, not giving the orders, not the masters of civilization. It was another life-defining moment, less pleasant than Ben and Kate's.

"The escort is waiting, sirs," Banichi said, and Bren translated. "Observe caution on the steps. —Nadi Bren, Jason has gone to the lounge."

"*Has* he?" He didn't let it show on his face or in his manner, and he didn't translate that part. He reined his reaction back hard, though he felt it as a blow to the gut. He'd raced all this distance, left his family early—he'd had to be the one to take the new ship-paidhi to the island

when he was ready to go, no question, but dammit! someone could have waited. He'd rushed to get back to have
time with Jason . . . and to no avail, it seemed.

Things suddenly didn't seem that right on the mainland,
despite Banichi's and Jago's presence, not with this mission,
not with Jase's.

"The aiji deemed best he welcome the passengers and
deal with them. Jasi-ji asks you meet him there."

"Let's go there, then, nadi-ji."

"Is there a problem?" Tom asked him.

"No," Bren said quickly, adjusting his coat sleeve past
the annoyance of the straight pin, relieved it had held, dignity preserved. It had scratched his wrist, minor pain, bringing a spot of blood to the cuff. "Jase Graham's gone to the
space center to welcome you there. The aiji, I'm sure,
thought you'd be more at home if he met you."

"Very thoughtful of him," Tom said, and at that unthought and rude familiarity, Bren found himself furious,
behind a diplomatic mask. *Thoughtful.*

Thoughtful, *hell!* Not of him, not of Jase, not of the unusual haste that was manifesting around him.

But having fallen already into the expressionless mode
of atevi among strangers, he'd also begun hearing things
through a Ragi filter, began to adjust his eyes, so that Banichi and Jago looked ordinary, and it was the humans who
looked strange. Such was the order of the majority of the
world, except for Jason Graham, and, briefly, Yolanda
Mercheson.

And he knew every nuance of his guards' expressionless
expressions, understanding by that immediate advisement
that he was being set on his guard, so far as Banichi could
go against the aiji's orders. He didn't know why, didn't take
anything for urgent information, guard-your-life information, but his bodyguard was just slightly on edge about
something.

Welcome home.

"Very thoughtful," he echoed Tom Lund. "I'm sure the
aiji hopes this mission goes well for both the island and
the mainland."

Three times was a charm, didn't the proverb say?

The fourth launch of a newly-built shuttle, however many

missions its exact predecessor had flown in the skies of the
earth of humans, still didn't feel secure, not to him. It didn't
feel that secure to Jason, either, not to anyone who'd
sweated through the first, problematic docking. Not to anyone who knew why there'd been an hour-long cabin blackout on the third flight.

Why the rush? he asked himself.

The haste couldn't feel that secure to the four Mospheirans, either.

Every time he thought about the possibility of a post-
launch emergency, with two places in the entire world with
a long enough runway, he found his palms sweating. Mercheson had made it safely to orbit. Jase would. He didn't
effectively give a damn about the Mospheirans . . . and did.

No cargo, well-thought test plans thrown to the
winds. . . .

"Shall we escort our guests to the facility, then?" he
asked Banichi and Jago.

"As you wish," was Jago's answer . . . elegant, smooth,
reasonable, and not a hint in her official bearing that there
was ever anything but business between them, or anything
in their meeting but well-oiled routine. "The van can accommodate us all," she said, "nandi."

With Banichi, then, she led the way down the stairs. The
usual van was waiting.

"Watch the steps," Bren said, starting down after her.
All the stairs on the continent were higher steps than standard on Mospheira. He didn't forget; he didn't trust them
to remember, and turned once and twice, hearing too much
haste and suspecting too much sightseeing behind him.
Rain slicked the ground. A brisk wind was blowing—tou-
sling the Mospheirans' hair, disturbing a strand or two of
his despite his braid, but never, ever disturbing the precise
single plaits that swung between atevi shoulders.

The van rolled forward as his bodyguard reached the
tarmac. Banichi and Jago opened the double doors of the
van and with the others settled inside, leaped inside themselves with a spring-rocking bound, pulling the doors to
after them with a businesslike thump.

The van rolled off on its way, comfortably appointed,

windowless, with no access to the drivers, whose identity Bren suspected as two more of his personal guard.

The van was armored: it was never a particularly quick acceleration. It heaved on bumps like a boat on rough water, while humans sat on seats out of human scale, sharing close, jostled space with a species who owned the planet by birthright. The humans stared at close quarters. In dim conditions, atevi eyes reflected gold under bounced light. Jago's gleamed from her seat in the dark corner. Bren didn't look to see the Mospheirans' reaction to that, only thought to himself that Jago damned well knew the effect on humans, knew it spooked him, knew it would spook the Mospheirans, and didn't take precautions against it.

Jago was mad, damned mad, at something.

Banichi added his stare to the chatoyant glare, and then looked away, not a word said at the moment.

Then, in Ragi, looking at Ben, "Pleasant flight?"

"Yes, sir," Ben said quietly, in Mosphei'.

Banichi was pushing it and knew exactly which ones of the humans were translators.

Beyond that, it was silence: Banichi prodded, Jago smoldered in silence, and Bren wondered in increasing desperation what could have gone wrong so quickly . . . besides Tabini's bloody-minded obstinacy and the Guild's picking a fight neither Jase nor he could win. Possibly both of them had understood Tom Lund's unfortunate, offhanded remark.

Ample opportunity for trouble. It was with them. It had gone to the space center with Jase.

The van, having made the long crossing of the security zone of the airport, bounced sluggishly and went down a steep ramp.

Somewhere behind them, massive hydraulics operated . . . the security doors, inside the space center at the northwest end of the airport, the new wing. Bren recognized the route, had absolutely no question they were on it, finally in it, and safe, at least in that regard.

The van leveled out, pulling to a halt with a low-tech complaint of over-burdened brakes. A thump sounded at the side of the van, someone hitting the doors, and a warning horn sounded outside.

Banichi and Jago left their seats, opened the doors in response to the signal from outside, and let them out into the dimly lighted concrete tunnel of the center. The white-and-black baji-naji emblem was conspicuous on the metal doors that faced them.

It was the emblem of Fortune and Chance, those governors of all cast lots, appropriate symbol for the shuttle as it was historically appropriate for the halls of government.

Nothing about the opening vista offended the eye. The columns that supported the roof were felicitously grouped. Atevi would be comfortable with all that met them, though the guests were doubtless oblivious to that felicity, even the two from the FO. It was concrete, black and white and gray, full of shadows and echoes . . . but it opened onto a table with a black vase, white flowers, a single, rising strand of blooms. It was a statement: felicity, ascent, under a stark white arch.

Banichi led the way up to the platform, stood at attention as an inner security door admitted them all at once to warmer, more decorated hallways.

Now, now it was the human reception area. The lowering of tension was palpable as his human companions met the soft brightness of the lights, the subtle pastels—felicitous colors to atevi, to be sure, soft green and blue, both quiet nature colors: that was what the human heart wanted. He and Jase together had picked out this scheme for the human comfort zone and approved it . . . he and Jase had planned this, as they'd planned everything about the center. They'd ordered human-scale furniture from Mospheira, and they'd translated the shuttle specs, a mammoth undertaking.

They'd defused the atevi resentments of the two-doored shuttle design, they'd found compromises . . . they'd ended up with three hatches on the shuttle, and atevi, who'd dug in their heels for decades—fighting every advance Tabini-aiji tried to bring them—had gathered enthusiasm for the most incredible advance of all.

For three years a handful of atevi engineers, he and Jase and to a certain extent, Yolanda Mercheson, with their respective staffs, had shared every breath, lived and breathed the shuttle, the space center, the program.

"Nice," Lund said of the decor.

Bren took a breath. Let it out slowly. Lund meant a compliment. He and Jase had *hoped* for just such ease in humans when they came to these rooms. Cope hadn't even said that much when he'd come down four weeks ago, yet Cope had lived those four weeks almost exclusively in these rooms because he'd had motion sickness *only* when he'd left this facility . . . had had it all the way across the strait at night on the plane, had had it in his new residence on Mospheira, probably would have it in his new offices, give or take the drugs that held it at bay, and despite his suggestions to State to try to limit Cope's exposure to changing light conditions and contrasts and open horizons.

He'd grown sensitive to such details, thanks to Jase. Irregularities in lighting were an indication of failing systems, to a ship-born human . . . large spaces were a particular fear, or so Jason had explained to him: a sensible fear of impact.

Make the corridors interrupted with cross-corridors and nooks that could be a refuge in acceleration: the center did that. Zero chance the space center would ever accelerate, but small chance that blue that comforted Lund and his friends was sky, either. It was something to do with hindbrain and childhood security, he supposed, not intellect.

So Lund liked the decor . . . didn't apparently notice that there were no steps to make humans labor or to trip up atevi strides. Elevators handled all level changes. Control panels and wall switches sat at intermediate height, a little high for humans, not too low for atevi.

And the flowers on the table, an atevi welcome in this area, were a carefully chosen arrangement—no different than the species familiar to Mospheirans, but felicitous in number and color, given the blue and green: they were spring, and hope.

"Lovely flowers," Kate was kind enough to say, perhaps making conscious amends for Lund. She and Ben might understand. The others might finally twig to at least that. Mospheirans were remarkably stubborn in their insularity, but the news channels had been full of unbridled analysis of atevi ways in the last three years. In the end, he'd sent his own reaction in an interview, trying to satisfy a burgeoning, fearful curiosity without weakening the strictures that kept the species from unofficial contact. Adventurous types on either side of the straits had tried contact in rowboats, and successful, live venturers, even escorted back by the authorities, were damned dangerous to have expounding in the press and over the airwaves.

How long could they hold two curious species apart, with a narrow body of water separating them?

That, apart from hostile aliens in some other solar system, was one of the worries inherent in the space program . . . in this launch, in Jason's recall, and in this mission. Atevi *would* grow close, again, to humans.

The door to the lounge opened.

And there Jason met them—his dark hair starkly, badly, shockingly cut. In three years Jason had carefully grown the beginnings of a respectable braid, that badge of atevi dignity, and now he'd cut it, along with his ties to the earth . . . God alone knew in what frame of mind when he'd gotten the orders from above. Jase wore a dark-blue jersey, black trousers, and, God save them both, that frayed fishing jacket Toby had given him three years ago.

"Jason Graham," he introduced himself to the Mospheirans, as if television hadn't broadcast his image all over the planet at least twice a week. He didn't quite look at Bren, not looking him in the eye, at least. "Jase is what I go by." Duly, Jase shook hands, smiled, did all the right and human things with the newcomers: Bren accomplished the introductions, wanting all the while to ask the essential question, but they were waist-deep in newcomers and unanswered questions.

"Mine's the first room," Jason said to the incomers, indicating the first of the twenty rooms in circular arrangement around the common room: no head, no seniormost: King Arthur's revolutionary arrangement. It set atevi teeth on edge. To atevi eyes, it was social chaos. War. "Plenty of room, this trip. We have space for more."

All cheerfulness . . . which certainly hadn't been Jase's mood when he'd gotten the order to fly, and was not what he expected from Jase, not with that haircut.

Bren waited, offered polite, required courtesies. Considered the coat, the performance, because performance it surely was . . . and God alone knew how Jase had gotten out the door past their major domo wearing that; God knew how he'd saved it from the servants.

But the jacket was a map of explorations. There was an abrasion on the elbow, where Jase had tried to fall in the ocean. Jase had begged, pleaded, and demanded his visit to the ocean—for ulterior motives, as it had turned out. But Jase had fallen in love with the sea.

And what did it say, that, going home, Jase chose that ratty, salt-weakened jacket and a shirt he knew had seen three years of wear? What had Jase been thinking, and what must the servants have thought, when Jase took something to his hair.

"Where's the shuttle?" Tom Lund was forward enough to ask.

Jason didn't give them the expected, verbal answer. He walked over to the wall and pushed the button that motored the blinds aside.

The gleaming white, bent-nosed bird out on the tarmac seemed about to lift from the ground of its own volition. It looked small . . . until the eye realized those service vehicles that attended it were trucks.

"God." Ben was the only one with a voice. "My God."

And Kate: "It's *big.*"

When ten men set their hands to a rope and pulled in unison, amazing amounts of weight slid.

When an entire civilization worked in concert to accomplish materials and training for a tested design, three years produced—this shining, beautiful creature.

"Shai-shan," Bren said, standing behind the group, finding a voice. *"Favorable Wind."* He'd seen *Shai-shan* from framework to molds to first flight, and now Jason's life, Jason's departure from the world, rode on these same wings. He'd translated every line of her. He'd all but given birth when she lifted off for her maiden flight, a curious emotion for a maker of dictionaries, a parser of words and meanings.

"Marvelous, marvelous thing," Kate managed to say, and the group stayed and stared.

Jason had a sense of the dramatic, and of diversion. Bren caught Jason's eye once for all as the group, Kate last, with a lingering glance at the shuttle, began to disperse, subdued, to make their choice of accommodations.

For a moment Jase gazed back at it, too, then looked at him with a subtle shift of the eyes that indicated the dining recess.

He went, Jason went. Banichi and Jago walked as far as the arch and stopped.

There would not be intrusion.

"So they want you up there," was Bren's opener.

"The aiji's order," Jason said with a brittle edge. "Packed in an hour. Hurry and wait."

"I'm sure I'll learn why," Bren said faintly.

"I'm sure *I* will," Jase said.

"Damn it."

"Damn it," Jase said. That much was Mosphei', and then, in Ragi: "Sit a moment. The tea's not bad."

"Shouldn't be," Bren said. "We ordered it."

So the parting they'd both dreaded came down to a cup of tea from a dispenser, and all Bren could hope for was a quiet, guarded conversation in the dining section. The Mospheirans wandered about. Banichi and Jago were forbidding gatekeepers, not moving a muscle.

"Wish I had answers for you," Bren said. "I wish I had *any* answers. You don't know?"

"Just . . . word came: get up there; and word came from the aiji. Go. Not a choice in the world. I suppose the aiji wanted me here to look over our guests, make sure they didn't steal the silverware."

Atevi joke.

"I don't know," Bren said. "I swear I don't know. Didn't know. Didn't have any more warning than you did."

"I believe you."

There were signs they used for truth, *I swear* was one of them. They never lied when they said that to each other, though lying was part of their separate jobs . . . or had been, and might be again.

"Might still be a weather delay," Bren said.

"What about the Mospheirans? Did the Guild want them, too?"

"Hell if I know," Bren said. "Not a clue. They asked to go. Tabini said go now."

They looked at one another. No sum of the parts made total sense.

"I've still not a clue," Jason said.

"Unless they're going to spite the Guild," Bren said, and warmed chilled fingers around a plastic cup. "Tabini might do that."

"Going to miss you."

"Get back down here if you can."

"I'll try," Jase said. "Get up there, if you can."

"I'll try that, too," Bren said. "If I can find out anything and get a message back to you, when I get to the Bu-javid, I will."

"Do we *ever* get word?" Jason asked, rhetorical question. He looked badly used, with the uneven haircut, wisps sticking out at angles. God knew what reason . . . maybe just a fit of anger at an unreasonable order. Jason wasn't immune to fits of temper.

Neither of them were that.

"Look, tell them that second shuttle won't make schedule if you're not down here," Bren said. "It's not entirely a lie."

"I know," Jason said. "Damn all *I* can do. Maybe . . . *maybe* there's a way back. I can't guarantee it."

"Ramirez?"

That was the senior captain in the Guild, Jase's sometime guardian, sometime chief grievance. Ramirez had his good moments and his bad ones.

"I imagine it is. Him, I can talk to."

"Talk and get back here."

"I want to."

"You're going to have to grow that damn braid again."

Jase gave a rueful laugh, shook his head, and for the better part of an hour they drank tea and reminisced, mostly about Toby and his boat . . . nothing about Barb, not a word about Barb, just . . . "How's your mother? How's Toby and all?"

"Oh, fine," he said.

Remarkable how little now they found to say to each other, when before this they'd had all the time and talked and talked about details, plans, intentions—time shortened on them, three years to recall, no time ahead of them, just a little rehearsing of the schedule for the two shuttles under construction.

"I'll write tonight," Bren said, damned well knowing the barriers of administrations, governments, and just plain available space in the message flow up from the big dish that was most of their communications.

Jason was quiet then, subdued, next to distraught. "Tell Tano and Algini I'll miss them," the word was. "Tell the secretaries, all the staff." It achieved a sense of utter desperation. "Banichi. Jago." He cast a look at them.

"Nadi-ji," Banichi said.

"I'll miss you."

"We also regret this," Banichi said.

A silence fell. And grew deeper and more desperate.

"I've got to get back," Bren said. "I'm going to get to the bottom of this. I'll come late tonight, if I can. Maybe spend a little more time." The launch was in the early hours. "As much as I can."

"I'd be glad if you could."

So there was nothing to do but finish the tea, get up from the chairs, and face one another. Bren offered an embrace. It was the Mospheiran thing to do. Jason met it awkwardly, hugged him fiercely; ship-folk were isolate, not prone to touch one another. Bren gathered a grip on the worn jacket and clapped Jase on the shoulder, feeling a burning tightness in his throat.

"Take care," Jason said. "Take care, Bren."

"I'll do my best." Bren let him go, turned in the futile attempt to find something to do with his hands, and walked away.

Banichi and Jago went with him, saying not a word as they followed him out of the residency and down the outside, gray hall.

He'd known for three years that, once the shuttle truly flew, he'd be alone again. He'd planned to be alone in his life.

And what was this . . . *alone?* He had Banichi and Jago, whom he loved . . . a human could say *love,* and they could be devoted in atevi fashion.

He had Tabini-aiji's high regard, he lived in splendid quarters, held an extravagant seaside estate where his mother and his brother and his brother's family arrived for family visits . . . visits no other paidhi had ever been granted—

Not to mention the hundreds of staff and servants and acquaintances . . . and the relationship, of sorts, he had with Jago, for good or for ill. He was not, whatever else, *alone.*

Yet losing Jason left him feeling used up, bruised to the soul.

In that light he knew he ought to open his mouth and talk, talk about something, anything, in the absence of a word from his companions. It wasn't their job to guess that the human in their midst wanted—*needed*—to be talked to. He was the translator, the cultural interpreter. He should initiate a word, something to give them a cue how to deal with him in this situation they'd never met.

But he didn't find one.

They escorted him in silence down to the security zone, into that area of grim gray concrete where the van had let them out. The next link would not be by van, but by rail, up to the Bu-javid, the palace on the hill, the center of Shejidan. He walked with them past the spot where the van no longer stood, in the echoing hollow of the place. They entered through a black security door, and saw, not unexpectedly, their associates Algini and Tano, holding place near the rail-access to this closely guarded facility.

"Paidhi-ji," Algini said, seeing him, and that was the first word he'd heard since he'd left Jason above.

"A good trip?" Tano asked him, as if that should be some consolation for what he was sure Tano knew.

"Very fine," he said politely. Tano was a good man, a very good man. In the paraphrase of Lund's question, Tano cared.

But this wasn't fine, his trip hadn't been fine, Jase wasn't fine . . . and on the island his family wasn't fine. He hadn't thought that, in this suddenly harried trip, but it hadn't been fine at all. His mother had wanted him to stay. Toby's youngsters were going through growing pains and grand-motherly spoiling, and were wretched company, grating on his nerves for the single day he'd been with them . . . he wasn't used to human children.

Where had he lost that sense of connection?

And what had he traded it for?

What was he losing, back there with Jase? The one human being on whom he'd focused all his remnant of humanity, in a desperate attempt to put together official policy for the aiji, trying to understand the ship-humans' mind-set?

He boarded the train, rode in absentminded silence, recalling a dozen and one trips over the years, the first launch . . . spiraling back in time, the first trip to Malguri, the return . . . going out to Taiben, once and twice, all jumbled together, Jase and before-Jase. Down to Geigi's estate, for one reason and another . . . those were the good times. Fishing.

What in *hell* was Tabini thinking?

"Do you know anything about this?" he asked his bodyguard, when they were alone, rocking along the rails.

Tabini's rail car—he'd used it more often than Tabini had, this specially secured compartment, armored against all eventualities.

"No, nadi-ji," Banichi said. "We, like you, wonder."

He leaned back on the comfortable velvet bench seat, red velvet, red carpet, a fresh bouquet in the vase on the counter, blooms of the season, the first in the lowlands. They shed a thick, sweet perfume.

A wake might have been more cheerful.

"I need to meet with the aiji," Bren said quietly.

"One will forward that request," Jago said.

"The dowager is in residence," Banichi added.

A new alarm began to go off, deep in his gut.

"Did she come to see Jason?" Bren asked. "What in hell's going on?"

"She invited him to tea," Jago said, "and they discussed the weather."

Well, it wasn't entirely unreasonable; she did come to Shejidan for visits. It was probably coincidence; she'd arrived, and heard he was leaving.

"He'll have no weather where he's going," Bren said, trying to settle himself to the possibility. "He'll have to get as used to being without it as he did being with it."

"He will," Jago agreed.

"So it was one of those conversations?" The aiji-dowager,

whom he'd thought safely and remotely at Malguri, was staunchly, provocatively conservative, a promoter of causes, a keen wit.

A good heart.

And a talk on the weather with Ilisidi, Tabini's grandmother. Lords of the Western Association would give a great deal for a social conversation with her.

But did she do anything . . . *anything* . . . by chance?

"Did she know he was leaving?" he asked his security. It was a three-hour flight from Malguri, for an arthritic woman who didn't like long sitting. He was prepared to be touched by that effort, if she'd heard and made the trip only for Jason.

"One has no idea," Jago said, "nandi."

My lord? Nandi? So formal? What signal was *that?*

Jason had said not a word about his visit with the dowager. But she was, though silently, a head of a potentially restive association, within the information flow. Tabini would have sent the dowager word of a favored associate's departure . . . or else. If *Ilisidi* couldn't press Tabini to resist this sudden request from the station, his own chances dimmed.

Jase hadn't mentioned the meeting . . . but what could he say? He and Jason hadn't talked much about the court, had talked instead about the first things they'd done, the things out in the countryside, then sounding each other out a last time, getting their positions on issues fine-tuned, for those who might ask.

It was their job to do that.

But that Ilisidi came to bid Jason farewell meant far, far more than a social discussion . . . nothing Ilisidi did could go without notice. By meeting with Jason alone, she had declared not only her past association with Jason-paidhi, but a current, live, and potent one.

She had just announced that, in a meeting sure to make the news.

She'd just announced it to her grandson, the aiji. She had an interest in Jason, in his people, in the space program and in the business the ship-humans had with atevi . . . she, the ecological conservative, the arbiter of taste and society.

He'd been walking about stunned since he'd gotten the news; now he began to wake up.

Much as he relied on the dowager's goodwill, it was never, ever to be taken for granted. If one lived among atevi, one asked oneself questions, like: was there any enemy or associate Ilisidi wished to slap in the face by making such a trip? He could think of several enemies.

He could even think of the dowager's grandson, Tabini-aiji, who had advanced Jason's trip to the space center by a full day, damned well knowing he was coming back with the expectation of a decent farewell . . . and why had Tabini sent him out there as he had?

Protective of Jason?

A reproof of the dowager for that invitation . . . disquiet, apprehension of what the dowager might have said or asked?

Why had the Mospheirans gotten their request faster than they'd wanted or expected?

He had to get his wits in order, or endanger the whole damned Western Association, not to mention himself and his bodyguard.

Wake up, paidhi-ji; that was very likely the thought in his bodyguards' minds, too. They were all but telegraphing signals at him. *Realize there might be danger. Defend us. Use your wits.*

There was some advantage in having Jason debriefing early, having a man they knew for certain was well-disposed to atevi go up there to counter any negatives Mercheson might have given in her report. Atevi didn't know Mercheson nearly as well, and didn't have that much confidence in her, not as they had in Jase-paidhi.

No atevi mission above the technical level had yet reached the station. Pilots and technicians had gone, in the shuttle tests. Those were canny, intelligent individuals under strict instruction how to react and what to do; but no one below could know how those contacts might have gone, off the set script. Tabini wasn't comfortable with Mercheson's recall; Tabini knew all the unpleasant history of the Pilots' Guild, being a student of history other than his own.

That was a hellish load of responsibility under which he

served. The Mospheiran government trusted him. The delegates from Mospheira had made gestures toward trusting him. Tabini trusted him. Jason trusted him and wanted to stay down here. He was overburdened with trust and vastly undersupplied with information.

"One does wonder what she wants," he said mildly, a question utterly without offense to ask in the context of his own bodyguard. He invited response.

"One does wonder," Banichi said, denying he knew anything worth saying, and Jago, with the equivalent of a shrug:

"She does regard him as within her influence."

Regarded Jase as an associate, in other words . . . one who couldn't be taken from her without dealing with her in some fashion: that was true; it was why Tabini would have called her with that information, probably personally, though the dowager disdained telephones.

"Interesting," he murmured to Jago's remark, and noted that Banichi didn't in the least disagree with his partner's assessment. *That* rang alarm bells. Jago, the junior in that set, speculated beyond Banichi's answer: not ordinary in a sober moment. He could conclude both of them thought so, then, but had no solid knowledge of Ilisidi's motives, and therefore Jago, juniormost, advanced what they could say . . . once they nudged him into question, dropping their small bombshell of information between them: She's here, and, She's involved.

"So what else is going on?" he asked his security. "Who cleared the visas for the Mospheirans?"

"They are cleared," was all Banichi could say. It was, then, all Banichi knew.

"The Atageini matter is resolved," Jago said.

"The staff has sent the requisite letters," Banichi informed him. "The contract is canceled."

That was a relief. The lord of the Atageini had complained of encroachments on associated territory . . . the minor squabbles were the bread and butter of court intrigue, rarely accidental, usually a maneuver for position. The land was in contention, and likely the subassociation resident on the land had set up the conflict; assassinations had seemed likely.

And a niece of the head of the subassociation was seeking a union with a neighbor lad who wasn't within her association. Social convention strained at the seams, interpersonally speaking, and that was how associations widened . . . if uncle Tatiseigi of the Atageini gave his approval, which at last report would be a cold day in a human hell. Tatiseigi, Tabini's uncle-in-law, was as hidebound as any lord on the mainland, and what hadn't been true three hundred years ago was, in Tatiseigi's book, suspect. They had *that* boiling on the border. It was suddenly quieter, for no good reason. *Tatiseigi* had changed his mind, then. Ilisidi, a distant associate, was back in court.

Go to the island for four days and the landscape rearranged itself.

"Damiri-daja favors the union," Banichi said, meaning Tabini's wife. "Nand' Tatiseigi does not."

"And Ilisidi?"

"She has had no known contact. But one asks."

Things shifted and shuddered: the structure of the associations changed constantly, but the overall outlines remained the same; and Tabini and his wife's uncle carried on a moderate, courteous warfare, within social limits. Men had died over it; but it looked as if violence was avoidable this time, only an old man asserting his power to be disagreeable and old-fashioned . . . and the aiji-dowager possibly bringing her foot down. He remained disturbed on that account. Tabini had been under siege in his own house. Jason was out from under the roof, unreachable.

The space center began to look like a refuge from the storm. *He* had to go persuade Tabini that sending Jase as the Pilots' Guild wanted wasn't a good idea, that perhaps Jase should catch some unanticipated malady, a contagion . . . the ship-folk had worried, at least, about contagion. But he didn't know, now, what the repositioning of atevi meant, combined with the moves of the two human governments.

He was still thinking as the train climbed the steep of a very familiar hill. The windows might be curtained in red velvet and sealed in bullet-proofing, but Bren had no need to see out when they entered the distinctive region of echoes and the more level pitch just after the hill.

They were coming to the station. Algini and Tano rose from their seats, stood poised at the door to secure its safety—routine. It was unlikely there would be any assault, but counting the high position he did hold, and things shifting in the court, there was always a remote chance of those doors opening on a hail of bullets.

The car wheezed against the hydraulic brakes, and the doors opened.

No bullets. Bren rose, shouldered his computer, walked ahead of Jago and behind Banichi as they exited down to the platform in the high concrete tunnel. They were in the bowels of the palace, beneath the hill they had seen from the plane. Palace and gardens were above them.

They were safe now, beyond the reach of all but the most adept assassins . . . there existed a short list of likely offended parties, but there always was that. His enemies were fewer now. They knew, he knew, the assassins they hired knew that taking him down would create far too disruptive a vacuum. These days a determined few did pursue him, but the most, he was in a position to be sure, pursued him only for policy, and would not be willing to meet the retaliation of the aiji: paper threats. Or less than paper: his bodyguard, empowered by the aiji, informed him there was no valid Contract in the Assassins' Guild.

In that relative assurance, his mind trying to form arguments for Jase's immediate usefulness . . . and the nature of a nonthreatening illness . . . he entered the lift with Banichi and Jago, Algini and Tano as usual seeing to the baggage, while the three of them rode up to the level on which he had his now-permanent apartment.

It was a historic residence that had lately been the abode of the Maladesi . . . center of an association which had been, since the debacle of resistance to the space program, utterly absorbed.

Small loss, Tabini said; upstart newcomers, Damiri-daja said, though Bren regretted the passing of anything so incredibly old it antedated Mospheira, and felt a small guilt for his improved fortunes. He didn't *need* a lord's estate . . . he'd once argued. Now he knew the need of it. It was for his staff. His servants. The convenience of his security.

The Maladesi servants had understandably remained with

elements of their historic association, absorbed into other groups. But certain servants had come in from the clerical staff, some had been recommended by Tabini, or through his security. Certain ones had even come from redoubtable Uncle Tatiseigi of the Atageini—a matter of some nervousness, but if the old man offered, one would assault the old man's sense of taste to assume he would use a festive gift to launch assassins . . . he would, but not as an invited guest at the birth of a grandson, Tabini's heir: it was old-fashioned manners, largesse and celebration.

And the apartment had been generally gone over with a fine-toothed comb for remaining bugs and security breaches . . . when a lord of the Association moved, it necessarily occasioned changes far more extensive than changing the locks on an apartment. Interior doors had been moved, screens erected, both to confound assassins and to change the numerology of the patently unfortunate rooms.

The locks, of course, were both changed and upgraded, some to lethal levels . . . all of that. His staff contained no one that Tabini's security had not passed . . . an atevi lord of older standing might have had reason to object to that thorough an infiltration from the aiji's estate, but he was grateful. Banichi and Jago were from Tabini's staff, before they had given him their man'chi. *He* was within Tabini's man'chi. There was no contradiction at all.

Jase was within Tabini's man'chi, too. *That* . . . was an argument.

The head of staff met him at the door, took his coat— Narani was the name of this major domo, an elderly and distinguished gentleman from the mountains. Two grandchildren, three former wives, and three sons were all on staff, not to mention lateral relations of wives and sons, including two current husbands . . . all staff.

Most remarkably and quite literally the heart of it was the population of a small fishing lodge, simply given to him in a very feudal fashion, along with title to the residence that was the source of the staff. The servants there had grown too numerous, in several centuries of marrying and begetting and birthing, to be confined to the maintenance of a lodge the aiji rarely visited. They were only half Ragi in ethnicity, ignored by Tabini's father—this was a recommendation—somewhat remotely tied to Lord Geigi, a thoroughly reliable lord of the south coast . . . and delighting in a lord who actually visited the district, and brought his very family and honored mother to visit, no matter their oddness.

Or as Narani had put it, they had rusted in their former service, little called upon by the aiji, and now luxuriated in a service in the very heart of the court, their historic lodge likewise elevated to unprecedented prominence and wealth. Tourists came to the district to see "the paidhi's country estate" in hopes of the exotic and outrageous, Bren was sure.

His staff survived his mother's residencies with remarkable fortitude, not to mention Toby's children.

Even Tatiseigi's former servants avowed his service to their liking.

"The mail, nadi." Narani assisted him with the coat, delivered the garment to a maidservant, and with a nod indicated the small silver bowl on the ornate, ivory-inlaid table by the entry.

Not unexpectedly, messages had accumulated, formally delivered message cylinders of silver, gold, ivory, and the like, each unique, most with some small felicitation or solicitation for the paidhi's office—these cylinders were from the lordly ranks. The ordinary run of mail, arriving by common post, now had a staff of hundreds in full-time employment: would the paidhi kindly respond to a small association in the hinterlands who suspected the sighting of three meteors was a landing of spacecraft?

Granted.

Would the paidhi tell schoolchildren whether they might write to a school on Mospheira?

They might exchange greetings, no more. They could not let down the barriers that prevented free access . . . not for lunatics in rowboats; not for innocent schoolchildren.

Those were the kind of things the staff handled, up to certain levels. Messages in the silver bowl were likely to be departmental meetings, committee meetings, and policy conferences. Some might have heard about Jase's departure. The whole court might know, it being late afternoon.

But why was he not astonished to see the dowager's message cylinder among the rest? And where was Tabini's?

"Rani-ji," he addressed his major domo. "When did the aiji-dowager's message arrive?"

"Within the last hour, nadi." Narani had not mentioned Jase. But the house was very sober, very quiet compared to happier homecomings. The servant who had taken his coat went away, head bowed, without a sound, and Narani had not a word to say about the shirt cuff.

They stood in a white circular entry hall, reflected in three massive gilt-framed mirrors, before which sat three gilt-and-silver tables on which sat very massive bouquets . . . gold seasonal flowers in blue-and-green porcelain vases. The marble floor held, three times repeated, the baji-naji symbol in black-and-white marble; the same design echoed on the ceiling in a great medallion; and one could suppose someone had counted the number of repeating reflections from every angle of the mirrors, to be sure nothing in the entry hall was infelicitous.

So were all the motives, all the implications, and all the politics around and above him . . . atevi. Tabini-aiji, effective ruler of the world, had not, to his observation, sent a welcoming message to him, and he could not approach the aiji without that invitation. He had to count on Banichi and Jago to get something through to Tabini's staff . . . and to send a message to Tabini reporting what was surely an invitation from the dowager, Tabini's grandmother, was exceedingly indelicate. Among atevi, one trusted a great lord *knew* what was going on. In the Bu-javid, messages flowed like groundwater, invisibly . . . tastefully.

Perhaps a commiseration in the loss of Jase. That would be reasonable to expect. And there was not, not from Tabini.

He opened Ilisidi's cylinder. Not a word of Jase. The message indeed asked him to supper, with scarcely enough time to bathe and dress in sufficient formality.

He was not surprised at all.

But wary of this invitation, aware of all the threads that ran under various doorways here and across the continent . . . oh, yes. He was that.

3

The dowager's apartment was very familiar territory, with a luxurious, red, gold, and black decor, the heraldry of the aiji's line, armed attendants, glorious, though faded, works of tapestry . . . a hall full of familiar faces that met the paidhi's visit. Time and events had forged that cordiality, and it warmed a human heart even while a wary official mind remained on the alert.

Check and mate, as far as getting to Tabini. Bren found himself here, instead, going through social motions. His hair was braided with the appropriate braid of rank. He had on the high-collared coat, quietly, houselessly beige—the fichued shirt, with gold cufflinks . . . no lack of cufflinks, this side of the straits. A little lace, above pale hands as conspicuous as the fair hair. A little scent, appropriately muted, one of the few that both came from an atevi supplier and blended with a human's natural scent: so Jago informed him, while Banichi wrinkled his nose and said it was decadently floral.

Narani, at least, had sent him out the door with professional satisfaction. Banichi and Jago had very naturally come with him, and met the senior bodyguards of the dowager's staff with wary cordiality. They'd saved one another's necks repeatedly, and had as friendly a relationship as their slightly divergent man'chi allowed.

Tano and Algini had brought Jason there, and avowed they had observed nothing untoward. The curious fact remained that Jason hadn't mentioned the visit . . . though human interactions were like that; in the hour they'd had, everything but what was human had fallen out of their minds.

Jason to this hour might be thinking, *My God, I forgot to tell him . . .*

But that Tano and Algini had not . . . *that* was more likely because they deferred to Banichi and Jago, and *they* knew there was something afoot that the paidhi needed to figure out for himself. They couldn't, psychologically couldn't, fight Tabini. He was on his own in that; but they were worried about the footing he was on, trying to guide his steps as accurately as they could through what was shaping up as a maze of intrigue.

"Nand' paidhi." The head of the dowager's security, Cenedi, met him in the dowager's entry, accompanied him from the foyer to the hall . . . and from there on into, thankfully, the dining room, not the cold fresh wind of the balcony, where Ilisidi, accustomed to fresh air and disdainful of assassins, had been known to serve meals.

The dowager waited for him instead in the warm heart of her apartment, a woman slight with age—for her species—leaning on her cane, beside a glittering dinner table centered with crystal, flowers, and candles. There was no grand entry, no keeping him waiting. This was the approach afforded intimates.

"Nand' dowager," Bren said with honest fondness.

"Well, well, so formal, are we?"

"'Sidi-ji,'" he amended that, but only on indication she welcomed it. "I received your invitation and came immediately as I reached my apartment."

"Sit, sit, flatterer." Ilisidi advanced a step toward the table, and her bodyguard whisked her chair into position. She sat; the cane went to the bodyguard's hand with never an interruption of movement, and Bren sat down in a chair as deftly moved and reset by Cenedi's partner. "I support your vices. I have imported *vodka* from the island."

"It's very good of you," he said. He was pleased. A measure of the times and the current size of his office. A subordinate must have passed it, so that she could actually surprise him with an import. His job had grown far, far beyond stamping import manifests.

"With appropriate fruit juice?"

"Thank you," he said, as a glass . . . with unseasonable

ice, decadence in the dowager's opinion . . . turned up in a servant's hand, and settled in place in front of him.

Another servant presented a glass of the dowager's own preference, one of those alkaloid stimulants that could kill a human, or make him wish it had. "So, so, nand' paidhi, how fares your mother?"

"Well. Very well. Complaining of my desertion on a holiday."

"The Independence Day." Ilisidi showed herself amused, and well-informed. "Independence from *us*. What a curious holiday, under the circumstances."

"A historic, a traditional occasion." The inference belatedly dawned on him, that there was in that human ship overhead another threat to Mospheiran independence. "Equally, Mospheirans secured their independence from the Pilots' Guild all those centuries ago by flinging themselves onto the planet in parachutes. I assure you . . . there's certainly no national urge even yet to rush into the arms of the Guild. Even those who wanted to go back to space have their doubts."

"When you first landed, atevi thought you'd fallen from the moon. Now the sun's a star and the morning star a planet. What a strange world we've made! Try the relish. It's from the garden at Malguri. I did inquire of its safety."

"A fond memory." He did help himself. Relish and other pickles were exceptions to the rule of propriety, of *kabiu*: nothing but what grew or was customarily hunted during the season was *kabiu*. What was preserved as a condition of its recipe and served during a subsequent season was acceptable: such were liquors and other products of time and fermentation, which had no season but readiness. Likewise smoked or pickled meats.

And the dowager would not be wrong about the alkaloid content. If she flatly meant to poison him, she would never, on a point of honor, assure him of its safety beforehand.

The relish was, if peppery, quite good with the egg, that standard of atevi appetizers.

"The sun is a star," the dowager reprised, serving herself another two eggs and a dollop of relish, "and the Pilots' Guild so mistrusted by the Mospheirans has now offended another species. So they say." Old, old news; but in that statement the dowager set the topic of the encounter. She knew about the human mission; she was well-briefed. He formed the hypothesis she'd come across the continent to have supper with Jase; and now with him; and that Tabini couldn't prevent her three-hour flight or her interference but might not be pleased with it.

"We don't know that it was an offense the Guild committed, nand' dowager. This strange species may have attacked the Guild for its own reasons."

"Ha. Simply ill-natured, do we believe? Humans launch out from their own star, lose their way, and come here—such is our great good fortune. They fall on our heads. Now they go out looking for their own misplaced planet and manage to offend unidentified neighbors. Given their record, I doubt it was simple bad luck."

"The Mospheiran government, frankly, shares that opinion. Though logically, one can't exclude bad luck."

"They have no sense of felicitous design. Baji-naji." That was to say, chance and fortune could overset the pattern however good or bad. "And this frantic exchange of paid hiin? Acceptable to you?"

"I'd like to hold Jason." They were on diplomatic and personal thin ice. Tabini hadn't asked yet. 'Sidi-ji asked for her own reasons, which she had not divulged. He tried to deflect closer questioning on the exception he was about to advance with Tabini . . . if he could find a way through Tabini's door. The dowager might be a resource, or fuel on a fire. "I'll mourn his departure. I need his help down here."

"They don't present us a successor. Just this fellow Cope who's made a nuisance of himself. Will they?"

"I don't know what they intend. One may come down with the next launch." It was what they'd done with Mercheson.

"They'll debrief our Jason before they send the next one."

"I think that's their intention."

"Understandable in them. Dare we take that motive for what it seems? —More to the point, do you take it that these ship-folk have interests in accordance with yours? I shall never expect they accord perfectly with ours."

"My interests don't diverge far at all from those of the associations, and I don't know, nand' dowager, in all truth. Mospheira doesn't know, either. No one does, not me, not Jase, no one but the officers of the Pilots' Guild . . . and possibly even not all of those."

"Hereditary officers. Lords of their association. Ramirez?"

"As a father to him. A stern father." It didn't mean quite what it did to a human, but it meant man'chi.

"This business of being one of Taylor's Children."

"Just so."

The servants took away the egg dish and replaced it with the seasonal meat, a large, fan-spined fish. It sat atop the platter staring at them from a bed of blue-green weed, but its body was a sculpted white pâté dotted with small green fruits.

The rule was generally to avoid blue foods and mildly suspect the white, but he trusted the dowager, and took a serving without question. A servant set a cruet of herb-flavored vinegar beside his hand, and he applied it.

"Excellent." A friend of the household could never take for granted the sacrifice of a life, however spiny, or the artistic efforts of a cook preparing the dish. "Truly excellent, nandi. My thanks and my admiration."

"Duly accepted, paidhi-ji." Warmly said. "Now. Tell me his tale, not as you told it when we were ignorant of stars and shuttle ships. Tell me the tale as if this time I shall understand destinations. What is this business of Taylor's Children?"

"Taylor was the pilot, the first pilot. *Phoenix* set out centuries ago from the earth of humans to a station construction site, going to a star within sight of the earth of humans. But the ship suddenly flew askew, and turned up instead at a deadly dangerous star, out of fuel, or nearly so."

"Sabotage?"

"It's given it was an accident of subspace, one of those mathematical questions the Astronomer Emeritus—"

The imperious wave of an elderly black hand. "So. Continue. The birth of the children."

"Proximity to the star would mean the early death of those who went outside the ship; but they had to acquire fuel. They used the construction craft intended for station

construction, craft with little protection. Heroic person
went out, knowing the exposure would surely kill them
Indelicate as it is to say—they left their personal legacy in
frozen storage, not out of vanity, but because if they were
so lost, they wished to have a community of sufficient variety for a healthy community. They knew they were in trouble. They died in great numbers."

"And they gathered fuel to move the ship to safety."

"Even so."

"Here. And this *Taylor-captain* guided the ship safely to
this harbor before he died."

"Yes."

Jason had been her guest yesterday, and he'd wager anything that Jason had told her the same tale in carefully
compared detail. He stayed close to the canon.

"So," Ilisidi said, and had a bite of fish. "All those born
of this *legacy* are named the sons and daughters of Taylor.
And they had come to the earth of the atevi. Taylor died.
The pilots wished to stay in space and search for home; the
ordinary folk instead chose to land and become a problem
to us."

"The Pilots' Guild respected the rights of atevi not to be
bothered or contacted. They wanted to move off to the red
star, leaving no station about this planet beyond what they
needed for a very small base. But the colonists didn't agree.
They saw a green planet much like their own. Certain ones
leaped off on the petal sails and fell into the world."

"To a welcome, after initial difficulties," Ilisidi interjected, more expert than he in this phase of atevi history.
"We were entranced with change and your technology. We
became addicted to these offerings."

"While the ship left on its search, leaving some persons
on the planet, others running the station. But as conditions
grew harder on the station, and as the atevi did welcome
the Landing, more and more humans came down."

"Increasing our good fortune," the dowager interjected
wryly.

"So many left the station couldn't function. They could
shut it down and prepare it to wait, in which case it would
take less damage, but shutting it down seemed to necessi-
tate leaving. When the ship came back, after elapsed

centuries . . . all the surviving humans were down here, and everything had changed."

"Yet the ship had had children. They populated the ship with this *legacy*."

"They rarely access it. When they do, they treat those children as special, outside the regular lines of descent. They don't tell whose child they were, so as not to create any sense of preference in their history. They call them all Taylor's Children."

"So Jase is a special person, of consequence within their association."

"A person they're disposed to view as lacking associations. Not as an aiji lacks them, but born for a specific purpose. Captain Ramirez authorized the birth of a number of them . . . with ordinary mothers . . . for the return journey to this earth. They hadn't known about the aliens yet. They were supposed to prepare themselves to contact the station; that purpose stayed. That's why Jase studied languages. He said it was a hobby, but he wasn't quite truthful at the start . . . not in that, not in a lot of things he later told me. He and the others . . . there were ten of them . . . they were purposed for something a lot happier than what Ramirez found when they received a distress call from the second station they'd built out there."

"Languages," Ilisidi echoed, and from her deliberate tone, he knew she'd seen the flaw in the reasoning. "To greet their own descendants. Does the human language change so rapidly, then?"

He had no answer to that. He and Jase had discussed the same question, had looked at Jase's existence in ways Jase had never considered. Jase had said, *There are factions aboard ship* . . . and Jase had acknowledged some of those did not gracefully accept the current negotiations with the atevi.

Ramirez had authorized the birth of the children, had had them encouraged into those very skills that would enhance their ability to negotiate . . . that Ramirez had planned the children to negotiate with the atevi from the start, that Ramirez had had the vision to see beyond human arrogance to welcome aid from any source available . . . that had been well within Jase's understanding of his captain-father, and well within the needs of peace aboard ship that Ramirez would keep such a purpose to himself.

But he couldn't say that to Ilisidi. That was speculation of a nature he hadn't even factual-basis enough to pass on to Tabini. But that Ilisidi, a veteran of subterfuge, had made the logical leap on her own . . . that he could well believe.

"So. Well," Ilisidi, her point made, continued. "With these strangely trained children in tow, they went to this other station which had called and which had suffered great damage in their absence."

"Exactly so. Ramirez questioned the station-folk there, and determined to come here, fall back to this base, thinking he'd find a large population and a thriving station. The ship was not happy in what it did find."

Not happy, yes, but that Ramirez had been surprised . . . that, he and Jase had decided, was highly unlikely.

"One does imagine so." Ilisidi silently finished a massive portion of the fish, and accepted a dish of spiced vegetables. "These are from the south. I've taken quite a fancy to them."

"A very wonderful presentation."

"—Does Mospheira continue to distrust the motives of the Pilots' Guild? Or have they taken alarm at the idea of foreigners chasing the Guild here?"

"Mercheson-paidhi tried to persuade them to cooperate fully. And to trust the Guild's modern leaders. Especially Ramirez."

"Did she succeed in this persuasion?"

"Not wholly." He made up his mind to give Ilisidi a little information, information that might reassure her, and that Tabini wouldn't mind her knowing. "The delegation that's going is suspicious. The Guild will have to work to convince them. They didn't expect to go this early."

"And now Trent Cope will attempt the same quick reconnaissance?"

"I don't know if you can call it that."

"And they take Jase."

"Just so. If I can't find a way to persuade Tabini to rescind the order."

Ilisidi gave a laugh, a very rude laugh. It said her opinion of how likely Tabini was to backtrack.

He tried further. She was an ally, if he could win her. " 'Sidi-ji, the Pilots' Guild would be fools either to offend the aiji or to deal with Mospheirans in any preference. Nature put the resources in Tabini's hands."

"Nature," Ilisidi scoffed.

"So to speak," he amended that. "But they already know they can't get a thing from the Mospheirans but workers who speak their language. A considerable resource. What they *don't* comprehend is the danger of having atevi and humans in close contact. We've warned them. They still don't comprehend because it flies in the face of experience. People who live together a long time should grow closer. Not more angry."

"And the Guild originally was the party to respect atevi rights."

"Just so. But they're desperate now. As a human, nand' dowager, and speaking with all my understanding of the situation, I believe that desperation is real, and that it may drive them to fear atevi less than they ought, or to listen to Mospheirans who may not be well-informed Mospheirans. Above all else, I know Jase knows the truth; it's valuable they listen to him, but if they get him up there, where he doesn't have current contact with information, we're left with Cope, who can't hold his food down, and whom I don't find agreeable; and with some other stranger they're going to drop in our midst, which I don't favor. There are aliens. There is a danger. There may be small omissions in that truth, but I haven't lived with Jason for three years without knowing he's more valuable to us than he gets credit for. If you can intercede with the aiji, do."

"Jason hasn't lied to us. On that, everything rests."

He swallowed a bite that proved just a little large, and took a slow drink to correct it, trying not to let nerves show. They might win. They truly might win. "I have no doubt of him."

"Do you not?" She rapped the table sharply with her knuckles, shaking the liquid in the glasses and causing ice to shift in the pitcher. *"Do you not?"*

He had not fortified himself against all her tactics. Some

still worked, and this one could shake atevi out of their certainties.

It made him think twice, however, how very, very much relied on Jason's truth: how much of their information came from Jason; how all their confirmation with the paidhi on the island did agree . . . but in all of it . . . in all of it . . . trust figured prominently.

"Nand' dowager," he said calmly, "I have asked myself that question for three years, the same I asked at the beginning. I know I'd entrust my life to him. But the responsibility I bear to the aiji and the association to be sure of the truth . . . doesn't allow me to believe anything without question."

"And this Mercheson-paidhi, whose associations you don't thoroughly know?"

"Just so."

"I'd thought a human might have a more exotic answer regarding trust and confirmation."

"My own mother has associations I don't thoroughly know, and consequently there are things I won't tell her. Man'chi doesn't apply, but gossip in the wrong places is a universal problem."

Ilisidi laughed, that short, sharp laugh that said someone had, after all, taken a turn she didn't expect.

"So does my *grandson* have associations of dubious connection," Ilisidi said, still amused, and utterly serious. "Tatiseigi of the Atageini still rests uneasy. —Paidhi-ji, you never lose your edge."

"I treasure the dowager's good opinion." God, were the gift-servants in his own household informing, however indirectly, the aiji-dowager, as he well knew even Banichi and Jago were informing Tabini? "I hope still to justify it."

"Is your amorous bodyguard one of those items you don't mention to your mother?"

He blushed. He knew he did . . . but Ilisidi had been in on this romantic intrigue from the first night.

"I try not to."

"Deceiving one's own mother." The fruit had disappeared. Ilisidi laid down her utensil and leaned her narrow chin on an aged fist. Golden eyes caught the light, wreathed in wrinkles. "I take it, then, she *would* still disapprove.

On the other hand . . . is *she* celibate? Or would she tell you that?''

His mother? He was shocked to think . . . no, she wouldn't tell him. She was completely isolated, completely cut off from relationships outside the family . . . give or take Barb. She'd separated from his and Toby's father and never had another man in her life that he knew. By now that was a fairly long record of no outside associations, but frankly, no, he didn't know what his mother did when he wasn't in town.

Ilisidi laughed, salacious amusement that was her wicked delight in a still active sexuality . . . in which he was relatively sure Cenedi figured somehow. He never understood atevi sensibilities in that regard. They had a great reserve outside an association; an unnerving lack of verbal reserve within one—and he suspected he simply didn't come wired to understand on what grounds she laughed—a fact which he was sure contributed to the joke.

"Your face turns an interesting color," she said.

"I'm sure it does." She'd learned the meaning of a blush: and in all the years of their association he hadn't quite figured out the precise point on which his embarrassment both charmed and amused her. God knew, with 'Sidi-ji, there were far, far more dangerous relationships. And he always played the game . . . won her help, sometimes against very heavy odds.

"So," she said, "are you embarrassed about Jago, before your mother?"

"My mother had far rather I'd married my former lover, who still courts her favor."

A wry smile touched the dowager's thin lips, inexplicable for a moment. Then: "Ah. Barb. And does your brother express an opinion?"

"He regards my staff very highly." Liked them immensely, but there was no atevi word for that. "I rest assured in his loyalty."

"Ha." Ilisidi was delighted. "Has he asked particulars?"

He blushed—again, surely to her triumph.

"Only in the most general way, 'Sidi-ji, and I haven't answered in any particulars."

"Such a gallant lover."

He didn't know on what grounds or on whose behalf he had just been examined, but he found himself on an unfamiliar shore, high and dry, and took, at last, a political risk.

"I would never lie to you, 'Sidi-ji. And I do need your help."

She smiled. Simply smiled. "Welcome home," she said and, perhaps with a touch of the arthritis that plagued her, winced. "Supper is done. These old bones need a rest. I hate old age."

She was not going to say a thing about Jase. And there was a time to stop, cease, let a subject rest where the person of higher rank had decided to leave it.

"I should withdraw, then," he said quietly, "and give you peace. In all high regard for your rest and well-being, nand' dowager. —But if you will I stay, I shall."

"Oh, flatterer." Thin fingers shooed him from the table. "Go. Out."

"Nand' dowager," he said, rose, and excused himself toward the door, attended by the dowager's servants, by Cenedi as well, who brought him to the foyer where Banichi and Jago waited.

"How is she?" he dared ask Cenedi. The dowager being the age she was, he did worry. He never knew; he never knew whether she would intervene or not.

"As ever," Cenedi said . . . no young man himself, but as indefatigable.

"And Jasi-ji?" He never remotely expected Cenedi would betray a confidence, he knew asking had a risk of offense; but pass him a message the dowager herself could not in dignity relay, that Cenedi might do.

"He was here," Cenedi said, "and now he is outside our security, paidhi-ji. We can't reach him. We are concerned."

"So am I," he said, having no answer. "But not for Jase's motives." He passed that word under the table to Ilisidi, who probably would ask Cenedi if he had said anything; and went out, with Banichi and Jago, out into the general hallway, in an area of elegant marble, antique silk carpet, carved tables, and priceless porcelains.

Then he heaved a sigh, finding the vodka had taken the edge off the day; the bruising encounters were at least at distance enough. But if he couldn't get to Tabini . . . then he'd go back to the space center, keep a promise . . . sleep tonight wasn't likely.

"Bren-ji," Banichi said to him as they walked, "the aiji has just requested your presence."

He had his audience. He didn't know but what Cenedi might have sent word through; he thought Banichi might have asked.

Or it was equally possible Tabini had his own agenda, and waited for the end of this supper—knowing Ilisidi had invited him.

Or there was collusion. That was possible, too.

The aiji called. There was no question he had to accept the invitation.

4

Eidi, the major domo of the aiji's household, admitted them to those historic precincts with minimal fuss, and just as smoothly Banichi and Jago, who knew the territory, knew the staff on a familiar basis, disappeared just past the doorway and went aside to the security station as Bren now knew few others would be permitted to do—Banichi and Jago were from this staff, originally, and maintained their ties.

So, technically, was he from the aiji's staff, once upon a time, and still technically was on the staff, in respect of feudal loyalty. Any other lord of the Association might have, as he and Ilisidi had discussed, extraneous ties of man'chi, but he did not, and the welcome over the years had varied very little. Eidi provided him a chair in the small side chamber and whisked up a cup of tea, welcome after Ilisidi's vodka. He sipped that while Eidi went to inform the aiji he had arrived.

A small commotion returned down the length of the foyer. It reached the door, and Bren rose.

Tabini came in still dressed in his court finery, black and red colors of his heraldry, and waved Bren back to his chair. "Well, well, Bren-ji. And how is Grandmother?"

"Very well, as I saw her. Complaining of her age."

"So. So." Tabini dropped into a chair. Tabini was a young man: aiji and paidhi-aiji, chief translator, were both young men. In a certain sense, they had come up together, together survived the tides that tried to wash civilization back onto known shores. "A blindingly quick flight from the hinterlands, and she complains of her arthritis. —Sip the tea, be at ease. I've no need of any. And how did the trip to the island go?"

Governments and theories of government had fallen; they stood, aiji and paidhi-aiji. On Mospheira, at his back, a very odd coalition of hitherto marginalized minorities with *nothing* in common but their detestation of the conservatives and their fear of war; while the aiji had gathered his former opponents, the bluest-bloods of the Association, to overcome the wealthy conservatives and get atevi into the space business.

"How fares Mospheira?" Tabini asked.

"As it has been. Always as it has been." *I was startled as hell to learn you'd admitted four humans to the space center* did occur to him. *I was upset as hell you'd moved Jase out,* was ahead of that, but he let Tabini get there at his own speed.

"The new paidhi was accepted?"

"There's no polite choice. They find no affront in Mercheson's withdrawal, but they're not happy and they wonder what she'll say."

"Since they tried to kill her, probably not a thoroughly positive report."

"But to recall her . . . Mospheirans accept this as the Guild's right over its own representative. I did talk with Shawn Tyers. And talked with the delegates on the plane. They were surprised you granted their visa, aiji-ma."

"Were they? And the meeting with Jase?"

"We talked at some length." He kept all expression off his face, out of his voice. "I advise the aiji against sending him."

"When shall we send him, then?"

A question, a challenge for an answer. "When the second shuttle flies," he said. "I need Jase."

"And if I say he goes as Ramirez-aiji requires?"

"Then he will go, aiji-ma. But I'll wish to go back to the space center. I was surprised, of course. We spent the conversation reminiscing. I fear I came away not having asked things I should have asked. I'm not ready to lose this man. . . ."

"What would you have asked?"

"Principally, what Jase thinks they'll ask next. He doesn't

think they'll let him come down soon. I find this alarming."

It wasn't no, not yet. He still schemed to advance a plan.

"He might take moderately ill. The shuttle cycles in six weeks. That would give us time, aiji-ma."

"Time. —And Trent Cope? Did he recover?"

"Jase doesn't favor him. I don't. Though it's very difficult for a person to be forthcoming when he knows he's sedated."

"Understandable. He has all of Jason's physical difficulties?"

"Moving at night did prove better."

"And your household? Well?"

"Very well, aiji-ma."

"And President Durant?"

God, what was this? A catalog?

"Very well. I introduced Trent-paidhi myself, though Trent-paidhi was mildly indisposed and took immediate leave to a windowless room. The President asked politely regarding your health, aiji-ma, and extended his wishes for you and Lady Damiri."

There was no reaction to the good wishes. Tabini, even seated, towering in the natural height of adult atevi, was a powerful individual . . . a hunter on opportunity, besides a student of every curiosity, and of technology. His gold eyes were pale to the point of ill omen, and the predatory look came naturally. There might never have been so progressive and enlightened a ruler as Tabini in all the history of the Western Association. But his direct, continuing stare unnerved his opponents.

"You were surprised by the delegation, paidhi-ji?"

"Utterly. I knew they were training a group to go, as of last year. I knew there was going to be a request as soon as the shuttle officially had a flight schedule. I did report that, aiji-ma, I'm sure I did."

"You did, nand' paidhi. I certainly attach no fault to you in this matter of the delegation; on the contrary, I sent directly to Tyers, and *suggested* this mission."

Without translation? It was impossible. Someone had mediated. Someone knew what was going on. He damned sure didn't.

No study, no committee, no hesitation. Bang! Stamped,

sealed, approved, and the team suddenly had a visa; use it or else.

In the same heartbeat came a footfall at the door, a whisper of fabric, a faint whisper of spice, to nostrils assailed with Mospheiran scents for days. Lady Damiri arrived in the room, and Bren rose in courtesy as Tabini's wife settled in the graceful chair at Tabini's elbow.

"We will miss you, paidhi-ji," Damiri said to him.

Miss? Bren thought in shock, and Tabini looked vexed.

"Light of my life," Tabini began.

"Oh, you haven't told him."

"No, I haven't told him, daja-ma. —Bren, nadi, there was a reason I sent Jase Graham to the space center in such haste. Your belongings are by now packed."

While he was at the dowager's apartment? In a matter of two hours? "And I'm going . . . where, aiji-ma?" To Ilisidi's estate at Malguri, perhaps. Perhaps that was the connection with Ilisidi's invitation, and this—he was needed somewhere, maybe another insurgency, some further difficulty with the anti-space conservatives. Twice before, he'd found himself moved out to regions of political stress under extreme security and with little notice.

"Do you approve, paidhi-ji, this mission of representatives to the station? Are these acceptable persons?"

"Two translators from the Foreign Office, Feldman and Shugart, belong to Shawn Tyers; or Podesta. She's department head now. They're advisors, very junior. I don't know the other two. One is from Commerce. Anyone from that department is a concern to me. That's George Barrulin's old power base."

"Translators of Ragi," Tabini mused. "To go to the space station."

"Awareness of nuance and context makes them valuable observers. I understand why Tyers sends them . . . I know why they formed the team as they did." *Four. Infelicitous four,* he thought. It was not a good number. He'd been functioning with the Mospheiran side of his brain not to see that at the outset.

But Jase was going. Set of five.

"What does Jase fear?" Tabini asked. "He expressed no fears to me."

"He wouldn't," Bren said. "He respects you. He knows he has no recourse. And I *still* ask, aiji-ma, that you not send him yet. The next flight. Not this one. They'll understand . . . they won't *expect* you to grant their request. A human would delay."

Tabini had a wry expression. "Delay, with these aliens coming."

"It's human, aiji-ma. And I need him. They won't argue. They won't take offense."

"In this additional time . . . what would you gain?"

"Questions. More questions."

"And three years have not sufficed?"

It was a very good question . . . one he couldn't outright answer, except they weren't either of them ready for this.

"Jase wants to see his ship again; and he knows, in the economy of things, he's become a valuable advisor to them."

"As to you."

"As he is to me," Bren acknowledged.

"He will go, advise his people, then return."

"Not likely. They've no reason to let him come back."

"I shall place a personal request for his return."

"I fear your request won't get him back, aiji-ma. Not from the Guild."

"Will Jase remain well-disposed to us? Will he wish, then, what he wishes now?"

"He'll feel emotional attachment. He'll fall into old associations."

"And this mission from the island? Will they find things familiar? Will *they* obey the Pilots' Guild? Or oppose them?"

"I don't know. There'll be an emotional context for them. The sites of history have their impact."

"*Naojai-tu,*" Damiri said quietly, "nand' paidhi."

"Like that," Bren said. The *machimi* plays were the collected wisdom of atevi history, the culture of the Western Association. In *Naojai-tu*, a cynical woman came face to face with relics she had thought remote and unimportant . . . and in the impact they had, in the context, she turned on her lover. Indeed, he knew the play, and its conclusion.

Unguessed association, unguessed emotional reaction, unguessed affiliations devastatingly realized.

And when one came down to analyzing the emotional impact of the human team seeing the station their ancestors had come from—or the feelings Jason would have face to face with his relatives again—yes, atevi could indeed comprehend that. Sometimes humans jumped the same direction atevi jumped when startled.

But you didn't take for granted it was the same reason for the reaction. Or the same outcome. "And what was Jason's reaction to the mission?" Tabini asked.

"He didn't meet with them immediately. He had a short time to see me; he chose that. We met, we talked, and I forgot to ask him questions I should have asked. He didn't ask me, either. On a certain level I think we knew we'd become separate in our man'chi, so to speak. When he goes back—he'll have no aiji but Ramirez. So we reminisced, and said good-bye."

Tabini listened soberly.

"That's very sad," Damiri-daja said.

"Do you have confidence in the President's intentions?" Tabini asked. "And Ramirez?"

Not—is the President of Mospheira lying?—which would be one question, but—do you have confidence in him; and in Tyers; and in the senior captain of the ship-humans?

"Aiji-ma, it's the same story: Mospheirans want to lead their lives and not worry. A leader who makes them worry isn't popular. Right now, they remember that the Heritage Party nearly took them to war. Now ship-humans make them worry about the chance there are unfriendly aliens out there. They'd rather not think about it. So they won't. All this mission learns will create a furor at first . . . then lose attention. All the President does and all the conservatives do about it will be quiet unless there's a direct, imminent threat. There's no energy for it, not so soon after the people kicked the conservatives out of office."

Tabini smiled. It was certainly the short version of the politics of Mospheira, but it compassed very similar emotions on the mainland: Bren knew it did. *Never* upset the midsection of the Association, never annoy uncle Tatiseigi . . . or Lord Geigi.

"One day I should meet the President of Mospheira," Tabini said, implying there would be no few frustrations in common with Hampton Durant. "So shall we proceed in tasteful silence through these machinations? Or shall we wake two populations from their sleep?"

"Only to tell them both we've found a good solution, aiji-ma."

"Therefore I asked this mission to go with Jase. Time is ours now; perhaps not, if these remote aliens begin to dictate the schedule. Therefore, paidhi-ji, I'm sending you to the station."

My God, he thought.

And: No. I can't.

It was the dream of his life, that the space program should have just gotten off the ground with him to witness it. That *Shai-shan* should turn out to be his creation . . . he'd stood on the side of the runway and watched its first flight half a year ago, watched the shuttle become a gleam in the sky, and a dot, and a memory and a hope. When, two weeks later, he had stood on that same runway and watched *Shai-shan* land as easily as any airliner—God, he'd wept.

But go *up* there? That wasn't for *him*.

His face, he discovered, didn't react, hadn't reacted. Like his predecessor, Wilson, who'd forgotten how to deal with human emotion, he'd stopped reacting.

"Aiji-ma," he said quietly, accepting that this would happen, "on this flight?"

"On this flight," Tabini said. And one could not say: but my business, but my possessions, my duties, my staff. One listened. "To remain until you've understood them, and then to return to me. You can conduct your other duties by radio, can you not? And your staff is adept enough to carry on without you, at least the commercial aspects. Diplomatic matters with the Pilots' Guild take precedence until there is an agreement regarding our station."

Our station. That was Tabini's position. Humans had built it, Mospheira didn't want it, didn't want to lose it, either. Atevi weren't historically happy about it being there, didn't want Mospheirans to have it, and Tabini wanted it under his authority.

He hadn't thoroughly explained that position to Mospheira, but Jase knew.

Get me the sun and the moon, paidhi-ji. Toss in the good will of the Pilots' Guild for good measure.

Everything was in motion. Everything had been in motion before his plane had set down on the runway. Everything had gotten into motion during his five days isolated and out of touch on Mospheira. Tabini started planning this the day the ship called Yolanda Mercheson home; they called Jason, the day before the shuttle launched, expecting a wrangling argument, and Tabini . . . simply complied, high and wide.

The ship-humans wanted the program to move faster?

It was about to move faster.

"You must take care," Damiri-daja said.

"Daja-ma, I will."

"Safeguard yourself," Tabini said with unaccustomed fierceness. "Your bodyguard need not return to me if any mishap takes you."

Then Banichi and Jago were going with him.

But no one would have asked them their opinion, either, and what had been sacrificed in cargo to add three more passengers with baggage . . . God, the baggage! . . . he had no idea. Everything . . . all the scientific packages, all the materials tests . . .

Where did those stand?

What *were* they taking?

What in hell was he supposed to do to make this miracle happen?.

"I'll work with Jase," he said to Tabini.

"If they prove intractable, leave."

"Yes, aiji-ma."

"I insist on it," Tabini said, and rose. Damiri-daja rose, and Bren rose.

Together, while he bowed, they left him.

He stood there a moment then, in the middle of the ornate carpet, next to the historic chairs. All the warmth had gone out of him.

He'd built it. He was going to ride it. He was going *with* Jase, who'd just been coopted back under the captains' authority. If Jase chose to have that happen . . . and probably he should; probably the captains shouldn't notice that humans who dealt with atevi tended to grow very strange.

So, well, he said to himself, drew a deep breath and went out, then, not forgetting to pay courteous notice to Eidi, as composed as if he hadn't just learned he was riding a plane into orbit, to filch change out of the Pilots' Guild's pockets.

An agency his compatriots on Mospheira thought of as the devil incarnate.

Had he somehow, somewhere failed to relay that to Tabini?

And Tabini had talked to Shawn?

He walked casually toward the foyer, where he regained his escort.

"Nadiin," he said simply, taking his leave of Tabini's security. "Nadiin-ji," he added, the warmer address to men he knew, and walked outside the heavy doors in his own security's company.

They, he suspected, had known something was going on from before they picked him up at the airport. They might not have known where he was going, but they'd known they were going with him, and were bound by the aiji's orders to let him go through this long evening of dinners and conversations—

While his personal belongings were doubtless packed, moved, attended to . . .

They walked down a hallway resplendent with antiquity and scrutinized by a hundred hidden watchers, electronics, spying devices, all of the panoply of the iron-handed ruler of a world civilization . . . who didn't damned much move anywhere without his knowing it.

"Well," he said to Banichi and Jago, not accusingly, only to assure himself the needful things were done, "not surprised, were you."

"Nandi," Jago said quietly. "To be sent up to the station? We were surprised by the destination, not by the fact that we would move."

"Nand' Jase doesn't know."

He considered that, as they approached the lift. "He's going to be shocked." As hell, he thought.

"I think he will be," Banichi said.

They stood at the lift. He suddenly realized he had no

notion which button to push, whether to go to his apartment, or down to the train. "The staff has packed?"

"While you were at supper," Banichi said.

"Tano and Algini are going," Jago said, and punched in for the lowest level. It *was* the train. "Likewise Narani, Sabiso, Kandana and Bindanda."

"Bindanda." One of Tatiseigi's. His mind went flying off on a suspicious tangent, involving Ilisidi's long association with Tatiseigi, Tatiseigi's occasional opposition to Tabini, and the likelihood more than one element of the Association had been brought in on this before he had.

Bindanda, a quiet, polite spy.

Four security, around a fifth point. Himself. Nine, with the servants. A very fortunate number: 'counters had devised it, in harmony with the space center and shuttle.

One wondered how those numbers fit in with the station and the Guild.

"Narani's quite old for this excitement," he said as the car arrived.

"He avows his health will withstand it. He's left Tagi in charge of your apartments, moved Edoro into Tagi's place in your coastal estate, nandi, with your approval."

The warmth hadn't yet come back to his hands. He stepped into the lift.

He hadn't his most comfortable clothing; he had only what he stood in.

He and Jase had made extensive preparations to set up an atevi residency on the station. There were items of baggage. There were pieces of equipment.

"Are we displacing all the cargo?" he asked.

"One believes so," Banichi said.

He didn't know what he was going to tell Jase.

5

It was back on the train . . . going the other direction, a passage punctuated by the click of the rails and the whisper of the car's passage against the wide and narrow portions of the tunnels.

He sat with Banichi and Jago, sure his baggage from the airplane would turn up, at least the needful things. The computer would turn up. He was entirely sure of it.

"Did the dowager know?" he asked, out of a moment of silence.

"I believe she made great haste in arranging a flight," Banichi said. "That's all we know."

Bindanda was one of the number. If Tabini had deceived his redoubtable grandmother, that deception would have meant very unhealthy things going on within the Association. Tatiseigi was always an uneasy ally.

"One is honored," he said of the dowager and her dinner. "I'm glad she came."

Jago lifted a brow. "She has no return flight arranged," Jago said, "that we know."

She might well have decided to stay and become a thorn in the side to Tabini, or so Tabini would claim.

Yet it was remarkable how close that apparently divided house could stand, in crisis . . . no few of the aiji's enemies had discovered it.

Ilisidi had brought herself and her security, for what was bound to be a period full of speculation among the lords: what would the paidhi learn? What would Tabini agree to? What would be the relation with Mospheira? . . . that was bound to follow his ascent into space.

God, he didn't want to think about the flight. He'd survived watching the flights, had nervous fits watching the landing. The switchover in engines was a miracle the technicians swore was flawless, but it always seemed a chancy thing to do, cut off perfectly good engines several miles above the ocean.

A part of him wanted to go to the one atevi physician who monitored his health and ask for total sedation. He wasn't sure he could do this; he'd been shot at, shot, and chased down mountains; but engine switchover scared hell out of him.

So did facing Jason at the end of this train ride with, *Oh, well, you know how Tabini can be. He decided to send me with you. I swear I didn't know. And by the way, we're taking the station.*

Sorry for the inconvenience, old friend.

He was still in that psychological dislocation that a trip to Mospheira tended to bring him, that sudden trip among people his height, furniture his size, steps his convenient dimensions, language and food he'd grown up with; and now, leaving Jase in the space center, he'd just definitively cleared the air of the island enclave from his lungs, human language from his head, and human expectations from his emotions.

Now, in the obliging silence of his security, he tried to jerk all that back into focus. Banichi and Jago, sitting across from him on the red velvet seats, became two stone-faced giants in the black leather and silver of their profession, black of skin, black of hair, gold of eye . . .

He knew, the patterns and the battles he understood . . . he was valuable *here,* dammit, the world's leading expert on the atevi-human interface. Someone else could do this part . . . maybe a year from now.

Jase was the logical one. *Jase* should be in Tabini's employ and reckon whether Tabini hadn't tried to get Jase's loyalty into his hands?

He knew that answer, suddenly, knew it hadn't played right from Tabini's point of view, and Tabini had played the hand he had left.

And what *was* the meeting Jase had had with the dowager? Fond farewell? The dowager had been her grandson's greatest opposition—on certain causes; but at times she was solidly her grandson's conduit of policy. Had that been a sounding-out?

And had Jase failed it . . . or had he never been in the running?

"Well," Bren said with a sigh, "well." The deep-welling panic about the shuttle flight took its place in a long queue, somewhere behind having to deal with Jase, and that itself was somewhere behind his knowledge that he himself was Tabini's . . . and that civilization rested very heavily on his being faithfully Tabini's . . . whatever Jase was or became.

It wasn't the situation he wanted to contemplate. Jase was likely to be mad; if he mismanaged the matter, things could get worse.

"How far in Tabini's confidence is the dowager in this matter?" he asked his security.

"One has no sure knowledge, nadi," Banichi said. "We were aware of movements; we did not investigate the aiji's doings."

"I understand that," Bren said. More exotic and more mundane affairs came flooding into his head. "Mospheira very carefully selected four persons, no staff: and I have— what, *eight*, with baggage? This will disturb Mospheira, I fear, not to mention the delegation; not to mention the station. We should be alert to that."

"The paidhi-aiji will *not* make his own supper," Banichi said. "These things were agreed."

Know to an exactitude the limitations of mass and cargo? Banichi's native gift for mathematics exceeded the norm for his species, considerably. In human terms, he would have been a prodigy.

"How much cargo did we displace?" he asked his staff.

"Sufficient," Jago answered, "to assure your safety and comfort."

They had their weapons on them; they always did; and he apprehended that the kitchen likely wasn't the only thing they were bringing along in cargo.

"They have never advised us our facility is complete," Bren said.

"Did not this station once shelter three hundred thousand humans? And do we not reckon the crew of the ship to be two thousand five hundred at largest?"

"They have the ship," Banichi said. "They can live there."

"We will claim a very fine accommodation," Jago said firmly, "for a lord of the Association."

And the weapons, he wondered?

"Will they be wise," asked Banichi, "to attack the paidhi-aiji on his first mission?"

"They're as fond of surprises as Uncle Tatiseigi."

"The paidhi is a very skilled negotiator," Banichi said with supreme confidence.

Get control of the station, for God's sake. He had to argue fast for that one. Mospheirans might not want a thing, but they didn't want their rivals to have it.

Looking at the microfocus, he'd thought of Cope as the principal problem, and assumed Yolanda's recall was all the Guild was going to ask for a while. He and Jase had assumed that the Pilot's Guild would take a long while to digest all that Yolanda could tell them. Consequently, he'd been utterly blindsided by this second request, this notion of having Jase back up there.

So had Tabini. Tabini didn't like it—but took, not the path of resistance, but the path of equal action in their system of half-formed agreements.

One wanted to know what atevi were culturally set up to expect? The machimi plays held a repertoire of treachery and double-cross. It was the common trick, in the machimi, to try to move some agents about distractingly and achieve a move not suspected, not even by the all-seeing audience.

Mercheson hadn't resisted going. Shall we send Mercheson-paidhi? Tabini had asked. And he and Jase hadn't seen it coming, hadn't drawn the line. Nor had Mercheson.

So now the ship captains asked more, and at the last moment. And Tabini reacted.

He couldn't claim he himself understood the Pilot's Guild. They were human, but they damned well didn't feel like Mospheirans . . . not the old familiar, frustrating debating and delaying of the Mospheiran policy-making apparatus. The ship's captains were autocrats. In that, they and Tabini understood one another better than the captains were going to understand what the Mospheirans were doing.

Across the barrier of gravity and distance, the maneuvering of subordinates was not easy: one couldn't, say, as in the machimi plays, ask a major player to tea and serve up daggers.

Now the ship suddenly had Jase, whom they'd asked for, plus a lapful of Mospheirans with their agenda, and worse, an atevi presence at the same time, instead of the test cargo it expected. He could almost see it in historical dress, the blithe guests at the doorway, banners flying: refuse us or accept us. Draw swords or deal.

If it wanted to turn them around and send them back down unreceived, it still had a two-week delay at minimum to service the shuttle. It still faced the fact it couldn't leave them all on board the shuttle for two weeks unless it meant to murder them all, because life-support wouldn't last that long . . . and it couldn't just shoot them, either, if it ever wanted to deal reasonably and cheaply for earthbound supplies.

It said it desperately needed those supplies, and thus far urged the world into a breakneck development of technology and materials.

The Guild also couldn't take over the shuttle . . . couldn't fly a complex surface-to-orbit craft themselves.

Let the Guild look across their steel battlements and figure all that out.

He drew a quieter breath, gazed at his two companions, at Tano and Algini, too, standing their somewhat more distant station at the end of the rail car, and he thought all these thoughts in a tumbling race while the wheels clicked over the joints of steel rails.

When he'd first arrived in his job as a very young paidhi replacing an old and retiring one, the paidhi's office had still been trying to convince atevi that an air traffic control system over large communities was a good idea.

Atevi had leaped centuries in a decade, unanimity of effort that was *only* possible because of the Western Association and the power Tabini-aiji could fling into action on a wave of his hand. Mospheira called it autocracy, and that was true on the surface, but only true if one backed far, far away from the workings of the government and the legislature and took a human-tinted view. Atevi had committees.

God, atevi had committees. Lord Brominandi could put a tree to sleep.

But the committees didn't debate what the aiji paid for out of his own pocket . . . and every subassociation on the continent had wanted a slice of the budget and a connection to the new materials and industries. The download of designs from the ship archive had become a feeding-frenzy of industrial sponsorship, because there was no question that the world was going to change.

Tabini had fought the requisite small skirmishes in the process, several of them, right to the brink of war, but never over it.

Take the kitchen? Damned right they would. Take his bodyguard, his servants, his staff—they didn't go with him to Mospheira, by virtue of the treaty that kept humans and atevi on this world separate and sane. But the station was going to be atevi territory.

The interface was a lot safer than it had been historically; atevi were a damned sight more sophisticated than they had been. Mospheirans likewise.

It was a question of what the Pilots' Guild had become.

But Tabini hadn't backed down yet: blood and conniving bone, yes, the atevi lord of lords, the one other atevi regarded as dangerous, simply waited for the moment the Pilots' Guild blinked.

Conversation stopped, in the group of Mospheirans gathered in chairs about the low table in the lounge. Bren walked the rest of the way in, scanned the room for Jase first of all, and didn't find him, not there with the Mospheirans, not in the dining nook.

Ginny Kroger got to her feet first, and asked the logical question: "Mr. Cameron. Is there a problem?"

"No, not as such. What I didn't know this morning was that the aiji's just formed a mission of his own. Atevi are going. I'll accompany you up on this flight."

The body language said they'd been struck, one and all, a second blow to their certainties when they'd been rushed into this mission not on their own schedule; and now they'd been finagled. Conned.

Lund got to his feet, and Feldman and Shugart, less certainly.

"Quite honestly," Bren said, "this came as a surprise to me. I suppose it shouldn't have, but here I am. I'll be lodging next door, this evening, in the atevi facilities, but I did come by to advise you. To advise Jase Graham, who doesn't know anything about this, either."

"You're welcome here," Lund said, as cheerfully as he might invite a known thief into their midst. But it was graciously done, all the same.

"That's very kind of you," Bren said. And at that, Jase did come out of his room, not hopefully. Jase hadn't seemed to have overheard the details, only the voice, and didn't look as if he expected miracles, or a reprieve.

"Bren?"

"He's sent me, too." He was very conscious of the witnesses. *"I'm* going."

"Are you?" Jase asked. It was the question of a man who'd known he was in a rapid river, and now heard the cataract. "The aiji's orders, is it? His idea?"

"Very much so," Bren said. *Jase* could speak of the aiji in the third person remote. Jase had a welcome in the aiji's apartment, had the familiarity to speak of him, if Lund didn't. "I think he figures things are moving, since the Guild asked for you. 'Go up and deal with them,' he said. So—here I am. Me. Banichi and Jago . . . four of the staff. With the galley." When he said that, Jase would know everything: it *was* the full mission, as they'd planned it. "I hadn't any notion until he called me in this evening, and then it was turn around, get on the train, go."

Lund had the look of a canny businessman. The junior translators were simply dumbfounded; Kroger, from Science, looked as if she had swallowed something unpleasant."So what does this mean?" Kroger asked. "Are you cooperating with *us,* or what?"

"The aiji has his requests to make of the Guild . . . one of the foremost to be sure there *are* adequate quarters for us. We will cooperate, if there's any difficulty in that regard. The other matters . . ." He let the statement fall, not willing to lie to them. "Our missions are separate. I don't know how long it will take. I hope for the same turnaround. If not . . . we'll hope they find somewhere for all of us. I do regret the surprise."

"Well," Lund said. "Well. It *is* a surprise."

They had to realize now that their job had just become far more complex, that they weren't going to get unfettered access to the Guild up there, if they had ever laid elaborate plans in that regard. They couldn't be pleased with that. Managing their own reencounter with the Pilots' Guild, when the Pilots' Guild was simultaneously face to face with atevi for the first time in all history . . . they'd been sand-bagged, in short. As he'd been, as Jase had been . . . as the Pilots' Guild was about to be. It was a three-way ma-neuver, and Tabini had assigned him, flatly, to get ahead of the Mospheirans.

"Well," Jason said faintly, "good. I'm glad of the com-pany.—Want to sit down? Fruit juice?"

"Madi," Bren said, deciding to force his way into the company from which Jase had kept himself isolated, in his room. It was an early fruit, green, biting and sour.

Jase went into the dining nook, bent down to take it from the refrigerator . . . took down a glass.

Bottled juice, poured into a glass: Jase had scandalized the staff, early on in the bottled juice experiment, drinking from a bottle; and not since.

"Glass," Jase said.

"Glass." Bren took his drink, settled . . . trusted Banichi, Jago, and the rest attended the questions of cargo and bag-gage. And weaponry. God knew what was going into cargo.

God knew what the station would say.

"So," Tom asked, "what are you going to ask them?"

"A working agreement. A means that doesn't get Mos-pheirans *or* atevi dying in the labor force. The aiji specifi-cally honored his agreement with you in his plans. In his terms, that's adherence to the agreements. Work with me. I'll work with you. Fact-finding, I'm very much in favor of."

"The facts," Jase said in a faint but carrying voice, "the facts are, there's a threat out there that may come here."

"Fact-finding," Kroger said, annoyed. "We're not pre-pared to make agreements."

"I am," Bren said.

"Mr. Cameron, this puts us in a difficult position. We need to contact our offices. Tonight."

"I intend to cooperate fully with your mission," Bren said, "and hope for the same courtesy. Contact your offices as you like. The phone will go through, I'm sure."

Lund said, "We've left scheduling to the atevi government. Does the ship even know we're coming?"

"Probably not," Bren said. "They will."

"Good God."

"It's not the aiji's style to make it possible for the other side to argue," Bren said. "We *have* an agreement amongst ourselves. You don't want to contract for labor in bad conditions; we don't; they need us badly. That adds very simply. If we on the world present a reasonable case that gets them what they want in a timely fashion, we get economic benefits and we all get some sort of preparation against whatever threat comes over the cosmic horizon."

"Until what?" Kroger asked. "Until the aiji decides to surprise *us* with another maneuver we aren't told about?"

"He will do that," Bren said. "It's my job to make sure it's as fair as possible."

"Mr. Cameron, you're *their* representative."

If he weren't Mospheiran he wouldn't have understood that statement. Jase probably didn't. And the species-based blindness that produced so obvious an observation ran cold fingers down his back.

"Yes," he said, "as I've made as clear as possible. I hold a rank *within* Tabini-aiji's court, I hold my Mospheiran office only because no other paidhi can get a visa, and over that I have no control. Your interpreters can tell you I don't control the issuance of visas in the aiji's government. I will negotiate on the aiji's behalf. I will speak on the aiji's behalf to Mr. Graham, here, who you might remember speaks for the Guild. That *is* his function. So we shouldn't burden him with witnessing too much. On my own, I apologize for the shortness of the notice. For the aiji, I don't apologize, because it's perfectly reasonable. Explaining that point is my job. You won't have to explain it to the Pilots' Guild. I will. If, on the other hand, you want to request a plane to take you home tonight, I can arrange that."

There was a lengthy, heated silence.

Anxiety, anxiety, anxiety, on every front. What new technology would arrive to disrupt the economy? How could manufacturers bet on known factors in the economy when something could fall out of space and throw all calculations awry?

At least within their imaginations, fortunes were at risk; their independence as Mospheirans was at risk.

"Ultimately," he said, "humans don't rule this planet, but you don't want to be ruled by the Guild, either. The aiji fully supports your position."

"Well, now," Lund said, clearly the peacemaker, while Kroger scowled, the lines of her face set in what now looked like a habit of fury. "We have political stability to consider; we're not splintering off into a second colony."

"That's always a hazard," Bren agreed. "The aiji would agree."

"And I say we aren't here to negotiate," Kroger said.

"And I am," Bren said quietly. "I don't negotiate for Mospheira. But I think the Guild will rather well expect something to result besides fact-finding. I think we'll exit with some kind of agreement, because I know the aiji's prepared to move to the next stage."

"Then let atevi die working for the Guild," Kroger said.

"I'm sure he's not prepared to have that happen," Bren said, "and I'm sure the Guild's perfectly happy to have the goods they want without loss of life. On the other hand, there *can* be profit in this for Mospheira, including the fishing industry, food, and electronics . . . the usual areas of specialty."

Electronics was lately in danger, but Mospheirans were still convinced of their superiority.

"Finished goods," Bren said, to Kroger's scowl. "That's what Mospheira has tended to do. We have the lift vehicles; you have specialized manufacturing and you process the kind of foods the station needs far more reliably." No alkaloid poisons, that was to say; humans were naturally very careful of that sort of thing. "You want the status quo. There's no reason to see that change. Humans who want to go into space, I'm sure will find a place. Humans who don't will have their way of life undisturbed, and the aiji's prepared to guarantee that point."

Kroger's face relaxed ever so slightly. "We'll hear your proposal."

"I'm making it. A guarantee of stability. Freedom to come and go. Protection for Mospheira against any demands or encroachment."

"You can't guarantee that."

"I know the aiji's position. I'm very confident of it."

"He can't withstand the Guild," Kroger said, and cast an uneasy glance in Jason's direction, as if for a heartbeat she'd forgotten who and what he was. "He's not able to withstand them."

"He can," Jase said, and drew all attention, but that was all he said.

"He will," Bren said, and set down the empty glass. "Jase. Mr. Graham. Will you allow me a brief consultation?"

"I will," Jase said.

Bren rose, resisted the habit of a slight bow. "Morning comes before dawn," he said. "Gentlemen. Ladies."

"Mr. Cameron," Kroger said. "Don't take us for agreeing."

"No," Bren said. They didn't have the power, and he was sure they didn't, but he had the uneasy suspicion he'd heard Kroger's opinion, the anthropocentric side of Mospheiran politics. If she wasn't Heritage, she at least cast that shadow across the proceedings, and he wasn't so sure Lund even realized it, if he had to guess. He'd have taken Lund for the problem, being out of Commerce, but he began to see compromise in the composition of this mission . . . Lund thinking he was in charge, but Kroger armed with understandings . . . he very much feared that was the case: understandings that had nothing to do with Mospheira remaining independent, and everything to do with the last regime's aims at getting into orbit, getting in power, running human society in a way that had nothing to do with the general will of the Mospheirans as they were and everything to do with old, old agreements with the Guild.

"But I will see you before daylight," he said, and caught Jase's eye as he left.

Jase went to the door with him, to the outer hall.

"Very much need to talk with you," Bren said. "Never mind what they think."

6

A diplomatic, an official action, this first venture into space. To Mospheiran humans, that meant a balanced array of powerful men and women, human interests that could wangle a spot on the team all represented by someone—hence the circle of rooms around a central meeting point—no one more important than the next. Well, give or take the two Shawn Tyers had put in, Bren thought, walking the hall toward his own quarters . . . gathering up Algini and Tano in the process: trust that his security was never that far from him. They met him, walked with him, overshadowing him, in the black leather and silver of their Guild . . . good men, both.

And surely Mospheiran dignitaries, given the chance to take more than two translators along, would like to have their secretaries, their whole array of support, including NSA and the appurtenances of Mospheiran dignity.

But those seats on the shuttle were not free of cost, and on the whole, they'd rather be assured that *if* their competition was going, they were going, too.

So they had four seats.

But to atevi, the fortunate gods forbid there should be a laying out of the interregional issues of the Western Association in front of strangers, a diplomatic mission meant the highest representative of the court appropriate to the task, with his supportive community.

And servants were more immediately essential than secretaries, although the four he had could double in that capacity. And security: no atevi lord was ever without security, day or night.

Algini keyed open the door for him into the atevi side

of the space center, and Narani met him, closely followed by the others, with deep, respectful, surely anxious bows.

"Nand' paidhi," Narani said. "We had orders."

"One knows, Rani-ji. You've done a wonder, I'm very sure. Thank you all."

Reception foyer, a dining hall, a sitting room, several bedchambers for the lord and his security, who were never far from him. A bath, what atevi genteelly called the accommodation, a cloakroom, a security post, a reading room, a kitchen—all that was minimal.

And when he and Jase had designed the place, in company with atevi architects, the requisite bedchambers and recreational facilities for, they had decided, a minimal four servants, since the servants had to attend the security personnel as well, and assure the security personnel had their minds utterly free to do their duties. Even if for some reason the aiji had sent a tradesman or craftsman . . . neither craftsfolk nor trades came as isolated individuals. The carpenter would have his apprentices, not to mention family and servants; the plumber would bring his own equipment, his apprentices, and if not servants and security, at very least some remote younger relative of a relative who made tea for the customers . . . how could one respectably do otherwise and answer obligations to the relatives? If the Mospheirans had a set of independent luxury rooms opening out onto a common room where varying interests could meet, the atevi answer was a single household, inward-turned, a hierarchy with a master or mistress at the top.

"Jase is coming," he said to Banichi and Jago when he passed the small security station.

"Shall we include Jasi-ji?" Narani asked, following him.

"He won't stay, I much doubt it," Bren said. "But he will come. We'll have vodka, Rani-ji, in the sitting room. Might there be a fire?"

"Immediately, nandi."

Jase being under other orders, it wasn't proper, he suspected, to include Jase in his personal arrangements, not for the sake of a few hours. If he undermined Jase's status as an independent representative of his ship, and if the captains took exception, that could prove a distraction.

Only if Jase asked. Then they should, and he'd deal with the difficulties.

He didn't want a fracture in his understandings with Jase—above all else, he didn't.

And sure enough, Jase arrived not a minute later, in his jersey and that wretched jacket.

The servants fussed and made despairing motions toward taking the jacket, but Jase complained of chill.

Bren said not a word, only showed him to the sitting room and offered him a chair by a just-lit fire.

Narani himself brought them ice, glasses, a crystal flask of Mospheiran vodka, set it on the side table and poured in that practiced efficiency that never seemed rushed, that seemed to urge the same deliberate slowing of pace on the whole household. Narani served them, received Jase's quiet thanks, and ebbed silently out the door, shutting it as he went.

"Cheers," Jase said, in his own dialect, lifted his glass and took a sip.

Bren took a sip of his own, second for the evening; but it was an uncommon evening.

A damned uncommon evening.

"I am sorry, Jase. I was utterly blind to this one; to the last, I didn't see it."

"I have no trouble believing it."

"You didn't say you'd had supper with Ilisidi."

A blink. "I did."

"I know you did. So did I. *Why* did she come?"

"I've not a clue," Jase said.

"Do you think she knew what was up?"

"I'm not surprised at anything where she's concerned. Or Tabini." Jase added: "I'd like to have stayed. Selfishly speaking. Is this, honestly, not cleared with the Pilots' Guild?"

"Of course it isn't. Does Tabini clear any damn thing?"

"No," Jase said. "Of course he doesn't."

"He doesn't want the Guild to build its entire impression of atevi from you or Yolanda, either."

"It wouldn't be an accurate impression."

"More accurate than the Mospheiran delegation would give them, I'll tell you. I don't trust Ginny Kroger."

"She's angry at you," Jase said.

Bren shook his head. "Angry doesn't matter with her. I'm afraid she's a type, and unless she changes her attitude about me, which she came in with, I don't like the idea of her shaping policy."

"You have to admit you've pushed them."

"I know that. I don't think it matters a damn to Kroger's opinion. She's set on her own way. Until she believes she's not on Mospheira, she won't modify her opinion; and I'm afraid she's going to discover it after she's gotten into negotiations."

Jase didn't say anything for a moment, then: "How long are you up there?"

"Two weeks. Just until the shuttle goes down."

"If the shuttle's on schedule."

"Fifty-fifty so far." That was the shuttle's on-time departure percentage. So far, the shuttle had had no serious mechanical problems, no disaster. "Crossing fingers. I'm not against staying longer. I'd *like* to get you back down when I go. If you *want* me to do that."

"I want to be able to go back and forth.—I want them not to blow up when they find out they've got unscheduled guests."

"You think they will."

"I know they will." A small laugh, not amused. "They'll survive it. They'll be glad, on one level. But I get to explain Banichi to Ramirez."

"Think the quarters are ready?"

"I damned well doubt they are. Nothing gets prioritized until it's an emergency. There's just not enough personnel."

"We can fix that. If you can get us Ramirez's seal on this."

Ramirez: senior captain, the one who'd managed all the atevi contact, the one Jase called something akin to a father, if fatherhood was a signature on an authorization. Of the four captains, it was Ramirez who'd had the vision of a trade empire uniting this station with their outpost at a distant star, and Ramirez who'd had all his plans fall in ashes with the alien attack.

It was Ramirez who'd brought *Phoenix* home to the station at this star, hoping for a thriving station, and help.

And the planner in all this grand design for how humanity in this lost end of space should reunite and support the ship, was likewise Ramirez.

"You're going to be our most valuable resource," Bren said soberly.

"Don't count on me for any say."

"I know. I understand you're in a difficult position. *And* in a certain amount of power, if you'll use it."

Jason's shoulders drew in as if, even with the jacket, he felt a chill. "Symbolic. Ramirez's project. We were that; we were supposed to inspire the crew . . . back when this contact was supposed to bring the whole circle together. But as far as power beyond Ramirez's good opinion, I don't have it. With Tamun . . ." That was another of the captains. "I certainly don't have it."

"Why did they call you back?"

Jase's eyes lifted, direct, worried.

"*Why* did they call you back?" Bren repeated the question. "We didn't expect it. Might Yolanda have said something?"

"She might have, inadvertently. Maybe they just think it's time.—Maybe it *is* time."

"Tabini thinks so." Bren drew a breath, took the plunge. "Tabini wants the station."

"I'm not surprised."

"I'm not surprised you're not surprised. That's the condition. Mospheira running the station? They can't site a public park without a chain of committees. If this alien threat materializes, someone's got to make decisions as fast as the captains do. Mospheira won't do it. They know one thing: the history that drove them onto the planet. Freedom is down here. The faction that wants to be up there—isn't the best of Mospheira. In my own biased opinion, the captains can't deal with them either. There's too *much* history in common, too many old issues."

"Tabini and the captains sharing power?" Jase said, his lips hardly moving. "That's not easy, either."

"It has to work."

Jase and he had talked about the eventuality before, even the complexity of Mospheira's quest after space, a quest Bren himself had furthered until the anti-atevi Heritage

Party had seized the government, diverted the program to their own issue . . . until criminal elements had applied force to scientists and idealists, scared some, killed some, converted some. It had been a narrow thing three years ago, when reasonable people, greater in number on Mospheira, had pitched the scoundrels out and discovered the game they were up to. Knowledge of a threat outside the atmosphere hadn't, however, convinced reasonable people they should go back to space when *Phoenix*, that old bugbear of Mospheiran legend, had just returned asking for laborers and foretelling wars in space.

The average Mospheiran wanted to go on having his job and his beachside vacations, raising his kids, believing that if there was a war in space, it wasn't a threat to the planet . . . and that linchpin of Mospheiran faith: if they didn't contact any aliens, aliens would be more likely to leave them alone.

It was even possible that Mospheirans were right. The question was whether the aliens in question would recognize the difference between Mospheirans and *Phoenix* crew, when *Phoenix* came here for help. Some bet their lives that the aliens would be wise, and discriminate.

Bren didn't. Tabini didn't bet atevi would remain immune from retaliation, either. Nonchalance was a position from which, if wrong, there was very little chance of recovery.

"You know where I stand with Mospheira," Bren said. "We *know* each other. That's three years of good faith any other negotiators would have to do over, and—we've talked about this before—I'm not sure *anybody* is going to understand Mospheirans *or* atevi who hasn't met us in our own environment."

"No more than you'll understand us without being in ours," Jase said. "Ramirez comes closest."

"On the planet, among atevi, Tabini comes closest."

Jase shook his head. "No. Among atevi, *you* come closest. Down to the last, down to the last, I think I hoped there'd be a personal miracle. Selfish hope. It's a dream, on this planet. You can dream there are no aliens. You can dream you can go on forever, going about your routine, having your pleasant times . . . that's what the Mospheirans do, isn't it?"

"And atevi," Bren said. "Atevi aren't immune to it."

"Living a fantasy is not what they created me to do. What Ramirez *did* create me for . . . was to make this leap; contact; understand . . . report. Ramirez was the only one who understood the possibility there *would* be Mospheirans. He thought the people we'd left behind us might have changed; the other captains didn't think so." A second sip, steadier. "He'd planned we'd meet a tamer situation, a safe, functioning station; that we'd present you a present: a star station and a starship to reach it, and we'd build another ship; and another; and weave this grand web that gave us all access." Jase shook his head. "Which the alien attack demolished. We ran home. Here. And when we found what *did* exist, then the other captains looked at me with my language study as something other than Ramirez's personal lunacy."

He knew this part. He sensed Jase was going somewhere new with it. The other captains? Josefa Sabin was the second shift captain in the twenty-four-hour rotation; then Jules Ogun, and the fourth, different than they'd started with, since that man had died last year, was Pratap Tamun.

"But they *don't* see me as having authority," Jase said.

"Then join our group. We'll make damned sure they listen to you."

Jase shook his head. "That would undermine Ramirez. He's had confidence in me; I'll back him. Just . . . don't push too hard too early. Give me a day or so to sit down with Ramirez, let us put our heads together. If you'll trust me, I'll see if I can level with him and get his agreement."

It posed a question, not Jase's honesty, but how much three years of rarified diplomatic atmosphere had prepared Jase to stand on his own feet; and how much internal politics of the Pilots' Guild would listen to reason.

"Chei'no Ojindaro. Pogari's Recall."

Another machimi play. Jason's gaze flickered first with an effort to remember, then with complete understanding. *"Hari'i,"* he murmured, sliding back into Ragi with no apparent realization of it. *By no means.*

The return of a long-absent retainer to a corrupt house:

a recognition of loyalties, a sorting-out of man'chi . . . a resultant bloody set of calamities.

"You're sure," Bren challenged him.

"I have to try."

"Don't tell me *have to try*. You know you can work with me. The issues here aren't for guesswork."

"Tamun," Jase said. "Ogun's the chief bastard, but that goes with the job. Tamun is our problem, hardnosed, Sabin's man, or used to be. Those two have split. Ogun's not a fool. I *can* explain a situation he didn't anticipate to exist. Pratap Tamun's the problem."

Straight out of the Council, Bren recalled Jase saying when he knew Tamun was elevated to the captaincy: the captains tended to be more moderate, the Council more inclined to go for a radical solution. And his appointment to what the Guild called the fourth chair meant that one of the captains tended to more volatile solutions.

"They won't risk relations with the planet," Jase said further. "It's not in their interest. There's every chance of getting what they want if they ask Tabini and ask politely. As *I* mean to tell them. —Bren, you've never asked me what I'll say; but you know I'll advise them to deal with Tabini."

"This is the question I will ask you: will they listen?"

Jase took a deep breath. "The same us-only streak that runs in the Heritage Party is there. There's a strong party that thinks aliens out there and aliens here are no different, and the way you feel about Kroger . . . I feel about Tamun. I think he'd rather deal with the Mospheirans. The whole faction might not even know yet that they'd rather deal with the Mospheirans, but I think there's a chance the Guild will go through that stage—until they get a strong taste of Mospheiran politics to match their first sight of atevi. That's going to scare them. No matter they've seen them on screen. They're impressive, leaning over you. But you know and I know the Guild has no real choice. Ultimately, Tabini is their best and only answer."

"He's going to be another shock to their concept of the universe."

"They already had a real shock to their concept of the universe when they lost a space station. They're scared of aliens. They're scared as hell of losing this base, and of being double-crossed by aliens they don't understand. Bren, understand their mindset. If we don't have this station, we don't have anything—no population, no fuel, no repairs, no place to stand. That's death. That's death for us. That's their position."

"You and I both know that, for reasons of state, friends lie. But *I'm* telling you, and I want you to tell Ramirez. Tabini's a master of double-cross, but stress this. He's also fair. He welds parties together; he's united the Atageini with his own. He's gained lord Geigi."

"He deals with his grandmother," Jase said with a wry smile. "*There's* the training course."

"And he deals with Tatiseigi. This is a powerful, progressive influence that's tripled the size of the Western Association, gained votes in the hasdrawad and the tashrid, and *not* conducted a bloodbath of his rivals, which is hell and away better than his predecessors. You tell Ramirez this. In this lifetime, you're not going to get better than the man who peacefully took the Association to the eastern seaboard and simultaneously took atevi from airplanes to orbit. And who has the resources under rapid, efficient development. There is not going to be a better association for Ramirez, human or atevi."

He didn't have to convince Jase. It was Jase's store of arguments he supplied.

"Ramirez will listen," Jase said. "Your Mospheiran history about the Guild's misbehavior might be true: I don't believe all of the accounts, figuring your ancestors as well as mine had their side of the story. The others will argue.— But here's the hell of it, Bren, and this I've realized slowly over the last three years. A ship's a small place, compared to a world. What you don't understand, what you *can't* understand by experience . . . you think Mospheira's small and bound by a small set of habits. *Phoenix* is smaller. Compared to Mospheira, *Phoenix* is a four-hundred-year-old teacup, same contents, same set of thoughts, whatever comes and goes on the outside, we're on the inside. On an island two hundred years? We've been spacebound in that teacup for four hundred. We have the archive; we have all the culture of old Earth; but all of us on *Phoenix* have in that sense been in one same small conversation for centuries. I've been thinking about contrasts, the last few days. And this is the big one. All of us on the ship have the same database. We don't encourage divergences."

Curious, he *had* always thought of *Phoenix* as the outgoing group of humanity, the explorers, the discoverers; and Mospheirans as limited.

But twenty-five hundred individuals, only twenty-five hundred . . .

"How many *are* on *Phoenix?*" he asked, that old, variously answered question between them.

"Fifteen hundred," Jase said, a thunderstroke in a deep silence. The fire crackled, reminiscent of Taiben, of Malguri, old, old places on the earth of the atevi, aboriginal places where fire was the means of heat and livelihood, far, far different than this most modern waystop. "Fifteen hundred. —Understand, when we built the station, out there, before I was born, there were six thousand; the ship was doubled up, full. When the station went, there had to have been nine or ten thousand people, just there. But we're the core. We sent out all our population to make the other station; and now there's just . . . just fifteen hundred humans alive in space, besides the population of Mospheira . . . thousands, tens of thousands, *six million* and more human beings on the planet, on the island. That's incomprehensible to us. Precious to us. And whatever you think, *nobody* wants to jeopardize that resource . . . an irreplaceable one to us. That Yolanda can go up there and talk about *millions* of human beings is so incredible to the Guild you can't imagine."

He could. Not adequately, perhaps, but he could.

"But in a certain sense," Jase said, "when you talk to the Guild, you have to imagine a far, far smaller politics. We differ. We do differ. But we have philosophical differences, personal differences; you can't even call it politics . . . certainly no regional differences. Generational differences. Experiential differences. Differences of rank: the engineers think one way; the services think another. We respect the captains; we don't see the same conclusions; but we have to take orders. We always take orders."

It was the reprise of a dozen conversations, some of it

exactly the same; other bits, and beyond the ship-population bombshell, were new, as if, with his ship-home a reality on the horizon, Jase was recalling details. Details not purposely withheld, only lacking a certain reality in Shejidan.

The same, but different, and Bren listened with all that was in him.

"What are you going to do?" he asked Jase. "You don't take orders."

"I'm going to tell them things that aren't in their database. I'm going to ask Yolanda what she said; I'm going to find her and remind her she can say no. I'm going to tell them they'd better deal with Tabini because they won't have a concept in their universe how to get an agreement out of the atevi without him. But when my gut knows I'm talking to the captains, I'm going to be scared as hell. All the rest of me is going to want to say, 'yes, sir,' and do what I'm told."

"But you won't do that."

"I can't do that anymore."

"You know we're armed. That was part of the understanding, that we would have our own security when we set up the atevi quarters on station. That there would be weapons, electronics . . . bare walls and life support; and we tie our electronics in with theirs, all that agreement."

Jase drew a deep, long breath. "I'll be damn surprised if it's there yet. It's not an emergency yet; it's what I said. And the rank and file isn't going to know what to do with it because it violates a dozen rules. You'll stare at them, and scare them half to hell. There'll be aliens among them. You know what kind of scare that is, when we've already lost one battle?"

"Not looking them in the eyes?"

Jase hadn't, when he first came. "They really don't like that. Try to make your staff understand."

The consequence of growing up in small corridors, narrow passages, managing some sort of privacy in nose-to-nose confinement. They'd discussed that sort of difference over the last three years.

"I rely on you," Bren said.

"That scares the hell out of me."

"We share that feeling," Bren agreed.

"Time for me to go back. It *is* time."

At the root of all their plans, Jason had known he had to go back as soon as the shuttle flew reliably—being too valuable a passenger to send up with the tests. He'd known when Mercheson flew successfully; they'd both known . . . that he'd get the call, eventually.

"We want you back down here to finish the job, if you want to come."

"I'll do what I have to do."

"So will I," Bren said. "And I'll work with you. Tabini will. He considers you in his household. That's an irreplaceable advantage. When they really want to talk to Tabini, they'd be wise to send you to do it. —Might at least work a fishing trip out of it."

Joke, but a painful one.

"Safer, this trip," Jase said. "At least."

"Flinging yourself at a planet?" It was the way Jason had landed, flung himself at the planet in a three-hundred-year-old capsule with two chutes, the first of which had failed.

"Don't say that."

He himself didn't like all he could imagine, either.

Jase hated flying. He didn't. But at engine switchover, he'd like to have the whole damn bottle of vodka under his belt.

"I promise," Bren said. "You want a bed here, tonight? It's late."

Jase shook his head. "I'm going to take half a sleeping pill. Try to get some rest. If I don't wake up for the launch, come and get me."

"I will."

"You're not nervous."

"God, yes, I'm nervous!" He laughed, proof of it, and didn't think about the engines. "I plan to enjoy it anyway. Experience of a lifetime."

"An improvement," Jase said. "Falling out of space on my second parachute . . . that was an experience. —Horizons. That was an experience. Riding another living creature . . . that was an experience. Being *on* water higher than the highest building . . . *that* was an experience. I want that fishing trip, Bren."

They'd been through a great deal. Even standing upright on a convex planet under a convex sky had been a visual, stomach-heaving nightmare for Jason.

Having a natural wind sweep across the land and ruffle his clothing had frightened him: a phenomenon without known limits. The flash of lightning, the crack of thunder, the fall of rain—how could Jason's internal logic tell the natural limit of such phenomena?

It hadn't been cowardice. It had been the outraged reaction of a body that didn't know what to expect next, that didn't know by experience where unfamiliar stimuli would stop, but that knew there was danger. He was in for the same himself, he was sure, tomorrow.

"Having no up or down," Bren said, his own catalog of terrors.

"There's up and down. The station spins. —Didn't when we docked; but it does now. Low doorways, short steps. It's the household that's going to have to watch it, and they never have."

Atevi, in Mospheiran-sized doorways. And furniture. "Well, an experience. That's what we're there to negotiate. Cheers." He knocked back the rest of the glass. Stupid, he said to himself. It wasn't wise at all, flying tomorrow, before dawn.

"Cheers." Jase tossed down his ice-melt, and rose.

7

A gleam of silver on a black, imposing figure in the dim inner hall, the gold chatoyance of atevi eyes . . . very familiar eyes, they were, never failing to observe; his staff had been there. He'd been aware of them. Jase had gotten a summons from outside, and now Jase was under observation, however benign. Someone watched, and that someone was Jago, who waited for him. She bade a polite farewell to Jase and, with Jase out the foyer doors, Narani properly attending, she came back to report as he walked toward his bedchamber, two more of the servants waiting in the hall.

"The staff reports baggage is boarded," she said.

Bindanda, imposing, roundish shadow, said, "The bath, nandi?"

"Very welcome." He was tired, mentally tired; he wasn't going to shake the events of the day by lying down and staring at the ceiling. He knew that Jago would oblige him sexually; he didn't ask that. She had her own agenda, no knowing what, and he didn't inquire.

Rather he walked on, down a hallway more comfortable to his soul these days than the geometries of the human-area conversation grouping.

Had it only been this morning he'd left Mospheira, and all that was familiar to him from childhood?

Jago walked behind him, catfooted.

"Mogari reports," Banichi said, also appearing in the corridor. "Nothing untoward, no messages passed concerning Jase, except expectation of his arrival." Mogari was the site of the dish, the source of communications from the station.

"Good." He left all such questions to his security, trusting they could manage it far better than he, and would.

"Get some sleep, Banichi-ji. If you can leave it to someone else, do. Tano and Algini, too. This all starts very early in the morning."

"One does recall so," Banichi said. Banichi had a new set of systems under his hands in the security station, ones Banichi had helped put together, and he knew Banichi had that for a powerful attraction. "Tano and Algini, however, have gone to meet Jasi-ji in his room."

"To sleep there?" He was astonished. Did they think someone in the Mospheiran mission might have any designs on Jason's life?

But they were careful; they were atevi, and they were careful.

"For safety," Banichi amplified the information, "Replacing two of Tabini's staff."

"Where are they sleeping?" he wondered, stupid question.

"Nadi, they will hardly *sleep*. We will survive lack of sleep."

"Of course," he said, as Narani, too, entered the central hall, this inner circle of fortunate encounter. A baji-naji inset was above, below, and several places about. No soft green and blue here: definite, entangling black and white and color that fought like dragons in every design.

"Will you have any late supper, nand' paidhi?"

"No," he said. "Thank you, Rani-ji, I can't manage another bite, and I fear I had at least half a glass too much tonight, with Jase." His head was light. He'd run from supper to late tea with Tabini, to here, all nonstop.

He turned, saw all the staff together, in various doorways all eyes on him.

He'd been afraid, a moment ago, thinking on the morning. In the moment Jase had left he'd mentally expected he'd be alone, like the Mospheirans; but he wasn't, he wasn't ever. They wouldn't let him be. "Nadiin-ji, thank you, thank you very much for coming."

"A grand adventure," Narani said, a man who should be, if he were Mospheiran, raising grandchildren . . . but here was a model of discretion and experience for a lord's house. "A great adventure, nand' paidhi."

"Your names are written," he said, bowing his head, and

meant it from the heart . . . meant it, too, for the starry-
eyed, enthusiastic young woman, Sabiso, who'd come primarily to attend Jago, for the Atageini who had come, ro-
tund Bindanda, who carried the eastern and old-line houses
of the Association into this historic venture.

"Nandi." There were bows from the staff, deep bows, a
moment of intimate courtesy before he went into his bedroom, before Bindanda and Kandana attended him there.

He'd used to think of it as an uncomfortable ritual. Now
he took comfort in the habit . . . carefully unfastened the
fine, lace-cuffed shirt and shed it, sat down to have his
boots removed, all the items of his clothing from cufflinks
to stockings accounted for and whisked away to laundry or
whatever the solution might be on this most uncommon of
evenings. He didn't inquire what they'd brought and what
they'd left or what they might do with the laundry. If he
named a thing they'd left, they'd send clear to the Bu-javid
to bring it, and God knew it would turn up.

"Good rest, nand' paidhi," Narani said, managing to turn
down the bed and to bow, quite elegantly and all at once,
as young Kandana, a nephew, hovered with a robe. "And
will you bathe?"

"Yes, nadiin." He accepted the bathrobe Kandana
whisked into place, stepped into slippers . . . should the
paidhi-aiji walk barefoot, even ten meters down the hall?
The staff would think him ill-used.

It was a very modern bath . . . porcelain, far newer than
the general age of the fixtures in the Bu-javid, but there was
absolutely nothing lacking in the quantity of water in the
sunken tub. Bren slid into the soft scent of herbs, slid down
to his nose and shut his eyes, while the extra half-glass of
vodka seethed through his brain, blocking higher channels.

A shadow entered, a dark presence reflected ghostly on
dark tiles: Jago, likewise in her bathrobe.

"Shall I bathe later, nandi?"

So meticulous in slipping in and out of the role of bodyguard. Perhaps they were a scandal. He was never sure. He
had no idea how Banichi construed matters, and suffered
doubts. He wasn't sure even how Jago construed matters,

except that he wasn't utterly surprised at her turning up now unasked, after this crisis-ridden day.

"Now is very welcome, Jago-ji."

Smoothly then she shed the robe, tall and black and beautiful as some sea creature . . . slid into the water and let it roll over her skin with a deep sigh. In the next moment she submerged and surfaced, hair glistening . . . still pigtailed: with that propriety alone, she could answer a security call naked as she was born, with never a sign of ruffled dignity: she had done so, on occasion, and so had he, and so had his staff. There was no mystery left, but there was admiration for what was beautiful, there was expectation. One didn't say *love* in dealing with atevi, as one didn't say *friend* or any of those human words . . . but bodies knew that despite differences, there was warmth and welcome and comfort. She might technically be on duty; there was a gun with the bathrobe, he was relatively sure.

But she pursued his welfare here, strong, graceful arms keeping him warm, when all at once he felt the chill of too much air-conditioning above the water surface, and the heat of an atevi body beneath. The water steamed in the refrigerated air, made clouds around them, steamed white on Jago's bare black shoulder, and on her hair.

Large atevi bodies chilled less rapidly than human, absorbed heat and shed it slowly, simply because they *were* larger; and tall as she was, she could pick him up and throw him with not an outstanding amount of effort. But that wasn't in their dealings, which were mutual. The dark blue walls reflected him more than her. She was always warm, and he was chronically cold. Across species lines, across instinctual lines, their first engagement had been a comedy of misplaced knees and elbows; but now they had matters much more smoothly arranged, and had no difficulty in a soap-slippery embrace. Hands wandered, bodies found gentle accommodation under the steaming surface. She enjoyed it; he did. He was recent enough from Mospheira that he was conscious of the alien, and fresh enough from converse with Jase that he still had his human feelings engaged.

And not knowing to this hour whether these interludes with the source of her man'chi were permissible for her or a scandal to her Guild, he still found no personal strength or reason to say no. He found a gentleness in the encounters that never had been with Barb . . . his weekends with Barb had been more intense, more desperate, less satisfying. He didn't know which of them had been at fault in that, but he knew that what he and Jago practiced so carefully respected one another in a way he and Barb had never thought about. There was humor; there were pranks; there was never, except accidentally, pain.

He struggled not to let his heart engage. But his heart told him what he and Barb had called a relationship hadn't been the half of what his heart wanted to feel. He had asked, or tried to ask, whether Banichi and Jago had their own relationship; and Jago had said, in banter, Banichi has his opinions; and Banichi never managed to take him seriously . . . never quite answering him, either; and it was not a question he could ask Tabini—how do atevi make love.

He was not about to ask the dowager, who—he was sure—would want every salacious detail.

It was sure above all else that Banichi would never betray his partner, that she wouldn't betray Banichi, not under fire and not in bed.

It was sure between him and Jago that the man'chi involved, the sense of association, flowed upward more than down, and that no human alive understood atevi relationships in the first place—

But the more he involved himself in the atevi world, the more he knew he wasn't in a pairing. He'd assumed a triangle; and then knew it wasn't even that, but deep in some atevi design, a baji-naji of their own convoluted creation, and deeper and deeper into feelings he knew he wasn't wired to feel as atevi felt, not feeling as they did, only as he could.

God help him, he thought at times, but she never asked a thing of him. And they went on as formally and properly in public as they'd always been, always the three of them, she and he and Banichi, and four and five, if one counted Tano and Algini, as it had been from the time Tabini put them together.

He'd been in love in his teens, when he'd gone into the program, with the foreign, the complex, the different.

She certainly was. God, she was . . . pure self-abandoned trust, and sex, and her exotic, heavily armed version of caring all in the same cocktail.

They rested nestled together till their fingers and toes wrinkled, while the heater kept the water steaming.

They talked about the recent trip to Mospheira . . .

"Barb came to the airport," he said.

"Did you approve?" she asked.

"Not in the least," he said.

They talked about the supper with the dowager.

"Cenedi looked well," he said.

But she never talked business in their interludes. She had, in whatever form, a better sense of romance than he did, twining a wet lock of his hair about her finger. She'd undone his braid. Her tongue traced the curve of his ear and traveled into it.

A shadow appeared in the doorway, above the steam.

Banichi.

He was appalled. "Jago-ji," he said; she was aware . . . surprised, but not astonished.

"Nandi." Banichi addressed him, incongruously, in the formal mode. "Your mother has called, requesting to be patched through wherever you are. She says it's an emergency."

Banichi had been exposed to his mother's emergencies. He himself certainly had. He was remotely aware of the rest of his body, and simultaneously of the rest of Jago's body, soft and hard in all the right places, as her arms and her knees unfolded from him.

He probably blushed. He certainly felt warmth.

"I regret the untimely approach," Banichi said, "but she says she's calling from the hospital."

"Oh, damn." He was on his way out of the water as Banichi procured him his robe.

Jago gathered herself out of the water as he slipped into the robe. He had the presence of mind to glance back at her in regret for the embarrassment, whatever it was, and knew that, in a Situation, Tano and Algini being absent with Jase, Banichi had left the security post rather than send servants into the bath to pull him out.

Bren yanked the sash tight on the robe, on his way out the door. His mother had had her spells before . . . had had surgery three years ago, one they thought had fixed the problem with her heart as far as age and life choices let anything fix the problem.

At least *she* was calling.

God, could anything have happened to Toby or Jill? He had enemies, and some of them had no scruples. He'd cleared Kroger to call the island. Word of the mission could be out, no telling where, and he'd not been in contact with Shawn, to advise him to tighten his mother's security, that *he* was on this mission.

Banichi had reached the security station near the front entry, that place which, with its elaborate electronics, held the phones.

"The ordinary phone, nadi," Banichi advised him, and Bren turned a swivel chair and settled onto it, picking up the phone that looked like a phone.

Banichi settled into the main post and punched buttons. Bren heard the relays click. "Go ahead," he heard the atevi operator say in Mosphei', that deep timbre of voice, and the lighter human voice responding: "Go ahead, now, Ms. Cameron."

"Mother?"

"Bren?" There was the quavering edge of panic in his mother's voice, real desperation, and that itself was uncommon: he knew the difference.

"Mother, are you all right? Where's Toby?"

"I don't know. I don't know. Bren, you've just got to get back here. Tonight."

"Mother, I'm sorry. I can't just—"

"You have to get here!"

"Where's Toby?" Had there been a plane crash? A car wreck? "Where are you?"

The line spat, one of those damnable static events that happened when the atevi network with its intensive security linked up by radio with the Mospheiran network. He clenched the receiver as if he could hang onto the line.

". . . at the hospital!"

"In what *city*, Mother? Where's Toby? Can you hear me?"

"I'm in the city!" That meant the capital, in ordinary usage. "I'm at the hospital! Can you hear me? Oh, *damn* this line!"

Not *in* the hospital. "You're *at* the hospital. Where's *Toby,* Mother? Where's my brother?"

"I don't know. He got on a plane this afternoon. I think he should be home. I think he and Jill may have stopped at Louise's to pick up the—"

"Mother, *why are you at the hospital?*"

"Bren, don't be like that!"

"I'm not shouting, Mother. Just give me the news. Clearly. Coherently. What's going on?"

"Barb's in intensive care."

"Barb." Of all star-crossed people. Barb?

"Barb and I went shopping after we left the airport, after we put Toby on the plane, you know. We were at the Valley Center, the new closed mall, you know . . ."

"I know it. Did she fall?" There were escalators. There was new flooring. The place had opened this spring, huge pale building. Tall, open escalators.

"No, we just came out to go to the car, and this *bus* just came out of nowhere, Bren."

"Bus. My God."

"She went right under it, Bren. I fell down and I looked around as the tires came past and she never said a thing, she just . . . she just went under it, and packages were all over, I'd bought this new sweater . . . "

His mother was in shock. She was the world's worst storyteller, but she wasn't gathering her essential pieces at all.

"Mother, *how bad?*"

"It's bad, Bren. She's lying there with all these tubes in her. She's messed up inside. She's really bad. Bren, she wants you to come."

He was dripping water onto the counter. His feet and hands were like ice in the air-conditioning. With the side of his finger, he smeared a set of water droplets out of existence, thinking of the new counter, the new facility. He was not at home. He was not going to be anywhere close to home, and he was trying to think what to say. He tried to choose some rational statement. "I know you're with her, Mother. —Were *you* hurt?" Setting his mother to the first person singular was the fastest way to get his mother off the track of someone else's woes. He'd practiced that tactic for years of smaller emergencies.

"She needs you, Bren."

It was bad.

"Are *you* hurt, Mother?"

"Just my elbow. I scraped my elbow on the curb. Bren, she's so bad . . ."

He winced and swore to himself. His hand was shaking. Jago had turned up in her bathrobe, with Banichi in the little security post, support for him. But he didn't know who was with his mother, tonight, or how bad the damage was. Shawn's people watched her. They always kept an eye toward her. But they'd damned well let down this time.

"Have they assessed Barb's damage?"

"Spleen, liver, lung . . . right leg, left arm . . . they're worried about a head injury."

"God." On medical matters his mother very well knew what she was talking about. She made a hobby of ailments. "Has anyone called Paul?"

"That useless piece of—"

"Mother, he's married to her! Call him!" He tried to assemble useful thoughts and quiet his stomach. His mother was acting as gatekeeper, *hadn't* called Barb's husband. He hoped the hospital had.

And the time . . . he wasn't sure of the time. It was well after dark now, east of Mospheira. If his mother and Barb had gone to the mall directly after leaving Toby at the airport, it couldn't have been that late when the accident happened, and she'd only now gotten through the phone system?

He was behind a security curtain. God knew how she'd made the entire worldnet and the aijiin and captains understand she had a real emergency, and now she came unglued. She was sobbing on the phone.

"Mother. Mother, you fell down. Has anyone looked at *you?*" He was honestly, deeply worried. "Are you sure you weren't hit?"

"Something hit me. I'm not sure." With the intonation that said it wasn't important, it didn't matter to her pain.

"Have the doctors looked at you?"

"They did." Dismissively. "Bren, Bren, you can get a plane. Tell the aiji. You have to."

"Have you called Toby?"

"She doesn't need Toby, dammit! She needs *you!*"

"*You* need Toby, Mother. I want you to call him."

"You listen to me, Bren Cameron! You damned well listen to me! The woman you were going to marry is lying in intensive care in there, and you don't tell me you don't care! You don't tell me you're carrying on an affair over there and you don't care. You straighten yourself out and you get back here!"

She did know. She guessed. On one of her visits, somehow someone had slipped . . . the tightest security in the world, and she knew.

"I can't. I can't, Mother." Barb's kiss in the hangar, Barb running, whole and healthy, across the concrete, and a *bus*, for God's sake . . . there was a sense of dark, and malign comedy about it, a grotesque sense of the impossible, and he didn't catch half the awful details his mother spilled to him, except that there were fractures, a punctured lung, internal bleeding.

And knowing Barb . . . knowing Barb who'd been his on-island lover and sometime contact point for relaying dangerous messages before their breakup . . . it was entirely possible Barb had shoved his mother for that curb and *that* was how Barb had gotten hit, and *that* was what drove his mother's grief.

Barb would. Grant all their failure to be a couple, Barb would. "What are her chances?" he asked, dreading to know. "What's the damage?"

"They're going to do a bone replacement and a brain scan." His mother drew a breath and grew calmer in a list of specifics. "She's conscious. When the ambulance was coming, she said, 'Tell Bren this really wasn't a scheme to get him back here.' And when they were putting her in the ambulance, she said, 'I need him.' Bren, she does. She really needs you. I had a feeling you shouldn't fly back today."

She hadn't seen the damned *bus* coming, but that wouldn't convince his mother she didn't have premonitions.

He'd done all he could. The personal phone wouldn't have helped her at all, once he'd gone through the security curtain that surrounded Tabini's intentions. Hours of trying to reach him.

And what did he say, after she'd worked a miracle to reach him?

"Mother, I absolutely can't come."

"Bren, don't you tell me that! Bren, you have to come, that's all there is! You're so damned important to Tabini, you get him to get you a plane, right now. I want you here!"

He had the receiver against his ear for privacy—thank God. "Mother, I'm involved in something I can't leave. I can't tell you. But this is important. I'm sorry. Tell Barb I'm terribly sorry. —Don't you dare tell her I love her. Don't you do that, Mother."

"You listen to me, Bren. You listen. This job is killing you. It's killing the son I knew. It's killing any happiness you're going to have. You don't decide when you're sixty that you ought to have gotten married, you don't wait till the end of your life to regret you didn't have children . . ."

"Mother . . . "

"You listen to me, Bren Cameron! I know what's going on with you and that atevi woman! It's not right!"

"Mother, where are you?" He was appalled that she knew, but more appalled to think she might be in a hallway, at a public phone. "Don't say that out loud. Don't raise your voice."

"Are you ashamed? Does it worry you?"

"It worries me when my mother might be saying things in a public corridor. It worries me for her safety if the extremists get themselves stirred up again because some damned rumor gets started—talk like that won't help Durant, either. Hush! Be still. Listen to me . . ."

"You really don't want to hear it, do you? You know Barb always loved you. She married that fool Paul because you broke her heart. You hurt her, Bren, and she was sorry, and oh, no, you were too self-righteous, too damned important with your fancy estate to take her back."

"I never promised to marry her. *I don't love her,* Mother! I'm sorry to say it under these circumstances, but I don't love her. I never loved her, she didn't love me; we slept together. That was the end of it. I tried to have something else, and she was the one who wanted something different."

"You don't *know* what she felt! You weren't here! You were traipsing about the continent acting as if you were some atevi lord! She decided to marry. To *marry,* respectably, as sensible people do when they want to have normal lives."

"I don't have a normal life."

"She was scared, Bren, she was scared and she was hurt—personally hurt, by the things you'd done. If you asked her to divorce Paul, she'd be there in a moment."

Dealing with his mother was like running a course under fire . . . and he feared his mother would tell Barb there was hope of having him back, wreck Barb's marriage, drive Paul off when Barb needed him, and hurt Barb more than she'd been. Most of all, he couldn't hold that out to Barb . . . because he wouldn't *be* back and Barb, all she valued and all she wanted to be, her fashion, her nightclub glamour, all the things she loved . . . didn't exist on this side of the sea.

"I can't marry her. End of statement. It's not a time to debate it."

"How can you be like this? You'd come home. You'd show up on a weekend, ask Barb to drop all her plans and go running off to some hotel, with the news people all trying to find you, and then you'd be gone, and then the news people *would* find where you'd been and Barb would have to duck out and lock herself in her apartment for weeks, Bren, sometimes in fear of her life!"

"I know that." It was true, Barb had played international intrigue as part of the shining, glittering game, until it turned bloody; and now his mother was working herself back into tears. He tried to get his point through while there was still rational thought to hear it. "But I can't help that. I can't *help* that, Mother; listen to me! The president's guard does look out for you. If there are spies at the hospital now, they're official. They probably are at the hospital right now. I want you to call Shawn Tyers. You know how."

"Don't you hang up on me!"

"Mother, you know I love you. That's the way things are. Call Shawn. Call Paul . . . I know you don't want to, but do it! Then go home, get some rest.

"Mother, what was between us is still *her* business and *my* business. Give me credit that I know Barb, I know her damned well, and I can't help her by getting involved in her life and ripping that up a second time."

"Bren, don't be like this."

"I'm sorry as hell for what happened. It makes me sick to think of it. But I can't fix it, and don't you dare tell her I love her, don't you dare tell her there's any hope of my coming now. There isn't. You'll just hurt her. Do you hear me, Mother? Go home! I'll call you as soon as I can."

"Promise to call Barb."

"I will *not* promise to call Barb. I've got to go now."

"Bren, call her."

"Mother, *go home.* Good night. I love you."

He hung up. He was aware of Jago in the doorway of the security station, aware of the fact some words were in her understanding and Banichi's, at least of his side of the conversation.

"Barb's had an accident," he said. "A bus hit her. My mother fell down and hurt herself. Barb's in the hospital. There's nothing I can do from here." They didn't understand love, they didn't understand the intricate details of failed human relationships, but they knew attachment persisted. Most of all they knew loyalty, and the urge to go to the scene of trouble. "There's nothing I can do."

Banichi said solemnly. "The aiji can request action of the President of Mospheira, and Shawn-nandi. Shall we do that?"

Tabini could do so much; and so damned little. "Not for this. Toby's not home yet. Patch me through to his house, Banichi-ji. I'll leave a message."

Banichi pushed buttons. The communications interface was a great deal easier than it had been, with security codes that automatically engaged when the messages crossed the straits. Even at this hour, the Mospheiran system produced an operator, better than in prior days, and the call went on its way to the north coast, where Toby's answering system cut in.

Bren was in some part relieved. It was easier to unburden the matter to a machine. He was sure their mother had put one of those nerve-jarring *Call me!'s* on Toby's system, and he hoped his message might at least advise Toby what the matter was, if their mother fell out of contact before Toby ran off into the night trying to hire a plane.

"Mother seems fine," he began his message, experienced in years of long-distance crises. "Scrapes and bruises, as I gather. Barb's in the hospital, Mother's with her. A pretty bad accident with a bus, and Mother saw it, might have been in front of it. She wants some comfort. Toby, I know you just got home, I hate like hell to drop this on you, but I'm behind a security wall at the moment and I absolutely can't get back there. I don't think you need to fly back, just give Mother a call at . . ." Professional coolness wavered. "I don't know what hospital." Their mother was probably one of the few people outside the government who didn't have forwarding on their calls: security precaution. And she was one of the very few, inside or out, who wasn't completely aware of all the security arrangements that surrounded them. He couldn't call her security and ask where she was. He hoped to God they knew and that his mother and Barb hadn't gotten whisked away out of security's sight. "She didn't tell me what hospital." He covered the microphone. "Banichi-ji. Get the origination on that call from my mother."

Banichi pushed buttons, wrote on a slip of paper, handed it to him.

"It's Central City," he said into the phone. He was relieved. He knew the number by heart. "Look, just give her a call through the hospital system, and if she's not there, call the apartment. It's possible Barb pushed Mother out of the way of a bus. She's really shaken. Barb's critical. God, I'm sorry, Toby, I'm really sorry. I wish to God I didn't have to put this on your shoulders."

Toby, however, wasn't there to assure him it was all right, or that some disaster hadn't delayed Toby and his family. There were watchers around Toby, too, all the same. Agents followed the kids to school. It was what the government had to do . . . what he thanked God they did, because the whole question of atevi/human relations provoked every borderline crazy in existence, on Mospheira and on the mainland. Even someone the random lunatics thought might be connected to him, like his former secretaries, had to have constant protection on the island . . . it went against Mospheiran law to round up the lunatics until they'd actually done something.

"You take care," he said, hearing the vast, cold silence. "Thanks, Toby. Hope we get that fishing trip one of these months."

He hung up.

No, he couldn't come back. And he couldn't let out, even on a shielded line, that he was going up to the station, not before launch. The aiji would announce it when the aiji chose.

The paidhi's personal crises didn't figure in the plans. He thought he should call Shawn . . . but if the other delegation had, or should, call the island, there were issues . . . a lot of issues.

A hand rested lightly on his shoulder, Jago's, calling him back to rational thought, reminding him he wasn't, after all, alone.

"Barb just stepped in front of a bus," he said. He felt distant from that information, as if it were some line in an entirely unpleasant, grotesque joke. But it wasn't. He didn't want to think what kind of damage she'd taken. "Possibly she moved to protect my mother. Likely it was my mother's inattention to traffic. It's quite heavy, where they were."

"One only asks," Banichi said, who, like Jago, had likely understood a great deal of it . . . more, because they both knew his mother and knew Toby. "Did you not advise your mother to go home and did you not say to Toby call the hospital?"

"My mother won't go home," Bren said. "Nothing we can do, any of us, from here. I have to trust Shawn will do something. That Toby will."

There were frowns, confusion on their part as to what the proprieties were. As for him, he could scarcely think.

"Nadi," Jago said, not *nandi—my lord*—but the common

sir. She wanted him to leave the matter. She wanted to take him out of the security station, away from the questions.

She was right; he rose, but he cast a look at Banichi, who'd be in charge, who *was* in charge of whatever came through these communication and surveillance boards, and who took his safety and his family's safety very seriously.

"It was an accident," Bren said. "It couldn't be otherwise. The buses are public. They move quickly, even recklessly. It's notorious."

"Sometimes there are accidents," Banichi said.

"Sometimes there are," he said.

He left the security center then, walked back in the halls, to the bedroom that was his, in a place quiet now. The servants had retreated to their own rooms, likely, hoping for sleep; or still working.

Jago followed him, stood a moment while he stared at the wall.

"Stay," he roused himself to say.

She shut the door behind her. He slid off the robe and went to bed, and Jago put out the main lights.

She came and eased into bed beside him, around him, not a word said.

I don't love Barb, he wished to say to her, but there wasn't a word for *love,* and it didn't matter to Jago; from her view, since he insisted Barb was still with his mother, Barb was still within his association, marginalized somewhat, but still there.

But if *love* wasn't in the atevi hard-wiring, sexual jealousy wasn't, he suspected, quite that remote. He couldn't trust his own human feelings to interpret hers, further than that, and his thinking wasn't outstandingly clear; neither was his feeling, his emotion . . . his heart, whatever one wanted to call it.

Was it that way for Jago, too?

He didn't relax. Couldn't.

"Shall I turn on the television?" Jago asked him.

"It might be good," he said. He didn't want sleeping pills. Couldn't bring himself to make love on news like that. They put a machimi on . . . a part of the culture close to religious, but not, having everything to do with the atevi heart, and nothing at all to do with gods.

In the play before them, he guessed the woman would learn her lord had interests conflicting with her sexual partner's. The uninitiated human, seeing the drama, might expect quite the opposite as would happen, but atevi had no doubt. One only waited for disaster.

He'd send Toby the funds. He had that. He always had that, and Toby knew it. In his absence from crises he could always contribute money for the airfare.

"We have boarding before dawn," Jago said against his ear. "Do you think of that, nadi-ji?"

"I do now," he said, realizing he'd slept, and that his arm was numb, and Jago's might be. "What time is it?"

"The depth of the night. Rest, nadi."

He sighed, and Jago, with the remote, without moving him, shut the television off.

8

Remarkable as it was to be going up to space, it was only a matter of walking out into the hall that had led them here. That hall led to double doors, and those doors let them into the departure lounge. Jase was there, Tano and Algini; Bren was so used to seeing them he hardly knew the sight was uncommon, except Banichi and his team had exchanged their habitual leather and metal for more form-fitting operational black, mission-black, the sort they'd hitherto worn only in clandestine work, and rarely with him. That was one thing different.

The other, patently, was Lund and Kroger and company, pale-skinned, reflecting in the glass. "Good morning," Kroger said frostily. "Good morning," Lund echoed, in slightly more friendly fashion.

"Good morning," he gave them back as if nothing at all had happened.

But what commanded his attention, what utterly seized his attention, beyond that wall of dark windows was a floodlit view of the shuttle, white as winter, long, sleek and elegant.

Shai-shan.

We're going, his mind chanted over and over, halfway numb and operating on far too little sleep, while the body manufactured a false, expensive strength. We're going. We're going.

Attendants of the space center had ushered them here, and now, time ticking away, opened the outer doors of the departure lounge, so smoothly on the edge of his arrival that he was sure he and his party had been on the edge of late.

"Well," Shugart said with a deep breath, and started off. Bren started walking without half thinking, fell in with Jason . . . then, willing to make peace, waited for the Mospheirans, not to outpace them.

They walked, far as it was. There'd been consideration of a mobile lounge, but the shuttle itself took precedence, every element of the budget concentrated on that and on its sister ship, still under construction. It sat farther away than any ordinary walk to a waiting airplane, slowly looming larger and larger, deceptive in its graceful shape.

Meanwhile the lingering night chill set into human bones, and uneasy stomachs had a long, long time to contemplate the fact that the engines were different, the wings were mere extensions of the hull. *Shai-shan* didn't look human or atevi. She looked alien, out of time and place . . . a design not state of the art when *Phoenix* had launched from the earth of humans, no, but one that might have served that age.

They arrived within the circle painted on the concrete. The embarkation lift sat in down position in front of them, a cargo lift with a grid platform, a railing, a boarding bridge up against the hatch, no more exotic an arrangement than that. They walked aboard, the four Mospheirans, Jase, Bren with his security, and after them Narani and the three other servants, carrying the hand luggage, bags that would have taxed strong humans. There was room on the sizable platform, but only a little.

The lift clanked, jolting them all, and rose up and up to level with the boarding platform that sat mated to the open hatch.

From it, Kroger pushing violently to the lead, they filed past a dismayed atevi steward.

Let her, Bren thought. She passed the steward because he had no orders to lay violent hands on a human guest, and had had no suspicion of the move in time to make himself a wall. He had no doubt Banichi and his team took their cues from his failure to object . . . and that Kroger hadn't scored points with the atevi.

She and her team, moving ahead, were under-scale in a cabin sized and configured for atevi . . . beautifully simple, completely fortunate in its numbers. Bren knew it intimately, and the harmony of the sight soothed away his annoyance at Kroger, showed him how little she did matter to the atevi's ability to launch this vessel. It might have been one of the mainland's best passenger jets, simple rows of seats, carrying a hundred atevi at most; the buff-colored panels were insets, not windows; that was one difference. And in every point the craft *felt* fortunate, and well-designed, and solid, an environment completely carried around the passenger, surrounding and comforting.

Screens occupied the forward bulkhead, high, large, visible from all the seats.

Stewards waited for them, showed Lund and Kroger into the foremost seats, not quarreling with the precedence; Ben and Kate looked troubled by the proceedings, uncertain in the disposition of their small handbags, and sat with their group.

Bren chose his own seat, on the aisle, midway down the row of seats—there were plenty available—and offered Jase his choice.

Jase eased past him and sat down next to the wall, while Banichi and Jago took the pair of seats across the aisle. Tano and Algini took the row just behind them. The servants settled at the rear, in their own society, doubtless commenting very quietly on the unusual man'chi-like manifestation among the humans—had a threat been passed? Had the woman in charge felt attacked? Certainly not by their will.

"Luck to us," Jason said anxiously, in the last-moment activity of the stewards.

"Baji-naji," Bren said. That black-and-white symbol was conspicuous on the forward wall, right beneath the monitors: Fortune and Chance, the give and take in the universe that made all the rigid numbers move.

The engines fired, whined, roared into life. The shuttle wasn't particularly good at maneuvering on the ground. Towed to its berth, it had a straight line to one runway going straight forward as it sat, and as the engines built, it gathered speed away from the space center. The cabin crew, too, presumably had belted in.

The shuttle gathered more and more speed . . . disconcerting for passengers used to taxiing and maneuvering.

They could see nothing; the craft quivered to the thump of tires.

"One hopes the small craft have heard the tower," Banichi said cheerfully, from the matching aisle seat, over the thunder.

God, Bren thought, and reminded himself all air traffic would be diverted away from Shejidan for the next half hour, sufficient for the shuttle to clear the airport, with the aiji's planes to enforce it. The shuttle was not as maneuverable as an airliner, in the air, either. One unanticipated fool, and the whole program was in jeopardy; not to mention their lives.

The center screen flicked on, showed a double row of runway lights ahead. A lot of runway yet. The pace still increased. The lack of side windows combined with the black forward view made a center-seat passenger feel like a bullet in a gun.

Not nervous, Bren said to himself, not nervous, not nervous, no, not at all. He locked his sight on those monitors, hyperfocused there to keep his stomach steady, trying to convince his claustrophobia that what he saw was a window. But the aft cameras had come on, retreating perspective of the lights warring with the forward motion. Then a belly camera came into operation, showing a spotlighted forward tire and a blur of dark pavement.

The engines cycled up and up. Thundered. The tires thumped madly. Where's the end of the runway? Bren thought. *Lift! Lift!*

The tires suddenly went silent, and the deck slanted up. A hand shoved Bren against the foam of his seat: he felt himself sinking back as the whole craft shook to the engines, found his fingers trying to hold him against that illusion.

Deep breath. He tried to relax, look casual in the moment, but his heart cycled in time with the engines. No easy circling of the city like the aiji's jet, just a straightforward climb, proverbial bat out of hell.

They climbed and they climbed before the press backward eased.

"Well, it worked again," Jason said weakly.

"It did," Bren agreed, convinced himself he dared let go the armrest.

But the tilt of the deck was still extreme; they were still climbing, if under less pressure; and every citizen of Shejidan would have been shaken out of bed, hurried into the open to look up and wonder . . . the wonder was still new, in Shejidan, and people forgave the handful of falling tiles, and filled out the requests for repair, which they would point to, doubtless, and say to generations to come, see, this crack was in the first days of the space venture: all Shejidan suffered this, and won. . . .

What? The space station? The Foreign Star that had shone in their skies for centuries?

A birthright?

Not every citizen of Shejidan welcomed roof repairs. But the aiji promised a new spaceport, conversion of the space center to an acculturation center, promised work for craftsmen, a great felicity, an ultimate association not with the humans but with the *associations* of humans, a method by which they could avert war and ensure the future.

Humans could read the translations of the aiji's statements and never understand. The aiji had received a deputation from representatives of the Gan, original tenants of Mospheira, heretics, of a sort. A whole bright new world was upon them.

The aft monitor showed a seam of dawn, past the running lights on white edges, the belly camera very little but black. The forward cameras picked up nothing but black. They were on their way.

And of all things, Banichi and Jago turned on their seat lamps and broke out reading material.

Look at the damn monitors! Bren wanted to shout at them. A miracle is happening! Look at the sky, for God's sake! The people pour into the streets of Shejidan! Are you numb?

They'd taken the technical manuals.

It was very like an airplane. It flew and showed no sign of malfunction. It was proved on several flights before. Should they be other than confident in the pilot and the design the paidhiin had translated?

"Much better than parachutes," Jase muttered, beside him.

That view persisted. Bren didn't even consult his memory of technicalities, just watched the monitors, time stretched to a long impossible moment.

The stewards rose, sheer atevi obstinacy, Bren thought, viewing procedures with dismay, procedures he would have disapproved if any ateva had asked him.

"Nadiin," one of the stewards said, walking up the steep incline of the deck, "fruit juice is provided, should you wish. Please avoid excess. Breakfast will be easier to provide now, rather than during free fall." The attendant repeated the same message in Mosphei', not too badly pronounced.

There was laughter from the front.

"Have I spoken badly?" the dismayed crewman asked Bren.

"Not at all," Bren said. "They hadn't expected service aboard." Impossible to explain near-hysteria, and the relief of humor. "They're in very good spirits, and if they were atevi, they would say thank you. —Ms. Kroger, Mr. Lund? Do you want breakfast, up there?"

Kroger said nothing. Lund leaned from his seat, a face at the high end of the aisle.

"What's available?" Lund asked.

"He is courteously inquiring," Bren said, "the nature of the offering, and means no offense."

"Nand' paidhi." The crewman offered a respectful bow, and proceeded forward to take the orders from the Mospheirans with a written list as the other steward came to take their orders. "Nadiin-ji?"

"I'll have just fruit juice, if you please."

"*Paiinai* for me," Jason said. "My last chance for a long time. Juice. Toast."

"Nandiin," the crewman said, and walked back the precarious route to the rear.

"You all right?" Jase asked.

"Fine," Bren said shakily. "Supposed to be like an airliner, isn't it?" The breakfast call still amazed him. "It's a bit wilder on the takeoff."

"No problems."

Don't say that, he wanted to say, at his most superstitious; and Banichi and Jago, having ordered a large breakfast, continued their manual-reading, probably because they hadn't had a chance in all else that had been going on. Tano and Algini were behind them, likewise possessed of an appetite.

The fruit juice arrived, in spillproof containers. Lund thought they might like another juice on the way to orbit, and the cabin crew stayed busy.

Bren confined himself to one glass of juice. Jase ate with good appetite.

No further calls from the island. That thought flashed through his mind as it hadn't since waking, since sleepwalking through dressing and last-moment details.

He supposed Toby had dealt with matters.

He supposed their mother had finally gotten home, and that none of his family had any idea the shuttle creating a sonic boom over the straits carried a Cameron back into space.

Back to a space station he'd dreamed of seeing . . . dreamed of seeing, like the surface of the moon; a station where all Mospheirans' political dreads were born, for its history, up there with the starship that was the ark in their ancestral stories, the beginning of all human life on the world.

At a certain point the engines grew quiet; and quieter. Ginny Kroger's laugh carried farther than she intended, doubtless so, but he was glad to hear it. Fear might have been a part of Kroger's anger, something Kroger herself might not have known; and now they were past the worst danger . . . technically the worst. That was what the reports tried to assure them.

The crew collected the plastic trays and cups, passed to the rear. Bren looked at his watch, knowing the flight profiles, knowing them as having crossed his desk, knowing them as having sweated through the launches.

Now he was where minutiae counted, degrees of the schedule that had seemed long on the ground, but that seemed both too short and too long, up here.

"Stand by for changeover," came from the cockpit, and the cabin crew translated to Mosphei': "Sirs, now the engines will switch over. Secure all objects immediately. There will be a moment of free fall. Place all loose objects securely in confinement, however small. They may fly back and strike a fellow passenger."

Oh, God, Bren thought. This was the point he dreaded. This was the point where they shut down the engines he knew worked, and the others were supposed to start.

The cabin crew went aft.

The sky in the forward monitor had almost brightened to color, but now quite suddenly a hole opened in it . . . not night, but the threshhold of space.

There was a moment of uncanny silence. A stomach-dropping moment of no-thrust. *We're falling,* apprehensions cried.

Suddenly the shuttle stood on its tail. That, at least, was the illusion. The whole world reoriented. There was a yelp from forward, cries from the servant staff in the back seats.

And a muffled yelp from the paidhi-aiji, Bren realized to his embarrassment.

Yet *up* was the direction of the central monitor, and that was black. Belly-cam showed nothing. Aft-cams showed the running-lights.

Banichi and Jago, damn them, hadn't done more than calmly comply with the safety instruction.

"This is what it *should* do," Jason said.

"I'm glad," Bren said. "I'm so very glad." He wished he hadn't drunk that acidic juice, he was not mentally prepared for this, and somewhere in his memory was a confused datum of how long this acceleration should last. It had been numbers. Now it was life and death, and he truly didn't want it to fall one second short of that, not in the least.

Slowly the sensation of being on one's back eased.

And suddenly there was no *down* and no noise at all but the fans and the general static noise of the systems. *We're falling,* the brain screamed again, growing weary of panic. Bren glanced to the left too fast: the inner ear didn't accommodate the change, not at all.

"God," he murmured, sternly admonished his gut, and turned his head far more slowly, looking about him to see whether items did, as advertised, float. His arms did.

Beyond Banichi, Jago experimented with a pen from her pocket. She seemed quite fascinated when it rebounded off the seat in front of her. Bren stared at that miracle, too, fighting his stomach.

Banichi seemed a little less entranced with the phenomenon, rather grim-faced: Bren took moral comfort in that. Atevi were not immune to disorientation: the first crew had proved that biological fact . . . the same crew, in fact, that was flying the shuttle at the moment.

"We're back," Jason said softly. "*I'm* back."

"Are we doing all right?" Bren asked.

"Completely," Jase said.

So Jase's stomach understood what was going on; and if that was so, damned, then, if he'd miss the trip he'd dreamed of seeing . . . the engines had fired, they were in free fall, and doggedly, seeking something to prove it, he searched up a small wad of paper from the bottom of his pocket, the paper Banichi had handed him with the hospital phone number.

He let it go, floated it in personal incredulity, a miracle. It shouldn't do that.

Or was gravity the miracle? Wasn't it wonderful that the world stuck together, and accreted things to it?

No, he didn't want to think about accretion.

The view in the monitors now was all black. He'd thought he'd see the stars. There was one. Maybe two.

And all the rules changed.

It was a lengthy universal experiment, this traveling in zero-G . . . even Lund and Kroger tried it, if only partially out of their seats; Ben and Kate held carefully to handholds, careful of transgressing that unspoken territorial limit in the cabin, but skylarked there like youngsters on holiday.

Even Banichi, which was the more remarkable, unbelted, and then the others did, but in his security Bren saw a purpose beyond curiosity . . . Banichi's experiments were of measured force, push here, bounce there, back again; and Jago and Tano and Algini did much the same.

A pen sailed by on intercept, lost by a rueful translator forward, and Tano plucked it from space.

Narani was delighted, the servants likewise, laughing with the stewards.

Bren regarded them in slow revolution, wondering at what his mind knew, that they were all hurtling at very high speed.

"The station," Jase said, then, catching his sleeve, directing his attention toward the screens, where a gleam showed against all that blackness, where hull-shine dominated the camera. Banichi and Jago, then Tano and Algini, ceased their activity and focused their attention on that point of light, and after that the four of his security drifted together to talk, a conversation obscured in the thousand nattering systems that kept the shuttle from utter silence.

The cabin crew moved through again, this time horizontally, assessing the state of the passengers, returning Kate's pen. Later, over the general address, the steward admonished all of them: "Be cautious of releasing hard objects, nadiin, which might lodge in secret and become missiles during accelerations."

It occurred to Bren that he wouldn't want to contest with Banichi's mass in any free-fall encounter. And he didn't want to receive Kate's pen on the return, either.

At a downward tug from Jason on his jacket, he secured a hold on the seat and drew himself back in . . . just before the senior steward said, in Mosphei', "Please be seated for the duration." The stewards had practiced that. "For your safety."

The Mospheirans did listen. Buckles clicked, instant obedience.

Bren fastened his own. Jason had reacted to the effect of leaves and sunlight on the planet in utter panic. He measured the fear of vacuum, the fear of movement, against other fears he'd suffered, fears of drawn guns, fears of falling off mountains. This was visceral, a war against lifelong experience, the laws of nature overset . . . as far as his body was concerned. But his senses weren't skewed, nothing except that tendency to look about in panic. Too many surfaces, he decided: all of a sudden too much change. He calmed himself. Thought of lily ponds on the mainland. A formal garden.

"We shall be braking, nadiin."

He wished they'd been able to have windows. He did wish that. The monitors weren't straight-line forward. The cameras had moved to track the station; he began to figure that out. Of course. They were gimbaled, to track anything outside they needed to. The crew was giving them a view. It was giving him extreme disorientation.

Jase talked to him, small matters, observations: "We brake to overtake," Jase reminded him. He knew that. Gravity-tied to the planet, they couldn't catch the station by accelerating: the result would be a higher and higher orbit, missing the equally-bound station. Their path was simply—simply!—to coincide with it and brake slightly, little by little.

That would drop them in the orbital path to line up with the docking stem.

"There we go," Jase said. Jase knew he was scared.

He'd sweated through this, every docking from the first one; knew this whole docking business was another troubled sequence. He bit his lip and prayed there was no mistake.

"Easy," Jase said, salt in a wound.

"I'm fine," he said. Jase had used to say that. Jase prudently didn't remind him.

The image, over a long, long nervous approach, resolved itself from one dot to two connected dots.

Finally into a ring with that second dot against the stem.

Kate pointed to it as the camera suddenly brought it up close, while Jason just said, in a low voice, *"Phoenix."*

9

The cameras on close-up, as they glided past, showed a battered surface, not the pristine white Bren had once imagined *Phoenix* to be. She was sooted, discolored with black and with rust-color, streaked and ablated on the leading edges.

Their ship. The ship. She carried the dust of solar systems, the outpourings of volcanoes on Maudit's moons, the cosmic dust of wherever *Phoenix* had voyaged . . . and the scars of the first accursed sun where *Phoenix* had lost so many lives. Jason's forefathers. His own.

The whole world had seen the scarred image on the television during the first shuttle flights, and the sight had shocked everyone, moving some even to question whether it was the same ship. *Phoenix* in all Mospheiran accounts was always portrayed shining white, though every schoolchild also memorized the truth that the earth of the atevi was in a debris-filled, dangerous solar system, that the colonists had rebelled against *Phoenix*'s plans for refueling principally because fatalities were so much a part of mining.

The image of authority. The ark that had carried all their ancestors on two epic journeys, and a third . . . without the colonists, but with Jase's fellow crew. Bren felt a chill go over his skin, felt a stir in his heart, an awe he hadn't entirely expected.

Now the outcome of this last voyage, this run home with hostile observers behind them. The captains had no disposition to die without a struggle, as hard a struggle as their compatriots back in this solar system could make of it, with or without their consent.

Welcome to the space age. Welcome to the universe *we've* made, and the consequences of all *we've* done.

"Stand by, nadiin, for braking. —Sirs, ladies, prepare your safety belts. Secure all items."

Bren tugged the belt tight, fastened the shoulder belt as Jason unhurriedly, confidently at home, did the same.

He glanced across the aisle and saw his security belted in, looking as calm as if they sat in their own apartment.

There was no stir from elsewhere. This was the sequence that had fouled on the first flight, nearly ended the mission in a dangerous spacewalk.

"Homecoming," Jase said.

"Nervous?" he asked Jase.

"As hell," Jase confessed, and took a deep breath. "I don't mind traveling in space at all. It's stopping short of large objects that scares me."

Bren felt safe enough to retaliate. "Better than skimming the surface of planets, isn't it?"

The engines cut in. Jase grabbed the armrests. "I hate that, too. I really hate this part."

Hard braking. Jase was not comforting.

Warnings flashed on the side-view screen in two languages: in general, stay belted, don't interfere with crew, and don't interfere with the pilot.

The mechanisms are old, figured in the explanation.

"There's an understatement," Jase muttered.

This time, however, the locking mechanism didn't fail: the grapple bumped, thumped . . . engaged.

"We have docked," came the word from the pilot.

There were multiple sighs of relief. A buckle clicked.

"Please stay close to your seats," the steward said. "We have yet to perform various tasks and assure the connection."

Bump.

Gentle bump.

Second jolt, second crash of hydraulics engaged. Bren told his heart to slow down.

They were in. Locked.

"Made it," he said.

"Bren," Jase said, in one of those *I've got something to say* tones of voice.

"What?"

"You think Tabini's ever advised them yet we're not the test cargo?"

"I'm sure he has. —Worried?"

"Now that I'm here, I'm worried."

Second thoughts were setting in, in a way he didn't have to entertain, because *he* didn't have any options here. "About them—or us?"

"Just—worried."

"Survival of the atevi, Jase. Survival of all of us. If you've got second thoughts about rejoining your crew . . ."

"I have no choice."

"I *can* claim you as a chargé d'affaires, under Tabini's wing, and I know he'll back me on it. You can talk to Ramirez from that protection, inside our quarters, if you think you need it."

"You don't have quarters here . . . you don't *know* you have."

"Believe me. We will have."

"I'm Ramirez's choice. I have to play this through, Bren."

"For you?" Bren asked. "Or for them? Or because it's wise? Second thoughts, I understand. Believe me, I understand: I've made my choice. Whatever you want for yourself, this is no time to make gestures. Too many lives are at risk here. What's the sensible truth, Jase? What do you expect?"

"I need to get to Ramirez. I need to talk to him. We *aren't* atevi associations. I remember that from the gut now."

Naojai-tu?

Association-shift? Rearrangement of man'chi? Damiri's cynic meeting the relics, in the play?

Humans, on the other hand, made and dissolved ties throughout their lives, even on so limited an island as Mospheira. Jase *was* human; the Pilots' Guild was human. In this whole business, everyone in the game could rearrange loyalties . . . so could the atevi, but under different, socially catastrophic terms.

"Still friends," Bren said, meaning it. "No question."

"Still friends," Jase said. "But, Bren, I can't *be* who I was down there. They won't let me be."

"Will they not?" He was determined to the contrary, determined, in this last-moment doubt, to recall what Jase had thought last week and the week before. "Listen to me. Will you turn against Tabini, or report against him? I don't think you will; you understand what the truth is down there. I know you won't ever turn coat for your own sake. I know you."

"Do you? I don't know *what* I'll do."

"I understand that point of view. Been through it. You *know* I've been through it."

"I don't know I can."

"Get your thinking in order. I know the dislocation you're facing. But think of Shejidan. It's real. The people you know are real, and depending on you, the same as I imagine people here are. Personally—I'll get you back, Jase. Damned if I won't. Politically, you'll do as you have to for the short term, but don't ruin my play and don't stray too far, not physically, not mentally."

"I'm not Mospheiran. I can't explain how different . . ."

"Na dei shi'ra ma'anto paidhi, nadi?" . . . Are you not one of the paidhiin, sir? Am I mistaken?

From a glance at the screens, Jase flung him a sidelong, troubled glance.

"Na dei-ji?" Bren repeated, with the familiar.

"Aiji-ji, so'sarai ta."

There was no real translation, only affection, loyalty, a salute. *You taught me, my master. I respect that.* Implicit was the whole other mindset, that back-and-forth shift that came with any deep shift in language, an earthquake in thought patterns. From panic in Jase's eyes, he saw a slide toward sanity and familiar ground.

"Shi, paidhi, noka ais-ji?"

Are you reliable, translator-mediator?

Jase heaved a small, desperate breath. *"Shi!"* I am.

"Think in Ragi, Jasi-ji. The language changes the way you think. Changes your resources. Your responses. So does your native accent. You've been on a long trip. You're going to remember things here you'd let slip. But stop and think in Ragi, at least twice a day."

"It's trying to slip away from me! Words just aren't there!"

"I've been through that, too, every trip to Mospheira. Fight for it."

"Please give attention to the exit procedures," the steward said, with the worst timing in the world or above it.

"Jase," Bren said. "What's your personal preference? Honestly. You don't *get* personal preferences. I don't. But tell me what it is."

"If I had personal preference," Jase said with a desperate laugh, "I'd be home. —God! I'm scrambled . . ."

"I know that," Bren said. "Think of the sitting room in the Bu-javid. Think of Taiben. Think of the sea."

"*Sha nauru shina.* I'll contact you," Jase said desperately, as staff rose and the Mospheirans rose to leave. "Or you demand to see me. They're going to want me to themselves for a number of days. Ramirez I can deal with."

"I'll raise hell till I do get to see you," Bren said. It might be a close, intense, emotional debriefing, a close questioning no one could look forward to. They would want to bring him back under their authority, even to crack him emotionally to be sure what was inside . . . Jase had never quite said so, but he had an idea what he was facing. No government could take chances with trust, not with survival at stake.

Likewise he knew what he was promising Jase, on the instant and on his own judgment of a situation. He *had* been in Jase's position. And he knew how Jase might both take comfort in someone saying *you matter*—and at the same time feel politically trapped. In the emotional impact of the ship that was his home, the atevi world was starting to leak right out of his brain, along with all the memories, all the confidence of what he believed.

"At Malguri," he said while bangs and thumps proceeded aft and Mospheirans drifted free of their seats. "At Malguri," he said, because Jase knew the story, "I had one of those language transit experiences; I think it helped make me fluent. I'll tell you honestly I don't envy you the debriefing. And this I can tell you. Don't ever let them take *time* away from you. Don't ever let their reality become yours. I'll be here as long as possible, and if I have to leave,

I'll apply every means I've got to get contact directly with you. I won't give up. Ever."

"You can't afford that."

"Hell, Tabini won't forget you. And I won't. You have power, Jase. I'm handing it to you, right now. *Aishi'ji.*" Associates. He laid a grip on Jase's arm. Tightened it. "We don't lose one another."

Jase concentrated on him with that wild look he'd had once, contemplating a very deep sea under his feet, and all that heaving water.

"Kindly file out to the rear hatch," the steward said.

They unbuckled, were able to rise . . . straight up . . . taking advantage themselves of zero-G.

His staff had gathered up their carry-on baggage, of which there was a fair quantity.

Tano was with the servants. "One has the manifest, nand' paidhi," Narani said to Tano in his hearing, "so that baggage may find the quarters. How shall I deliver this document?"

This, in a space increasingly complicated by loose passengers, baggage, straps, and elbows.

Something banged. Nothing advised what the various bleeps, beeps, bangs, and thumps were, but he thought it might be the hatch, and in the next moment a wave of cold wind came through the shuttle.

He had to forget Jase then. He cast grim looks at his security, sure that he needed to stay with them, because, being atevi, *they* would assuredly stay with *him*, and he wanted no misunderstandings. The possibility of abrupt, wrong movement all rested with him, with the relative position of him, his guard, and threat. He dared not let overzealous station security create a moment of panic.

"If they do jostle us, nadiin," Bren said, drifting up beside Banichi and Jago, "recall they don't feel man'chi, and may make apparently hostile moves. They are foreigners. Be restrained. Be very restrained. Don't show weapons."

"Yes," Jago said, that disconcerting Ragi agreement to a negative.

The Mospheirans pushed through their midst, evidently intending to be first out. "Let them, nadiin," Bren said, by no means inclined to argue with Kroger's sense of proprieties.

Kate and Ben, more hesitant, drifting free, looked distressed, worried as they passed, clutching drifting luggage.

"Understood," Bren said to the junior staff. "Go on past. Best if you do go out first. Best if the first thing they see isn't atevi. Good luck to you." His servants waited, cramped to the side, while Kroger and her team exited.

"Go," he said then, and went forward, using the seat backs for propulsion. Jase stayed close, experience and unthought confidence in the environment in the way he gauged distance ahead of him and checked a small movement with unthought precision.

A little of the motion sickness quivered through Bren's stomach, or indigestible fear. He imitated Jase, using the same technique of small pushes and stops against the seats to avoid bumping into his servants. "Nadiin-ji. Follow Banichi and Jago. Do not make sudden moves, no startling of the humans."

The air in the ship had turned from mere cold to truly bitter, breath-steaming cold. His hands were numb. Within the air lock, it was worse still; the chill turned any moisture in the air to ice. He met the handline there, took hold, regretting gloves had not been part of the arrangement in their shirtsleeve environment, as he followed Kate's feet out into the bitter chill of the access.

There a handful of ship worker-personnel, suited against the cold, wearing masks and goggles, likewise clung with gloved hands to the rigged line. The Mospheirans had gone on, a line of bodies the brain kept saying was ascending a rope through water. Perception played tricks, in a stomach-wrenching glance at an environment of metal grids and pipes and insulated walls.

In the same moment the workers saw what was coming: the body language wasn't as definite in zero-G, but Bren saw it. First: *Jase; we know him, glad to see you.* Then: *That's a stranger,* coupled with, *Omigod, they're large, they're alien, and there are more of them than us.*

Jase reached out a bare hand to one of the anonymous workers and caught a gloved grip. "Luz?"

"Jase." The word came muffled through the mask. Josefin was the name on the orange protective suit. "Jase!"

"This is Bren Cameron behind me. His staff. Atevi security. And his servants. I hope the message got here."

"Yes," Luz said. "Yes. Mr. Cameron." Bren drifted along with the assistance of the rope. Exposed flesh, face, ears, and fingers—burned and chilled in the dry cold. The inside of his nose felt frosted, his lungs assaulted. He held out his own hand, had it taken, gingerly, in a grip that hurt his cold fingers.

"Thank you for the welcome. My bodyguard and staff, thanks. Glad to be aboard."

"Yes, sir," was the answer. Luz Josefin, a woman with dark eyes behind the goggles, seemed paralyzed an instant, then said, "Yes, sir. Hurry. You'll freeze. Watch your hands. Warm your ears when you get inside."

"Thanks." Bren moved along rapidly then, fingers having lost all feeling. Jase was with him. His staff followed. The atevi crew hadn't exited—wouldn't yet; they and the pilots, with their separate hatch, would still be at work, checkout and shutdown. Bren concentrated on getting himself and his security to the end of the rope and the doorway he saw ahead before he lost all muscle coordination . . . and before Kroger might shut the door in their faces.

"Air lock." Jase shoved him through, using leverage. "Watch those controls. Don't push any buttons." He bumped Mospheirans, couldn't help it, tried not to kick anyone.

"Are enough of us going to fit?" he asked Jase in Mosphei', and was glad to see another crewman, wearing bright yellow, standing guard over the lift controls.

His staff packed themselves in. There was a directional arrow on the wall, and the attendant hauled at the Mospheirans, saying, "Feet to the floor," until they had squirmed and rotated into some sort of directional unity, "Feet down," Jase said. "Watch the luggage, nadiin, push it to your feet." The door shut by fits and starts, wedging them and their baggage in, and Bren blew on the fingers of one hand, asking himself how fast frostbite could set in on the one maintaining a hand-grip.

"Never been this way but once," Jase said. "Should have remembered gloves. Sorry. Sorry about this."

"Yes," Bren said with economy, teeth chattering. "Gloves have to go on the list."

The car moved.

"Hold on," Jase said. "*Jai! Atira'na.* Don't let go."

"Hold on!" Jago echoed, amused, as it proved understatement. Bags settled, forcing themselves among atevi feet. Kate's bag traveled to the floor and thumped.

"We'll go through the rotational interface," Jason said in Ragi, and repeated it in his native accent. "Don't let go the handholds at any time."

It was a curious sensation, a little like going from flying to mildly falling, resting very lightly on a floor, then weighing more and more. Where does this stop? Bren's senses wanted to know with panicked urgency.

The Mospheirans had been told *no large hand baggage.* This was a point the Mospheirans had clearly noticed, and probably resented like hell right now, as his four servants fought desperately to keep theirs organized. Tano and Jago helped, shoving items back in the shifts of stress.

A lift, hell. It didn't *lift*, it suddenly moved sideways, like a small plane in a thunderstorm.

It dropped.

Came to a stop. Definitive stop, Bren decided, and relaxed an ice-burned stranglehold on the safety grip.

The door opened on light, warmth, a beige wall and an official welcoming committee, men and women in blue uniforms, all the expected signs of rank . . . uniforms identical to uniforms in historical paintings, in old photographs, in plays and dramas.

It wasn't teleconferences anymore. It was living history looking them in the face as they got off the lift, one of those perception shifts: home, for Jase, to him and the Mospheirans, history, like someone dressed up for a play— while the atevi saw this uniformed lot as . . . what else? . . . the very emblem of the foreigners who had dropped from the sky.

Bren immediately recognized two of the faces he'd seen previously on a viewing screen: Captain Jules Ogun, third-shift, dark-skinned, white-haired. In real life, he had curiously few wrinkles, as if some sculptor's hand had created them, then smoothed them out again. He was over eighty years old, and had the body of a younger man.

"Captain Ogun, Lieutenant Delacroix," Jase said quietly. "The Mospheiran delegation, Mr. Lund, Ms. Kroger; and Bren Cameron, the aiji's representative."

Ogun offered a hand, shook Lund's, and Kroger's, then Bren's, a thin-boned, vigorous grip.

"Sir," Bren said, "a pleasure to meet you."

Ogun gave him an eye-to-eye stare, not a happy one, not an angry one either. "Mr. Cameron. I take it this mission was the aiji's sudden notion. And the President's."

"We were sent," Kroger was too quick to say, "on the aiji's schedule. It was hurry up or lose the seats."

Coldly, Ogun turned his attention past her to Jase. "Jase. Welcome home."

"Thank you, sir," Jase said quietly.

"As for the suddenness of this move," this with a sweeping glance at Bren and Kroger, "the quarters aren't prepared. Not a priority, since we'd received no prior word and I don't hold my crew accountable. I can explain we don't have the space. I can explain that when we occupy a section of this station we have to secure seals, check the power conduits, turn on power, check the lines, and bring up a section the size of our ship from the extremes of space and vacuum . . . which we don't damnwell have the personnel to accomplish without risk. Our occupancy is of two sections, plus the core transport, plus the ship. No room. That's first. Second, I understand there's cargo you don't want opened, that you want put under your control. Unacceptable."

It had been a long flight. If Bren had a wish, it was for facilities—soon, but the aiji's dignity was life and death. Ridiculous as this standoff got, it was everyone on the planet's life and death.

He launched into a translation for his staff, occupying attention, making clear that there was a communication problem which no amount of shouting could cure, and hinting that his staff didn't communicate, which might become a problem to the station.

Then, giving the captain a direct look: "Space, under

your constrained circumstances, is negotiable, sir. Our cargo is diplomatic baggage, which falls within the previously agreed circumstances, and any interference in it will compromise all negotiations. This has been cleared; it is agreed. We're prepared to be understanding regarding your degree of preparedness; but not about our necessity for appropriate food."

The silence stretched on—two, three more heartbeats.

"If you can eat it, they can eat what we eat."

"Your pardon, sir, but their physical requirements involve alkaloid poisons, as I'm sure we've made clear; their religious and philosophical requirements insist they have their own diet."

"Baggage passes our inspection. Your people can stand by."

"No, sir," Bren said calmly. "That's contrary to already negotiated agreements. We state that we've brought nothing aboard that's on your forbidden list, and we'll make no open fires. The fact you don't have the facility ready is your side of the agreement; the fact that we have equipment we're bringing aboard is our side, and failing one of our arrangements, we stand by the other."

"Captain," Kroger said. "*Our baggage* should not be at issue. We have our clothing, our small personal necessities. Inspect what you like, but this is an official delegation, negotiated as of two years ago; that the aiji in Shejidan hurried it is not our choosing."

"We won't be hurried," Ogun said.

"We've heard for three years," Bren said, "that haste serves all of us. The baggage is not renegotiable; trade agreements depend on our ability to maintain a mission here under our own seal, to feed our people in our own kitchen, and we will not give on that point."

"From what I can see, you're human, Mr. Cameron, and you can tell them this, and you can tell the aiji this: we won't tolerate being pushed!"

"He's being obdurate," Bren said in Ragi, and in Mosphei', "My security officers are armed, tradition on the mainland; they will always be armed. So will the security that attends any atevi representative. That, and the kitchen, will not change, sir. My staff understands as well as yours the hazards of discharging weapons in this environment, and likewise the hazards of interfering with your communications. All this was worked out two years ago, both for us and for Mospheira. Inspection violates those agreements. Your negotiations with the aiji are all tied to those agreements, and we will not give on that point. The contents of diplomatic messages and baggage must be respected, or this shuttle will go back down, and the aiji will consider constructing his own space station and reserving work for himself."

"The hell he will!"

It was possible to stare down another human being, someone on eye level. And he already knew watching the changes in expression that the captain was not going to throw up two years of agreement on his source of supply; the captain wanted him to back down on the details of the request.

More, he knew this man, at least second-hand and from Jason.

"The hell, yes," Bren said, and in Jase's accent. "End report."

"We can't admit weapons to the hull. Or biological contaminants."

"The greater hazard is in ourselves, sir, and frankly we're more worried about you, since the Mospheirans and the atevi have never had a major disease outbreak interchanged. We don't carry crop pests, and if we did, we could settle them. Processed flour, sir. Cooking oil. Our galley is self-contained and uses electricity, not open flame, a *considerable* cultural concession, components we've designed to function with station electrical systems on your own advisement, captain, *with* all due respect. I'm here to talk deal on your supplies, not our baggage."

"All right, we'll arrange a stopgap. Settle it for now. Our security will take you to quarters. You can settle in and we'll discuss the rest."

"On the baggage," Bren said, not disposed to move . . . resistance to discomfort was a requirement of tenacious negotiation; and if this man was difficult, a session in the atevi legislature was hell itself. "If those seals are broken, sir, if there should be an accidental breach, we go down without negotiating, and we may be another two years negotiating another mission."

There was a long, long silence.

"This will go under discussion during the next twenty-four hours," Ogun said. "Along with the quarters." He shifted an eye distastefully over all the staff, and the hand luggage, a waist-high mound of it. Then gave the same look to Kroger and Lund and party.

"Mr. Delacroix. Quarters for the lot."

"Yes, sir," the lieutenant said.

"Jase," Bren said, aside, with a glance at Jason. "Join us for supper?" Meaning: if you don't like what you hear, accept. Now.

"Mr. Graham is *Phoenix* crew," the captain said. "He'll join the captains for supper. Contact them later, Mr. Graham."

"Yes, sir," Jase said.

"Meanwhile, Mr. Delacroix."

"Yes, sir," Delacroix said, and passed the next order to the human crew that waited. "Mr. Kaplan, Ms. Ramsey. Quarters."

"Yes, sir, come this way, sir."

Quarters, then, had been an item understood, probably debated with raised voices ever since Tabini's advisement they were coming up. Mr. Kaplan and Ms. Ramsey evidently had a completely clear idea where they were going; Bren was no little amused, resolved not to let it affect his judgment . . . and not to jump quickly to oblige the captain's maneuvers, no matter the personal discomfort.

Meanwhile Narani and the servants had gathered that they were moving out, and gathered up the baggage. Banichi and his team, likely subtle origin of the signal to Narani, looked to him for orders.

Bren delayed, smiled at Kroger and Lund. "Hope to see you tomorrow," he said, offering a hand, and went through the entire hand-shaking formality for no other reason than to set his imminent departure as his choice, his schedule.

"Mr. Cameron, sir," Kaplan urged him, wishing him to go to the left. Kaplan, a young man, wore a kind of headset, and had swung down an eyepiece, appalling-looking creation. It looked like half of eyeglasses; screens, set only a minute degree from the eye, quite transparent to the outside view.

Such eyepieces could be used for targeting. Bren recalled that. Mospheira didn't have any survivals of that technology, not outside the close confines of the Defense Department.

And on a thought, Bren delayed for another moment, regarding transmissions down to Mogari. "Ginny, give Shawn my regards when you talk to him," he said.

"The same to the aiji," Kroger said, with less than atevi-style formality, annoyed as hell, Bren thought.

"See you," he said to Jase, before he acquiesced to the guidance offered. It was the parting he least wanted, and Jase knew he meant it: *See you.* It was another of those mutual codes. But for now he obediently led his group after the crewman, down a short hall to an automatic door.

They passed through that and into a hall that, incredibly, curved upward, exactly the reverse of the situation that had turned Jason's stomach when he'd faced planetary horizons.

Remarkable, Bren thought . . . and was glad to know his stomach tolerated it. It didn't feel as bad as it looked. There was just more upward-curving hallway. And a lot of intersections. He'd seen the diagrams of the station; had studied them with interest, when, two years ago, the whole business of diplomatic establishments had come up and they'd talked about what he could do about the doorways, the sanitary facilities, all the modifications that evidently hadn't been made as agreed.

But, damn, he thought: he had them in his computer, that small machine Jago carried for him. Since he'd gotten this new portable, and since it went in the highest security Mospheira and the mainland could mount, he'd never dumped a file that he feared he might regret. More, he'd loaded everything in that he could possibly lay hands on, everything Shawn *let* him have.

Everything they knew of *Phoenix* design was in there; station design was; the architectural modifications, and ten or fifteen card games and any other piece of extraneity he'd used in the last damned year, and he hadn't even thought about it, except a passing connection of neurons about having it with him, asking himself, under hasty circumstances, if there were *atevi* files he could compromise.

But he didn't keep the sensitive ones in the portable. Those were in the office computer, under guard. He didn't take them back and forth to the island, only files atevi and the island shared. Thank *God,* he thought, for that.

His staff was coping with the perspective and the maze they traveled. Keeping his own steps straight seemed to want conscious effort, but at least the nausea didn't recur. Most of all, he was glad to have played the hand right in the encounter with Ogun . . . not to have been settled into siege in a rapidly-cooling shuttle cabin while Tabini slugged it out verbally with the Pilots' Guild, as could have happened if he'd overshot his limits. Atevi, who chilled less readily, could have lasted longer than he could . . . but it could have been damned dangerous, no credit to Kroger . . . none to him for antagonizing the woman.

But that he'd win the question with the captain who didn't want atevi cargo on his station, he had little active doubt. It was not in the ship's interest to offend Tabini, as it was not in his own interest or Tabini's to declare war with an orbiting power.

Ultimately, agreements had to work. Ultimately, Kroger, who seemed to get harder to deal with when fear reared its head, had to work with him.

And with luck, he would do what he'd come to do in the same two weeks as the Mospheirans planned to use. He'd get an arrangement with Ramirez and his brother captains, Ogun included, that let him come and go . . . and that let Jase come and go. He had no right to add that to the bottom line, and couldn't spend the aiji's credit to get it; but he was forming an opinion that if Bren Cameron had any personal credit in this affair, he knew where he was going to spend it.

Seeing this place with its wrong-curving corridors, its endless, same-textured, cream-colored corridors, he understood how frightening Jase had found the variability of a planet. He found *this* morally frightening. A machine had extruded this corridor, a huge, unvarying machine. The door insets were just that, inset in an extruded-plastics form, not fighting the curvature except for a slanted sill, and every one the same, every door human height, as the corridor overhead was interrupted by absolutely regular translucent light panels.

It was absolutely the antithesis of hand-crafted Malguri. His ancestors had made this place . . . and he didn't recognize it. Heart and mind, he didn't recognize it.

Banichi and Jago walked just behind him, clearing the ceiling by not too much, trusting his leadership without question as they went deeper and deeper into this maze, deeper and deeper into places human authorities knew and he didn't. Tano and Algini walked behind them, the staff with the hand-baggage two by two behind that. He was aware of the order every time they passed a section door, and there were no few. The escort took them on and on.

And finally right-turned down an intersecting corridor, through a doorway—theirs, Bren hoped, in acute discomfort, only to be disappointed. There was more corridor, another turn, and again a corridor, another door. Kaplan had to be using that eyepiece to navigate, giving no advantage to anybody who wasn't receiving the information. Scuffs on the flooring gave the only proof of prior traffic.

Security . . . for the holders of the information. They'd refurbished this area. Put *no* identifying marks anywhere on walls or doors or floor.

"Here you are," Kaplan said confidently, at an apparent dead end that might be only another turn in the corridors, and opened a door.

Light came on inside a room with a bed, a desk, several chairs, and a dressing-area.

"Thank you," Bren said. "And what for the rest of my team?"

"I've no instructions, sir. Far as I know, this is what there is."

"Nine persons won't fit."

"I can relay that, sir."

"And how do we come and go to our meetings? I have to make an appointment with your officers at the earliest. How do I contact them?"

"Someone will come for you."

"At very minimum we'll need more beds."

"I have no orders, sir."

"You have a request. This is one bed. Obviously there are other beds elsewhere." He waved a hand, Tabini-esque. "We need more beds."

"They're built in, sir. Can't move them."

"Then mattresses. Bags with stuffing in them. I don't care. My people are not going to sleep on the floor or step over one another. We need more rooms. We need mattresses."

"I don't know what I can do, sir."

"You know how to find out, however. That *is* a communications link you're wearing; you *can* talk to your officers on that communication system, and I insist you do that or accept all the responsibility for not doing it. Tell them mattresses. Or padding of some sort. I want those within two hours. Rooms by tomorrow. I'm sure we'll work it out. Will you show me the phone?"

"Phone?"

"Communications, sir."

There was contact, behind both eyes, glassed and unglassed. The young man stepped inside and touched a wall installation, fingers flying over buttons. "This is communications. This is light. This is up heat, this is down. This is the fan setting. There's an intercom. You just punch in and wait."

"What about the other rooms neighboring this one? I'm sure you won't mind if we open them up."

"There's personnel assigned there, sir. There's personnel assigned all over. This is living quarters."

"Do they have mattresses?"

"Look here, sir, we're not under your orders!"

"No. They are." This with a conscious reference to the living wall of atevi waiting around them. "We need the mattresses, we need more room, and we're going to be persistent. I don't care what you find, sir, or how long it takes, but this is the team that's supposed to supply you with *your* needs, I assure you, not ours. I do appreciate the inconvenience and the difficulty involved and I'm sorry it's fallen on you, but I know, too, that your captain places confidence in your judgment and your resourcefulness, or he wouldn't have sent us off with you. So what can you do for us?"

Likely suggestions occurred to the man, but he adopted an aggrieved, respectful expression and heaved a sigh. "Sir, I'll do what I can, sir."

"I'll expect success, then. I'm sure of it. Thank you. Thank you very much."

"Yes, sir."

The guard left, probably saying more on his personal communications than a request for mattresses.

Bren, on the other hand, looked at Banichi, then cast a look at Jago, and then, with the indisputable privilege of rank, ducked inside in desperation, and to the back of the room, to what atevi politely called the accommodation.

In hardly a day and a night he'd antagonized a Mospheiran ambassador, one of the four *Phoenix* captains and an innocent crewman. It was not unpredictable that the aiji's notion of presenting a fait accompli to the Pilots' Guild had lodged them sideways in the throat of the station, but he had to reflect, once the adrenaline had somewhat fallen, that he'd had to do it, that Tabini had put him into a position, and he had no choice but make it clear . . . he couldn't lie to the Mospheirans.

He couldn't tell them the entire truth of his intentions either, much as he'd gone out of his way to level with them. He'd told most of the truth to Jase, his one wholehearted ally. But as far as human relations went, he'd had to clear a working space, make it very clear to the Mospheirans they weren't participant with him in agreements he might make, make it clear to the captains one and all that if bargains weren't kept, bargains wouldn't be kept.

It was one policy in the elegant halls of the aiji's residence.

It was another here, where they settled, the staff on the floor . . . himself in one chair, Banichi and Jago sitting on the bed, Algini and Tano standing in the corner. The place was too cold for human comfort. Though the fan was on high and the heat coming out of the vents was substantial, it seemed to produce only a fever-chill in the air. The surfaces stole warmth: walls, even the bedding seemed cold through.

"I do regret this discomfort," he said to his servants. "Nadiin, I am hoping to improve this."

"They do not, seemingly, adapt well to surprises," Banichi remarked, and, caught by surprise himself, Bren had to laugh.

"We don't know," Jago added quietly, "whether this represents the standard of their own quarters."

"One certainly hopes not," Bren said. "More, one doubts it."

"We can sleep on the floor," the juniormost servant, Sabiso, said softly. She had banged her head quite painfully on the door of the facility, and had been mortally embarrassed, knocked half unconscious. It had raised a sizable lump on her brow. "We can use our baggage for mattresses, perhaps."

"I don't intend so," Bren said. "I do *not* intend so. I don't wish to move in with the shuttle crew, but if we get no better from the captains soon, we may have more words. We won't tolerate this for two weeks." Dismissing his servants to that greater comfort did occur to him; but it was not the atevi way of managing things, and it could not be his choice, not without shaming his staff. Tabini would much prefer a standoff.

And ultimately . . . ultimately, Tabini would have his way.

"We have brought sandwiches," Narani said cheerfully, "in case of a long flight, and delays, nandi. It is the hour, in Shejidan, by the clock, and nand' paidhi may have his supper, if he will."

"Brought supper, Rani-ji!" He'd never even asked the servants what was in the huge, heavy baggage. "Beyond hope. Marvelous."

Narani was delighted to have surprised him; the servants were entirely pleased and encouraged, and scurried about opening baggage, setting out unbreakable plastic dishes on the desk and the vanity counter.

Another piece of baggage opened up packets of sandwiches. A third produced fruit juice in unbreakable containers besides other black canvas packages, which Tano quietly abstracted and gave to Banichi.

What have you brought? he thought of asking, and thought perhaps he'd face the captains more honestly not knowing. Besides, familiar, homemade food sounded very good at the moment, and he was very glad to accept a plate and juice, in a glass, not the scandal of drinking from a bottle. In no wise would nand' paidhi have other than a plate, and proper utensils.

"Excellent," he said. "Excellent, nadiin. —Sit, sit down, nadiin-ji. I wish you to sit and share all this with me."

The offering was meat of the season, pickled eggs and dried fruit, juice, with tea still hot in the flasks. And eat together, and in front of nand' paidhi and his security? The servants were rarely comfortable with such an arrangement . . . and he was sorry for his failure as yet to provide them their own place, quarters of their own, their own dining room, their own place for jokes and camaraderie, their domain which Narani should rule.

But they all settled to eat, then, and the sense of ceremony with which they shared their meal made it a quiet, reserved time.

"We've become a village," Jago observed then, recalling the more informal culture of field and farm, and that struck the servants as strangely funny, for reasons a human found difficulty figuring.

"We should have *goda,*" Tano said, which made them laugh aloud. It was country fare, boiled grain on which one slathered butter or fruit jelly or fish sauce, in season: Bren had had it.

"No fish sauce, nadiin," said Bindanda, the outsider; all the servants well knew Bren's distaste for that, and they shyly thought that was very funny, too.

"No fish sauce," they echoed.

In that laughter came a beep from somewhere in the room, which drew immediate attention from Banichi and his staff. The servants, lifelong accustomed to the goings-on of assassination-prone lords and their armed security, fell instantly silent.

"Mr. Cameron," a voice said from near the door, from the wall unit.

Banichi leaped up, and immediately the rest of the security staff was on their feet.

"I'll deal with it," Bren said, and rose and went to the wall console. Green, white, and red buttons were lit.

Green button, he decided, green for go, certainly not what an ateva would have chosen. "Hello?"

"Mr. Cameron, this is the officer of the watch. Your cargo is released, orders of the captains. It's on its way."

"Thank you," Bren said, not entirely surprised, but very glad it would arrive before they wished to sleep. "Please relay our delegation's satisfaction, captain, and its appreciation. My servants and staff will assist in moving it, at need."

"No need," the gruff reply came back. *"We're sending a cart."*

"And the other problem? The mattresses?"

"Mattresses?"

"I thought this was understood."

"What mattresses, sir?"

"My staff, sir, averaging well above two meters in height and numbering eight, besides myself, cannot rest on the floor, nor do I lodge with my staff, sir, excepting my security. This insults the aiji in Shejidan, it was agreed, and I am still waiting." With whom it had been agreed he neglected to say. "On the other hand, I'm sure more rooms would solve the problem. Five rooms would be adequate. We are prepared to move."

There was a lengthy moment of silence. *"Let me ask the captain on shift."*

The captains damned well knew how one had to deal with the aiji of Shejidan. He glanced at his watch, knew by the usual ship's schedule that it was past Ogun's watch. "Shall I wait on line? Let me talk to Captain Ramirez."

"He's asleep, sir." That meant it was either Tamun or Sabin. He strongly hoped for Sabin. *"It may have fallen between watches. Give me a moment on the problem, and I'll get back to you."*

Bren punched the switch to off. The quarters might be bugged, but they could only detect riot or silence and the occasional drop of a recognizable name. No one aboard spoke Ragi with any fluency. Jase, and to some degree Yolanda, was the ship's only chance of translating it on the fly. There had been a dictionary sent up; he was sure they would make use of it. But learn Ragi? In years of dealing, there had been no request for that.

*   *   *

"The baggage will arrive," he told his staff, cheering them. "They're pursuing the question of additional quarters. The captains go by shifts. Ramirez is asleep, Ogun has left duty, and we wait to see whether Sabin or Tamun happens to be aiji of this ship at the moment."

The servant staff had risen. They bowed, pleased at the news.

"Let us resume our supper," Bren said, and everyone settled. He made short work of his own sandwich, fortification for combat.

Within a few minutes the intercom beeped again.

Banichi punched in this time, quick study.

"This is Bren Cameron," Bren said with the comfort of good food on his stomach.

"This is Captain Sabin. Mr. Cameron, despite the apparent size of the station, we don't have unlimited facilities. Not all areas are livable. Quite bluntly, sir, we can accommodate the Mospheiran mission; but we're finding difficulty accommodating your special needs."

"The aiji will not take that into account, captain; nor should he. But we're willing to make adjustments for your situation, quite understanding your position. We can forgo the modification of doorways and accesses."

"It's not doorways and access, Mr. Cameron. I doubt the native government will want to accommodate an unannounced lot of us, either."

"The aiji has prepared your guest quarters exactly to human specifications, captain, on schedule. Send down a complement on the shuttle, and they will be treated as guests." It certainly couldn't be a credible threat of invasion, not unless they wanted to drop their several hundred crew members in capsules, and only atevi goodwill would put a second shuttle within their reach. "We understand your schedule has been subject to pressure. But I must say this situation was not of our making . . . and we met schedule. The Mospheirans responded with extreme suspicion when you abruptly recalled their translator; when you recalled Jase Graham, the aiji took that as a statement as well, indicating a new phase in our dealings."

"Mr. Cameron, the aiji is proceeding on assumption."

"You made the gesture, captain. You alarmed the Mospheirans, the Mospheirans appealed to him for seats; he granted it. He *is not human,* captain. He responded to your gesture and to the Mospheiran delegates in a thoroughly logical way for an ateva. He sent me up here first to ask why, to be sure the Mospheirans tell you the truth, and to assert his agreements with you and your Council. I find, unfortunately, that the quarters we require aren't ready. I'm ready to accommodate that, within reason; but for the reason you came to ask our help, we need to arrive at a working relationship. That begins with adequate space."

"We don't have space at our disposal."

"And I believe we've already made it clear that atevi representatives don't come in ones and small sets. They have staff to provide for security that is never absent from them, waking or sleeping, on the planet. This substitutes for weapons. You don't *want* a solitary ateva, sir. If you found one, I assure you he's crazy and probably dangerous to your lives and property. An ateva with his household, however, is someone who can be dealt with, genially, and the more comfortable he is, the *easier* he is to deal with."

A long silence followed his lengthy rehearsal of matters already settled. Clearly, the woman on the other end of the connection was not speaking without thinking . . . or consultation . . . or at very least, getting control of her temper.

"We have a difficult situation here," Sabin said. *"Two competing delegations."*

"Not at all competing. If you have an interest in minerals and shuttles and work done up here, talk to us. If you want to talk to the Mospheirans, they will refer your requests back to their government. I, on the other hand, can deal in specifics and have an agreement to train workers up here as soon as I'm convinced quarters are adequate. You can meet with the Mospheirans, but without the aiji, you'll have no transport for that labor and you'll mine the asteroids for supply."

"This is a matter for the Council."

One saw the origin of the Mospheiran fondness for councils and committees; the third captain was not about to commit the others.

"This is not acceptable accommodation, captain. I'm afraid this doesn't encourage me to sign a damned thing."

"All right. We'll meet. Thirteen hundred hours, to-morrow."

"Excellent." He deliberately let the slight accent of long habituation to the atevi language creep into his voice, wondering to what extent Jase was going to spend a sleepless night on the schedule he'd pushed, because he had a notion they'd recorded every word he'd said. The captain was trying to get him to talk, and that they'd talk to Jase . . . in detail, after sleep if he didn't push it; with no sleep if he did. Not to mention the captains. Ramirez didn't seem destined for a peaceful night, nor Ogun and Tamun rest off-duty. "Granted adequate rest for myself and my staff, I insist on expansion of these quarters."

"This is an orbiting facility, Mr. Cameron. A centuries-old, jury-rigged, malfunctioning orbital facility. We cannot manufacture space on demand. We haven't the manpower. We understand that's likely to be Mospheiran. The raw materials and transport have to come up from the mainland, and your atevi are prone to slaughtering humans for no damn good reason. We find that just a little damn worrisome to be accommodating."

"Your emissaries have been taken ill on landing, to the point of nausea and incapacity. I believe we've understood for three years that atevi would be coming to this station, and I believe we transmitted our specific requirements years ago. I don't think requesting to use them now that the shuttle is operational is at all beyond reasonable expectation, since in that time, we've upgraded our industry, produced one shuttle, have another well along, and have *your* quarters operational. That's the first point. The second: you don't get transport or supplies if the atevi aren't happy, you don't get labor if the Mospheirans aren't happy; and you're damn right they don't live together, and that's not making your job easy. I, however, am Mospheiran by birth, *do* live together with the atevi, very successfully, and I'm willing to tell you all I know about the how and why of it, granted I get any sleep with no mattress and on a cold floor."

"Members of our crew will be forced into zero-G accommodations by the aiji's maneuver, Mr. Cameron."

"Members of my staff, all somewhat over two meters in

height, have nowhere to sleep otherwise. One has been injured by a low doorway and the floor is unacceptably cold. Nor will the furniture adequately accommodate them. Thus far, we're maintaining a sense of humor about this situation. However, it is wearing thin."

There was a silence. Bren waited, cast a glance at his staff, and the voice on the intercom said quietly: *"We'll vacate the sector to you, down to the security door. An hour to move our personnel out. Understand that I'm granting this as a stopgap and in extreme displeasure at this maneuver. Don't expect further modifications until we have labor that meets our needs."*

"As an invention of the instant, more than generous, captain."

"We'll meet. Thirteen hundred hours tomorrow, no delays. Our security will bring you to the offices."

"My security will also attend, captain, as provided for in the agreements. That is not negotiable on the aiji's part. And we're still waiting for our baggage."

"We have not opened your baggage, Mr. Cameron. I trust you know how fragile this environment is. I trust you've briefed your delegation."

"Completely. Please brief your personnel never to move or stand between me and my security. It's the same as a drawn weapon. We make adjustments in our procedures; we likewise expect the courtesy returned."

"I'll see you at thirteen hundred, Mr. Cameron."

In the middle of her off watch, likely. The slight whisper of electronics vanished before Bren could touch the button.

"This device might receive without announcement," Banichi said, leaning above him for a closer look. "I believe I can prevent that."

"It might," Bren said. "But don't. Yet." He'd been speaking Mosphei' to the captain's responses in a mutated mother tongue, of which some of his staff had some knowledge, but not all. He suspected Banichi might not have utterly penetrated the captain's accent, or grasped the nuance, any more than Banichi would have an understanding of the green light as go, when atevi would have chosen white.

In such small matters lay the least of the problems they faced.

"Nadiin-ji," Bren said, looking out at the whole staff, across the small room, "that was one of the captains. She's given us the whole hall up to the safety door, the baggage is on its way, and she wants me to come to a meeting, probably with several of the captains, at early afternoon tomorrow. She proposes to send security to fetch me tomorrow; she doesn't sound at all pleased when I say I'll bring mine with me."

"Were we to send you alone, nadi-ji," Banichi said, "Tabini-aiji would have a contract on our heads."

"I made that clear," Bren said. "Captain Sabin doesn't like us having weapons, and wishes discretion. Banichi, you and Jago come with me tomorrow, that is, assuming the baggage arrives and we get the quarters we want. Tano, Algini, you'll take care of the premises."

"Nandi."

Contrary to what he'd said to Sabin, he knew Tabini-aiji had gotten them onto the station by what amounted to sleight-of-hand, one that would have played very well in the hasdrawad's chambers or the machinations of the associations.

So he had the consequence of that: a very rattled, very angry Pilots' Guild who'd had a few experiences with Tabini-aiji at a distance, and who'd probably—wisely—begun to count their fingers in every transaction they had with his government.

Courtesy, however, was a cultural fault line that crossed more than atevi-*Phoenix* relations. The captains weren't exactly adept in courteous suggestion, a trait that was bound to rattle the Mospheirans, who for ancestral reasons were already disposed to suspect the Pilots' Guild leadership of nefarious doings. Conspiracy theories bred on Mospheira, part and parcel of Mospheiran life, and the most prominent had the aliens as a complete lie and the captains bent on conquest of the island, from which they would launch out to conquer the mainland.

Neither the Mospheirans nor the Pilots' Guild had reasonable expectations of one another. *He*, however, had had Jase for three years. Assuredly, the Guild hadn't sent their most senior officer onto the planet in the first place, but he could have had worse advisors. . . .

God, he hoped he was right; it was always seat-of-the-pants navigation on an alien interface, where the paidhiin operated. It was bad enough trying to keep the Mospheirans out and yet not overdo the pushing, either. Now he had to stand nose to nose with a captain of the Guild and tell the Guild he wanted the sun and the moon on a platter. He hoped Jase had reached Ramirez, that Ramirez was inquiring about what Jase knew . . . and that Jase, perhaps with Yolanda Mercheson listening in, was shaping up a pyramidical negotiation: atevi with Ramirez, if they were lucky, the Mospheirans with Sabin. That left Ogun and Tamun to distribute somewhere, possibly to stand off and analyze and pose their own threats.

The servant staff meanwhile was gathering up belongings, to rearrange their living space after hardly more than a couple of hours aboard the station.

Banichi and Jago, Tano and Algini, were in a close four-way conversation in which the communication panel figured. On the one hand, he was too preoccupied to inquire and yet thought he should find out.

And he had to tell them, too, what he knew of station structure. "This communication center will be much the same in various apartments," he said to them, "linked to the central control systems of the station. The ship will be linked into that system, with all its equipment. There might be bugs of all sorts, more sensitive and harder to find than anything that Mospheira's ever heard of, nadiin, or anything we might have given the aiji. We don't know what these people have developed in two hundred years, with all they've been through."

"We ourselves have nothing to conceal," Banichi said, "nandi, and trust our associate will not translate for them."

"No," he said: Banichi didn't use Jase's name, and for the same reason, he didn't, himself. "Because they're humans, nadiin, it's very easy for me to assume I do understand them. I resonate to certain things in this culture the way metal resonates to the right pitch . . . but Jase and I speak different languages with the same words. One's own ancestral culture is not the easiest thing to ignore; not always the easiest to identify, either, or to tell from instinct."

"So one understands," said Banichi, who owed man'chi to a human.

"So one understands," Bren said somberly. He looked at the servants as he spoke. "We doubt the ship-folk's security has become fluent in Ragi. They've had three years to do it, but use either the most courtly or the most vulgar language. I forgive you any impropriety. We doubt they'll acquire the skills to deal with either extreme, no matter what they find in a dictionary. I intend to annoy the aijiin of the Guild; too much comradeship will let them make dangerous assumptions, and I have no wish to repeat the mistakes of the Landing. Let them detest me, nadiin, let them think me entirely unreasonable, so long as they assume nothing and presume nothing. That may not make matters entirely comfortable from moment to moment."

"Shall we fear for our lives?" Bindanda asked.

He at first thought, *Ridiculous,* then had to take a heartbeat to be honest with what was at stake. "Recall there's no air beyond the outer wall, and that delicate machinery maintains air and light and heat within. They fear mistakes, and fear them justifiably. Every door will be too low for you, every seat too small; security will take alarm at your height and your manners, which are contrary to their own. Bow often. If a human looks at you with hostile appearance, smile, however you may think it rude, or however you may find it difficult. Smile even to persons of high rank. Smile at me, as well, even in public. Remind yourselves to do it. Even if their intentions are the worst, we have a mission here, in the aiji's man'chi. I rely on you all for my life."

"Nandi." Narani bowed deeply.

"Smile doing so, Rani-ji." He did so himself, instantly, and provoked anxious laughter from the staff. "Even you, Banichi-ji."

Banichi turned from his examination of the television, gave him a dour look, a dire smile, and all the staff laughed, including Jago, including Tano and even Algini.

"So," Bren said with a small ironic expression, "we await the baggage, we await the betterment of our quarters, and we prepare to deal with whatever comes. Nadiin-ji. My machine, please."

Jago gave him his computer, and with it he settled in the smaller of the chairs and set to work finding files. Yes, the ship records *were* available. And Jase's notes, on particulars of every member of the Pilots' Guild, every acquaintance he had, every officer, every piece of history.

Trust that information?

Yes. He did. He discovered even his scruples were useful to Tabini, that his human nerves remained sensitive to human concepts of betrayal . . . that served the aiji. The penalty was a live and touchy conscience about what he did, but intellectually, yes, he knew Jason had hedged the truth and then, in later years, amended it, quietly, just changing a detail or two.

Now he did believe the record, as he believed Jason. His file regarded more than a hundred of the crew.

Senior Captain Ramirez was seventy-one as the ship counted time.

Senior captain, a son, a daughter, both privileged into command training: command within the Guild had descended down very narrow lines, all but hereditary unless the offspring failed the academic tests.

A wife of fifty-some years, deceased. Marriage on Mospheira was often transitory, sometimes lacking entirely. Marriage on *Phoenix* was lasting, rank-linked, alliances of power that just didn't break, not without dire consequences.

He'd asked Jase whether to believe Ramirez. Jase had written: *Ramirez picked me and Yolanda to go down. In a sense, if I have a father . . . he is. He signed the papers, at least, that drew the samples out of storage. He wanted us born because it was a new age. He didn't expect what happened.*

Jase had written it in Ragi. They'd been talking late that evening, in the sitting room in the Atageini apartment, inhaling a wind laden with *djossi* flowers.

He still could all but smell the flowers and the fire when he thought of that conversation . . . when Jase had repeated in Ragi, "We have no man'chi, except to the ship. And our mothers. We have ordinary mothers. But Ramirez sent me.

He's looked out for me all my life. Encouraged what I studied. I suppose that's having a father."

"I couldn't tell you, either," he'd said to Jase.

No man'chi, except to the ship.

Jase had pursued the old knowledge for its own sake, because Stani Ramirez had had the notion of returning to the world they'd left behind to set up a trade route, a stellar empire. Things had gone monstrously wrong, then, within Jase's lifetime.

Jase said . . . and they had cast everything on believing Jase . . . the Pilots' Guild was here to set up a defense of the world. The station they'd left at that other star hadn't stood a chance.

"I saw the pictures," Jase had said, that night that Bren had found himself absolutely believing the alien threat. "Only a few of us actually went aboard the station. There was a meeting then, when we'd pulled away. Some of the crew said we ought to try to find the aliens and settle accounts; some said we should just run elsewhere and not risk an enemy tracking us home. But there were all the records on the station. There were the charts. Some thought the station crew might have destroyed them; but most thought they didn't have the chance. We voted to come here, hoping they'll wait to digest what they took."

In due time there came a great deal of thumping and bumping in the hall.

"Shall one investigate?" Jago asked.

"Let them proceed in their own way," Bren said, much as his security chafed to be of use, and to know what was going on. *Moving out,* he thought, *probably crew quite, quite annoyed with the guests from the planet.*

The thumping went on.

Banichi settled to reading, Jago, Tano, and Algini played a game of chance. The servants were similarly engaged, casting dice, darting glances at the door.

In time the light by the door flashed once, twice, and the door opened.

A man in uniform said, "Mr. Cameron?" as if he couldn't tell which was which. "The area is yours."

"Thank you," Bren said, keying a total shutdown.

He rose, walked unhurriedly into the corridor, and sur-

veyed a pile of baggage, three more humans, two with sidearms, and a space of corridor which he gathered had just
become an atevi residence. "Very fine, I'm sure. We appreciate your work, nadiin."

"Captain's orders," the man remarked coldly, and
walked off, stiff-backed.

Bren's nerves twitched, cultural reaction bristled just
slightly, but he'd triggered that; he'd done it consciously,
and he didn't answer, just stood and watched as the crew,
likely the displaced personnel, stalked out.

Well, well, well, he thought, wary of creating lasting
anger; or the assumption atevi could be insulted with
impunity.

"Crewman!" he said sharply.

There was a fast look, a wary look.

"One regrets the inconvenience. Those dislodged will receive compensation, if they will make me aware of their
names."

"Johnson, sir." The jaw was set. "Johnson, Andresson,
Pressman, Polano."

"Three names known on Mospheira," he said, disobeying
his own instructions to his staff, to smile. Possibly they were
doing that. "One I don't know. Interesting. We will import
goods once cargo delivery begins; let us know what you
think fair return. Jase Graham may recommend certain
items."

The stance was less hostile, though uneasy. The foremost
crewman returned a sketch of a salute. "Yes, sir. Where
do we turn that in, sir?"

"There will be a desk here. Tomorrow if you wish. It
may take a while, but we have a long memory."

"Yes, sir." The man wavered into a move backward, and
all four left, to talk, perhaps to officers, not unlikely to
other lower-ranking crew. Likely bribery and compensation
broke a good many rules.

The door shut.

Banichi arrived beside him. "Shall one inspect for bugs?"
Banichi asked. "Or leave them?"

"Search. Let the staff unpack. One shouldn't, however,
remove their bugs . . . or destroy the communications panels. Yet."

"Yes," Banichi said, satisfied.

The search they would make was technical, beyond his competency. He did trust Banichi wouldn't short out the station's power systems or ring a fire control alarm.

And there the cargo stood, a mountain of black canvas and white packing crates, the galley, kitchen supplies, Banichi's own gear, clothing . . . weapons, if the Guild had kept its word and stayed out of their baggage. Their electronics surely weren't as sophisticated as the equipment they passed through, but there was, to be sure, the quality of the persons using it. He thought of a shipful of technologically sophisticated spacefarers spying and eluding one another for centuries; and he couldn't quite imagine how adroit competition could make them, whether worse, or better . . . but knowing the aiji's court as he did, Bren rather bet on his own allies.

10

The servants would not possibly permit the paidhi to enter the apartment they had chosen for him until they had, of all improbable things, produced from the baggage and arranged three small scroll paintings by the doorway.

Farther, in the main corridor they spread out a mat with auspicious and harmonizing symbols, a unification of one in a hallway otherwise appallingly blank.

It all depended on numbers of items with which they had to deal, which they could not possibly have judged without seeing the place, and Bren had to wonder what other adornments they had brought that rested unused. Narani's sense of felicitous design was undisputed. His ingenuity was extreme.

More—Bren had tried to ignore the racket, and not to ask—they had shifted furnishings, taken other chairs from tracks, traded between rooms, hung small, portable art-works, and set up a kitchen, all in four hard-working hours that by now had entered the mid of the night down in Shejidan.

"Nadi-ji," Bren said to his major domo, standing in the central hall to view it, "you've worked a wonder." He walked farther, considered the positioning of a desk in the center of the room they proposed for his, and how, within the outside corridor, and by tools and options they had likely found in security's kit, they had removed and taped a small table to the corridor wall, managed a vase containing dried grasses with three small stones meticulously arranged, and a dish for message scrolls, should any miraculously appear.

Loose furniture might horrify station authorities. But he was vastly touched.

The chairs within his room numbered three, the bed had a piece of tapestry draped across it catty-angled, and he had to imagine how much better his staff felt. *He* felt the rightness and the devotion in their arrangement . . . in human terms, felt warmed and comforted in senses that had learned to count flowers and colors of flowers in a vase almost as naturally as atevi brains registered that kind of information. They had made it far warmer, far more welcoming, a brave atevi gesture in a world otherwise steel and plastic.

"Thank you, nand' paidhi. At what hour will you have breakfast?"

Minds were more comfortable with understandable decor, and bodies were happier with things on schedule.

"Nadi-ji, a small breakfast, on schedule as Shejidan judges it, if you please. I may nap, but wake me."

They were happy in the praise, and went off to perform their miracles in whatever they had arranged as the official kitchen, likely as well their own quarters, where the servants' hall would develop its customary jokes and pranks and irreverence, free of the lord's affairs.

"Much, much better," Jago said. "But tiny doorways. Poor Sabiso."

The lump on her head had not gone down.

"Even on Mospheira doors are taller," Bren remarked, one of those small windows of information which once in his career had been restricted. "We must have compromised, when we built houses together, before the War. Beware of ladders and stairs, nadiin. Either they saved materials and heating and cooling as best they could when they built this place, or this is actually the scale of the remote ancestors."

"Never considering felicity," Algini said quietly. "Does one think so? Perhaps we'll adjust those numbers, nandi, and this time the station will be fortunate."

As if the lack of flower vases explained all the calamities that had befallen this station and the other . . . not that any of the staff attached to Tabini's court believed the numerology with the fervor of the religious.

"One might say," Bren replied, "never considering harmony among the residents; and that is infelicitous in the extreme. Let's hope we can set things in much better order, baji-naji." Given the workings of chance, the devil in the design.

The message tray set outside was so hopeful, so gently expectant of proper behavior.

And considering that, he truly felt he had a base from which to work, a base from which any *other* delegation from the aiji could work.

He entered his room, sat down at the desk, and opened up his computer.

"The clock says rest," Jago admonished him.

"One small task," he said. He looked at his watch and performed a calculation. "It's a number of hours until my meeting with the captain. The Mospheirans are surely first on the agenda. They don't get to rest. And *they* have to eat the local food. Jasi-ji didn't recommend it. I, on the other hand, look forward to a fine breakfast."

"Nandi," Jago said, amused, and withdrew.

There was no question of pursuing what they had pursued in the apartment in Shejidan, under Tabini's roof. Some questions simply were not to be asked, and Jago reverted to grand formality, left, probably to have no more sleep herself. Banichi and Tano and Algini were doing setup within the room they had appropriated, however quietly. The security module, like the very carefully negotiated galley, was meticulously thought out, very portable, piecemeal. Crates and baggage had disappeared in the general transformation. His security was happy.

He ticked down the list of crew, with a mind accustomed to numbers, in a language that utilized calculation in every simple statement . . . a skill at memorization acquired over years of study and experience in the very dangerous years of Tabini's court. He reviewed names, everything Jase had told him about persons he might meet, their relationships, their spouses. Monogamy was the rule, occasionally serial. Offspring of high-ranking crew tended to be preferred into slots, but had to be capable of the rigid, computer-mediated training courses. Families had been split in the colonization. There'd been a lot of fatalities before the ship had returned, over a thousand lost with the station, and many still-extant families had lost members . . . it wasn't considered polite to talk about the fact. In a society where everyone knew everything, discussions about such things were shorthand, and interpersonal understandings were intense and fraught with assumption. There was no one to tell. People swallowed their grief and just went on. The mere notion of people Jase regarded as essential to his welfare vanishing over a horizon had disturbed him, but more to the point, Jase had taken two years even to mention how it troubled him, or even to figure out why he paced the floor and grew furiously angry in their separations.

Jase had gotten better about it. He hadn't mentioned it in their parting with the world, but it was implicit in his regret for leaving, his wish to have the freedom to come back . . . there was not a whole damned lot Mospheiran or easygoing about Jase Graham, and he called himself normal and sane.

He had assembled that kind of data on Jase into a profile that might fit the captains: quick explosions, a tendency to compromise their way through conflicts on the one hand and yet to store up points for future explosions, all grievances carefully inventoried. No one on the ship could get away from anyone else. Resolutions had to happen, sooner or later, and bare-hands fights happened, weapons anathema in a family dispute. But the captains enforced absolute order, and isolation was a heavy, dreaded punishment among people who were never, ever, separated from each other.

Jase had volunteered to drop onto a planet among strangers and aliens. Jase had learned to speak a language of the earth of humans, that no one else spoke, because Jase, born of a father dead for centuries, had been destined to *be* different. He'd been born to make contact with the former colonists, no matter how they'd changed.

Jase . . . and Yolanda Mercheson.

This . . . from two of the *Phoenix* crew: separate by job, separate by choice, in their own strange way competitive and *jealous* of their relationship with Ramirez . . . it was likely foredoomed not to lead to friendship, even if it had led to lovemaking.

And both of them were different from Mospheirans—
how different he hadn't quite figured until he entered a
verbal shoving match with Ogun, and saw the responses
that had unnerved him in Jase ticking into action, one after
the other.

He took notes for a paper he meant to write, notes in
Ragi for a paper in Mosphei'. He'd been a maker of dictionaries, once upon a time, and still could find common
ground with scholars like Ben Feldman and Kate Shugart,
on Lund and Kroger's team.

But in the contents of that paper, an explanation of foreign ways, he found himself possibly unique, possibly the
only one but Jase who could see in what particulars they
were strange to one another . . . possibly the only one but
Jase who could spot the shoals and rocks onto which the
Mospheirans might well steer; or the crew of *Phoenix,* since
there was no right or wrong in it. Foremost of Mospheiran
hazards, the Human Heritage Party had not the least idea
how strange humans could get, on a world, on an island;
on a ship, locked in close contact, communicating only on
things everyone already knew. They thought "original humans" were their salvation; and there were no longer any
"original humans." Both sides had changed.

His staff came and went in the corridor . . . easy to know
the servants' soft footsteps and his security's heavier booted
ones. He found himself surrounded by sounds far more
homelike, despite the prospect of the encounter tomorrow.

Then, unintended, he thought about the island, the city
where he'd been only a day prior, Barb running across the
gray, stained concrete of that hangar, dignity thrown to
the winds . . .

Flinched, inside.

A damn bus.

He wondered whether Barb was improving . . . or wasn't;
wondered what lasting damage there might be. With the
faults she did have, if their places were reversed, Barb
would have moved heaven, earth, and the national borders
at least to communicate with him.

Not to reach him, not to live with him in a world where
she didn't want to be; but at least to call him, to say, "Bren,
are you all right?"

Barb didn't deserve to be hurt. His mother didn't deserve to be pacing the hall of a hospital all night, scared out of her wits. They fought, they disagreed on everything, and still cared, that was the crazed sum of it all, one he'd begun to accept and one he wasn't sure Barb yet realized.

He wondered whether his brother Toby had gotten a flight and gotten to their mother, and whether Toby and Jill were doing all right . . . Jill had happened into a life she'd never contracted for, watched over by security agents, national security haunting her street, following the kids. Toby's marriage had had its rocky moments, and now Toby's kids were getting old enough to understand how their freedom was circumscribed by their uncle's unique job, and how their lives were complicated by a dozen random lunatics who under Mospheiran law couldn't be arrested.

The whole family was kept balanced on edge, waiting for his visits, as if somehow he kept defining and redefining things, as if he was the one keeping them from living their lives. The fact was, they were bound together, hurt one another: Jill, involved by marriage, didn't put her foot down hard, and should.

Small hours of the morning. Those kind of thoughts.

He rested the hand with the stylus against his chin, concentrated on the computer screen, buried the files in arcane atevi code which no one on the station would likely crack.

He got up then, called Kandana, undressed, and lay down in a bed Bindanda arrived to turn down for him.

"Sleep soundly, nandi," Kandana said, and Bindanda echoed him.

"And so must you both," he said, and shut his eyes, refusing to think of where he was, or what he faced, or what he had to do—beyond take out a title on the station.

The door shut, leaving the room in utter, depth of space, dark. Air whispered briskly through probably ancient duct work.

And in that deprivation of senses he drifted down, waking once or twice, asking himself in panic where he was, and whether he was blind.

"Jago?" he said once.

But realizing, remembering, calming himself after the

separate frights, he found it impossible to resist rest, of which he'd had notably less than his body needed.

As deep a sleep, while it lasted, as he'd slept in half a dozen weeks.

The door shot open, and light flared into Bren's face.

He waked in alarm, finding one central reality: Banichi dressed, immaculate, and backed by Narani and two servants.

"Time to wake, nadi-ji," Banichi said.

He collapsed backward into the pillows, telling himself he was in orbit.

Truly in orbit.

Jase wasn't there. Banichi was.

Jago. Narani. Tano and Algini.

He had a meeting with the captains.

The mind had been very, very far away. He'd been walking on a beach, somewhere in his childhood. He'd heard kids laughing.

"Nadi?" Banichi asked.

Banichi could come through a firefight with his hair unmussed. Bren did not find himself in that condition. Restarting his heart was one priority. Convincing exhausted limbs to move took second place.

Getting his brain organized was a mandatory third.

"I'm moving," he said. Banichi, over the years, had learned not to assume until he saw a foot out of the bed; and he put the necessary foot out, into very, very cold air.

"God, I don't think I want to do this."

"Shall one wait breakfast?"

"Bath," he said, gathered himself up with an effort, and went to the small bath, hoping desperately for hot water.

It was instant. He hit the wall, managed to get the water adjusted, told himself it wasn't the shower he was used to; but soap was there, oiled soap with familiar herbal scents: Narani and the staff had everything in order. And when he came out of the bath, his servants were ready with his robe and his clothes.

He sat down to have his hair dried and braided in its single plait.

"Did you sleep, nandi?" Narani asked.

"Very well. What's the time until my meeting?"

"Two hours," Narani said serenely. "One thought you might wish to sleep."

"One was very correct," he murmured, having his hair tugged at. He discovered his eyes shut. "Tea," he said. It arrived in his hand, preface to breakfast.

Narani finished.

He stood up, passed the teacup to Kandana, after which he dressed, taking time to assure the set of his cuffs, and walked out into the hall that now was the heart of the atevi mission.

Servants bowed.

Tano occupied a canvas, atevi-sized chair in the room opposite his, the chosen security station, next to the outside access . . . with a fair stack of electronics and a massive console.

Where in hell did that come from? he asked himself. He was moderately shocked, and turned to find Banichi waiting for him at what was now the dining room.

Certain things he didn't want to know. Certain things he might investigate only if the captains asked him. God knew what else might exist, besides the galley that he and Jase had carefully designed to work with station electronics.

Doubtless, that set of equipment found compatible power supplies, too. If it was patched into the room electronics in any unreasonable way, he didn't want to know it, at least not before his meeting.

Inside the next open door, that which, with two desks secured together, served as their dining hall, places were set for three, himself and Banichi and Jago, two canvas chairs of atevi proportions, and his. Algini was there to draw back his chair for him, and as they three settled, Sabiso brought in a tea service.

He couldn't bear the curiosity.

"You aren't doing anything I need to know about," he said to the two of them, Algini having melted out the door. "Banichi, Jago-ji, surely nothing hazardous."

"We know what comes and goes," Banichi said, "and we listen, Bren-ji. Should we not?"

"Listen as you wish," he said, as Narani arrived with Kandana, who bore a great, wonderful-smelling serving dish, the contents of which he could guess as a favorite of his. "Nadiin, you amaze me."

Kandana set down the platter, and Narani removed the cover. It was *amidi ashi*, a delicately shirred egg dish.

"Eggs, nadiin?"

Narani was delighted with his success. "We have a few," Narani said.

Dared he think that all his security wore their operational blacks, not courtly elegance; and that made into the uniforms were devices the function of which he generally knew as location, protection against sharp weapons, and objects for quiet mayhem? There were small needles, and several sharp edges within what otherwise seemed stiffening.

He ate breakfast, not saying a thing more on that matter.

And a little after the final cup of tea, Tano came in to report a human at the outside door, the promised guide.

11

I t was not the guide of the day before, but it might have
been. The eyepiece, the uniform—the quick sweep of a
glance around.

"You can't have that table in a corridor, sir," was the
first comment, and Bren smiled.

"This isn't a corridor."

The young man clearly didn't know what to do with that
statement. The door of the security center, fortunately, was
discreetly shut. Algini was inside. Tano, Banichi, Jago, and
the servant staff stood in the hallway, three of them in
operational black, the servants in their usual formal dress,
bowing when stared at.

The guide looked at him, clearly disquieted. "Come with
me, sir."

"Lead," Bren said, and the guide opened the door. The
man wasn't prepared to have Banichi and Jago come with
him, or didn't like it. He stopped there, looking uncertain,
then led on, and Bren followed, with Banichi and Jago last,
very clearly wearing sidearms.

There was no conversation, no pleasantry, no
curiosity . . . just a handful of looks at corners, doors, and
other excuses to look back, and the young man reported
into his communications that he had, "a couple of the aliens
coming, too."

What the answer was to that indiscreet remark Bren
didn't hear. The young man wore an earpiece.

Not the most communicative guide he'd ever had. Bren
tried to keep the corridors in mind through the changes,
gray and white and beige corridors, endless, same-looking
doors, two lift descents, one of which went forward, now

down . . . he'd looked at the map last night, tried to figure where the administrative portion of the station had been, and thought they were in it, but where the captains lodged, whether even on the station, he had no idea.

Three corridors on from the only conversation, they entered more prosperous territory, a place with sound-deadening flooring, spongy, odd-feeling plastic, a bracketed, white-light row of prosperous-looking potted plants, which he didn't recognize, but they had a fresh, not unpleasant smell. The original colonists didn't bring many plants; weren't supposed to, in ecological concerns . . . though some scoundrels had smuggled down tomatoes and a handful of other seeds from the original station stores; but the ship reasonably had whatever ornamentals had survived. Beside a doorway an airy green-and-white thing sent down an umbrella of runners and little plants. Another, at a turn, had improbable large leaves, unlike anything in the temperate zones of the mainland or Mospheira.

The hallways were no longer blank. Turn right at the green-and-white one, be sure to pass the giant-leafed monster. Jase hadn't said they had plants aboard . . . hadn't known anything on the mainland; but these . . .

Could they be from the stores on the station?

Or from some completely unknown world?

The doors become more impressive as they walked.

And centermost, at the end . . . two potted plants and a gold-metal door . . . clearly they'd reached some place of importance, but he'd learned never to assume that a door led to a room and not another hallway.

But their guide led them to it, pushed a button, opened the door, showed them into a council room with a T-shaped table, four seats at the far side. Ogun was one; Ramirez was the other. Thin hair combed down and cut straight across the brow, hollow cheeks, a mouth that didn't give a thing to anyone; Ogun's dark, square face was unsmiling.

But Bren smiled, taking his own advice. He walked in on the even numbers, even balance of seats. No round table here. The captains clearly dominated the arrangement.

"Sir," he said, "captains." He walked the length of the table to Ramirez, offered his hand, forcing the reciprocal gesture, and Ramirez rose, the first Mospheiran-style politeness he'd met. "Glad to meet you in person, captain; Captain Ogun, a pleasure." He extended his hand there, too, and Ogun frowned and rose, taking it.

"Cameron." Ramirez said, settling, and shifted a glance toward Banichi and Jago, just the least admission of their presence, about which he said not a thing, nor lodged any objection. Ogun sat down.

"Delighted you could find the time," Bren said. "I trust you've spoken with Jase."

"Extensively," Ramirez said. "He says you're here with authority."

"That's so."

"To offer what?"

"What do you want?" Bren asked.

"What we *want*, Mr. Cameron, is a skilled work crew that we can communicate with."

"Failing that, a skilled work crew who communicate accurately with their group leader."

"When do we get the full set of shuttles?"

"I saw number two six days ago. No skin yet, but soon. Fast as it can be done. You want a job done . . . we have personnel who will be interested in coming here. You came here wanting a base. You didn't have a way to reach us. We built it. What else?"

Ramirez waved a hand about him. "Make the station work."

"That can be done."

"Can you do it?" Ogun asked with a dour, flat stare. "These people of yours have a size handicap, fitting into places."

"They also have talents, captain, as I'm sure Jase *has* told you, which enabled the shuttle out there."

"Human-designed," Ogun scoffed.

"More convenient," Bren said. Ramirez, if he was senior, said nothing, and tempting as it was to come back with wit, Bren restrained it in favor of a calm, respectful demeanor. They were autocrats, no question. This *was* the heart of the Guild. "You wield absolute authority here. The aiji has the same. The aishidi'tat, the Western Association, is a misnomer: the aiji rules the whole of the continent, can manage the industry you need, with minimal difficulty, and will keep his agreements."

"And push," Ramirez said, "like hell."

"He's an impatient man."

"Man," Ramirez said.

"You *are* in communication with an alien authority, captain. *Man* is the term they use for you and themselves, which is fortunate. Their customs aren't yours. Their instincts aren't yours. The first contact of humans with atevi was a success that led to a disaster. If you'd come a century ago, I don't want to guess what might have happened. No supplies. No help at all from the planet. But very fortunately, now there's a small association of trained personnel who know how to work with one another, a handful of leaders on the mainland and on the island who understand how to avoid problems, and with a good deal of luck we'll agree, and make you very happy."

"Not by throwing schedules to the winds and pressing us!"

There it was, natural consequence of the situation, and it was a case of tiptoeing past it or confronting it, keeping the aiji's position his own secret, or laying it on the table and playing the pieces where they fell.

He made his choice.

"Being one of that small association of trained personnel," Bren said, arms on the table, "I would have urged the aiji to proceed differently. Unfortunately, no one on your side asked me or Jase about recalling the paidhiin. That looked like a fast move. It touched off the island, it touched off the atevi, and that was exactly what happened. Jase couldn't explain why he was recalled. Yolanda Mercheson hadn't called back with reasons. You may have had good reasons, but I couldn't tell the aiji I understood, and the aiji decided to find out, by honoring his agreement with the Mospheirans and sending one of their delegations up with his and not announcing the fact beforehand, even to me, since I happened to be on the island and not within secure communication range. That, gentlemen, is a very good example of the communications difficulty we hope to avoid in the future. Fortunately, this misunderstanding didn't harm anyone. I might have argued with the aiji not to do it; but it was already fairly well in progress. My instincts said not to; I came here on twelve hours' notice because, frankly, I want to know who I'm dealing with before I advise the aiji what to do."

There was a small, stone-faced silence.

"Mr. Cameron, you're pushing us."

"No, Captain Ramirez, I'm being completely honest. I stand between, admittedly, not a foreign power, but an alien one, and you. The Mospheirans will have promised you the sun on a platter. We in the aishidi'tat know their virtues . . . and their limits. I, as a one-time representative of the Mospheiran government, know their limits; and I say in all desire to have Mospheira benefit from your protection, that I hope you don't rely heavily on any offers from the island, because I know who makes them. Fortunately, that's not relevant. The resources critical to your needs are on the atevi side of the straits, except for a little tin and a little silver, which I'm sure Mospheira will be glad to sell you. That's my opening position." He drew a breath, seeing he was already pressing most of the way to the wall. He went the rest of it. "The specifics of my position are actually quite generous, unless you have personnel to spare to run a space station, as I know you don't. This is the atevi's star, the atevi's planet, the atevi's native solar system; you have a ship that looks to have had hard times, and you want supply. *We* think we can arrange a bargain."

"You're insane."

"No. By all you say about an oncoming threat, we and you don't have two hundred years to learn one another and fight a mistaken war over trivialities. Ask the Mospheirans what they think of sharing the station. They won't like the idea at all; but they may not refuse it. Atevi don't want to share it, either; but they know Jase, they think he's been telling the truth, and they're disposed to work with you and with the Mospheirans to gain their own say. It's a situation they know they have to live with."

"You mind my conveying this to them?" Ramirez asked, sitting in a similar attitude, arms on the table. Ogun frowned, no different than his other frowns.

"I'd be happier with free access to the Mospheiran delegation, but I don't think you want us to have that, as much chance as we've had to do it beforehand."

Ramirez cast a glance aside at Ogun.

"What do you want in exchange," Ogun asked, "to arrange this delivery of goods? What coin are we going to trade in?"

"Ideas, captain. Atevi understand that commerce. Knowledge. The agreement that they'll run this station." It wasn't the end of the agreement; there was the question about whose law was going to prevail, but the first objective was possession of the station. "Tabini-aiji declared the terms he wants; I've relayed them. I've relayed to him what I know about the kind and amount of supply *Phoenix* has used; I think he can do it."

"Can he build another starship?"

That stopped him cold, for at least a handful of heart-beats. It was the logical extension of the request. It was completely reasonable, in that sense.

"I can relay that request."

"Can he do it?"

"Yes. I think he can. How many are on the ship? How many does it take?"

"Jase didn't tell you?" Ramirez asked.

"I ask the senior captain, who probably has figured the size of the request he's making of the planet: how many does it take?"

"Up here? To man the station and handle the equipment? Five hundred minimum. To build . . . varies. Several hundred at mining; several hundred at refining; several hundred at fabrication . . ."

"The old figure, the first figure, was three thousand."

"Twice that. Twice that."

"Five shuttle trips to start."

"Mr. Cameron, this station is holed in a dozen places."

"That's not as difficult as not having a station, is it?"

"Why was there a war?" Ogun asked. "The Mospheirans say the atevi are inclined to war."

Bren shook his head. "The War happened because humans moved in with atevi, allied with the wrong party in a chaotic situation, ignored their boundaries, and didn't know what they were doing. Atevi didn't see it coming, either.

That's why we have paidhiin. That's why only one human after the dust settled was licensed to live on the mainland and mediate trade."

"You turned on your own leaders."

"Mospheira still pays me. I've objected. They keep putting money in my account, and I just don't spend it. It's their position I still somewhat work for them, despite my advisements to the contrary, and the plain fact is that I do mediate. They don't want a war; the aiji doesn't. None of us want your war, but if it comes here, we don't see any chance of ignoring it."

"Do they understand?" Ogun asked, shifting a glance to Banichi and Jago.

"Perhaps some," Bren said.

"The solar system, is it? Do you have any concept?"

"I can tell you that if unwary humans thread themselves among the atevi, or ignore atevi presence on the planet, there might be another war. Territorial integrity is an imperative, a biological imperative with atevi. Living with atevi is simple. Living among them is difficult, *impossible* for humans who can't understand that imperative is gut-level, emotional, life and death. If you work with atevi, the interface will be limited, regulated, and very narrow, exactly as it is on the planet, the same people, the aiji and the President of Mospheira, will control that interface; but the goods you want will arrive and *you* will never notice the inconvenience."

Ramirez gave a strange half laugh and shoved back from the table. "I've dealt with you for three years, and you've been a pain in the ass."

"I tell you the truth."

"Your own security," Ramirez said, with a look up and at the end of the room. "Banichi and Jago?"

"Nadiin," Bren said, without quite taking his eyes off Ramirez and Ogun. "The captain inquires whether he knows you."

"We are the paidhiin's security," Banichi said.

"Assassin's Guild."

"Yes, Ramirez-nandi." Banichi was very polite in his salutation.

"He calls you Lord Ramirez," Bren said, and saw Ramirez take that in with mild embarrassment, in the Pilot's Guild's long pretense of democracy. Bren added: "Banichi and his partner aren't security as your Guild defines it. They also have the aiji's ear, and rank very high in their Guild."

"Would they care to sit?"

"It's not their tradition. But they will report, to those places where they report. You always have to assume their Guild knows what's going on. It has to. They're the lawyers."

"With guns."

"That custom limits lawsuits," Bren said.

"And this Guild enforces the aiji's law?"

"The aiji himself enforces the aiji's law by hiring certain of this Guild; but likewise his opponents may do the same. But the law *they* enforce, the law as the Assassins' Guild sees right and wrong, has no codification, only tradition: that rule of theirs is the one constant, sir, in the whole flexible network of man'chi."

"Man'chi: loyalty."

"Don't fall into the trap of defining their words in human terms. Man'chi: an ateva's strong instinct to attach to an authority. As long as man'chi holds the organizational structure steady, there'll be more smoke than fire in any dispute, and you negotiate with the head of the association. Man'chi transcends generations, settles disputes, brings atevi to talk, not fight. The War of the Landing happened because humans insisted on making associations in one man'chi and turning around and making them in another. We call that peacemaking; to them it was creating war. I can't emphasize enough how dangerous that is."

"So we don't agree with them?"

"Agree with their leader. Not leaders. *Leader.* What we bring to this association, sir, is more than resources and engineering. There's an expertise to contacting foreigners and finding out their intentions, one that might well have saved your outlying station. It's the most important resource we have in this solar system, one you have now, in Jase Graham, in Yolanda Mercheson. There's also an art to listening to your interpreters and not letting politics or your own needs reinterpret what they're telling you. The

Mospheirans have something you need: companionship, a nation, a place to belong; the atevi have something else you need: mineral resources, industrial resources, mathematics, engineering, a highly efficient organization, but more than all of that: adaptive adjustment to a species you don't instinctively understand. You could stand on the ancestral plains in front of a lion, sir—I believe we both agree what a lion is—and you'd biologically understand what it might do. I submit to you that you can't ask the lion, but that you'd more or less recognize a hungry one and one that wasn't. With the atevi, with any species that didn't evolve in earth's ecosystem, all those signals, all those assumptions don't reliably work. We'll teach you what we've learned on this world. *That,* gentlemen, in your situation, is the most valuable thing."

"You think we could *talk* to a species that blew hell out of our station and that probably got our records."

"I think that if you're dealing with a species which might be numerous, sophisticated, and very different, coming from a place we don't know, the ability to figure them out and to talk, if it's appropriate, might save us. I don't say you have to like them. I'm saying you need to know *why* they shot at you."

He left a long silence.

"And your atevi can figure that out."

"No, sir, though they might, now; I'm saying an atevi-human interface might manage to make smarter moves. As a set, we may figure out what we otherwise couldn't."

"Makes no sense," Ogun said. "Confusion's confusion."

"No, sir. You aren't responsible for understanding the atevi; your gut never will do that. Just learn what you should and shouldn't do. I happen to *like* them, but I can't translate that word and they don't understand. They've given me their man'chi, passionately so, and I can't figure that from the gut, either, except it's a feeling like *home* and *mine,* and I know the quality of these two honorable people. You're not in familiar territory here. *Confused* is a condition of life on the interface, but you *can* know when you're with people you can trust. *Trust* intersects directly with *We're confused,* sir, and I know for people who deal in exactitude on both sides, trust comes hard. But trusting the *right* people is absolutely essential here, or we take on additional enemies when we might have had allies."

He watched physiological reactions across the table, body language, two men who'd unconsciously leaned back from him leaned forward; Ogun had just heaved a long, deep, meditative breath—thinking, getting rid of an adrenaline rush that probably urged Ogun to attack him, his ideas, and the whole situation that pinned *Phoenix* to an agreement the Pilots' Guild had hoped would be very different.

"Think of the planet," Bren said softly, "as a very large space station with a two-species cooperation that already works."

"Yes," Ramirez said wryly, "but docking with it is hell."

Bren laughed, and immediately there was less tension in the room, less critical thought, too.

"There's no need," Bren said. "We do that. You do the technical operations your crew knows how to do, and you teach where we don't know. You have our cooperation, and with us, the deal's done, if you agree. Technicalities have to be worked out with Mospheiran authorities, with your various sections . . ."

"The Guild itself has to meet," Ramirez said. "You will have a majority on the Council."

Bren replayed that, replayed it twice for good measure, asking himself if it was really over, if he'd actually done it. He saw a more relaxed body language on the part of Ramirez and Ogun, consciously projected consideration and solemn thought on his own part, and nodded.

"Then we can proceed to numbers, and matters the aiji will govern. The fact that he will have to assure fair, decent supervision of labor is entirely his problem. The aiji will deal with station repairs, the training, labor management, and his own relations with Mospheira. The aiji proposes the area of the station where you have your headquarters and your offices be under your law and your regulation, the same with your ship, in which he has no interest. He proposes that an area of the station of sufficient size be under Mospheiran law, for their deputies and business interests. And he further proposes that the aishidi'tat will govern the entire rest of the station and its general operations under its own law and customs, build to its own scale, and provide your ship with its reasonable requirements of fuel and supply at no charge." He said nothing of ownership of the station, of policymaking, of war-making, and command of that effort. That all waited on the growth of atevi presence in space, but he also had a very clear idea that Tabini had not an intention in the world of allowing the Pilots' Guild to dictate to him, once he owned the establishment that fed *Phoenix*. If the Guild should study the history of the aishidi'tat, it might learn how Tabini had ended up running the continent and, to a certain extent, Mospheira . . . in the sense that Mospheira nowadays didn't work against Tabini. But he hoped they wouldn't concern themselves with old history, not until or unless it repeated itself. Given the history of the Guild, including bringing them a war, he had every determination to see the whole station under Tabini's guidance. They could shoot him if not . . . and various interests had tried.

Ramirez and Ogun listened intently, unmoving, perhaps not unaware that Tabini had steered the situation to this point, and meant to go on steering it . . . perhaps as uninterested in running this station as Tabini was in running their ship or ruling humans.

"We may have an agreement," Ramirez said. "You will need to present the case to the Guild in general session, but I think you see very clearly what our interests are."

"I think our interests are entirely compatible."

"You have to explain it to Mospheira."

"I have no difficulty explaining it to Mospheira. Ms. Kroger and I seem to have a problem, possibly of my making, but President Durant and Secretary of State Tyers and I do communicate quite well."

Ramirez gave a small, short laugh, indicative, perhaps, of chagrin at the rapidity of the negotiation.

"Interesting to meet you in person, Mr. Cameron. Jase is quite emphatic we shouldn't deal with the Mospheirans. Yolanda, interestingly, just says believe *you*."

He hadn't expected that. He gave a slight, tributary nod of the head. "My compliments to Ms. Mercheson. I'm flattered."

"Jase says you're the best asset we have."

"Jase roomed with me for three years. If he and I, given our starting point, haven't killed one another, peace is possible between our parts of the human race."

A slight smile from Ogun. There was an achievement.

"Jase has seen what you wanted him to see," Ogun said.

"Jase could go anywhere he applied to go. He was rather inundated with the workload that descended on both of us. Your shuttle flies, gentlemen. We, on the other hand, worked a very large staff very long hours."

"The shuttle is a damn miracle," Ramirez said. "Another *Phoenix* is far, far harder. Fabrication in space. Extrusion construction. Simultaneously repairing the station."

"The population of the continent is a classified matter, but suffice it to say, if that is a national priority, labor is no problem. Leave that matter to the aiji."

"How many fatalities are you prepared to absorb?" Ogun asked.

"None," Bren said flatly. "But that's the aiji's problem. Accidents are possible. Carelessness won't be tolerated."

"And meet the schedule?" Ogun asked. "Three years for a starship?"

"Depends on your design, on materials. Transmit it to Mogari-nai with my order, and translation on the design starts today. Materials inquiry starts on the same schedule. We have a good many of the simple conversions automated in the translation, with crosscheck programs; we've gotten quite quick at this. We build the ship, we turn it over to you, *we* run the station our own way."

"You don't understand. It has to be built in orbit."

"Yes, Captain, I do understand. That's why we have to make immediate provision to get the other shuttle in operation and to get crew housed reliably and comfortably. We'll rely on you, I hope, to determine what materials are available most economically in space, with what labor force, and what we have to lift."

"Are you remotely aware of the cost involved?"

Bren shrugged. "There *is* no cost so long as the push to do it is even and sustains itself. Materials are materials. You won't deplete a solar system; you won't pollute a planet; you won't push atevi any faster than they choose to work. The critical matter is who's asking them to work, whether their quarters are adequate . . . and all I say about the second ship is subject to the aiji's agreement that it should be undertaken as an emergency matter. —Does your ship work?"

That question startled them.

"She works," Ramirez said.

"That's a relief."

"Fuel," Ramirez said. "That's a necessity."

"Can be done."

"You talk to the general meeting, Mr. Cameron, and we have a bargain."

"No problem that I see. We'll straighten out the details, and I'll go down again." He added, as if it were ordinary business, not looking up at the instant. "I could use Jase. He can come and go, but I need him, urgently; he's the other half of our translation team for technical operations."

"He said so," Ramirez said with some humor, and didn't quite answer his request, but the response sounded encouraging to Bren's ears.

"When, for this meeting?" Bren asked.

"Two days," Ramirez said. "Oh-eight-hundred."

Ramirez said a majority was a given, and wanted two days. Bren didn't raise an eyebrow, but thought the thought, nonetheless, and gave a small, second shrug as he drew out a common notepad with a pen, and made a note.

"Meanwhile," Bren said, so doing, "we'd like to feel free to move about."

"Mr. Cameron," Ogun said, "there's hard vacuum on the other side of certain doorways, and we don't allow our own personnel to wander about."

"Access to crew areas. Guides, if you like. Integration into your communications."

"Not until there's agreement," Ogun said.

"We need radio contact with our own government. As, I'm sure, Mospheirans will ask the same. Resolution of outstanding points on the agenda the last several years, release of historic records, archived files . . ."

"Classified," Ogun said.

Now Bren did lift the eyebrow, and stared straight at the captains. "Centuries-old records, gentlemen?"

"Mospheira wants them. There's ongoing negotiation on the matter."

"It's been ongoing for three years. We see no reason for these files to be withheld. Was there any secret in the original mission? Were we *targeted* to the white star? Or here? That *is* one of the conspiracy theories, generally promulgated in small handbills throughout the island . . . has been, I think, for over a hundred years. Of course, that flies in the face of the competing theory that atevi, having just made the steam engine practical, secretly sent out energy waves to divert our navigation to this world to take us over. The fact is, sirs, there are theories; the more reasonable ones do find credibility, where there's secrecy with no evident, rational explanation for that secrecy. *Were* we targeted to the white star? *Is* there some mammoth conspiracy? *Have* you always known where Earth is? Was Taylor's flight sabotaged?"

"Release the files," Ramirez said. "The short answer is, Mr. Cameron, there's no secret. They've been retained because negotiations have remained volatile, because we haven't known how certain historical information would intersect your government's opinion . . . the Mospheiran government, or the atevi. There were a couple of murders. Inflammatory history. And a damned lot about old Earth that we weren't sure how the atevi would receive, and consider, frankly, none of their business to worry about. But no one's history's perfect. The main reason's simply that they're something Mospheira wants and something the atevi want, and we have them, until we know more about *you.* But in earnest of the agreement you set forward, I'll release them. They didn't exist on the station when we arrived. We theorize you must have lost them, probably in your notorious War of the Landing. We and the station storage now have redundant copies, and between you and us, Mr. Cameron, I'm anxious to see the collected works of our species replicated in a storage deep in a gravity well. We've stared extinction in the face, Mr. Cameron, and we *want* those files duplicated. They'll be available within the hour. When you order transmission, we will transmit, in your name."

Promoting *him* as an official contact point, not the Mospheiran delegation. He understood the game, he knew what Ramirez intended, and gave a solemn nod. "I'll look at the nature of them as soon as I can; but again between us, I'd rather release them outright. Rumors are bound to fly on both sides of the straits, and I'd rather have those records for the theorists to digest right now, rather than let them work over the entire question of the agreement itself before they get them, or doubt that there might be anything in those files that might be associated. The more volatile elements are the very ones most interested in those records . . . and that have most to lose if those records contradict their universe-view. I say that in some faith they aren't right and they likely won't like all they read. But the news on Mospheira, I can tell you, will cover the records much more thoroughly than it will the details of the station agreement. If you want a smoke screen over what we do, yes, release the records. They'll be an item in some footnote on the news of Shakespeare's missing plays."

"You evidence cynicism, Mr. Cameron."

"Gentlemen, if I wanted to make Kroger a lasting hero on Mospheira, I'd give them to *her*. As it happens, I don't want that. She's not been in the position, and I rather cynically doubt she wants it, or would, if it happened. Mospheira's hard on its public figures. It's too small an island, with too many people, and too damned deep a dividing line between factions. I'll rather ask you to transmit the files to the State Department and to the aiji tonight simultaneously, under your seal, and just let the pieces fall where they may, without politicizing Kroger. As far as I'm concerned, the agreement we reach will stand. The transmission is your way of proving your goodwill in current negotiations. It particularly favors Mospheirans, who value those files extremely; the atevi aren't all that interested, since they reached technical parity with human culture, and you don't need to say that the files in any way came from me. I don't need the credit, but being in orbit, you can take the credit and not have lunatics phoning you in the middle of the night with religious visions."

"You don't want Kroger's name on them."

"I damned sure don't want to give them to Kroger."

"Personal animosity runs that deep."

"No." It did, potentially, but he wasn't that mean-spirited, not against Kroger. But against those who might feel she was their representative, or who might turn her into that, definitely he held grudges, and suspicions. "Give the files to the world, gentlemen. Say it's your gift. You'll win good feeling on both sides, and if there *should* be an informational bomb in those files, you'll have defused it by being the one to release it, and Kroger and I will be completely safe. From that position, you can argue that you've been entirely open. That you've withheld them for three years becomes irrelevant. And if the Heritage Party on Mospheira discovers something it doesn't like, that's too bad."

"Kroger doesn't like you."

"It's her job to suspect the worst of me. *Someone* needs to question what I do. Too damned many people take my figures without checking them."

Ramirez gave a slow, quiet smile. "Dealing with you over three years, Mr. Cameron, I've acquired an understanding of your ability to maneuver, to answer, and to calculate. You came up here prepared to agree; you have agreed. I'll tell you I'm still astonished."

"As I've dealt with you, I have considered you an ally. A sensible man. So is the President of Mospheira, so is the Secretary of State, and so is Tabini-aiji. The world is fortunate. The human race and the atevi are fortunate. We have reason to believe what you say and take you seriously. After all, the world's been invaded from space once. Twice and three times would not be an astonishment."

Ramirez' brows lifted, then contracted in thought as he examined that concept, and perhaps realized he was the alien invader in question. "All right, Mr. Cameron, we'll transmit the archive. Your channels will be open to it henceforth, in your quarters. Examine the files as you will. I do caution you that the designs you're going to be working with are part of that download, however buried in detail. If there's anyone on the planet you don't want to have that technology, they will have it."

That was worth a small, wry laugh. "Furtive construction of a starship?"

"Of weapons you don't have, perhaps."

"Mospheira's manufacturing is good, but no better than the mainland, and falling behind by the hour. We've reached parity. Some few might want to misuse the files; but we've already come to mutual destruction and declined. We've learned to get along, Captain; in some part you've watched it happen."

"Are you planning to go back at shuttle turnaround? Is that our time limit? I'll tell you, we consider you too valuable to be running up and down in a gravity well in a relatively untested landing craft."

"I can stay longer, but if you want my office to undertake a major new project, I'd rather be there to deal with my staff. And I intend to come and go. I'm worthless if I'm not where I can settle things. We have a limited time to set the details. If we're to get workers up here, we have to arrange quarters and intensive, rapid training. We need room for five hundred, by our designs. Can I tour a similar, refitted area?"

"I can arrange that," Ramirez said. "Whenever you ask, you'll have a guide."

"And a point we must agree to in principle. As you wouldn't house the Mospheirans within totally black walls, you'll expect certain aesthetic accommodations where atevi reside."

"Aesthetic accommodations."

"They are important, Captain. You want workers to work, there will be aesthetic changes, changes in the way the rooms connect . . ."

"We have no time to spend on aesthetics."

He was very, very glad to hear that word *time,* a corroboration of every single point of negotiation over the last three years.

"So there are aliens."

"Can you still ask that?"

"Damned right I can. And the walls won't be this particularly objectionable yellow and the doors will be differently arranged . . . while we build your starship. I must warn you that the time will be a little longer than the three years we've already taken on the shuttle."

"You've worked a damned miracle," Ramirez said. "I need another one."

"Another point. Potted plants will be very popular on the station, but these have to be removed to some other facility; we can't have yours going down to the planet, no matter how innocuous the intent. We will observe a quarantine zone."

"Understood. That becomes your problem."

"It will be." He drew a heavy breath. When he engaged with Ramirez, common sense arrangements tended to happen at a breakneck pace, and he wanted a space to consider the details. "I'm very content, gentlemen; the only other request I have is for radio contact with the planet, my schedule, my initiation." Amid all the rest of the preparations, the designs on a vast, space-spanning scale, anguished small realization dawned on him, that he couldn't honestly use personal privilege and call Mospheira on the phone. The best he could do was ask his office to mediate, or send off a letter or two he greatly feared wouldn't pass Mospheiran security unexamined.

"Any communications of that nature," Ramirez said, "can be patched through to your residential communications center. I'll give those orders."

"Thank you, captain."

"Any other requests, requirements, observations?"

"I'm very glad we have time, gentlemen. We officially believe you. We'll use that time as efficiently as possible."

"Very welcome news," Ogun said, and Ramirez rose; Ogun did, and Bren did, too.

In parting, there were handshakes, far happier faces, even Ogun looking relieved as they made their polite adjournment.

"I'd like to contact Jase. Can he get in touch with me, or how do I contact individuals?"

"C1 is the communications center," Ramirez said. "They'll put you through to whatever you need."

"Very kind, sir, thank you. Captain Ogun. Thank you."

"Glad to reach agreement," Ogun said. "Kaplan will guide you back."

"Good, sir, thank you." They were offered no further formalities. Bren cast a look at Banichi and Jago, walked toward the door, and Kaplan was outside, waiting, likely all through the meeting.

They'd gotten down to discussing, God save them, potted plants and ecological concerns. They'd agreed to build a second starship.

It was time to talk to the home office.

12

"It went well," Bren said to Banichi and Jago, while Kaplan gave them the guided tour back past the various potted plants. There was some chance Kaplan, twice specifically chosen to guide them, understood whatever words of Ragi existed in the dictionary the mainland had sent aloft, and he hesitated to speak with Banichi and Jago too freely, but then, what he knew would go out over radio with even more likelihood of someone listening . . . even Yolanda, even Jase, so he simply abandoned pretense. "We're building them another ship, nadiin-ji, pending the aiji's approval; we're going to run the station for them. And no one's told the Mospheirans yet, but we've freed the library archive they've been trying for three years to get out of the ship's records. It should come through the wall units in the rooms, but it will be on its way to Mogari-nai by tonight and disseminated to the aiji and to the island at the same time."

"One is amazed," Banichi said.

"Indeed," Jago agreed.

"And Jase-paidhi may be part of this agreement," Bren added, "seeing we need his help with the arrangements we're making with the captains."

"A very fine negotiation," Banichi said. Banichi remained conservative on what he did say, clearly conscious of exactly the same possibility some of the crew knew a handful of words in Ragi.

Spy on one another? They surely would. He would, as far as he could.

And what *was* he to do about the Mospheirans, and about the President, and the State Department, and a delegation representing, essentially, distressed business interests behind the Department of Science and Technology, which had historically had ties to the National Security Administration, and likewise behind the Department of Commerce . . . which had ties to some of the richest, most powerful interests on Mospheira?

"Mr. Kaplan."

Their guide, stopped at a door, looked at him, half through the eyepiece. "Mr. Cameron, sir. I'm not *mister*. I'm just Kaplan."

"There used to be a business level on the station. Know anything about that?"

"No, sir. Never heard about it."

There was an answer. "Interesting," he said. "So that wasn't restored."

"No, sir."

He thought about that as Kaplan took them back to their own territory, a considerable trek.

He thought and he thought about that.

Narani met him, the servants ready to take his coat in this linear, human-made place. Tano and Algini waited in the doorway of the security station, likewise observing.

"Kaplan," Bren said, "tomorrow morning, you'll take me to see the Mospheiran delegation."

"I have to get clearance, sir."

"Do that, will you?"

"I'll ask, sir."

The doorway shut, sealing off Kaplan.

Bren turned to face his staff. "It went very well," he said. "We have agreement."

He made the staff happy. There were respectful bows from Narani's staff, very quiet happiness from his security.

The first order of business was to detour into his own quarters, write a small message to Tabini, set up his computer, and apply himself to the wall unit communications . . . a direct test of what Ramirez and Ogun had said.

Not unexpectedly Banichi and Algini turned up very shortly after he'd pushed a button . . . knowing something, at least, was activated.

C1, the man had said, and Bren pressed the requisite keys on the panel while his security took mental notes.

Static sputtered. *"Yes, sir,"* the answer came back. *"This is* Phoenix*comm."*

"This is Bren Cameron. Establish a link to Mogari-nai, Bren Cameron to Tabini-aiji, Capt. Ramirez' clearance."

"Verification required," the answer came back, and Bren waited. And waited, hoping there was no deception, no glitch. He had, for a view, shadowing the light from the overhead fixture, Banichi, Algini, and now Jago. Tano presumably was at the security station. "They're seeking authorization," he said, and in the next instant another button lit on the panel,

"You're cleared with the captain's compliments, Mr. Cameron. Stand by."

It was going through. He didn't expect to talk *to* Tabini, only to relay his message, and did not intend, in his message, to relay the heart of what was going on. Dropping major news into the court except through personal courier had its sure hazards, in the less stable members of the Association, and they had held suspicions of the Messengers' Guild, which ran Mogari-nai, where the big dish drew down messages from the heavens. The aiji could be extremely efficient, since the aiji had gathered power enough to pay the bills himself and keep detailed design authorizations out of the hands of the hasdrawad and the tashrid. But damned right there was debate on the issue, that the aiji didn't submit designs, but presented the bills after the fact . . . and he asked himself, pending time to think, just how what he dared transmit might hit the mainland if there were a leak.

Emergency reimbursements were Tabini's primary budgetary tactic of the last several years, when the hasdrawad *had* tamely voted the funds to reimburse the household accounts to build two space shuttles—granted one had whispered in the ears of the lords of the Association that the Association was in a race for time and survival.

Thus far the economy had never lurched, not with the industrial shifts, not with the new materials . . . it had only *grown* at a frightening rate. And there had been far less debate about the reimbursements than might have been.

The Association was seeing benefits from Tabini's expenditures. In some cases there was a *rush* to approve the new expenses, because innovation was pouring back into the economy, and thus far the sumptuary laws held. Conspicuous consumption could only be of art, no other luxury goods.

And *art*, as the law provided, could not be mass-produced. Even with the introduction of fast food, meat, traditionally, philosophically, had to be seasonal. Populations could not intrude onto green space and transport could not involve highways. A hundred and more years of developing mechanisms to assure the smooth fit of technological advances arriving on the mainland had worked this far.

Equilibrium. Prosperity.

Tabini's enlightenment, shining down from the heavens, where he at the moment stood, hand on switch.

He heard, in a reasonably brief time, the operators at Mogari-nai, bidding *Phoenix* go ahead.

And *Phoenix* relayed the message.

"This is Bren Cameron reporting to the aiji: *Aiji-ma, favorable. We have substantive agreements. I'll courier down many specifics when I return, likely on schedule.* End transmission. Mogari-nai?"

"Yes, nand'paidhi."

"Message to the office of the paidhiin, Shejidan: *Work is going well; maintain full staff.* End transmission. Mogari-nai, nadiin: you may be getting long files. Have you received any yet?"

"No, nandi."

A disappointment. "Have I messages?"

"Under seal, nandi. Will you receive now?"

"Send and receive, both."

A blast of sound followed, rapid, unpleasant, protracted; his computer squealed and squalled back. A second blast came from the speaker, and that was that. The computer storage light went on, went off.

Stored.

"Thank you, Mogari-nai," Bren said, figuring that burst should trigger alarms in *Phoenix*comm, that computers in any security installation would probably be very busy for a bit, that anyone with his ear pressed to a receiver was going to be damned unhappy, and that he would shortly hear a human voice.

"Mr. Cameron, this is Phoenixcomm. Was that intended?"

"Completely," he said. He was truly vexed about the files. "Thank you. I'm expecting a lengthy download."

"I've heard there's supposed to be a long 'un, sir. I'm supposed to set up for it when the terminator's past the island, to minimize traffic conflict."

Encouraging. Very encouraging.

"You mean after dark."

"Local 2400 hours, sir. It'll have been dark a while there."

"Thank you, C1. That's good to hear. Excellent. Can you put me through to the Mospheiran delegation on this station?"

"Clearance required," the voice said, and the unit went quiet for a moment. Bren cast a look at his audience, lifted brows, unconcerned by what was fairly routine mail pick-up, these days, and keyed up the mail display. Excited, however. Delighted.

He had a report to write to Tabini, to send by the next call. Now they knew they could do it. And the archive was going. God, the archive was going down. One day up here and they'd collectively worked what three years hadn't done. What they'd feared was lost was found.

There was only one message from Mospheira, from Toby. It said: *Delayed flight, weather at Bretano. Got your message and mom's; she's on painkillers. Very upset. I called her doctor; he's on holiday at Bretano, sending records. Flying back tonight.*

So how bad is Mother, Toby?

Toby had written in haste, gotten it through the system . . . probably hadn't triggered his mail until he'd gotten home, not expecting a problem: Toby had been on one long flight and somehow had gotten another, back again. It was Independence Day weekend, their mother's doctor was out of town, but they were getting another doctor? Was their mother having difficulties, or was it more than a scrape she'd suffered on the curb?

What about Barb? he wanted to know—What about Barb?—but there was nothing on that score. Toby likely didn't know the answer, forgot to mention it, or thought he wouldn't want to know.

He couldn't distract himself with family problems. At a certain point he had to pretend his family was like any other that didn't have a son on the mainland, and Toby and their mother had worked out something within their means. He had the aiji's agenda. He couldn't think about the island, couldn't do what Toby could do, wasn't responsible for it, dammit all to hell.

Calm, he said to himself.

He punched C1 again. *"Phoenix*comm, give me the other delegation, Ms. Ginny Kroger or Mr. Tom Lund."

"Mr. Cameron, this is Phoenix*comm. Stand by."*

It was going through.

"Hello?" he heard, *"Ginny Kroger."*

"Ginny," he said cheerfully. "Are you up to a visitor?"

"Cameron?" Not cheerfully. *"Where are you?"*

"At our apartment. I'd like to drop by tomorrow morning. Mind? I have something to discuss."

"Can you get here?" Incredulously.

"I can get there, I'm pretty sure. See you at ten." He punched that off. *"Phoenix*comm?"

"Yes, sir."

"I'll need an escort for the morning, ten o'clock, Ramirez' orders. Can you send Kaplan?"

13

It was a very curious seal-door they reached under Kaplan's guidance, a gray metal door that looked as if it belonged in a boiler room, very heavy, where the hall was beige and much like the rest of the station; it had an untidy seal around the edges of the frame.

"Temporary seal, sir," Kaplan said when questioned. "Seals off the area, safety concern, sir."

Safety concern, hell. *Security* concern, Bren thought as Kaplan opened it with a keypad.

"They have the Mospheirans safely contained," he muttered to Banichi and Jago behind them, and smiled at Kaplan as the door opened.

He walked through into a cubbyhole of a hall section, with four open doors facing one another, before the hall ended in a more ordinary security door.

They'd kept the room assignments equivalent, at least, a little diplomatic evenhandedness, Bren said to himself. The numbers involved could set atevi teeth on edge; but the Mospheirans would be quite happy in them, two and two, he supposed, like the fabled ark.

Feldman came out to meet them with a mild gesture toward the farther right hand door. "Mr. Cameron. If you please."

"Thank you," Bren said.

"Shall I wait, sir?" Kaplan asked.

"If you would, Kaplan, please. —Would you mind giving this very obliging gentleman a cup of tea, Mr. Feldman?"

"We don't have any tea, sir," Feldman said.

"Then, Kaplan, would you walk back to our quarters and

ask my chief of staff if he'd provide a generous packet of tea for the Mospheiran delegation?"

Kaplan began to obey that order, then looked taken aback. "He doesn't understand me, sir."

"Feldman, go with Kaplan. Translate. For that matter, take Shugart with you. Get some exercise."

"I don't know if we—" Feldman began, looked at Kaplan, looked at Lund, who'd just come out the door. "Mr. Lund, he wants me to take Shugart and get a packet of tea from their quarters."

Bren folded hands behind his back, looked down, looked up, and gave Lund a direct look; translators from the Foreign Office were not need-to-know on the proposals he had to make.

Lund caught the notion that something was up, apparently. "Tea would be welcome," Lund said. "Go, do that. Both. —Mr. Cameron. Come in."

Bren walked back with Lund toward that rear room, while Feldman turned out Shugart and explained the mission; and in the remote recess of his hearing as he walked into the room with Kroger, Feldman and Shugart were explaining tea to Mr. Kaplan.

"Mr. Cameron." Kroger was seated at the table. They had not moved tables for the conference. They still had a bed in this room, but had moved in an additional chair, or had moved one out. There were four floor braces, three with chairs, and Bren found himself moderately curious whether the four ate together and interacted in this room, or whether it was routinely two and two. He rather suspected the latter.

"We're attempting to secure tea," Bren said lightly as he slid into the third chair. "Good day, Ms. Kroger. Ginny."

"You're up to something, Mr. Cameron."

Lund swiveled a chair and sat down, the three of them at indecently close range at the little table, if they should lean forward. Bren did exactly that, arms on the table, and watched Kroger lean back.

"I've just sent to Mospheira and to the mainland, and I think things are going very well. Talks went very well yesterday, frighteningly well, in fact; and I have a proposal for you."

"The nature of *which*, Mr. Cameron, if you please."

"The nature of which is very commercial. The Pilots' Guild wants a functioning station. Commerce of an atevi pattern is very dubiously suited to a human ship's needs; they hardly want artworks or tea services. It does strike me, instead, that if we're to set up this station to function as it might, according to the historical capacity of large commercial stations—"

"We're talking about a war, Mr. Cameron, their war with these damned aliens."

"Eventually. Perhaps even sooner than we wish."

"We don't *wish*, Mr. Cameron. We don't ever *wish*!"

"Nor do we. But the commercial potential of this station . . ."

"We're talking about invasion and murder and a damnable atevi tendency to settle their disputes by assassinating the opposition!"

He blinked several times, considering that forceful declaration of Kroger's position. He did not retreat, rather leaned where he was.

And smiled. "Very precisely. War. Stupid, mistaken war. We don't *want* that sort of thing, either, I assure you. Atevi have absolutely no interest in dockside concessions, entertainment, or other things that one human community can very readily provide another . . . do you know Mr. Kaplan out there had not a clue what a tea service is?" Jase had come down to the planet relatively ignorant of varieties of food, having experienced very little in the way of fresh produce. "The potential market, fellow humans, the extension of island companies to the station—do you know there's not a single teashop, no paid entertainment, no *pay* for anyone on the ship, and no clothes that aren't simply drawn from ship's stores?" He had had the picture from Jase, and reckoned that Yolanda had likely explained that matter on the island fairly thoroughly. "Think of these yellow hallways endlessly extended, no commercial zone, no such thing, not even a soft drink dispenser? We could well do with a SunDrink stand."

"You're talking nonsense, Mr. Cameron."

He didn't let his smile vary. "They want us to build a ship."

"Build a ship," Kroger echoed, and blinked.

"The aiji's effectively agreed." It *was* so, since the aiji had sent him to make agreements, and he had made them. "However . . . wherever there are increases in personnel, supply is a problem; franchises for station operation, for, say, SunDrink, Inc., would be a fairly valuable commodity. Atevi happen to like it moderately well. Especially given the difficulties of transporting fresh juice."

"We're not empowered to agree to human personnel up here. We're against it."

"Atevi, however, are interested in this shipbuilding. In mining. You don't need to do these things. I believe we've tried to make that clear. But these halls filled with workers simply drawing uninspired rations from some ship's store . . . atevi simply won't put up with that sort of thing. Think rather of human industry supplying a vital commercial zone, with all interested companies selling goods and services tailored to crew and, of course, an increasing dockfront presence . . ."

"They don't have currency."

"Oh, but that, that can be solved. Think of Port Freedom carried into orbit, think of stores, shops . . . Isn't that what the stations used to be? Isn't that our historical image of the station?"

"We've got a damned alien menace out there!"

"I don't think it's arriving next week, or if it is, we're absolutely hopeless. We're not going to fold up shop and refuse to develop because we're anticipating being blown to hell. I'm quite serious in this. Atevi prefer fruit juice to yeast cultures. There's a thousand or so people in orbit who have never had a cup of tea. I'm told the food is no inspiration at all."

"Understatement," Lund said with a small twitch of the shoulders.

"A modern economy is not monofocused. You can see there's a market for a widening humans-in-orbit population. Everyone who wants to go up, can go, so long as they have a job to do up here."

"What side are you *on,* Mr. Cameron?" Ginny Kroger asked.

"The aiji's. There's not a single item of the aiji's business that proposal interferes with. Pizza definitely has a future on the mainland, but atevi generally find the Mospheiran diet quite bland and far too heavy on the sugars. Not to mention their absolute rejection of the meat preservation industry, which they have absolutely no desire to emulate. It would be ethically and morally ruinous to them to try. There's not going to be any objection whatsoever to Mospheiran companies expanding to in-orbit operations, small now, very small, but increasingly important as the population up here increases, and it will. I'm sure it will."

"What do you get out of it? What does the aiji get?"

"What do the atevi get? A sizable orbital population of their own which *they'll* maintain, in their own ways. We're not going to crowd one another, not up here, not in this whole wide solar system. We can engineer our unique facilities, each do what we do best, both benefit."

"And what about these aliens?"

"They haven't shown up yet. They may never. They may come tomorrow. In the one instance we have no problem worth worrying about. In the other, our whole discussion may be moot, but in the eventuality we have time to do something, I suggest there's a great deal we can do. First, take possession of our shared orbital space. We know how to do it. Our economies have been interlocked for two hundred years, increasingly so in the last several decades; it was a decision of several administrations to allow what we called *independent but interlocked . . .*"

"Not *living* interlocked."

"Nor living interlocked here, either, not changing our ways of doing things. *Respecting* our separate ways. You noticed that rather substantial door out there . . ."

"You're proposing to set *doors* between our two populations."

"As we reconstruct this station, yes. Two separate authorities; *we* do the gross construction, and the mining, which atevi do very well. You do the interior refurbishment and start the cycle of light industry up here which can make the shipments to and from the planet profitable. The atevi economy can support more heavy construction below and provide a certain amount of raw materials supply; but the very part of the economy that serves dense, linear human populations, the food preservation and the mass-production approach to manufacturing . . . all that is completely alien to the atevi economy and hurtful to their psychology. We proved that in the War. We also proved over the last two hundred years that we can interlock our efforts up here, profitably, sensibly, and get that linear multiplication of population linked into a prosperous economy. I've had some very substantive agreements with Guild authorities; they're willing to make gestures of goodwill on their side . . . I think there's every opportunity for us both to make sensible agreements with the Guild."

"We're here to study that," Lund said.

"Tom, *agreements* are on the table. I'm here to make firm commitments. And I know my responsibility to the aiji; I know he'll honor agreements I make with *you*. I'm proposing them."

"We're not empowered to negotiate with the Guild, let alone with you."

"What's this, 'Let alone with me'? We've *been* negotiating for two hundred years. That's what I do. That's what my office is. We collectively, in this room, *are* the planet. What's more, I know the State Department, I know Tyers on a personal basis; you take notes back to him; you talk to the President, personally; you just *hand* the government a workable agreement and trust they'll get it through the committees with their recommendation."

"Mr. Cameron," Kroger said shortly, "you can omit to tell us our business."

"Bren," he said with a fixed smile.

"*Mr.* Cameron, —we have instructions *from* the Secretary. We can manage."

"I'd be damn surprised if he knew I was coming up here, since I didn't know it, although who knows? He's very sharp. He might have guessed. *Did* he give you instructions regarding cooperation with me?"

"Damn you, Mr. Cameron! —No, he didn't."

He smiled his smallest, gentlest smile. "Take it from me that I regard him as a friend . . . *that word,* which I don't use on the mainland."

"I'm gratified you still recognize it," Kroger said, not pleasantly.

"I do. Believe me. You're from Science. Tom, from Commerce. You're not Tyers' personal picks. I think *you* might be someone the President relies on." This with a look at Tom Lund, who didn't immediately deny it. "But *you're* out of Science." A glance directly at Kroger, who sat thin-lipped and furious. Then he cast a deliberate sop to pride and party. "The *scientific* point of view. I don't expect decisions until there's proof."

"Exactly, Mr. Cameron."

"I respect that, Ms. Kroger. A fair mind-set, sharp judgment, objective examination of the facts. The Mospheiran point of view . . . you're *not* a friend of Shawn Tyers; not of the President, either—and a damned good thing," he added, as Kroger opened her mouth. It was not what she expected. "I think it's very well if multiple points of view on the island have their independent fact gathering. But I also know that a distinguished member of the Department of Science and Technology, with your background isn't going to be gathering anything *but* fact, no matter who appointed you, and anyone who thinks to the contrary isn't going to find damned much political value in you. You're no one's fools, I very much think you're no one's fools; certainly *not* Gaylord Hanks' fools, no matter what the source of the university's grants and funding."

Kroger's face actually colored. But she stared eye to eye and leaned forward, *her* elbows on the table. "Mr. Cameron, you have more gall than any human being I've ever encountered. Does that attitude come from the mainland or did you get *that* out of the University on some grant?"

"Ms. Kroger, how *do* you feel about atevi?"

That brought a slight twitch, a flare of the nostrils, a widening and narrowing of the pupils.

"How do *you* feel about them, Mr. Cameron? Damned fond, so I hear."

If he didn't react, it was a miracle. But there was no implication she knew more than the rumor mills said.

"Entirely. As I have a naïve affection for the human species, one I was born with. I'm not going to destroy my species, and I'm not a fool."

There was a prolonged staring match—him, and Kroger.

"Ms. Kroger, I *want* to deal with your committee. Give me some cooperation."

"We *haven't* the authority. We weren't *granted* the authority, Mr. Cameron."

"It wouldn't be the first time someone's *taken* it. Call me Bren. And let's deal sensibly with the hand we've been dealt here. Let's get this settled. Whether there are aliens out there who give a damn about us one way or the other, we've got two halves of the human species in renewed contact, we've got the atevi who have their first ticket into space, and at this start of everything all of us have a prospect of control over our own destinies if we don't hand this over to some damn Mospheiran committee for political wrangling. Paralysis follows. —Ginny Kroger, you *know* that. Represent your view, but for God's sake, lay it out on the table."

The steady, angry gaze shattered like a mirror, became an expression of outright fear.

"I'm *nobody's* fool, *Mr.* Cameron."

"Bren."

"Mr. Cameron, *sir*. You have an island-wide reputation for fast and shady dealing."

"Fast dealing. Never other than honest. I intend to maintain that record."

"Damn your attitudes, Mr. Cameron!"

"You're in charge, aren't you? Mospheiran committees are always committees, but if they're ever going to work, they tilt. It's always understood which way they tilt. Tom, here, won't be listened to, except by the President and the Secretary of State, who'll hear him. You have legislative backing. I know damned well where, and you won't be listened to by the other side. But *you* still rate yourself independent-minded."

"I'm *Dr.* Ginny Kroger, Mr. Cameron, and I damned well *am* independent-minded. As you'll discover!"

"You're going to fight. Good. About damned time. So do you take my deal?"

"God!"

"It's a fair deal," Lund interjected, "if we could rely on it."

"I'll assure you the last thing Tabini-aiji wants is the

SunDrink concession on this space station. Mospheira and its economy, on the other hand, its whole lifestyle, are set up to use that opportunity and to innovate in its own directions, which is exactly the difference between humans and atevi. You leave our section to us, to the atevi, and you handle trade with the ship, for whatever coin you can get out of them. We're not going to charge for building the gross structures of the station, or for building the second starship."

"You can't do that! We're not about to—"

"We charge, however, for shuttle space. We charge you not in coin, necessarily, but various things which we hope you'll supply, and those supplies are the matters I hope to start working out with you at least in gross detail before we even return to the planet. Mospheira understands the way to trade with the aishidi'tat. Mospheira knows we're a very, very different system. We didn't go bankrupt building the first shuttle; you won't lose by paying us for seats and cargo room, especially if you deliver contracts to SunDrink and Harbor Tea. We'll make sure the Mospheiran economy doesn't run short of grain or fruit. If we're waiting for an alien invasion, we might as well be comfortable and progressive about it."

Lund had leaned forward. Kroger had, too. It was now three heads together. "We're not talking theory now," Lund said. "It's a damn economic miracle you got the shuttle to work at all; I *know* what went on, on the mainland—"

"Damned scary," Kroger said, tight-lipped.

Bren shook his head. "Not a bit of it aimed at you. That Tabini *is* in charge of the mainland right now, with the various subassociations all cooperating, is the atevi response to what turned up orbiting over their heads, and a constructive response: *Build. Compete. Trade.* There are far worse responses possible. He does not see it possible to associate humans with the aishidi'tat. It's not good for the two species, damned sure not good for the atevi; and Tabini frankly doesn't want you under his rule. By no means does he want to rule Mospheira. He does want to cooperate with you, viewing you as having notably good ideas, amid your nerve-wracking disadvantages to his species. And that's the most constructive model of our cooperation you're going

to get on short notice, but that's the economists' jobs, which
they've been doing for two hundred years. *I know how i*
can work."

"Mr. Cameron," Kroger said, drawing a large breath.

"Bren."

"*Bren,* damn you. All right. What's the gist of it? Lay it
out. Let's see this nonsense."

"Delighted," Bren said. Remote from them, he heard the
seal-door open, heard footsteps in the hall, and heard a
small disturbance of voices speaking Ragi.

Then Kaplan, saying, "Just hold right here. Here, you
understand? *Stop!*"

"Stop here," he heard Feldman say, in unfortunately im-
polite terms, but he trusted his staff took it in high good
humor.

In a moment more Bindanda arrived carrying a tea tray
with a small service, as Jago and Banichi took up station
in the doorway.

"One assures the paidhi there is no alkaloid in it," Bindanda said, and graciously bowed.

"Danda-ji, thank you very much." Bren leaned back as
the others of the mission leaned back from the table to
allow the tea to be served . . . not the entire pot, to be
sure: Bindanda was a little baffled by the lack of a serving
table, but Jago offered her help, holding the tray, so that
tea arrived on the table with ceremony.

"Your health," Bren said, lifting his small, very fragile,
very antique cup, which its creator had surely never
dreamed would circle the earth. He sipped. Relaxed. "Very
much better."

14

It was one round of tea, a reasonable discussion, and a lengthy one, before a lengthy walk back, Banichi and Jago doubtless having learned a great deal of what was going on simply by listening, Bindanda mostly unenlightened, but having had ample chance to exchange pleasantries with Kate and Ben.

Bindanda had left the valuable tea set as a gift to the Mospheirans, properly to serve the tea, of course, and left empty-handed, doubtless confused and baffled by humans, considering the traditional manners of the ancient house that lent him, but mostly looking introspective . . . and surely to deliver an interesting report when once he found his feet on solid earth.

The meeting had ended much more reasonably than it had begun. They had all achieved civility, and the archive's release as a goodwill gesture had become, instead of a flashpoint, a positive matter. They were very excited about that prospect . . . a little resentful that they hadn't achieved it, but Kroger, the scientist who wanted her hands on that archive, and who now knew it was supposed to be available on the wall panel, was at least smiling and encouraged when they'd parted.

He had omitted to say, however, that the manner of it was not entirely Ramirez' idea. And he hoped it never came out to the contrary.

Kaplan escorted them back, saw them safely into their section.

And—once the section door was shut, having Kaplan out and his party in with him, safe and secure in the foyer of their own small, comfort-adjusted section—Bren heaved a deep breath, undid buttons and surrendered his coat to Narani.

Supper was cooking . . . one couldn't detect it before it was served, in the apartment back at Shejidan. Noble houses took great care not to have that homey, cottagelike state of affairs. But it smelled good; it smelled of home, tables, and comfort, and he was very glad, having had tea for lunch.

But otherwise a profitable day. A very agreeable day.

"Brief Tano and Algini, nadiin-ji," he said to Banichi and Jago. And to Narani, who handed the coat to Kandana: "We believe we've made progress." He was cold, even chilled, as he went back into the depth of his room. He considered asking for a light coat, but he was too anxious to know what might have come through, and what might have come of the transmission of the archive . . . midnight, C1 had said. And he'd collapsed last night; had the meeting this morning . . .

He set up the computer again, breathing on his fingers between strokes, requested Mogari-nai of C1, and after some small delay for authorization, got it, downlink, uplink, all in a burst.

A message had arrived from Tabini: it read: *One expects further word and commends the paidhi on his achievement. Large files have reached Mogari-nai.*

It was short, but went on to give dry notice of committee meeting outcomes, and a general minutes of the hasdrawad's oversight committee on the second shuttle, a positive report. He was interested, but he set it aside.

Of all things, God help him, an *advertisement* had made its way to Mogari-nai. He didn't delete it. He wanted to know how it had threaded its way into his account.

A message from Toby: *I'm in the capital. Delayed again. Rotten weather.*

A message from Mogari-nai: *We are receiving an immense download of information from the ship which is directed toward the Mospheiran President and to the aiji. Under prior agreements we are retransmitting without question or examination. We are scheduling the information, however, in packets, to allow normal flow of commerce.*

That was it. God, that was *it*. That was the total load, the fabled archive, and Ramirez had kept his word.

At least he *hoped* to God it was the archive and not some diabolically designed set of files designed to seize control of the communications system. The planet wasn't as vulnerable to computer attack as the ship or the station; and the mainland far less so than the island. To send anything that massive that was less than honest would not be the action of an authority ever wanting cooperation or productivity from the mainland.

It had to be going through. Disseminated.

"C1, do I have access now to all those files you transmitted to Mogari-nai?"

"Mogari-nai?" The rendition of the name as he'd pronounced it was almost unrecognizable. *"Yes, sir, captain's cleared it to your E10, as of . . . 0200 hours."*

Last night he'd slept, early, exhausted, completely. He'd found only scattered files this morning, and hadn't penetrated the communication system. "I'll need precise instructions, C1. This isn't familiar equipment."

"Easy-do, sir, just punch E10, that's the E and the 10 and then just S for scan and V for view, M for menu."

The whole literature of mankind? The missing technical files? The accumulated station records? Design for a starship? Press M for menu?

"I don't suppose Jase Graham would be available at this hour. He'd be very helpful with this."

A hesitation. *"Jase Graham isn't available right now, sir."*

Continuing debrief, several days of it. He was disheartened about that.

But in Ramirez's place, he'd certainly do the same . . . wouldn't allow Jase contact with people whose veracity he was testing. He only hoped Jase was getting sleep and meals in the process. It would have been a perfect cap to the day if he could sit down to a supper with Jase.

But, God, the archives!

"Message for him," he told C1. "Same message: say I called; tell him call me; I'd like to see him. No emergency, rather friendly reasons. A little help with this panel."

"Yes, sir. I can contact the captain, sir, if you need a technician."

Emphatically not, not with Banichi's rig across the hall.

"I think I can solve it myself, C1, thank you." It wasn't an unknown principle. M for menu was a good start. "Thank you very much."

He punched out on the contact, went across the hall to the security post where Banichi and Jago were conversing with Tano and Algini. "The missing archive. E10, the M key . . ." His security knew the Mospheiran alphabet, read it with some fluency by now. "Have a look at it, such as you have time to do."

"Yes," Tano said with a wondering look. "Yes, nadi."

He wanted to see it for himself; but he couldn't distract himself with it, couldn't slide aside from present business in a meander through human archives, if that was the treasure he had won. He had done what he could. Toby by now must have gotten through; Jase couldn't reach him. Mercheson if she had authority and access to communications might call him, but he rather thought she was engaged in exactly the same business as Jase: talking to her captains.

The cold by now had gotten to his muscles, a thorough chill as he walked out, back across to his apartment. His teeth were all but chattering as he passed Narani, told him he'd shower before supper.

Kandana and Bindanda showed up before he could do more than shed the shirt. They gathered up boots and clothing, offered a bathrobe to lie about his shoulders for the four-pace walk to the shower . . . proprieties, proprieties.

He turned sideways to enter, shedding the robe, closed the cabinet door, activated the jets at the temperature he'd last set, and shivered convulsively as cold water in the pipes came out first.

He'd been utterly unprepared except by the life he'd lived.

He'd guessed. He'd estimated. Solo, he'd pulled up his best recollections and his ideas to cover one damned serious, selfish mistake on the plane to the mainland, when he'd antagonized Kroger.

He'd made another mistake over the last several months, not foreseeing what Tabini was up to, not anticipating how Tabini would react when Jase did go up.

And he'd just now promised two parties an elaborate, jury-rigged structure of hopes, all with a manic focus, memorizing details, freezing concepts in his mind, trying to patch his mistakes with the authority he'd been handed. . . .

He'd assumed more and more and more details could be true . . . and now the whole structure of his plans evaporated, flew apart, deserted him so that for an instant he didn't know what he'd done or proposed or agreed to, whether it was well-thought or whether Tabini had a lunatic dealing his foreign policy. Millions of lives and two species' futures were at stake, and for the duration of his arguments with both Ramirez *and* Kroger, God help the world, he'd *enjoyed* the dealing. He'd proceeded on an adrenaline rush the same as a downhill race, just coping with what came up moment by moment.

He began to shake all over, suddenly doubted everything he knew, everything he'd done. He desperately wanted Jase with him to consult, he desperately wanted to talk to Tabini at this juncture. Most of all he wanted to know what he'd done and what he'd agreed to, because he couldn't for a second remember a damned thing of how it fit with reality.

He slipped down to the bottom of the shower, tucked up while the water finished its cycle. Long after the hiss of the jets had cut off and long after he'd informed his body, he wasn't truly cold, intermittent tremors rolled through his limbs like waves of the earthly sea.

Who am I to decide?

Most of all, what have I become, to *like* this? To gamble with the whole world's future?

Tabini. Tabini. Tabini, who's the only power *fit* to rule the world.

His own species calls him ruthless.

What do they call me?

I can't let *any* side dominate the other, for its own sake; but, God, God, God! where in *hell* have I appointed myself to impose conditions on the world, the ship, the station?

"Bren-ji?" he heard Jago say, through the door, and, sitting there, trying to control the shivers, he wondered how long his servants and his staff had fretted before one of them appointed herself to say something.

But the next step was his staff dismantling the door; and that would never do, never in the world do, at all.

Who was he to do what he'd done? He was the man in the middle, that was who he was, the one officer two nations had appointed to stand between them. He was appointed to do exactly what he'd done. He'd reacted strongly when Kroger, who didn't know what she was doing, had challenged him in his own territory, and he'd jerked her about in hopes of her realizing there were dangers. He hoped it had done some good.

More, Ramirez had leaped to agree with him . . . and it wasn't as if they hadn't been talking for three years, as if they didn't know what, essentially, they faced in the way of costs and necessities. Jase knew, he knew, Ramirez knew, and Shawn Tyers and the President of Mospheira knew that the station had to operate and the present situation had to keep some sort of balance, or the world went to hell and took *Phoenix* and two or three species with it, granted these far-space aliens had a future at stake, too.

He'd spoken for the balance.

He'd stolen some of what the Mospheirans wanted, control over the station. He'd given the Mospheirans what Tabini could have gotten for himself but which would have proved a poison pill: control over *business* on the station, as the humans in question expected to exchange goods and services. They'd sell hot dogs in any season, and atevi would shudder and look the other way as they'd learned to do, contenting themselves with ship building and station building.

He'd committed the atevi economy to another long push, but the social structure hadn't taken damage from the last one, in building the shuttles . . . the provinces had thrived, in fact. The complaint of certain associations had been not enough public projects to go around.

The station and the ship was the *answer* to what followed the explosion of the economy in the shuttle project. In a far lower-consumption society than Mospeira's, what did he *do* besides go to neon light and fast food like Mospheira's north shore, in order to keep the atevi economy moving at its breakneck, profitable pace?

Easy. He built a starship.

He *gave* it to the Pilots' Guild, true; but if you took any vehicle and compressed it to a cube . . . you had a lot of scrap worth so much the kilo. It was the labor and the shaping that had value; most of all, it was the learning that had value. They paid the raw materials and the labor and gained the knowledge and the technical skill with no R& D, sure designs, incremental learning of new theory. . . .

Damned right someone had to keep a tight lid on the economy; damned right it was time to sit down and hammer out answers until a handful of translators, diplomats, an economist, a ship's captain, and a damned angry woman from the Science Department all agreed they could keep the station running, get the needful things done, and assure that things in their respective cultures didn't blow up.

It was as he'd said. *Good* that Kroger was still to some degree mad at him and good he was as suspicious as he was of her. Angry, she wouldn't fall worshiping at his feet or take his seniority or his solutions without question. He no longer thought she was entirely Gaylord Hanks' minion, but she had that mind-set. Aliens and the devil were nearly congruent in her thinking, at least foundationally, he suspected. Fear was implicit in her attitudes, and those might be from the cradle. But a scientific career overlay whatever she'd absorbed from earlier influences. The woman had a mind, and a keen one.

Win her and she was an asset. More, she was someone who could talk to the most radical self-interests on the island, from the inside, trusted. Toss Lund into that equation: Tom Lund had influence in Commerce, and could be invaluable in moving business interests.

Tabini, meanwhile, put the brakes on volatile atevi interests on the mainland and dragged the lords, resisting, into an interdependent age and a boiling-hot economy. Mospheira and even some atevi might curse Tabini for a tyrant; but Tabini, alone of leaders, had a clear concept of how to steer this creaking, shuddering arrangement past the shoals of unmitigated self-interest on either side of the straits; and the Durant-Tyers combination on the island could move Mt. Adams, if it had to declare an emergency. It still had political punch. It just couldn't use it prematurely, on a non-issue.

And God, this was going to be a big issue—full cooperation with the atevi and the Pilots' Guild that trampled cherished party dogmas on both sides of the divide.

"Bren-ji!" A thump.

"Yes, nadi!" He hastily levered himself up to his feet, in case Jago should break down the outer door and leave them to explain the wreckage. Banged his head. "Perfectly fine, nadi. Thinking! One does that in baths. . . ."

"Dinner will be ready," Jago said, undeterred, still suspicious. "Will you wish a delay, Bren-nadi?"

"No," he said. "No, no such thing. I'll be right out." He had banged his head on an unfamiliar water-nozzle, checked his hand for blood in the running water, and found to the negative.

He left the shower stark naked, put the robe on for respect to the servants' prim propriety—and respect, too, for the imposition Jago didn't make on his time or his mind with sexual demands. She was simply concerned, was simply there . . . he was profoundly grateful for that, still prone to shivers, but had them under control.

It was still exhaustion, he decided. He needed sleep. He'd slept last night; he thought he could sleep this time. He wondered about asking Jago into bed, just for the warmth, just for the company.

A damned too-small bed.

"Ordinarily, alone, you take less time," she remarked, "Bren-ji."

"Sometimes I think," he said, still thinking of bed, wanting that, after the enervating heat of the water, more than he wanted food right now; that was itself a cue. He'd learned to pace himself. He tried, at least. "Thank you, Jago-ji."

"There is supper," she cued him, "of which Narani is quite proud."

How could he complain? How could he beg off and fall into bed.

It was, he decided, a good day, a very good day. Bindanda came in with Kandana to array him in his more casual attire, still with a light coat, but less collar, less lace to have to keep out of the soup. Together with Jago they walked to the room dedicated as a dining hall, where Narani had indeed worked a wonder, setting out a formal service . . . even a setting of cloisonne flowers in a jade bowl.

Banichi came in.

"Tano and Algini have chosen supper together in the office, nadi," Banichi reported. "But Rani will supply them very well, all the same."

"Sit, please," Bren said. Banichi and Jago sat, gingerly, in straight-backed flexible red chairs that made them look like adults at a child's table; but the plastic chairs held, and the first course followed, a truly magnificent one, difficult of preparation.

"Narani-ji, a wondrous accomplishment. Do say so to the staff."

"Honored, nandi."

One could not possibly talk business past so grand an offering. And it did put strength in him.

Afterward, afterward, there was a little chance to linger, to declare themselves in a sitting room, while the dishes disappeared, while a very fine liqueur splashed into glasses, clear as crystal. Banichi and Jago sat on the floor, on luggage, against the wall; it was doubtless more comfortable than the red chairs. Bren tried the same, on the other side, and accepted a glass from Kandana, from a small serving tray.

"The health of the aiji," he said, a custom they had learned to share.

"In this place," Banichi said, and they all three drank, the merest flavor against the lips.

"One would wish a little consultation on figures," Bren said. Banichi, who hadn't known the sun was a star because it hadn't affected his job in those days, did know every potential factional line in the Western Association, and did know the fine points of industry and supply. "I intend to do some work if I can stay awake. You haven't found any visual monitoring."

"None within the rooms," Banichi said, "but we remain uncertain about the corridor."

"I have the structural plans," he said, to Banichi's thoughtfully astonished glance. "I am a fount of secrets," Bren said. "I should have purged the contents of the machine before we left; nothing that the ship doesn't contain, or shouldn't. Nothing that isn't duplicated in the archive, or available to them for the asking: I think a search should turn it up. I've no trouble with them knowing *what* I know, but I'm a little more worried about them knowing *that* I know certain things. The very size of the archive buries things; but we *had* part of the archive. I do know the location of the search key *in the original archive.* It used to be extraneous information. Now . . . not so."

"One completely comprehends," Jago said.

"Have you followed much of what we said today?"

"And the day before. A good deal of it," Banichi said. "Does the paidhi wish an opinion?"

It was a measure of the relationship of confidence that had grown between them that Banichi did ask him that question, and would give it thoroughly.

"Yes. Very much so."

"I think the aiji will approve," Banichi said. "I think he will very much approve."

"One hopes," Bren said fervently. *Do you think so?* welled up from the human heart, but one didn't ask Banichi obvious questions. "Thirteen more days before the mission goes back down. But we ourselves may go down and up again on the shuttle's return flight. Can we can manage it? I know we have materials tests that need to run. But if we place a permanent presence here, *they* can manage those tests much more quickly."

"Indeed," Banichi said.

"Shall we leave an establishment here?" Jago asked.

"I hesitate to ask it of staff. They didn't agree to a protracted stay."

"They agreed to accompany you, nadi. And if we establish our security in these quarters, I would be reluctant to interrupt it for any reason. This is our center of operations, however we branch out from here."

"I think so, too," Bren said.

"Tano and Algini would stay, perhaps Kandana. That would suffice."

Bindanda's role as reporting to Lady Damiri's irascible and very powerful uncle was in fact an asset: to abandon

Bindanda up here unable to report . . . Tatiseigi would immediately suspect it was no accident.

And the old man probably knew that they knew Bindanda was a spy. Between great households there *were* courtesies. And some courtesies they could not violate.

While Narani . . . a possibility as head of a continuing station presence . . . yet he was an old, old man.

"We should ask Narani," Bren said. "Do offer him the post, but stress I value him equally going with me. I would trust his experience in either post. How is he faring?"

"Very well," Jago said. "He worries excessively that you and Jasi-ji were not accorded greater respect. He's quite indignant the officials haven't come here to pay their respects. He wonders if he has failed in some particular. One attempts to assure him otherwise."

There was some humor in the statement. Narani was exceedingly set in his devotion, but it was not an outrageous sentiment, in the atevi mind-set.

"By no means has he failed," Bren murmured. "These are not atevi. And for the two of you, for Tano and Algini, too, I understand their manners; I give way to them more than I ought, perhaps, but I still believe we will gain what we need."

"We defer to your judgment."

"Tell the staff. I would willingly place Narani or Kandana in charge here, with the understanding this area must remain sacrosanct. Jase may come here. Or Yolanda."

"One wishes Jase were available now," Jago said.

"They still refuse me contact with him. I intend to see him before we go down."

"So the paidhi, too, doesn't trust implicitly."

"I don't trust. I find out."

Banichi gave a wry smile. "We saw two captains," Banichi said, accurately nailing one of his apprehensions, with all the psychological infelicity that expressed. *Never* . . . never in atevi management of a situation would there be *four* captains in charge over anything, and two, by no means.

"They don't see the difficulty," Bren said.

"Yet even on the earth we have dealt with the same two

aloft. We never hear from the others. Should we be concerned?"

"Two captains," Jago added, "two days until a second meeting . . ."

"It's natural to them, these twos. They don't find infelicity in the number. They don't think it insulting or ominous."

"They have not sought to discover our opinions, either," Jago said.

"Baji-naji," Banichi added in a low voice, which was to say that there *was* a duality in the atevi mythos, the dice throw of chance and fortune, that black-and-white duality that governed gamblers, computers, and the reach into space. *Twos* allowed division. *Two* was implicit in the dual presence, and dual absence.

"Baji-naji," Bren echoed, thinking, in fact, of the old troubles with the Guild. Ramirez on every point was far better than their fears of the Guild . . . thus far. Ramirez had made negotiation possible, was, indeed, consistently the one they dealt with by radio; a handful of times with Ogun, a few with Sabin, very few words with Tamun.

Ramirez *said* that Guild agreement was a foregone conclusion . . . and it certainly would be hard to find disadvantage to the ship in having all their requests met, the same way the shuttle had leaped into production, the same way those files were going down.

But Banichi and Jago remained uneasy, in the strangeness of the culture . . . in the lack of relaxation, and the infelicity of numbers. Could atevi ignore that, psychologically?

And Jago was right. Might they not have thought of that, and tried to amend it? Three years in contact with the world might have taught them something.

He couldn't ignore the duality, for all of those reasons: the Pilots' Guild was in some senses an autocracy, but it was an autocracy on a twenty-four-hour, four-watch schedule, with *four* captains who shared absolute power on a time clock; and they'd consistently heard from the two seniormost . . . on the surface that was good; but in the subsurface, Jago was right, and Banichi was. It did raise questions.

"We've agreed for three years," Bren said. "Most compelling, they have reason to deal with us, the best reason . . . supposing they're telling the truth, supposing Jase is telling the truth, which I do believe: they at least haven't time to start a war here. And they are sending down the very large files. I've heard from the Messengers, and they confirm it. The local communications post says I can access the files here, just as Ramirez said."

"And we shall be building that second ship for them," Banichi said. "Do we understand that is still agreed?"

"Yes." There wasn't a thing yet the atevi hadn't pried apart and learned, not least of it the mathematics, not least of it computers, which they were taking in their own direction. "I have the commission from the aiji to agree to this, nadiin; I don't say I'm without misgivings." One couldn't say, of all things, *half have agreed* in the atevi language: it came out an oxymoron, agreement meaning *agreement.* "We haven't seen all of the captains; we assume their agreement. Let them teach us how to build a starship. Atevi have something as great to teach them, nadiin-ji. If they've started a war with strangers, then we and the Mospheirans have very important things to teach them. The Mospheiran economy and the mainland economy . . . both have things to teach them about how to build. We can't be the same as these ship-humans, but we don't need to be. We won't be." He caught himself using *we,* as he used it in his thoughts. "Atevi don't need to be. And atevi won't be."

They listened to him very soberly, and remained silent a moment after.

Then Jago said, "So, this starship. Shall we have one, too?"

"If the aiji wills," he said. That was the answer to all official policy; and he knew what Jago asked: separate command, on the station, was a problem. Establish another aiji and there was a potential rivalry within the aishidi'tat, an unsettling of the balance of power. "But with atevi, every outpost, every separated community must find honest aijiin who can agree with the aiji in Shejidan for good and logical reasons; as we may have to find an honest lord to command a starship. A hundred, two hundred, a thousand years from now, who knows what will be possible for any of us?"

"Perhaps we'll all be so virtuous there'll hardly be aijiin, or presidents," Jago said.

"One doubts it," Banichi said.

"More than starships, nadiin-ji, far more than starships is the skill to absorb change, and atevi do excel at that. Atevi managed the resolution of the War. We, Mospheirans and atevi, wrote the Treaty of Mospheira, and the atevi economy every year makes technology transfer an asset, not a detriment. It's taken two hundred years to refine the economy to do that. Now we absorb an immense rate of change without social upheaval."

"Without much social upheaval," Banichi said.

"Give or take what happened three years ago. But to accomplish what atevi and Mospheirans have done, nadiin-ji, welding together two completely different economies, peacefully, prosperously, that's no small thing."

"No," Banichi said, "nor managed by fools, as delicate as it is."

The mathematical gift of atevi was prodigious. They hadn't needed computers at the start of the relationship, and in the last few decades of this two-century partnership, the University and the Foreign Office on Mospheira had stalled . . . very, very fearful of releasing computers into the information pipeline.

They had done it, truth be told, because atevi knew *about* computers and had begun to understand them as more than an aid for humans. As trade proliferated, the economy expanded, the population bloomed, and—second truth—the Mospheiran economy could no longer fine-tune itself fast enough to sustain its more advanced industries once atevi competed with them, unless there was closer contact. Atevi, who made a rug or a vase to stay in the economy for centuries, had discovered a use for fast food and ephemeral gains . . . as a blunt-force weapon in an economic war and as a useful communal experience in an ethnically diverse province.

Highways had once started wars. Trains were the appropriate answer.

Computers had helped atevi understand how humans perceived the universe. Atevi were reinventing them, hand over fist.

But dared one think of a space station and a starship as the equivalent of a provincial fast food chain, feeding a carefully-modulated interprovincial money flow?

They sipped their liqueur, and he had his misgivings.

The banking system, with its new computers, was set up to do that kind of calculation down to the small exchanges. Coinage as such was one of those imports from the human side of the straits, more token than intrinsically valued.

Coinage was going to be a problem on the space station, getting crew into possession of coinage was another question.

And within the aishidi'tat there were questions. Provinces, however loosely they defined borders, still had borders in terms of economic interest, and that was going to be a touchy problem.

They had to be careful of the ethnic composition of the work force the aiji sent, keeping the provinces and great houses from seeing advantage to their rivals; and keeping the ubiquitous number-counters from seeing calamity in obstinate human dualities. Computers, God knew, had been a controversy in that regard.

He felt a headache at the mere thought of the provincial lords. The hasdrawad. The tashrid. The committees. Mospheira was not alone in its proliferation of committees.

"So," Banichi said, in this post-supper discussion, "we shall set up, shall we, nadi, as a permanent installation? And then, shall Tano and Algini look to stay?"

Tano and Algini struggled to learn the language. But outside of Banichi and Jago themselves, whom he would not give up, there was no choice, much as he hated the whole idea of leaving atevi unbuffered up here, without him, even for a few weeks.

"Ask them to consider the assignment. We should widen this zone with every shuttle flight. More, the next flight should bring technicians to assist, and staff to support them, and so on. Increasingly more personnel, until they see it possible to turn the matter over to subordinates. We can't forgo the materials tests, but we do need to establish several other working modules here, on the station."

"Refurbish those areas immediately adjacent," Banichi said.

"And areas useful to us . . . all those things, granted we gain the agreement of all the captains . . . and the aiji. We get the other shuttles into operation . . . hire more staff. The dedicated spaceport will have to move on schedule, no matter what. Shejidan can't spare many more roof tiles."

Wry smiles from Banichi and Jago. "The Ragi have a fondness for history."

The Ragi of the capital mailed broken tiles to relatives as valued mementos. He'd signed a few.

"But when their roofs leak, this fall, they may think less of it. We've met schedule. We're up here. *We're* up here, unlikely as it still seems. The new runway should be complete as soon as possible, before Shejidan soaks in the winter rains. I have the manager's word on it."

"With the tourist center?"

"With the tourist center." He lifted his small glass to atevi determination. Two small industrial towns near the new spaceport—a runway accessible by rail-link and a short flight from the airport space center—had turned out on various holidays to assist the crews driving spikes, to establish a second link with their quaint local steam locomotive, which would run back and forth, half an hour's round trip to the modern spaceport. The towns anticipated genteel atevi tourists, and prosperity, and perhaps warehouses of goods and a modern rail-link to the national system . . . all in the concept of what a tourist facility meant. They had not yet grasped what was taking shape at their very doorstep, were contemplating a name change to *Jaitonai-shi,* Flower-about-to-open.

Could one look about these cramped, small quarters, austere as the harbor town that might become Jaitonai-shi, and see, as they sat on the floor on their baggage, a place of dreams?

"I think of the folk of Jaitonai-shi," he said. "How very strange the world may become."

"It's already done so," Jago said.

He massaged his eyes, which stung with the dry air of the station, and asked himself, given the labor of townsfolk who turned out with hoes and shovels to link supply to the new spaceport, how he could think of going to bed in the next hour.

He could take notes. He needed to take notes.

"Nadiin-ji, most of all . . . *most* of all, I believe what I've done is the best thing to do. An enormous effort." He gazed across into sober, golden eyes, the two of them his absolutely trusted allies, advisors, protectors. "But over all . . . one that I still fear to report to the aiji-dowager. Do you think she will at all understand?"

There was no fiercer proponent of the old ways than the aiji-dowager, no more ardent defender of the land, the earth, and its sanctity. And he brought down a proposal for a change that would sweep atevi right off the planet and into an unknown, dangerous future.

But he saw no choice.

"The aiji himself supports what you do," Banichi said to him in that deep, quiet voice. "I have it on the best authority. —Change is the paidhi's business, is it not?"

"It remains my business," Bren agreed, feeling still that change rushed through his fingers, almost out of control, marginally within his grasp.

"Even before the Foreign Star rose," Jago said, "the world changed."

There had been changes even before the station appeared in the world's skies . . . changes wrought by steam engines, wood fires.

An association of noble houses hellbent on larger and larger associations of interests . . .

The ruler of the largest association on the planet remained hellbent on his ancestors' course, insisting the paidhi make sense of it all.

"Change there was," he agreed, "before there were paidhiin." He drew comfort from these two who, blood and bone, did understand things.

And he finished his drink, and sighed. "I'll work tonight. I have the meeting tomorrow. I'll prepare my case; we may have a very quick return trip, so it's best I go tomorrow with my proposals in some sort of order. Will you read them and check my proposals for common sense and provincial mistakes?"

"One expects to do so," Banichi said, and finished his drink.

*　　　*　　　*

Bren sat on his bed, made computer notes, nothing quite in Ragi, nothing quite in Mosphei', a great deal simply in code-labeled graphs that bounced numbers off each other in complex interrelation. He didn't let himself think about the archive, which might be done by now, which was surely available. Most urgently there was tomorrow's meeting to prepare for, careful consideration of what specifics he could propose and what he had to insist upon . . . all the traps, all the considerations on the planet that might blow up into interprovincial matters, or stress between Mospheira and the mainland. Banichi read what he did, discussed it behind the closed door of their small security post with Tano and Algini.

And, minor point of excitement and relief, larger mattresses arrived, simple cushions, very thin, but exceedingly welcome and curiously new, exactly like the mattresses of the bed, a sealed rectangle of foam in a bright blue plastic skin. New, Bren thought, as if the ship had manufactured them; and by what little he knew of the ship's resources, that was possible, granted the raw materials.

So they had gained another point of their requests. There were beds for the night that did not involve stuffed baggage, that were tailored for his staff, and his security passed the stack in, examining them behind the door for any sign of electronic output or potential for it.

It was encouraging that when, unable to resist temptation, he keyed in the E10 material and hopscotched around the content of the archive, it was accessible as promised. He found unguessed gems, a fabulous treasure of microimaged books, an encyclopedia he had never seen, languages he could by no means read, but which some isolated families on Mospheira might even recognize. Certain households had maintained knowledge and recorded it, recreating some things that Mospheira had lost, and scholars would have entire careers comparing the two . . . granted the world survived the next several difficult centuries and developed the leisure.

He scanned that material until the headache he attributed to the thin, dry air had reached an acute level, and bed began to seem a very good notion.

But before he did, he made one more call to C1, and to Mogari, and executed another send and receive.

A message from Tabini took priority on his list: *We congratulate you and your staff on a successful flight. We have received your prior message and await word of your progress.* With it came more files that needed examination, but they had the common prefixes of committee reports.

From his own office, in the Bu-javid, his head of the clerical staff: *Toby Cameron has called us three times and we have attempted obfuscation and delays. What shall we say?*

There was, in effect, nothing to say. Until he received clear word that the populace knew where he was and there was no problem with revealing that fact, there was nothing at all he could answer, but an enigmatic: *I am answering Toby Cameron's messages myself. Thank you for reporting them. You may ignore any future ones that do not evidence an emergency, but relay them all to me for my action.*

And an even more enigmatic message to his brother.

Toby, I'm receiving you at a considerable delay. I'm off on assignment and I can't reach you directly.

Understatement. He erased his signature and added:

Please write. I'm very worried for Mother and for you. How is Barb? Don't forget Shawn. He could rely on Shawn Tyers, personally.

His response didn't help Barb. Toby's letter didn't answer how she was and he had no idea why Toby didn't tell him that one simple piece of information: maybe because Toby thought he didn't want to involve himself with Barb's worries, or because he'd asked Toby to handle their mother's worries and Barb was one of them . . . God knew. The potential reasons were legion. The headache reached a lancing crescendo, riding just behind afflicted sinuses.

Humidity. When atevi had the station in their hands, humidity had to be higher than it was. Temperature was bearable, but the air was incredibly sterile.

Why in bloody *hell* didn't Toby put simple facts in a letter?

Is she alive, Toby? Is she doing any better? For God's sake, Toby . . .

He made what he foreknew would be another no-information attempt, through C1 . . . wanting some sort of consolation before he attempted sleep: *Toby, I'm sorry, but I* *need a specific answer, no matter what it is. Do you have any information on Barb? . . . *with all its attachments and addressing.

Don't give her any encouragement about our relation-ship. That's over. We do care about each other. I care how she's doing. I don't know how you can convey that.

Hell, don't tell her. Just tell me how she is so I know how much I have to worry. Don't you pay for those plane tickets. I will.

"C1, I have another send. Please transmit."

"Yes, sir. Done."

"Is Jase Graham reachable yet?"

"No, sir."

"Yolanda Mercheson."

"No, sir, they're both on duty."

"Relay the following message to both: Call when you can."

Debriefing, still, doubtless both called in, both going over a recording of everything he'd said to Ramirez and possibly all he'd said to the Mospheirans . . . no linguistic barrier stood between the Guild and the Mospheirans.

And not mentioning the chance the Mospheirans had wanted a second conference with the Guild, after the agreement he'd asked of them, untidy as dual agreements might become . . . there was never a thing done on Mospheira but that someone wanted another study . . . would they do differently up here?

The headache was splitting. He searched into a drawer, where personal belongings had miraculously appeared, located a headache medication, and took it with the remnant of a cup of tea.

After that he called Bindanda and Kandana and went to bed, arranged with every comfort, with every indication from his hosts that things were on schedule. Banichi reported no fault with anything he had read. *I see no flaw,* Banichi said. *One might mention there must be an adminis-trative Guild establishment on the station.*

By that Banichi meant his own Guild, which attended all civilization; and in the security post they had established, he supposed they had made a start on that. Their section might well become the core of it. And when the Pilots' Guild knew that, there might be arguments.

There might well be arguments. But he would *not* bring it up tomorrow.

He listened to his staff coming and going in the hall, beyond the open doorway, on some business one thread of his thoughts found both mysterious and ordinary.

He was very sure his security was on watch, completely in control of their small section of the station, while he listened to the slight sound of conversation in the hall, a little louder than the fans and the movement of air. Banichi's Guild *was* here, watchful and protective. Certain things the Pilots' Guild didn't need to know until Banichi's Guild office was a fait accompli and the Assassins were there to keep atevi mannerly and sensible. Banichi was right. Atevi respected their own institutions, and that had to be part of the plan. The Assassins' Guild, in fact, was one of the only neutral institutions on the mainland, and engaging them early in the negotiations, getting them to establish that presence on the station . . . that was a very good idea. It would reassure the provinces that no one's office was getting the advantage, and it was an obvious first, not technical but essential, silent, but needful he make an official approach to the Guild leadership. Banichi was very right to say so. He could begin that, immediately as he reached the planet.

But that was tomorrow. Days from now. Best *approach* that Guild, because as in every operation atevi undertook, it had someone involved. In this case it had four of the best, and probably Bindanda . . . if Bindanda wasn't a Messenger, which was also possible. It was a Guild almost as secretive.

He couldn't get to sleep on questions within his reach. He preferred to think about the archive until the possibilities overwhelmed even Toby's difficulties and Barb's, and when his mind grew foggier and foggier, he played red-and-blue economic graphs in his head all the way to sleep, simultaneously hoping the spaceport was another few feet of runway toward completion.

He waked confused in the morning, couldn't find the edge of the bed for a moment, or where the walls were . . .

but there was the comforting smell of breakfast and the same stir in the hallways.

He sat up, heaved himself out of bed, and wandered to the computer and the communications setup, where he keyed up communications and called C1, the same as he'd done last before going to bed.

"Any answers to my messages?" he asked C1 aloud. "Any word from Graham?"

"No, sir, I don't have any messages." It was a new man.

"Link to Mogari-nai," he said, and the new man on shift wanted to get clearance.

"Confirm it," he sighed, brusque before morning tea. It had been so convenient to have C1 cooperating yesterday. "Do it on a priority. This is Ramirez' orders. We were doing it all yesterday."

"I have to check, sir," the answer came back, on the suspicious edge of surliness, but cautious in tone all the same, and a moment later, far more officially: *"Yes, sir. I'm putting you through."*

Bren let go a pent breath. The computer and the wall unit squealed and spat at one another, an affliction to the nerves.

"Sir," C1 protested.

"That also is cleared, C1. It's the ordinary. Also I want a confirmation that my messages are getting to Jase Graham's quarters. Can you assure me of that?"

"Yes, sir. Just a moment, sir." Again a surly tone: it seemed one of those unfortunate voices that had to make whoever heard it bristle. And the man was, of course, in charge of communications. *"I'm putting the message through myself, sir."*

Bren made not a sound, and pulled his temper back from the brink.

And the answer came back: *"Jase Graham isn't in his quarters. System says he's on call, backed up personal messages."*

"Yolanda Mercheson." The man was informative. Bren liked him better of a sudden. "Can you reach her?"

"Just a moment, sir . . . No, sir. She's got messages, too. She's in conference."

"I'm expecting a call through from Captain Ramirez, or his office."

"Let me check, sir."

A lengthy wait.

"I don't find anything, sir."

Well, he said to himself, keenly disappointed, the date had been soft. Maybe the two days included this day. If there was an inherent imprecision in the language, it was counting the day one was on . . . or not counting it. And Ramirez had been deliberate in not being more deliberate. The man wanted room.

"C1. Thank you."

"Yessir."

Bren heaved a third sigh, went off to dress, settled to work after breakfast, and waited, continually expecting a call.

At mid-afternoon he put through a call via C1: "This is Bren Cameron. Could you confirm the meeting we have arranged with Ramirez' office?"

"I don't have it on schedule," the answer came back from what turned out to be not Ramirez' aide, but an aide to whatever captain was on duty.

Push too hard, too fast could blow things.

"I expect a call," he said, "and a firm time."

He expected a call back from someone. It didn't come.

Before supper he did a send and receive via C1, and discovered more committee reports.

But there was, too, a message from Toby: *Barb is recovering from surgery. Mother wanted to be there.*

He was appalled at his brother. *Is that all, Toby? Is that it? What's going on, here?*

Toby was angry at him. Angry, and picking a damned bad time for it. That had to be the answer. He couldn't think of any other.

After breakfast, the servants moved about very quietly, with downcast looks: the word was clearly out, a small indiscretion of the staff, that there was to have been a meeting of very great import; and one had not materialized.

Bren attempted to lighten the mood. He felt the failure, if it was a failure, on his own shoulders. By now he suspected Ramirez of placing far too much confidence in the agreement of brother captains. He suspected Ramirez had tried some sort of maneuver that had failed, and that was all right. Ultimately it had to succeed, since there was no other sane course for *Phoenix* to take. He refused to be glum about it, but the silence wore on his nerves.

"I haven't heard anything, either," was Kroger's response, frankly delivered via the intercom. She might be relieved to know, at least, that he wasn't meeting in secret with the Guild Council. "The download's complete," Kroger told him. "We've been in communication with Mospheira. It's hit with quite a commotion."

"I'm very happy," he said.

"It's one thing we've done," Kroger said. "One benefit from this."

At least they weren't working at cross purposes. He wasn't sure about Ramirez and his brother captains.

He tried to convey the Mospheiran indecision about days-one-was-on versus days-ahead to Banichi and Jago, after supper, and succeeded in astonishing them, though they had made a close study of humans and their ways.

"I know," he said. "I find it alarming, too. I find it disturbing that there's not at least an advance notice about the precise time of the meeting. But the fact is though we said two days, we didn't set one. I suppose I should have made sure of a date; but our calendars aren't congruent. And it was a signal not to push him."

Jago and Banichi alike had worn their most formal looks all through the day, all through dinner. *Now* they asked their questions.

"Is Jasi-ji safe?" Jago asked first.

"I think that he is."

"Is Ramirez attempting something we should know about?" Banichi asked.

"I wish I knew."

"Does not this great ship work by numbers, and precise numbers?"

"One would think so. But humans work by less precise ones." He could not keep his security ignorant of his worries, but he had no idea how to give their innate sense of precision a real appreciation of what was going on with the ever-lengthening two days, except to say, "This is a game.

It's a game as humans mean it, the sort one plays with one's enemies, not yet to fight, but not to agree, either."

That enlightened them. There were looks of complete comprehension.

And in fact, atevi were quite good at such games: Bindanda's presence was such a move, which must not be challenged.

"One does see," Jago said, seeming much more relaxed.

"I find it exceedingly annoying. It's a signal to me to back off. I perceived that when he chose to be that vague; I took it for something that might shift, and shift it has. But I will not let this situation go much further."

"And then?" Banichi asked.

"Our greatest risk is my annoyance and his, at this moment; and the aiji's, if I don't bring him back to the table before I leave, which seems what this game is about. I don't think the captains want to get to specifics yet, they want as much as they can get, they think a little more time might solve their problems, and among us . . . nadiin-ji, I think the trouble is that some of them want agreement with the Mospheirans and the Mospheirans aren't interested. I think that's quite upset certain officers of this Guild."

"To what extent, nadi?"

"To the extent that they're running this operation like a committee. I think Ogun joined Ramirez and the two moved too fast for the other captains' liking. What weighs on my thoughts most is that if I've made a grievous error and offended them by dealing with Ramirez and Ogun, then it's my doing for pressing it *too* fast, and I have to take the entire responsibility for it."

"Would they agree with Kroger in some secret matter?"

"I can't conceive of what it would be since, in plain fact, Kroger can't give them what they want, and if Kroger claims she can pull something out of nothing, that doesn't bode well for their understanding. I think they know damned well she has nothing substantive to offer. As for confidences I've shared with her, I don't worry about her telling the ship-humans all we've said. That can't affect what the captains think."

"Would it not affect Mospheira?" Jago asked.

"Oh, very much so. It's more to Mospheira's advantage

to keep the details hidden from their own more radical elements—to which I still think Kroger may have some ties in the first place—but if there's one way to create political furor on Mospheira, it's to suggest mass emigration and coerced labor. It's just not going to happen."

"The captains can't insist."

"No." A thought occurred to him as it had occurred earlier in the day. "If she's gotten anxious, if she's simply asked Ramirez for a delay or posed some kind of problem, there'll be annoyances and expressions of annoyance, and I'll be damned mad; but that's nothing to the difficulties we've sorted out on the planet over the last two hundred years. We'll sort this out. We will get our agreement and take it home with us."

"One worries," Jago said.

"The signs that worry me are that my calls to Jase aren't going through; my calls to Yolanda, none successful; I haven't even been able to get through to Kroger at will. The young gentleman in charge of communications doesn't have authorization to connect us, but more to the point, hasn't gotten it, and that means he hasn't gotten it or hasn't asked for it."

"Blockage at a low level?" Banichi asked ominously.

"I certainly hope not. This may be the action of subordinates instructed to cover for Ramirez. It may be the action of subordinates set as obstacles by someone opposing Ramirez. I'm not going to take any action. I am going to advise them how provocative this is." Not least of all, meeting times among atevi held numeric keys to fortunate or unfortunate numbers.

"They should not do the like with the paidhi-aiji," Jago said.

"We've had persistent difficulties. Three years of difficulties on this point," he said in some exasperation. Ramirez had persistently failed download appointments when they had dealt with him via Mogari-nai. He'd excused the behavior and allowed Ramirez to get away with it; he'd told Tabini it wasn't unknown among humans. He'd wanted to get the agreements that were otherwise in jeopardy. Now Ramirez was doing it again, in an environment where safety might be at risk; that would not do.

He went back to the console after he and his security went to their separate quarters, and sent a message to Ramirez, who—not surprisingly—proved unavailable.

"That's fine," he said to C1. "Record a message. *Captain Ramirez, contact me at earliest, at whatever hour.* Thank you, C1."

There was no call in the night. There was no call at all. Before dressing in the morning, Bren punched in C1. "Get me Ramirez."

"Sir, I can't do that."

"I want Ramirez, C1, and I want him now. I've waited all night. I'm not in a good mood."

"Just a minute, sir." A several moment delay: Bren sat down and turned on his computer, set up files, shivering in the cold air, before tea, before breakfast.

"Mr. Cameron? What may I do for you, sir?"

Different voice. Female.

He rose. Faced the wall unit. "Where's C1?"

"This is Sabin. What's the problem, Mr. Cameron?"

"Captain." He adopted a quiet, reasonable tone. "Thank you. You and I haven't had a chance to talk. Have you a moment today?"

"Not this watch, Mr. Cameron."

"Captain Sabin, most reasonably, and I've stated this during three years of negotiations: if agreements with atevi are not completed *at the fortunate hour* and *on time*, all agreements are subject to change, in however small detail. Moving appointments can't be the condition of discussions with the aiji."

"This is our deck, Mr. Cameron. You do things our way."

"No, Captain, quite respectfully. If you want this deck repaired and in running order, atevi ways matter. If today is inconvenient, can we set a firm time? Afternoon, 1300 hours, day after this?"

"I'll see you at 1400."

"Delighted. Meanwhile, another matter. Could you arrange for me to phone Jase Graham?"

"Mr. Graham is a member of this crew, under our authority. He has no duties to you or to your offices. Two days; your schedule. You have your meeting, with me. Are we agreed, now?"

"Two days, and I will continually hold out for Jase Graham, Captain."

"Then you'll wait in hell."

"I doubt your ability to create hell and obtain what you want from Tabini-aiji. *We* will likely survive your alien invasion."

"Don't rely on it."

"There's no need to argue, Captain. Let's save it for the meeting."

He heard a lengthy silence on the communications system. Then a restrained: *"Two days, and persistently no, to your request for Graham. He's not your citizen."*

"We will have it on the table, Captain. Thank you." He punched out on Sabin at that point, likely not what Sabin was accustomed to having happen, but he wasn't going to allow agreement to dissipate in further discussion.

He wasn't at all satisfied with the situation he'd set up.

He dressed, still in a glum mood, only involving Bindanda's help toward the end of the process. Breakfast waited.

But having settled his nerves from the adrenaline rush of one negotiation, he decided to observe routine and get his messages, never sure at what time ship command would lose patience and close off his access simply to demonstrate they *could* close it off.

He punched in C1, dealt pleasantly with the communications officer, and did a send-receive, picked up his messages, and sent the ones he'd written, all without incident.

From the mainland, head of the list, he found a veritable flood of personal notes from members of the legislature. He skimmed the likelier of them, found them much as expected, locally focused, various lords asking about their various interests, all felicitating him on surviving the perilous flight up in the shuttle, all interested in profit for their districts, their businesses, their concerns.

The word of his presence up here was out, then, likely with the download of the archive: news of the whole mission would break. He *could* advise Toby where he was; he *could* break the news to his family that he couldn't come back to the island this week or next, no matter the need.

From Toby, however, there was also a brief word: Toby, knowing the facts of his whereabouts, now, had written first.

I've heard where you are; it's all over the news . . . now I know there's a reason you left as fast as you did.

I talked to Barb's husband. He seems a nice fellow, quiet. Barb's undergoing more surgery, showing some awareness of surroundings now. Excuse the word flow. I'm writing this with no sleep. Jill's talking about a separation. I don't know why now, but I do know. My running up here isn't making it easier right now; we talked about it on the plane; she told me make a choice and I don't want to lose my kids, so as soon as I can I'm going back north and staying there. I can't do this anymore. Mother won't listen to me, says Barb is a daughter to her, and that's her choice.

Most of all I'm not going to lose my wife and my kids. I'm going to get a car, take mother home, and if she gets back to the hospital, she'll do it after I'm back at the airport, and after that it's not my problem. I'm sorry as hell, Bren, but if you can't do this any longer, I can't, either. My wife and my kids are as important to me as your job is to you, and much as I love you and much as I love mum, I've got a life to live.

He read that twice, hearing Toby's voice, knowing how much it had cost Toby to write it. He sat down and wrote back.

I have no blame to cast. I've felt deeply guilty for what I've asked. I've asked of you and mum both to turn caring for me off and on like a light switch, all to support me when I tried to stand in both worlds. Now I'm wholly on the mainland, and have to be. I can't change the job, I can't change myself, and we both know we can't change our mother's desire to have us both back . . . which I think hurts worse because one of us is permanently out of reach and involved in things that upset her. But generations can't absorb one another. Time we both stopped worrying, and that's not easy, but no one can ask more than you've already done. Tell mum I love her, tell her truthfully where I am, tell her there's no way in hell I can get there, and that Barb and I don't have a future.

Barb knew it before I did. Barb did the best thing when she married Paul. It made me mad as hell when I found out, but she was always smart about things like that, and she knew better than I did what our association had gotten to be, and what she needed, and that I was killing her by degrees. Her job was always placating me, it wasn't a healthy relationship, and she went on faithfully trying to do that after she married, I think because she and I do love one another in a caring sort of way. She couldn't be happy if I wasn't happy, and she saw how upset I was about the marriage . . . when I was the one who'd told her our life was always going to be occasional weekends. The simplest truth is the one we couldn't work around: that she'd be miserable where I am and I'd be miserable where she is, and there just can't ever be a fix for that, because I won't come back to live on the island and she deserves a man who's there through the thick and the thin of life, not just arriving on flying visits.

If she and mum have a friendship, I have no right nor wish to upset that. They both need friends, especially now.

But above all else, I owe my brother more than I can ever say. You've done more than any human should for the last ten years. Take care of Jill and the kids now, make them your priority. Mum's tougher than you think. Especially don't worry for me: people take care of me. You take care of your own family, love Jill, take care of those kids, and take any of my advisements of problems from here on out as simple advisements, not requisitions for miracles. Like Barb, you've known what's good and right, and instead you've been trying to satisfy me. I'm reforming. No more demands. I'm sending a copy of this to Mother. All my love, for all our lives. Bren.

And to his mother:

I'm on the space station, Mother. I'm attaching a letter I wrote to Toby. I love you very much, always. Bren.

He contacted C1 and sent both before he had a chance

to change his mind, or before the difficulty of relations with the captains cut him off. He tried not to think how his mother would read it, and how much it would hurt.

But one hard letter beat a decade-long collection of niggling apologies that kept his mother hoping he'd change and kept Toby and Barb both trying to change him. That had eaten up years of trying; by now it was a lost cause.

His emotions felt sandpapered, utterly rubbed raw. He'd said good-bye to his mother, his brother, and the one human woman who loved him all in one package, all before breakfast.

He thought he'd done, in the professional case and the private one, exactly what he ought to have done: professionally, physically, for a moment on the line with Sabin he'd reached that state of hyperactivity in which to his own perception he could all but walk through walls, a state he knew was dangerous, since in the real world the walls were real. But the chances he took were part of his moment-to-moment consciousness; his position was something he didn't need to research; his dealings with their isolate psychology was something he'd laid out in three years of working with Jase and hearing his assessments of the individuals. He wasn't a fool. He scared himself, but he wasn't a fool, not in his maneuvers with the captains.

The captains' anger was real, however, and backed with force which—yes—if they were intelligent, they wouldn't use.

Many a smart man had been shot by a stupid opponent. Not at all helpful to the opponent, but there the smart man was, dead, all the same.

And the psychological shocks bound to reverberate through his family . . . those were real, too. And he couldn't avoid them. He couldn't get to Mospheira. He wouldn't be able to in the future. It was only going to get worse.

He went to breakfast, forced a smile for his staff, apologized, and felt not light-headed, but light of body.

He was still in that walk-through-walls state of mind.

The staff that was supposed to support him recognized the fact and went on doing their jobs in wary silence, and Narani went on bowing and doing properly the serving of tea and the presentation of small courses . . . he tried to restrain the breakfasts, seeing his nerves hardly left his stomach fit for them, but Banichi and Jago came to join him, and their appetites well made up for his.

"I've just insulted Sabin and told my mother neither I nor Toby can meet her future requests," he said to them, "all before breakfast. What I sense around us, nadiin, is a set of people on this station attempting to contain us, and to contain the Mospheirans, and to contain Jase . . . to hold, in other words, their accustomed power up here, or at least, to maintain their personal power relative to Ramirez. And by our agreement with Ramirez, none of these things should be happening. We have to push, just gently. I think we should take a small walk, if I can engage Kaplan-nadi."

"And where should we walk?" Banichi asked him calmly, over miraculously fresh eggs.

"I think I'll ask Kaplan," he said. "I think we should survey this place they wish us to restore. I think we should walk everywhere. I began my report last night; this morning I have nothing but questions."

"Shall we arm?" Banichi asked.

"Yes," he said, and added, "but only in an ordinary fashion."

15

Kaplan appeared, kitted out as usual, electronics in place, opened the section door himself at the door with a beep on the intercom to announce his presence, and just came inside unasked.

Narani bowed, the servant staff bowed. Bren saw it all as he left his room.

Banichi, the security staff, and Kaplan all stared at one another like wi'itikiin over a morsel. The door to the security center was discreetly shut, good fortune having nothing to do with it, Tano and Algini were not in sight, and Bren didn't miss the subtle sweep of Kaplan's head, his electronics doubtless sending to something besides his eyepiece as he looked around.

"To the islanders, sir?" Kaplan asked.

"That, for a start," Bren said, and went out, sweeping Kaplan along beside him, Banichi and Jago walking rear guard down the faded yellow corridors that looked like something's gullet.

And he asked a flood of questions along the way, questions partly because he wanted to know, and partly to engage Kaplan: *What's down there?* he asked. *What's that way?*

"Can't say, sir." For the third or fourth time Kaplan said so, this particular denial at what seemed to be a relatively main intersection in the zigzag weave of corridors.

"Well, why don't we just go there and find out?"

"Can't take you there, sir. Not on the list."

"Oh," Bren said, lifting both brows. "There's a list."

At that, facing him and with Banichi and Jago looming over him, Kaplan looked entirely uneasy.

"Can we see this list?" Bren asked him.

"I get it from the exec, sir. I can't show it to you."

"Well," Bren said, and cheerfully rattled off in Ragi, "I think we might as well nudge gently and see what will give. Kaplan-nadi's restricting what we see, but he's not in charge of that decision himself. He's getting his orders from higher up. —What would *you* like to see, nadiin?"

"Where does the crew live?" Banichi asked.

"Excellent suggestion," Bren said, and looked at Kaplan, who did not look confident. "Nadi, where is the crew?"

"Where's the *crew,* sir?"

"What do you do when you're not on duty, Kaplan?"

"We go to rec, sir."

"Good." In some measure, despite the ferocious-looking equipment and the eyepiece, Kaplan had the open stare of a just-bloomed flower. "We should see rec, then, Kaplan-nadi. Or is that on the list of things we definitely shouldn't see?"

"The list goes the other way, sir. It's things you can see."

"Well, that's fine. Let's go look at all of those, and then when you're tired, we can go to this recreation place. That's rec, isn't it?"

"Yes, sir. I'll ask about rec, if you like."

"Why don't you do that while we tour what we're supposed to see? Take us to all those places."

"Yes, sir," Kaplan murmured, and then talked to his microphone in alphabet and half-words while they walked. "Sir, they're going to have to ask a captain about rec, and they're all—"

"In a meeting."

"Yes, sir."

"Well, tell them we just walked off and left you. All of a sudden I'm very interested in rec. I suppose we'll find it. Are you going to shoot us?"

"Sir, don't do that."

"Don't overreact," Bren said in Ragi, "and above all don't kill him. He's a nice fellow, but I'm going to walk off and leave him, which is going to make him very nervous."

"Yes," Jago said, and Bren walked, as Banichi and Jago went to opposite sides of the corridor.

He'd give a great deal to have eyes in the back of his

head. He knew, whatever else, that Kaplan wasn't going to shoot him.

"Sir?" he heard, a distressed, higher-pitched voice out of Kaplan. Then a more gruff: "Sir! Don't!"

Bren walked a few paces more, down a hall that showed no features, but the flooring of which had ample scuff on its sheen, leading right to an apparent section door.

He heard an uncertain scuffle behind him, and he turned, quickly, lest mayhem result.

Kaplan, going nowhere, had Banichi's very solid hand about his arm.

"Sir!"

"He's distressed," he translated for Banichi. "Let him go, nadi-ji."

Banichi did release him. Jago had her hand on her holstered pistol. Kaplan didn't move, only stood there with eyes flower-wide and worried, and rubbed his arm.

"Kaplan," Bren said, "you're a sensible man. Now what can we do to entertain ourselves that won't involve your list?"

"Let me talk to the duty officer, sir."

"Good," he said. "You do that. You tell them if we're going to repair this station, we have to assess it. Why don't you show us one of the not-so-good areas?"

"I can't do that, sir. They're cold. Locked down." He gave an upward glance at Banichi and Jago. "Takes suits, and we can't fit them."

"We have them. We could go back to the shuttle and get them. Or we could visit your ship. We're supposed to build one."

"Build one, sir. Yes, sir. I've got to ask about that." Kaplan had broken out in a sweat.

"Come on, Kaplan. Think. Give us *something* worth our while. We can't stand here all day."

"You want to see the rec area, sir, let me ask. —But you can't go in there with guns, sir."

"Kaplan, you're orbiting an atevi planet. There will never be a place an atevi lord's security goes without guns. And you really don't want them to, because if you have *two* atevi lords up here at any point, without the guns, the lords are going to be nervous and there might not be good behavior. Banichi and Jago are Assassins' Guild. They have rules. They assure the lords go to the Guild before someone takes a contract out on one of the captains. Think of them as law enforcement. There's a whole planetful of reasons down there that took thousands of years to develop a peaceful way of dealing with things, and I really wouldn't advise you to start changing what works. Why don't we go somewhere interesting?''

"Yes, sir, but I still have to ask.''

"Do,'' he said, and looked at a sealed, transparent wall panel with a confusing lot of buttons. "What do these do?''

"Lights and the temperature, sir, mostly, and the power, but *don't open that panel, sir,* some of the sections aren't sealed, sir.''

"Relax,'' he said with a benign smile. He began to like Kaplan, heartily so, and repented his deliberate provocations. "Let's go. Let's go to rec. You're a good man, Mr. Kaplan, and a very sensible one.''

"Yes, sir,'' Kaplan said, still breathing rapidly. "Just let me ask.''

Kaplan was nothing if not dutiful. Kaplan engaged his microphone and did ask, passionately, in more alphabet and numbers, and nodded furiously to whatever came back. "Yes, sir,'' he said finally. "They say it's all right, you can go to rec.''

"Let's go, then,'' he said. "And do you have a cafeteria? The mess hall? Shall we see that?''

"That's on the list, sir.'' Kaplan sounded greatly relieved.

"Good,'' he said. "Banichi, Jago, we'll walk with Kaplan-nadi. He's an obliging fellow, not wishing any trouble, I'm sure. He seems a person of good character and great earnestness.''

"Kaplan-nadi,'' Banichi said in his deep voice, and with a pleasant expression. "One would like to know what he does transmit to his officers.''

"Banichi wants to know what you see and send,'' Bren said. "Such things interest my security.''

"Can't do that,'' Kaplan said, all gruffness now.

"Buy you a drink?'' Bren said. "We should talk, since you're to be my aide.''

"I'm not your aide, sir. And I can't talk, sir. I'm not supposed to."

"Aren't you? Then I may request you. I'll need someone when I'm on the station. Are you married?"

"Married, sir, no, sir." Kaplan's nervousness only increased.

"Where do *you* live?"

"238C, sir."

"That's a room?"

"Yes, sir."

"Alone?" Bren asked.

"Two and two, sir, two shifts."

"In all this great station? You're doubled up?"

"On the ship we had more room," Kaplan said. "But they're working on the ship."

"Doing what?" Bren asked.

"Hull, mostly."

"Damage?"

"Just old, sir, lot of ablation. And when she's in lockdown, it's not easy to be aboard; you can't get a lot of places in zero-G, sir. See those handholds? Not much use on a station, but on a ship, that's how you get by if you have to crawl."

It gibed with what he knew from Jase. While he kept up a running interrogation on points of corroboration, it was more corridors, more turns, twists, and descents, not a one of them distinguished from the other except by the occasional wall panels. It was an appalling, soul-numbing stretch of unmarked sameness.

They came to a corridor with one open door.

"This is rec, sir," Kaplan said, and led them to a moderately large room with a zigzag interior wall—a safety consideration, Bren knew by now—and a handful of occupants. The decor consisted of a handful of very faded blue plastic chairs, all swivel-mounted, at green wall-mounted, drop tables. Most astonishing of all there was a decoration, a single nonutilitarian blue stripe around the walls. There was, besides the stripe, a bulletin board, and a handful of magnetically posted notices.

Crewmen, doubtless forewarned, rose solemnly to their feet as they came in.

"Gentlemen, ladies." Bren walked past Kaplan, walked around the walls, keeping a careful eye to the reaction of the crew to Banichi and Jago . . . fear, curiosity, all at the same moment. The crewmen wanted to stare and were trying not to. "Good day to you," Bren said, drawing nervous, darting stares to himself. "I'm Bren Cameron, emissary from the aiji at Shejidan. This is Banichi and his partner Jago, chief of my house security, no other names. Think of them as police. Glad to meet you all, gentlemen, ladies."

"Yes, sir," some said. Those terms had fallen out of use. He was an anachronism in their midst, or he was their future.

"Seems we have an agreement," he said, curious how far news traveled among the crew. "We're going to be building here. Mospheira's going to provide you all the comforts of the planet, up here, according to what we've settled on, everything from fruit juice and hot dogs to seat cushions. Jase Graham. You know the name?"

They did, though there wasn't a clear word in what they answered. It was Kaplan's wide stare replicated, one and the other, men and women.

And he'd bet the place had been cleared of anyone not on a List, too.

"Jase is a friend of mine. *Friend.* You may have heard—or you may hear—you can't say that with the atevi: that they don't quite work that way. That's true. But it doesn't mean you can't get along with them and that they aren't very good people. You have to figure out *associations* with them. For instance, if you get along with me, you know you can get along with my security, my staff, my associates, and everyone I get along with. There's no such thing as one ateva. It's really pretty easy if you ask the atevi what they think of the other ateva you plan to be nice to. Glad to meet you all. My security is glad to meet you, no one's going to shoot anyone. Don't mind that they don't smile. It's not polite to smile until you know each other. Kaplan."

"Sir!"

"Introductions, if you please."

"Yes, sir," Kaplan said, and proceeded solemnly to reel off every name, every job, and rank: there were Johnsons and Pittses and Alugis, there was a Shumann and a Kalmoda and a Holloway, a Lewis, and a Kanchatkan, names he'd never heard. They were techs and maintenance, all young but one, who was a master machinist. "Glad to meet you," Bren said, and went around shaking hands, doggedly determined to put a face and a name to what had been faceless for two hunded years and three more in orbit about the planet. "My security won't shake hands. Our culture is foreign to them. They find you a fortunate number, they compliment you on that fact; they find you a comfortable gathering. I believe your library has a file on protocols when talking to atevi: I know I transmitted that file a couple of years ago, and hope it's gotten around."

No, it hadn't. He could tell by the looks. And he was far from surprised.

"Well, I hope you'll take a look at it on a fairly urgent basis, since there will be atevi working here. And don't take humans from the planet completely for granted, either. From your viewpoint, they're quite different, and words don't mean quite the same; I was born on the island, myself, and I can say you don't at all sound like Mospheirans. What *do* you do for entertainment, here?"

"Games, sir." That from a more senior crewman. "Entertainment files."

"Dice," another said.

Jase had said entertainment was sparse and opportunities were few. Jase had been vastly disturbed by rapid input, flickering shadows, any environmental phenomenon that seemed out of control: Jase standing on a deck on the ocean under a stormy sky was far, far beyond the bounds of his upbringing . . . an act of courage he only comprehended on seeing this recreational sterility. "Jase enjoyed his planet stay, gathered up some new games. I know he sent some footage up."

It hadn't made it to the general crew. There were blank glances, not a word.

"Definitely, we have to talk about the import situation," he said, with a picture he really, truly liked less and less. "I'm sure the Mospheirans will offer quite a few things you might like." Give or take the whole concept of trade, which he wasn't sure they really understood on a personal level. "You'll have a lot of things to get used to, among them the very fact of meeting people who aren't under your captains' orders, who speak your language and mean something totally different. Who don't mind surfaces bouncing around under them and lights flashing and who are rather entertained by the feeling." The looks were somewhat appalled. "We, on the other hand, will be largely involved in construction: improving the station, providing fuel, materials, that sort of thing. And we understand you found a problem out in far space. We're used to dealing with strangers. We hope to deal with your difficulty and solve it."

That struck a chord, finally. That was something they understood . . . and didn't believe.

"Yes, sir," came from another one, whose name was Lewis. Bren hadn't forgotten, didn't intend to forget a single name.

"Have you talked to Jase since he's been back?" he asked.

"No, sir," one said, and there were various shakes of the head.

"Interesting," he said, and had a very uneasy feeling about this place, about the crew, about the whole situation. "But you do know him."

"Yes, sir." They seemed to take turns talking. Or they were all wired, like Kaplan, getting their answers from elsewhere.

"Kaplan," Bren said.

"Sir!"

"Why don't we take a walk to the Mospheiran delegation, and then over to the mess hall?"

"They're in the same section, sir."

"Well, good," he said. "Why don't we do that?"

"Yes, sir," Kaplan said.

"Would any of you like to walk along?"

"We have to get back to duty," one said.

"I'm sure you do. Well, good day to you all. Hope to see more of you." Bren smiled and made his withdrawal, saying, in Ragi, still smiling, "Jase was wildly extroverted when he arrived, compared to these people."

"They seem very afraid," Jago remarked.

"They seem afraid," he repeated, following Kaplan. "They were likely put here for us to see. They haven't seen

Jase, and they haven't seen any of the files we've transmitted up, the ones about atevi."

"One certainly asks why," Banichi said.

"One certainly does ask," Bren said. "Kaplan, what are these people scared of?"

"The aliens, sir."

"Banichi and Jago aren't aliens. You and I are. That below is *their planet*."

"Yes, sir." Kaplan didn't look reassured. Nor was he reassured, regarding the ship.

"Ever been in a fight?" Bren asked.

"Sir?"

"Ever had to fight, really fight, hand to hand?"

"No, sir," Kaplan said.

"Has anyone on this ship ever been in a fight?"

"I don't think so, sir, well, a few scrambles between *us*, but not outside, sir."

This from a man overburdened with direction-finding, recording, and defensive equipment, a man who looked like a walking spy post.

"Bren."

"Sir?"

"Bren's the name. You can call me Bren. For formal use it's Bren-nandi, but Mr. Cameron is my island name. Is Kaplan what you go by?" Last names were stitched on every uniform, and it was all uniforms, completely identical. Textures had frightened Jase. Differences had frightened Jase. He saw now that everything on the station was one color, the uniforms were all alike: the haircuts were generally but not universally alike . . . one size fit everyone and one had to train one's eye to look at subtler differences, which probably were quite clear to someone who knew the body language of every individual aboard. He supposed that Kaplan could recognize an individual from behind and at a distance down the oddly-curving corridors, and that he himself was relatively handicapped in not knowing. The difference he posed must certainly be a shock; the Mospheirans no less so; and what they thought of the atevi was likely like a man looking at a new species: the ability to integrate patterns and recognize individuals utterly overwhelmed by a flood of input, not knowing what was a significant difference.

Three years to build a shuttle?

Three years to bring Jason, who was trying, into synch with atevi ways?

It wasn't the engineering that most challenged them in building here. It was the psychology of individuals on the ground who for various reasons didn't want to comprehend, the pathology of individuals having trouble enough inside their own system of recognitions; the pathology of a human society up here walled in and sensitized to a narrow range of subtle sensations, subtle signals.

He'd been uneasy regarding Jase. In Jase's continued, defended absence, he was growing alarmed, pressing harder. He knew the hostility in his own mind toward these people who were behaving in a hostile way, and dare he think he was part of the difficulty?

It was a long walk through unmarked territory. More and more unmarked, unnumbered territory before they reached the Mospheirans, before sentries admitted them, unquestioned, at least, on Kaplan's presence, if nothing else. They walked into the small district, drew a curious response from Lund and from Feldman, who walked out from separate rooms.

"Come have a drink," Bren said. "The cafeteria's buying."

Lund and Feldman stared at him. Kroger and Shugart showed up, equally suspicious.

"Our hosts are hostile in manner," Bren said cheerfully in Ragi, a simple utterance, given the basic vocabulary of the translators, and Feldman and Shugart betrayed a quickly-subdued uneasiness.

"A good idea," Feldman said with some presence of mind. "We should go."

"Go, hell," Kroger said. "What are you up to?"

"Listen to him, nadiin," Jago said, and by now Kaplan was looking at one and the other of them.

"Kaplan," Bren said, laying a presumptive, hail-good-fellow hand on Kaplan's wired shoulder, "Kaplan, my friend, is there a bar to be had?"

"There is," Kaplan said.

"Is it on the List?"

"Yes, sir," Kaplan said.

"Well, let's all go there and have a drink." He tightened his grip as Kaplan began to protest. "Oh, don't be a stick. Come along. Be welcome. Show us this bar."

"Sir, I can't drink on duty."

"I'm afraid for what the stuff is made of," Bren said, ignoring Kaplan's reluctance, and pressed to turn him about. "But I've gone long enough without a drink."

"Sounds good," Lund said, but Kroger was frowning.

"Feldman, you stay," Kroger said. "All right, Cameron. I hope you have a reason."

"A perfect reason. Kaplan, is there any chance you can liberate Jase to join us?"

"I don't think so, sir. He's with the captains."

"Well, come along, come along. Feldman, my regrets."

"Yes, sir," Ben said confusedly.

At least Kroger hadn't robbed the bar party of both translators. And she'd left security behind.

They set off back past the sentries. Another walk, a short one, and there was, indeed, a small bar, the most ordinary thing in the world to the Mospheirans, one he himself hadn't thought of *until* he'd walked in among his own species, and one of the most astonishing places in the world for Banichi and Jago, surely. It was dim, it smelled faintly of alcohol, a television was playing an old movie on the wall unit, and every eye turned toward them.

"This is a place," Bren said in Ragi, "where humans meet to consume alcohol, talk, and play games. Hostilities are discouraged despite the loosening of rules, or because of them. It substitutes for the sitting room. Here you may sit and talk while drinking. Talk with the young paidhi while I talk with Lund and Kroger, find out what she knows, advise her honestly of our concerns, advise her how to communicate this discreetly to her superiors. It is permissible and encouraged to lean on the counter where drinks are served while one talks."

"One will try," Banichi said.

"Shugart," Bren said, "go practice your translation with them, using no names."

"No names." The word was difficult in Ragi.

"Lund," Bren said, flinging an arm about the delegate from Commerce. "What will you have? More to the point, what have they got, Kaplan? Vodka, more than likely."

"There's vodka," Kaplan said. "There's vodka and there's flavored vodka."

"I'm not surprised," Bren said. "Is there anything you *can't* make into vodka?"

"I don't know, sir," Kaplan said. The eyepiece glowed in the dim lighting. Unhappily, so did atevi eyes, as gold as Kaplan's eyepiece was red. The phenomenon drew nervous stares around the room . . . from the single bartender, the five gathered at a table. The stares tried not to be obvious, and weren't wholly friendly.

"Anyone here know Jase Graham?" Bren asked aloud. If there was anyone who didn't, they didn't say so, but neither did the others leap up to say they did. "Friend of mine. Missing on board."

"He's in the captains' debriefing, sir," Kaplan said under his breath.

"I know you say that. Here. Sit down."

"I can't . . ."

"Can't sit? You look perfectly capable to me."

"Yes, sir," Kaplan said, "but I can't drink."

"You can have a soft drink; I'll assume there's something of the sort here."

"Yes, sir," Kaplan said. They sat. The bartender came over as if he were approaching hostile lunatics. "Fizz-water," Kaplan said.

"What flavors does the vodka come in?"

"There's lemon and there's pepper."

"I think I'd play it safe," Kroger said, "and ask for plain. With ice."

"Sounds like good advice," Bren said. "Plain." Lemon was a flavor; historically it had been a fruit, but there was no such aboard *Phoenix*; and peppers, while some grew on Mospheira, were mostly native. It was a matter of curiosity, but not when one courted information, not new flavors.

The drink orders went in. Banichi and Jago talked in Ragi with the wide-eyed young translator. The drinks arrived, indifferently served, and their guard had a fizzwater while they knocked down untrustworthy vodka.

"Kaplan's been touring us about," he said in his thickest Mosphei' accent. "We'd really wanted to do this with Jase, who can't be found. I did get a call through to the mainland and sent one off to Mospheira; Tabini-aiji is quite pleased; I hope the President will be."

"We've put in a call," Kroger admitted, continually looking at her glass and her fingers, as if there were high counsel there. "We're going to work up some figures. We've been at it, actually."

"So have I," Bren said, and they proceeded to talk detailed business while Kaplan sipped his fizzwater and the vodka worked on their nervous systems. Kroger relaxed a degree; Lund grew positively cheerful; whether either took the warning about Jase's disappearance Bren remained uncertain, but he hoped Banichi and Jago were getting past the language barrier. He heard nervous laughter from Shugart, saw her duck her head in utter embarrassment, and saw Banichi and Jago both laughing, which was encouraging.

The whole bar relaxed, with that. The conversation between Banichi and Jago and Kate Shugart began to involve the bartender, evidently regarding the television. First the bartender changed the channel and punched buttons and then while business talk proceeded at their table, Banichi and Jago investigated the buttons, while Shugart translated and investigated the buttons herself.

And after two drinks, numbers exchanged, opinions exchanged in some quiet amity, and definitely more relaxed than he had been, Bren called an end to the visit. "Well," he said, "better go get back to quarters, see if there's a hangover in this stuff."

"Doesn't seem too bad," Lund said, who'd had three.

"Best we go, though," Kroger agreed.

"But we should give an official hello," Bren said. Perhaps it was the vodka, but his motives were sheer public relations, since things were going so well at the bar. He went over to the other table and had Kaplan introduce him and introduce the others, including Banichi and Jago, who never yet had spoken a word of Mosphei', and who met the five crewmen with uncharacteristic smiles.

"Very glad to meet you," Bren said, and went through

the most of the routine a second time with the bartender, whose name was Jeff, and who, yes, had shown them the workings of the entertainment system.

"Can they see in the dark?" Jeff wanted to know, further, on what Bren estimated was the chatoyance of atevi eyes.

"A little better than we can at twilight," he said, knowing as a human how people who saw in the dark played off human fears . . . and then remembering this Jeff would have no visceral concept of twilight. Dusk and dawn were no better. "Like in here," he amended that. "Not sure about the color range, well as we know each other; don't think it's ever been tested scientifically. But it's not that much different."

"Huh," Jeff said thoughtfully, and Bren gave the polite formulas and gathered his party out the door into the corridor, Lund tending to stray a bit. They were cheerful, the lot of them, even Kroger looking flushed.

"Well, probably time we got back to our various sections," Bren said. "Why don't you drop by tomorrow? We can give you something a little aside from the cafeteria fare. I have to let my staff know in advance, but no great difficulty to set a few extra places."

"I don't know," Kroger said.

"Anything but the food up here," Lund said, and then cast a look at Kaplan. "With apologies."

"Everything my staff brought accommodates human taste," Bren said. "Kaplan, can you bring them for supper tomorrow, say, oh, local eighteen hundred? You're welcome, yourself. Plan to eat with us."

"I can't, sir, not on duty."

"Your duty is a bother."

"Yes, sir," Kaplan said. "But I have to do it."

"All the same. You can have a cup of tea and a wafer or two. The universe won't end."

"Eighteen hundred," Kroger said.

"Granted we survive the hangover," Bren said. "Lead on, Kaplan. Show us the way."

16

"One does apologize, nadiin-ji, for curious behavior," Bren said when they met the staff, he and Banichi and Jago with Tano and Algini as interested bystanders from the security room door.

"It was a curious place," Banichi said.

"Indeed," Jago agreed. "But we were able to advise Kate-ji of the situation."

"I heard laughter."

"She said she was an endangered fish and again, that we were three amorous old men."

Bren had to smile, though the vodka had not improved the dry-air headache. He'd tried inhaling water that morning, tried a headache remedy during their stay in the bar, and still felt far too dry, which the vodka he'd consumed had not improved. "Relations with Kroger and Lund are definitely better, though I don't think we're communicating much better than you are with Kate Shugart. There's far too much apprehension around us all, far too much fear of strangers. I don't know whether the crew is more worried about you or about the Mospheirans. I think they're beginning to understand they're not the same as themselves."

"These humans will not have met even other humans at all," Jago said. "Jasi-ji was afraid, the first time he saw how large Shejidan is."

"Jase was afraid of very many things, but he improved quickly," Tano said from the side. "Is there word of his welfare, nadiin-ji?"

"Not to our satisfaction," Bren said. "Always they say he's with the captains. They claim he has no further relationship with the aiji's court: they wish to assert command over him, and I'm not willing to have that state of affairs. Nor will the aiji. What did Kate say, nadiin?"

"That Kroger-nadi was very angry at first," Banichi said, "and that she's still angry over the archive, but reconciled, one thinks, and glad to have an agreement which may turn out to her credit. Kate says that all of them are communicating in confidence they're being observed. One doubts they have that great a skill at it, judging what I've heard, but they are attempting to be discreet in their most sensitive policy discussions."

"The translators believe they're privy to those?"

"Yes, but with only small occasion to contribute. Kate stated they all like the notion of atevi mining and building; they believe they can interest commercial enterprises in venturing here, but they're worried about losing all economic initiative in manufacturing to the mainland."

"The translator was doing very well, then."

"She makes egregious mistakes," Jago said, "but goodwill and courtesy are evident in her manner. She is cautious of offense."

"Despite naming us noble thieves," Banichi added.

"Forgive her."

His security was amused. The words for assassin and thief were similar, for the antique word noble and guild even closer. "Perhaps we are noble thieves. Perhaps we might steal our associate from them when we go. Perhaps we will steal all manufacturing."

"I intend the one. Not the other. Medicines. Electronics. Refining. Food production in orbit. We can stake out interlocked domains. The principles are well-defined, nothing we have to invent."

"They have not yet opened their defenses," Banichi said, "and do not trust. One must ask," Banichi said, "nandi, how far one should go with them, or with Kaplan-nadi either in confidence or in allowing untoward movement."

Serious question. A very serious question. "Defer to me in this. If I strike anyone, then observe no restraint. But I rather like Kaplan."

Like was for salads; it was an old joke with them, but they understood it well enough for one of those transitory attachments humans formed, one subject to whimsy and change by the hour . . . when for atevi such changes were emotional, associational, life-rending earthquakes.

They might know, at least, how he read the situation. He added, "I rather *like* Lund and Feldman, too; Shugart is, well, Shugart's fine. Even Kroger improves with acquaintance. She and I had a bad start, on the flight to the mainland. I rather think she's Heritage in associations, but too smart for Heritage, too smart to bow to its leaders, too educated in her field, too innately sensible to swallow what they say. I think she's seen now how things *can* work between our species and she's not going to give the hardliners in her party a report they'll greatly favor. For political purposes, *they* want to regard us as enemies, they want *all* the station, and I don't think she'll accommodate them. I think she's honest. I think she sees the Heritage Party as a means to half of what she wants, better than those who'd rather not think about space at all, but I think if she sees a way to get Mospheirans up here without being directly under Guild authority, I think that satisfies most of what she wants."

"Kroger is aiji in that group," Jago mused, "one suspects. An aiji indeed, then."

"I'm still not sure what Lund's authority is. Possibly he has the same inclinations to leadership. Possibly he's even Heritage himself and quite canny at it—his department is rife with that party; but he seems far more skilled at getting along with other humans. Kroger is leader, in terms of having her way, and not owing man'chi to those who think they're her leaders. She has thorns, doesn't like what's foreign, but she also has a brain; and I think—I hope—she's used it in the last several days. I'm coming to respect Kroger, however reluctantly. I hope that lasts."

"One also hopes it does," Banichi said.

"Supper tomorrow evening; a meeting next afternoon with Sabin; one hopes we make contact with Jase. Not a bad day's work."

"Shall Tano and Algini attend you at supper this evening?" Banichi asked.

"Certainly." He had no objections to his staff doing turnabout at the luxury of the formal table and food served at the moment of perfection; more, he counted it a chance to brief the junior pair in more detail, and to give Banichi and Jago a break, or conference time, or time for a lengthy, self-indulgent bath . . . whatever they might want. They'd gone short of sleep in recent days; and whether something of a personal nature ever went on in that partnership he still had no idea, not a clue.

No jealousy, either. He owed them both his life and his sanity.

"One will dress," Tano said with a bow of his head, and that matter was settled.

Bren himself went to change shirts . . . *how* freshly-pressed shirts appeared on schedule was a miracle of the servants' quarters, but he took them gratefully as they were offered, a small indulgence of rank, and allowed Narani the smugness of small miracles.

He fastened buttons, turned on the computer, gathered messages, in the interval before dinner.

There was a short one from Toby:

Bren, Jill and the kids are gone. I can't find them.

His hand hit the wall panel, dented it.

"Nadi?" It was Sabiso's inoffensive voice, concerned. He collected himself, faced the young woman in formal courtesy.

"A difficulty, Sabiso-ji, a small difficulty."

Her glance surely took in the damaged panel. She lingered. "Shall I call Jago, nandi?"

"No," he said mildly. "No, no need." He wanted to put his fist *through* the wall, but a broken hand wouldn't help the downward spiral of the situation. He didn't want to alarm Sabiso. He didn't want to explain the situation to his security.

He was furious with his brother, didn't even know why he was brought to the irrational brink.

Not rational. Not at all rational. Not professional, damaging the wall panel. Downright stupid, leaving a trace of his temper. It wasn't like him. Accumulated stress. Short schedules. The frustration of his position.

He walked over to the vanity counter and tried to calm himself with cold water, the single frustrating handful he could get from the damned spring-loaded tap.

Sabiso still lingered, not about to leave a madman. He

could hear her small movements. "You may dismiss worry, Sabiso-ji. Please go about your duties."

"Yes, nandi." Confronted, she did leave. He gave it a very short time before he might expect Jago.

Why did he want to throttle his brother? What in hell was it in a perfectly reasonable message from his brother about his own personal distress that made him dent a wall panel?

Simple answer. Toby had just asked him to leave him the hell alone in one message; and he'd agreed, and sent an irrevocable letter to their mother. And now Toby broke Toby's own new rules and wanted him to worry . . . for a damned good reason; he could only imagine Toby's state of mind.

But, dammit, it was part and parcel of the way his family had always worked: first the ultimatum to leave the situation alone; then two hours later a cry for help he couldn't possibly ignore, and in most cases couldn't do a thing about but lose sleep.

He couldn't do a damn thing in this instance about Jill and the kids. He figured, somewhere in his personal psychological cellar, that the last straw in that marriage might have been his call to Toby to come back to the capital, when things between Jill and Toby were already strained. It was his fault. He'd done it.

And they had to quit the cycle they were in. He *couldn't* fix Toby's problem. He couldn't go on a search for Jill.

He had to take it just as Toby doing what he himself had reserved the right to do: send an advisory. Toby had that right, too. Toby's wife and kids were missing . . . in a world where political lunacy had flung rocks at windows, pegged shots at perfect strangers, and had a security guard from the National Security Administration guarding his brother's kids from a distance.

Where in hell were the guards when Jill took the kids? That was Shawn's office, at a primary level. Did Shawn know where Jill was, and would he tell Toby?

Dammit, he was up here releasing the archive files to the planet, the world had just found out there were missions going on up here, and Jill picked a damned hard time to do a disappearing act.

He settled down and wrote exactly that, in a far calmer mode. *I'm sorry as hell, Toby. It's all I can say. Likely she's at the cottage or she's gone to her family. I'm sure she's all right. Tell her I said it was my fault and she should be angry at me . . .*

He deleted the last sentence, one more interference in Toby's household, in favor of: *Contact Shawn. Get answers immediately. Don't assume. This is a safety issue. Pride is nowhere in this. Protect them.*

The message was stark, uncomfortably brief. He knew Toby was absolutely right to have told him, dared not reject the possibility it *was* more than anger on Jill's part.

He was the one who'd brought his family the necessity of security measures, armed guards, all those things. They'd begun to lean on them. *Surely* Toby had already been to the security people. And they didn't have answers?

He couldn't do anything, except fire a message to Shawn, on restricted channels. *Toby's wife and kids are missing. Need to know where they are.*

. . . and knowing that if that inquiry reached Jill and embarrassed her in a marital spat, it might be the true final straw in her marriage.

He'd done all he could. He couldn't spare personal worry. He couldn't afford to think on it. He calmly wrote another message for Mogari-nai, this one to relay to Tabini.

We have spent an interesting day touring the station and meeting with various crewmen. We have not yet located our associate, and have assurances the authorities are asking him close questions. I am concerned at this point but find no alternative. Particulars of my negotiations with all parties did attach to my last message. Please confirm that those files reached you, aiji-ma. I remain convinced of a felicitous outcome but find that certain representations are dubious. I was far too sanguine not of the early progress, but of its scope. Relations with the Mospheiran delegates have become smoother and those with the ship-aijiin more doubtful. Also my brother's family is missing and I hope you will pursue queries with Shawn-nandi, aiji-ma, discreetly. Personal argument preceded the disappearance, but the unsettled times are a worry.

On the other hand, after some inconvenience we have scheduled a meeting with Sabin-captain, and hope that a session of close questions will allay the concerns of the two less available captains and bring us closer to reasonable agreement. We have repeatedly asserted and I still believe, aiji-ma, that future association with the ship-humans is to the good of all parties including the Mospheirans and the only reasonable course for the protection of all living things. I am more than ever of the opinion that the long experience of Mospheirans and atevi in settling differences between our kinds may prove both confusing and alarming to the ship-humans; but that it also offers a surer defense than any weapon of their devising.

He sent. And hoped to God that Shawn readily had Toby's answer about where Jill and those kids were.

Supper was, for the first time, a vegetable preserve: such things were *kabiu,* proper, without going against the prohibition against preserved meat. Tano and Algini shared the table with him, and he mentioned nothing of Toby's difficulty, there being nothing any of his security could do about it. He'd developed a certain knack over the years, of dismissing things on Mospheira to a remote part of his attention, of shifting utterly into the mainland; and now further than that, into complete concentration on his staff, on the problems of Sabin and Kroger, on the regional labor resources, shuttle flight schedules, and station resources. Tano and Algini in fact had been working the day long on the security of the section they now held, on what went on behind the skin of the walls and the floors and arching ceiling, what possibility there was of being spied on, or of spying.

And at the very moment Tano was about to explain the console, the one in their dining hall leaped to life and let out a loud burst of sound.

"God," Bren said. Tano and Algini were out of their seats. It was not the only source of the sound, and it ceased quickly, as running steps approached the door.

Jago appeared.

"Apologies," she said. "We have found the main switch, nadiin, nandi."

The servants laughed; Tano and Algini laughed, and Bren subsided shakily and with amusement against the back of his chair.

The screen went dark again.

Supper resumed, in its final course, a light fruit custard.

From down the hall it sounded like water running, or a television.

Ultimately, after the custard, he had to send Tano and Algini to find out the cause, and he answered his own curiosity, taking a cup of tea with him.

By now it sounded like bombs.

He walked into the security station.

On one channel, insects pollinated brilliant flowers, unknown to this earth. They were bees, Bren knew from primer school, bees and apple blossoms. On another screen a line of crowned human women dived into a blue pool. On a third, buildings exploded.

The servant staff gathered behind him at the door, amazed and stunned.

Pink flowers gave way to riders in black and white.

"Mecheiti!" Sabiso said, wrong by a meter or so and half a ton.

"Horses," Bren said. "Banichi, what have we found?"

"One thinks," Banichi said, "we have discovered the architecture of this archive. There is an organization to it."

A varied set of images flowed past. He might have delighted in it, on any other evening. He might have laughed.

But while the staff watched, intrigued by human history, he went across the corridor to his room, to the computer, to check his messages via C1.

Toby *had* written back. *Call off your panic. Jill's at her mother's.*

Bren sank into a cold plastic chair.

Not . . . *thanks, Bren.*

Not . . . *security knew.*

Not . . . *I'm going there now.*

Not . . . *it's going to be all right.*

The chill sank inward, and lay there. He didn't move for a moment.

All right, Toby, did Shawn know, did Tabini send something through?

Did I mess things up, Toby?

I want you safe, dammit. It's not safe there. This is no time for Jill to be running from her security. . . .

He wrote that: *Toby, impress on her this is no time . . .*

And wiped it. Jill had left her home, run out on Toby. This was not a woman thinking clearly about her personal safety. Or she was rejecting it.

The news of atevi presence and *his* presence on the station was about to break on the island if it hadn't done so already, touching off every unstable element, from the mainland to Mospheira, in an ultimate paroxysm of paranoia. He was not persona grata with the Heritage Party, which made a fetish of armed preparation for invasion; his mother and Toby's accidentally stepped in front of a damn bus. If *that* accident had stayed out of the news, it would be a wonder, and that report would taint anything he did, as if there was something sinister and personal in the action. *Anything* was substance for the rumor mills, *anything* might touch off the unstable elements who searched the news daily to substantiate their theories, and the theories were no longer funny. It might be announced on the island at any moment that atevi were going to *run* the space station; even if the majority of Mospheirans didn't *want* to live under the Guild again, and didn't want to run the station, they didn't want to give it up, either.

And Jill picked this moment to ditch her protection.

He couldn't write plain-spoken things like, *The kids are in danger.* The Mospheiran link wasn't secure enough to be utterly frank; he didn't know whether their mother was on a bus bound for the hospital, whether she'd called a taxi, or even ditched *her* security. He knew there was danger, knew there were elements that would unhesitatingly strike at the innocent to wound him, and he'd had his try at gathering his family onto the mainland behind Tabini's much more extensive security. *That* hadn't worked.

He couldn't protect them. Not any more than he could have prevented the accident.

He bowed his head against his clenched hands, muscles tightened until joints popped. He wanted . . .

But he couldn't intervene with Toby, or Jill, or Barb, or his mother.

He couldn't beg off from his job or ask why in hell human beings couldn't use good sense. He'd asked that until he knew there was no plain and simple answer.

And he couldn't blame his brother for being angry with it all. He was angry, too. He could move things in the heavens, shift Tabini's Opinion and move the mechanisms of the *aishidi'tat* on personal privilege, but he couldn't do a damn thing to prevent unintended consequences.

Get to her, he wished his brother. *Get to Jill. Get her and those kids back under protection. Don't hesitate. Don't quarrel. Just do it.*

And for God's sake, write to me when you're all safe.

17

Aiji-ma, we still wait for any confirmation of agreement from the other captains, notably Sabin, third-ranking, who has set a meeting with me for tomorrow station time, whether with her alone or with others of the captains I still have had no word. I have been unable to contact Jase, whom they continually say is in conference with the captains. Nor have I been able to contact Mercheson, nor has the delegation from the island. I find infelicity in the condition of the halls, and their lack of all numbers and designations. Numbers and colors were erased from such facilities in historical times when occupants wished to prevent intruders from knowing their way about. A local guides us whenever we leave, and he receives a map image, I am sure, through an eyepiece and instructions through a hearing device. Neither device is unknown to the island but their use under this circumstance is somewhat troubling, when a small number of painted signs would indicate the route through what is a very confusing set of hallways.

I have received word directly from my brother. His wife is angry with him and has taken up residence with her household, taking the children with her. I have strong security concerns in this move, but will not allow these to override my good sense in the performance of my duties to you, aiji-ma.

Bren re-read the message, searched for words that might cue any other reader as to subject, decided to send as it was, and set up his computer on the table next the wall console.

He punched in. "Good morning, C1."

"Hello, sir."

"Send and receive."

"Yes, sir."

The squeal went out and came back.

"Good day, C1. Thank you."

"Out, sir."

C1 didn't readily know about mornings. Bren had a notion to ask C1 what his name was . . . at least the one that was there of mornings, or this shift, as the ship and station reckoned time.

And breakfast was waiting for him, but he wanted to see first what he had caught in his net this morning. He ached for a message from Toby, but Toby had his mind on other than sending to him, he was sure, and no news meant Toby had gone on his way and likely reached Jill's mother's house last night. If something went wrong, *then* he might hear from Toby.

And there was no message from that quarter, none from the island, none from Mogari-nai.

There was a message from Tabini, a simple one: *We have been in contact with the Foreign Office regarding matters of your concern. My devoted wife has transmitted a message through your office to your lady mother by the State Department offering her concern and her wish for the lady's early recovery.*

He was astonished. And grateful.

And hoped to God his mother sent a civil reply.

No, no, Shawn would mediate that. It would be decorous.

He had to thank Lady Damiri. And he very much suspected it was a signal. Tabini was aware of everything, and meant to reassure him.

He was moderately embarrassed to have had Tabini do that . . . though it was not an outrageous proceeding if it were some notable man of the province or of the court: a matter of courtesy, it was. He didn't know how his brother might receive any word from Tabini. He didn't *trust* his family to behave, was what it boiled down to, and he was vaguely ashamed to realize he held that opinion . . . justified as it might be.

There were messages from various others, more business of the committee heads to whom he had sent messages, he was quite sure, a few outraged ones, who were put out that a human should be leading an atevi delegation and had no shyness in saying so. The traditionalists had their opinions, and in fact he somewhat agreed with them, but couldn't speak against the aiji's decision that had put him here. He left them to Ilisidi, and hoped for the best.

There was a message from students of the Astronomer Emeritus, who were astounded and pleased at his voyage, and who asked what wonders of the stars he could see from his vantage.

What celestial wonders? Human obstinacy and suspicion was not the answer the students wanted. The captains, damn them, had sent down images from other stars but had ungraciously declined to give their coordinates or to tell where they were in the human system of reckoning.

He'd arranged for the University to transmit its own stellar catalog and its own system of reference and nomenclature three years ago. And Jase had drawn them a map . . . a hand-drawn, crude thing, but referencing the charts; so the reticence of the Guild on that topic had passed quietly unnoticed, except in certain close circles.

And the students wanted pictures?

In the press of things strange and hostile up here, he'd utterly forgotten there was an outside, that there was a reality of stars and forces more universal than the captains' will.

He went off to breakfast, thinking the while what he was going to do about those images, putting them at the head of the mental queue, since there was so damned little he could do today about the rest; and then thinking: damn, of course, the archive. Images had gone down to the planet with that.

Locating them in that universe of data meant having an appropriate key. And he had an idea where to find it, knew what the keys ought to be, in words like *navigation* and *data* and *star* and *map*, with which his staff might search the download. Simply comparing the two areas of the Mospheiran maps and the maps in the download . . . *simply!* There was a bad joke. But it could be done.

"Thought?" Banichi asked him, and, distracted, he had to laugh and explain he was thinking of dictionaries and starcharts.

"Usefully so?" Banichi asked. Banichi had learned that such things as the stellar nature of the sun had some relevance to his job, quite a basic relevance, as it had turned out, but hardly relevant to the performance of it.

"We're contained and without sight of the stars," Bren said. "And the students of the Astronomer Emeritus ask me for pictures and data."

"Are there windows?" Jago asked.

"I imagine that there are, but not necessarily of the sort you might imagine. Most that this station sees, it sees through electronic eyes, through cameras."

"Interesting," Banichi said. One wondered why, and, with Banichi involved, came up with several alarming possibilities.

"Of course," Bren said, "on the other side of all walls and windows and out where the cameras are is hard vacuum."

"One does recall so," Banichi said. "But a view of the exterior might be useful. One would like to know the relationship of pieces."

"That, I might provide. I can ask C1. There might be a view available."

"Interesting," Jago said, too.

They finished breakfast. And after the accustomed compliments to cook and staff—in this case Bindanda—Bren went to the dining area wall panel and punched in C1.

"C1," he said when he had an acknowledgment. "We've been here this long and we haven't seen the stars. Can you show us a view?"

"Not much to see from the cameras," C1 said. *"But hull view's active."*

The screen came live on a glare-lit, ablated surface, and absolute shadow.

"Where is that?" Bren asked, having an idea what Banichi was after, and now Tano and Algini had come in haste, Jago having apparently informed them what was toward.

"That's looking back over the hull from forward camera 2," C1 said.

"Is that the shuttle?" Bren said. There was a reflected glow on a smooth surface, the edge of a wing, perhaps.

"Should be," C1 said. *"I can angle for a better view. This*

isn't the deep dark, here. There's planetshine, for one thing, not mentioning the star. You want stars, sir, you should be a little farther out."

It must be a slow morning in the control center, Bren thought, gratified. It was, in fact, the shuttle.

"Got to close the show," C1 said. *"I'll leave you attached to camera 2 on, say, C45."*

"That's wonderful," Bren said. "Delighted, C1. Thank you."

"Interesting," Tano said, much as Banichi had said, as C1 punched out.

"More cooperation than we've had, nadiin," Bren said. "That man is not cautious with us. Others are. Interesting, indeed."

His security returned questioning looks. "We had early cooperation," Bren said, "very wide cooperation, and easy agreement with those who were already agreed. I don't think it attributable to my powers of negotiation, rather to understandings generally made verbal. Now we have these long delays."

"Dissent," Jago said.

"And placatory gestures from the servants," Banichi said.

It did, however atevi the view might be, seem to describe the situation with C1.

"It's not safe to press, however," Bren said. "No more than in an atevi household. The man is a subordinate."

He settled to work after that small show, imagining that someone thinking more down a human track would have negotiated that camera view much earlier; that very probably Kroger's team had asked; and that it was something C1 could grant on request, something to amuse the guests and, like the unmarked hallways, to tell them very little.

They were due to meet with Kroger this evening, supposing that came off on schedule. Certainly Bindanda came to question him diffidently about his selections and his menu: "Excellent," he said, "and one might have a sweet or two. That will please them."

"Nandi," Bindanda said, and went off to their galley stores, with Narani in close supervision.

The household ran without effort; it moved and buzzed

about him, rarely disturbed him except to renew his supply of tea, while he sat at the small desk and composed letters and replies to various correspondents.

To Toby:

> *Write when you can. My love and my apologies to Jill and the kids.*

There was no letter today. He wasn't that surprised in the silence.

To his mother, with ulterior motives, both to hear from her and to hear whatever she might have heard about Toby . . . *if* she had heard a thing from Toby, which she might not have.

Double reason for checking up on her.

I'm doing fine. It's an interesting place up here.

He struck that beginning. She might take offense at his doing fine in an interesting place; it was somewhat self-centered on his part. He tried again.

> *I'm just checking to be sure you're all right. I hope Barb is improving. I want you to take care of yourself, and be assured I'm fine. I hope you'll keep me posted on everything, and I want you to be sure to get enough rest. I know how you tend to push yourself. I think I inherited it. Do stay to sensible places. You know how certain elements are dangerous when I'm in the news, and I think I am now. I imagine that I am. Know that I love you.*

He'd achieved a certain distance in his communication, after sending that other letter, that possibly hurtful letter. He worried about it, worried about it a great deal, and thought now that he'd been too harsh, too self-centered on his own part, to take every move his mother made as self-serving and self-centered. She *was* concerned for him, God knew. She was a mother. She had a son off on a hitherto unreachable space station telling her things were fine while armed security watched over her and everything she did. He'd been desperate; he'd shoved too hard to be free.

*What I wrote was honest at the time but one of those
things that one starts thinking about; and both your sons
love you a great deal. At something over thirty I've
reached that stage of wanting to be free and to pursue
my own course. Kind of late, but there we are. I haven't
taken Toby's course, home and house and all. And I
shoved far too hard when it came to it. Now that I've
done that I find myself regretting it and wanting to know
how you are and to tell you I care. Not to change my
mind, but to tell you I care. Both are human, I think.*

The *I think* loomed out at him on rereading. In all honesty, it was an *I think*. He *didn't* know for certain any
longer, or hadn't since his teens, when he'd gone into the
University program and begun to separate from the culture
he'd been born to.

*I don't know what more I can say, except to take care
of yourself in all senses. I wish I had been able to stay
longer. We both needed that. But I'm doing a job here,
the results of which I think you are able to see now,
and which I hope will give those kids of Toby's a future.*

He wrote to the heads of committees.

*We are making progress and hope for your patience.
While there are agreements in principle, there are many
details yet to work out of what I hope will be a good
cooperation between our peoples.*

He wrote it until he began to see every flaw in the hope.
And he settled down with Jago for a lengthy talk over
the southern provinces of the *aishidi'tat,* their ethnic questions, their material resources and willingness to mobilize,
those divisions of loyalty and wealth he knew, but which a
human didn't *feel* with the accuracy an ateva felt the divisions, and which a human couldn't know with the breadth
and depth of an ateva's being immersed in them lifelong
while being wired to feel the tides of provincial resentment.
Was a little town building a railroad to a spaceport? Ask
what various provinces might do once they saw prosperity

within their reach. An ateva might make a pot to continue in the economy for a hundred years, and an ateva might utilize every scrap of a fruit, down to the peelings; but atevi also might have a color television in a house in which electric wiring was strung along the side of a stone floor, under exposed wooden rafters, some of which might have been replaced in the last century.

Atevi made families and ties within man'chi, and passed these houses, and their debts and their projects, from one generation to another, and had both the most informal barter arrangements and the most rigidly traditional activities . . . give or take what humans sent them.

Atevi when they came to the station might bring families, including aged aunts and grandfathers, which humans in their economy and focus might not understand.

"Will it be like taking service in a household?" he asked Jago. "Or will husbands and wives come?"

"Perhaps both," Jago said. "As husbands and wives make unions in a household."

Atevi unions, like human ones, could be ephemeral. "Unions within a household last. They seem obliged to last."

"Or part amicably," Jago said. "As one can. Or part for children, and come back again."

That was so. Lovers within a household might get their children elsewhere, by agreement, so as not to bring children into a household that was otherwise childless.

"I would never forbid children," he said, half wishing there were some.

"But the Bu-javid is a bad place for them," Jago said truthfully.

They were there to talk about the space station; but he looked at Jago, with whom he shared a bed on occasion, on opportunity, and wondered about children, which were not in the cards for them, certainly, biologically; and not for him, personally . . . he'd never wanted to leave a family of his own on the other side of the straits.

"Up here there might be children. Or not, as people prefer."

"There were children," Jago said, "who rode the petal sails."

Frightening as it was, certain pods had dropped onto the world with children aboard, all those years ago.

"So there were," he said. "And so there are on the ship itself." Jase had told him so.

"Like Jasi-ji," Jago said.

"And those with two parents," Bren said. "Jase and I talked about it, how the crew knows who's allied with whom; but outsiders wouldn't. And they *haven't* confined their children outside the Bu-javid, so to speak. And politics of personal relationship does exist."

Jago raised a brow. "One sees where there is no choice."

"No choice indeed. No other place."

Jago heaved a deep sigh. "And how shall we map these relationships? How does one perceive them?"

"One simply knows who's in bed with whom." He laughed. "It's a saying, in Mosphei'. It changes their man'-chi. Or flings them out of it, when the relationship fractures. And it's common, Jago-ji; the fractures are common. We have social structures . . . I'm sure within the ship they exist . . . to make interaction possible. Feud isn't allowed."

A second lift of the brow. "That was not a feud that invaded the mainland? One could have mistaken it, Bren-ji."

It was worth a wry smile. A shrug. "Politics is ideally separate from bloodline," he said. "Not historically true, but true nowadays. Humans did have ethnicities, once. And family ties, even smaller. But humans here have had no ethnicities, until the ship came back. Now they don't know what's happened to them. Now the Mospheirans may learn to think *atevi* are the more familiar culture."

"One doesn't know what the world would be like without humans," Jago said somberly. "Different. I don't think many would like to go without television, without the *aishidi'tat.*"

"I think humans have gotten rather used to fresh fruit, and the knowledge the aiji will stop any armed conflict. It's a sense of safety. Since the ship came back, that safety is threatened, at the very moment we seemed to have realized we had it."

"So for us. Just when we realized humans were valuable, we discover they have inconvenient relatives."

He laughed; he had to. "Our lives are *machimi*," he said. "The relatives come over the hill, and want a share of the hunt."

"And shall they have it?"

He considered what was at issue. "I think there's room,"

he said, "considering all of space, considering they've been industrious on their own. We simply have to add another wing to the house."

"So," Jago said. "Up here."

"Up here," he said, "where it doesn't spoil the view. — How will it be for atevi to live here? It's an important question. My household is the first to be able to judge. And you *have* to judge. I can't know whether what I'm doing, to gain the atevi their place up here, can be tolerable for you, or whether I have to modify everything to allow atevi to come and go continually. Might atevi be born here, and live here? On what you say, Jago-ji, I set great importance. Can you think of such a thing?"

Jago looked up, at the ceiling, at the lights, around at the room, very solemnly, before she looked at him again. "Atevi who live here will have man'chi to whoever leads them," she said. "And will they be within the *aishidi'tat?* I can't foresee. But when there are children, when there are households, they will not be under the captains, Bren-ji. They will never be under the captains."

"I don't think the captains worry about that so much as they worry about having no port at all." He had to amend that, in all knowledge he had of humans. "To teach the captains that they simply have to deal differently . . . that's a frightening task, Jago-ji. It does daunt me."

"It daunts anyone who thinks of it," Jago said. "They must be very wise, not so *kabiu* atevi who come here to deal with the ship-humans."

Not so *kabiu.* Not so proper. Not so observant of traditions of food and manners and philosophy.

"Not to be *kabiu* makes for rapid change," he said. "Perhaps unwise change."

Jago thought about that a moment. "The paidhi might see very clearly on that point," she said. "Perhaps we *would* change very rapidly here. And there would be problems."

The thought haunted him. He wrote to Tabini:

I have conversed with my staff regarding the attitudes that this place engenders within atevi at the sight of these corridors and this stark sameness and have discussed with my second security personnel the matter of kabiu, *whether it may be an essential safeguard to atevi against too rapid a change of man'chi. I think there may be merit in this view and wish that wise heads consider the matter. I brought no camera. This is an error I intend to remedy on my next visit. It is difficult to describe how foreign this place is to atevi.*

Yet the very foreignness may assist to confirm man'chi within the aishidi'tat: and certainly the small touches my staff has added have provided relief to the eyes and heart.

I wish that the aiji might give particular thought to deep questions of man'chi for those generations resident here, considering a residence as foreign as a cave strung with lights combined with the difficulty of maintaining close ties with relatives on the planet. The psychological elements are beyond my judgment, yet I continue in my belief that atevi authority here must be represented. Therefore I do not alter my course, and depend on others' judgment as to my wisdom in doing so.

Meanwhile I expect the Mospheirans to be our guests at supper, and hope that we may achieve agreement among representatives of the planet in the face of what may still be hard and divisive negotiations.

Kaplan brought the Mospheirans, at the appointed hour . . . lacking only Shugart, a fact Bren noted as Narani opened the door and admitted them to what was, de facto, the reception hall and their central corridor at once.

Shugart, clearly, was the home guard, the defense against tampering in their absence. Kroger continued to be cautious . . . as they were cautious. Algini had shut the door to their own guard post and had no intention of opening it at any point the guests might be in a position to see into that room.

Just for symmetry, and not to make too much of an issue of one closed door, Bren had likewise shut the door to his own room, leaving only the dining room and the servants' quarters doors open, across from one another at the end of the hall.

Kroger, Lund, and Feldman, the latter of whom had no status with the other two, clearly, and who stood somewhat to the rear as the hand-shaking and greeting proceeded.

So did Kaplan, a walking listening post who had to be shut out or otherwise occupied.

And who, like his own security, would have no supper with the rest.

When in Rome, a very old saying went. And this whole station was Rome, and the customs uncertain.

"Kaplan. Would you like something to eat?"

"Duty, sir."

"Sure?"

Kaplan, behind all the gear, inhaled deeply. The galley fragrances permeated the corridor. The visible eye was wide, nervous, the mouth . . . a little less resolute.

"Tano, would you see Kaplan-nadi has food?" He changed languages. "Ms. Kroger, Kaplan's going to have supper with Tano, here. Tano-ji:" Another language switch. "I think we have some of those fruit sweets, don't we, the ones Jase is fond of? Kaplan might find those a novel taste. Have we enough to spare, nadi?"

"One believes so," Tano said.

"Ben might have supper with them, perhaps." Kroger leaped on a chance to shed the translator, who looked somewhat disappointed, doubtless at missing the formal meal.

But if Kroger wanted to talk business at supper, that was the Mospheiran habit: and they might supply Ben quite handily. "Do," he said. "Ginny. Tom. Come along. Supper's delicate, doesn't like waiting."

"I trust they've watched the poisons," Kroger said.

"Oh, absolutely," Bren said. "We'll send along a dinner for Shugart, too. We'll have one made up."

"You're very well supplied," Lund observed.

"Always," Bren said. "It's just the habit. One I like very well." He escorted his guests into the room, translated the amenities to Narani and the others of his staff, seated himself and them. Banichi and Jago absented themselves, on prior protocols . . . not that they necessarily took for granted the lordly rank of the Mospheiran delegation, but out of convenience. Kandana deftly whisked away extra settings for Feldman and Shugart, changed bouquets to a felicitous combination for three, and added a dish of candy so deftly the Mospheirans hardly missed a word in the running chatter.

"Have you heard from the captains?"

"Nothing beyond the appointment I have tomorrow,"

Bren answered. "With how many at once wasn't clear. Definitely with Sabin."

"Mmn," Kroger said. "And what do you propose to discuss?"

"Anything Sabin wishes to discuss: reconstruction of the station, agreements for the building they want done. I utterly reserve the discussion of business interests *on* the station for you and your mission."

Kroger by no means looked unhappy at that.

"Have *you* had any message from them?" Bren asked.

"From Ogun, a request to meet, on what business isn't clear."

"Interesting. Divide and conquer? I think we should communicate what we learn and agree. More, I think we should *coordinate* what we agree, present a unified package to our governments."

"No exterior work for our citizens," Kroger said definitively.

"Franchises," Lund said. "Coordinated to atevi opening sections up for settlement."

"Both very agreeable," Bren said, "and I leave the distribution of the franchises to wiser heads than mine. The exterior work . . . atevi will undertake with appropriate safeguards."

Kroger heard him out, leaning back in her chair, eyes narrowed. A pause that lengthened into significance later, she said slowly, deliberately: "Let me tell you a theory, Mr. Cameron."

"Bren."

"Bren." By now, Kroger seemed amused. "Let me give you a word. Robotics."

"It's an interesting word."

"A very industry-heavy word. And the means by which you *might* operate—the only means by which Mospheirans *would* have worked outside, had I anything to say about it. Robots are the prevailing thought in Science about how to proceed with station repair, but we've lacked certain key information. Information that was in those archives, those *damnably* hard to obtain archives. I've found the records— two days solid, I've spent chasing the information down."

He'd heard the theories, in passing, but had paid little attention. He was listening now.

She leaned forward. "We lost the robots at the first star, such as we had, which was only the handful necessary to gather materials to manufacture the numbers required to construct a station, is the official word. Instead, our ancestors found themselves forced to use that handful in an environment that chewed through metal as fast as it ate human flesh. We arrived here, found an only marginally less hostile environment, and rather than use the resources, we risked lives to obtain or to repair those robots, and to build new ones, we risked more lives."

"Why?" Bren asked, not quite the first time he had heard the story, but never in this environment, never with the sanction of a senior representative from Science, never coupled with the understanding *why* robots hadn't been a viable option. It was something ruled out long ago. Wise agencies had said robots failed where heroic human beings succeeded. It was part of the legend of the arrival at the star.

Kroger's mouth tightened into a hard smile. "Offically? Officially, two things militated against that piece of common sense, first that we didn't have the resources to build the robots to get the resources, second, that in the Guild's management of things, getting the resources was an extreme priority."

"And unofficially?"

"We suspected but could never prove that the Guild wanted to keep the colonist population busy: by maintaining the extreme emphasis on heroism, on risk, they might keep the colonists willing to relocate. The Guild, according to those records, had a two-step plan for getting out of this system. The Guild, according to those records, wanted to relocate to Maudit."

This was new, utterly. Maudit, the place Kroger was saying the Guild had wanted to go, was the next system-site out from the earth of the atevi, a not-quite-planet in a thick asteroid belt.

"The Guild *hoped* we'd go on to our target star once we'd just gathered resources here. This spot, in orbit around an inner planet, was safer—or so they believed—for interim measures, but the Guild *hoped* we'd simply establish a small base until we had population enough to go out to Maudit's orbit and operate there, where off-planet metal is hazardously

nore common. The well-known fact is, we damned near lost
he colony, as was. This is a dirty system, Mr. Cameron, in
very sense. This planet meets meteor swarms. We didn't
ave that tracked; we were strangers to the system; we had
no wealth of advance data on that fine a scale. Where we
ame from, we knew these hazards, but not to this degree,
nd this degree was lethal to the equipment."

Lethal. The possibilities he'd begun to imagine took a
evere blow.

"Do those mining robots still exist?"

"Hard to say. The big robots, the extrusion molders, survived—the station itself is evidence of that. They seem still
o exist—somewhere on this station, according to the records.
But the smaller ones, the machines that could safely mine the
asteroids . . ." She shrugged. "The Guild has only opened a
raction of the station up so far. From those records, I believe
one or two might still be in storage in Section Five. Most
vere cannibalized for their metal: in those first days it was
he *only* nearby metal we could lay hands on."

"Can we make them work?"

"Mr. Cameron . . . Bren . . . *if* they still exist, *if* your atevi
an make them run, they may well *function,* but they won't
vork. Hardening. That's another word I give to you. The lack
of it on our initial equipment is why we suffered so much
damage: we weren't prepared for the environment we went
into; we damnsure weren't prepared for this one. The prob-
em with making the miner-bots work, then, launched in a
dirty system with minimal information, was getting the resources for spare parts. The problem with making them work
now and with any degree of economic viability is making
hem less vulnerable. In that archive, we have specifications,
however none of them are going to enable a robot *or* a
manned craft to operate safely in this system, let alone
efficiently. What I am *also* sure of is that we can do better.
You want atevi to do it all, Mr. Cameron . . . *Bren.* But
et me suggest that atevi manufacturing and design *linked*
o Mospheiran resources for electronics, optics, *and robotics,* can save a good many lives. *We can do better.*"

He was a translator, a maker of dictionaries, who had
had to learn far more about physics and engineering than
he had ever planned to know in the process of performing

his job. There were certain topics on which he was naïve and the specifics of items locked up within specialized departments of the Mospheiran establishment contained many such topics.

"I find this very interesting," he said. He utterly forgave the tone. "Go on."

"Joint effort, joint development."

"An atevi-Mospheiran company," Tom Lund said. "Manufacturing these things."

"Still interesting," Bren said. He'd envisioned shielding, to protect atevi operators. But shielding meant mass, and it became another worm-swallowing-its-tail situation: fuel to run the miners that gathered the fuel. Removing all that mass from the equation—atevi, shielding and the life support—meant fuel savings, but the same problem held true, as Kroger had pointed out, if robotic equipment ate up all its profits in repairs. If their proposed space industry ever entered diminishing returns, the situation could become again what drove colonists off the station and onto the planet, when *Phoenix* had drunk up all the fuel, all the resources, all that the colonists could do, because the captains of that long ago day had believed they could go off and find the earth of humans.

A lot of history had happened since then. The captains that had come back were dealing with a planetary population and an industry base that *was* capable. Capable not only of the manufacturing the Guild knew it wanted, but of analyzing what went wrong the first time and doing it right the second.

The solar system had proved capable of delivering nasty surprises, he'd known that from the incomplete records. He'd known, when he came to propose the atevi as miners, that those nasty surprises were a problem needing a solution. *How* extensive a problem, he'd had to wait for those archived records to determine.

Astronomical observation, the tracking of celestial objects, had been lacking for several centuries among the atevi: astronomy having become a science in disgrace since the astronomers had failed to predict the Foreign Star in their skies. Even with the new revolution in the field, with the Astronomer Emeritus and his work, atevi were *still* unware of cosmic debris that didn't make annual appearances as falling stars.

The Mospheirans had been even less curious about the lethal environment from which they'd escaped. The region of the solar system where they had to work to supply *Phoenix* and the station, let alone this new ship the captains wanted, was unmapped except in historical records he hoped were in that download.

He had expected bad news from those records and the initial surveys; but this . . . this robotics development . . . was an interesting piece of information from outside his domain.

He began to see much more accurately what they were up against.

He began to see all his proposals as achievable.

Still, she had raised questions . . . questions that definitely touched on his realm of expertise.

"You're saying it was a political consideration that killed the robots."

"Political and practical," Kroger said. "Political, because manned mining was part of the mystique; because the colonist faction was doing the mining and possibly the leaders feared if the robots replaced the miners they'd lose their political clout."

"Is there proof of that?"

"It's my own suspicion," Kroger said, "and there's no proof. But I don't think there were saints on either side. There was *some reason* the colonists didn't push for robotic development when they were dying left and right; there was *some reason* leadership didn't press for a delay of the ship fueling and a rearrangement of priorities, to get robots that worked. Possibly it was simple ignorance. Possibly it was ideological blindness. We've seen a bit of that in our generation. The fact was, the radicals among the colonists suspected *everything* the Guild proposed, by that point in time. If the Guild proposed it, there must be an ulterior motive. And the radicals were in charge. As long as their people kept dying at a sustainable rate, the anger of the colonists kept them going."

"I don't like to think so," Bren said, "but I've no way to deny your thesis."

"It *could have been done,*" Kroger said. "And they didn't do it. The political pressure for a landing built and built."

"The question is," Bren said, "whether the robots weren't built because they *couldn't* work, or whether you're right. I'd hope there's a third answer. I really hope there's a third answer, that we can't have been that venal."

"Both factions had a greater good at issue," Kroger said. "Both factions thought they were right, that if they gave in on one point, they'd erode all they had. Desperate, suspicious times. Both sides thought they *all* would die if they didn't have their way. *Robots.* Common damned *sense,* Mr. Cameron!"

"And a joint company," Lund said. "Your large-scale engineering, our electronics, our control devices."

"I see no difficulty in agreement," Bren said. "I see no difficulty at all." His own people had a plan, buried deep within the departments of the government, but, thank God a *plan,* and a viable one. He was for the first time in a decade *proud* to be Mospheiran. "Can you deliver it?"

Kroger let go a long, shaky breath. "Mr. Cameron, seventeen of us have spent our *careers* assuring we can deliver it. We *know* the metallurgy—and damned hard that's been to develop with all the materials having to be imported from the mainland—but damn, we've *done* it. For the robotics, the specific designs . . . that was a problem. The records had been lost. We just got those records, Mr. Cameron."

"If the archive *should* have those plans," Bren began, and Kroger lowered her fist onto the table.

"The archive *does* have them, Cameron. It does. I looked. I knew what the files ought to be, where they ought to be. I've worked my whole *life* around that hole in the records, and believe me I know where to look in the archive."

Her whole life . . . was that merely a figure of speech?

How long? Bren wondered with a nervous and sudden chill. How long had Kroger been working on this notion? More than three years back threw her into the whole pro-space movement, which had its roots in the Heritage Party, Gaylord Hanks' party, with all its anti-atevi sentiment.

But that didn't mean everyone who'd ever taken that

route because it was the only route for pro-spacers was automatically Gaylord Hanks' soulmate. Their proposal, just voiced, was a pro-space proposal, but it wasn't anti-atevi. That the Heritage Party might have drawn in the honest and sensible, the dreamers with a willingness to ignore the darker side of their associations . . . it was possible.

Kroger, whatever else, was not a fool. She sat enjoying supper in an atevi household and proposing, with Lund, *cooperation*. Proposing a program that would save atevi lives if the aiji undertook the rough part of the operation. Proposing to better what he'd envisioned and give her benefit to the project.

"I thought you might be Hanks' partisan," he said. "And now I don't think you are. I think you're an honest negotiator, Ms. Kroger. *Dr.* Kroger. Mr. Lund, the same. I think this might be entirely viable."

Kroger said: "Damn Gaylord Hanks, Mr. Cameron. No *few* of us damn Gaylord Hanks."

"Damn Gaylord Hanks?" Lund said, with a sudden, cheerful smile. Kroger had somewhat neglected her main course in the passion of argument, but Lund had demolished his, looking up sharply now and again, clearly paying attention. "I *know* Gaylord Hanks. I've known him since school days, and now a lot of people know him. The Heritage Party has another wing, I'm glad to say, and Hanks can take a rowboat north for what most of us think."

"So I have the Heritage party for guests." He'd picked up the prior signals of Kroger's attitudes, the unconscious statements of prejudice; he didn't see them in evidence at this table, in this room. He took that for a signal, perhaps, of a woman who'd adopted protective coloration, perhaps in a bid for survival.

"Certainly not Hanks' followers," Kroger said. "Neither one of us. I'm not a dogmatist; I'm a scientist. Tom's an economist, performs wizardry, odd moments of magic, I don't know what; but he's no more a follower of Hanks than I am or you are."

"That's quite good news."

"There was quiet cheering inside the party when the invasion bounced off the shores," Lund said. "That's not publicized, but, God, that wasn't a direction we ought to have gone, and no few of us knew it. We didn't have the means to stop it. There was cheering in some quarters when the ship came back; there isn't, yet, in others, and in some surprising quarters: some of the pro-spacers don't want it. They'd wanted to do it themselves, if you want the honest truth; they damned sure didn't want another Guild dominion."

"I know these people," Bren said quietly.

"Robotics," Kroger reiterated. "What we should have done from the beginning, what we couldn't do then, what we *can* do now."

And from Tom Lund: "You're not alone, Bren. Not you, not the atevi. Others share your enthusiasm for this new opportunity. Believe that, if nothing else."

"I do believe you," he said. "And I'm very willing to take this to the aiji with a strong recommendation."

There was a small silence at the table, a trembling, hope-fraught kind of silence.

"Well!" Lund said. *"Well!* Good! But I trust this room is secure. We understand your principals are rather good at that sort of thing."

"They are."

"Promise Sabin what you have to," Lund said quietly, "and let's get our own agreement nailed down, together, present a deal signed and sealed. *Then* tell the captains."

Bren gave a small, conscious smile, thinking to himself that these two were a tolerably good team. Sometimes Kroger seemed in charge, sometimes Lund, and he began to get the feeling that they were accustomed to sandbagging their way to agreements, much as the aiji was.

But these two were from inside the Heritage establishment, the pro-space wing, perhaps, perhaps some more convolute—*association* was an atevi word, one with emotional depth, and implicit unity. *Coalition* of interests seemed more apt, a human way of operating quite similar and quite different from ways atevi would understand.

"I'll reserve what we've discussed," he said, "and we'll continue discussing it. This venue *is* secure. It's one reason I encouraged you to come here. I hope you'll come back."

"Every intention to," Kroger said.

It was a success, an unqualified success, Bren said to

himself. Obstacles were falling down left and right because
the situation mandated cooperation and old, old rivalries
and attitudes didn't survive the encounter. It wasn't *his* triumph; it was the triumph of basic common sense, after a
long night of bad decisions. Three years of diminished
power for Gaylord Hanks and Mospheirans had gathered
up their wits and brought the likes of Ginny Kroger into
striking distance of a patient, lifelong work. The pro-spacers had made their move.

Thank *God*, he thought.

The servants had carried on their business in near-si-
lence, dealing in small signals, whisking courses onto and
off the table. Only at the end, Bren signaled Narani to
come and meet the guests, whom he introduced in Ragi,
with translation, and said, in Mosphei', "A nod of the head
is courteous. One doesn't rise or take their hands."

His guests showed that courtesy; the servant staff lined
up and bowed in great delight, and there were smiles all
around, that gesture both species, both remote genetic heri-
tages, shared . . . he'd never so much wondered at it or
thought it odd until he saw Bindanda and Kroger smile at
each other, both looking entirely self-conscious, each in
their own native way . . . convenient in an upright species
to unfocus the hunting gaze, perhaps, this bowing and smiling: hard to glare and smile simultaneously.

"Very fine," he said in Ragi. "Thank you, Narani-ji, so
very much. Is the staff managing with Kaplan-nadi and with
Ben-nadi?"

"Very well, nandi," Narani said, sounding pleased with
himself; and courtesies wended toward a late drink and a
social moment, which stretched on uncommonly at table.
They were short of a sitting room and the lord's bedchamber seemed less appropriate for foreign guests.

Narani had put together a supper for Shugart, alone at
her post; and that ended up in Feldman's hands as the
guests departed, with Banichi and Tano and Jago there to
bid them all a farewell, Kaplan in his array of electronics .
. . he had at least put off the eyepiece to have supper, and
had stuffed himself with food and fruit sweets, so Bren
discovered.

"He liked them quite emphatically," Jago said, "and had

eaten far too much to enjoy them, and wished more. So we quite by chance suggested through Ben-nadi that he put some in his pockets."

"He was very pleased," Tano said. "Like Jase, he had never had such strong tastes."

"One hopes he *is* careful," Bren said.

Fruits. Vegetables. Jase called them water-tastes and earth-tastes, and said they made his nose water. It hadn't stopped him making himself sick on them. Tano knew, and he trusted Tano had warned Kaplan before stuffing his pockets full.

Fruit sweets.

Kaplan's first taste. *There* was one of the likely first imports. Jase had said he would miss the fruit most of all.

And wouldn't have to miss it long, if the meeting tomorrow went well, and if they gained agreement with the captains.

Send and receive produced no messages from Toby. A *hello, Jill and I have made up our arguments and everything's fine* would have capped off the evening beyond any fault.

But that there wasn't . . . that was understandable. He'd been too damned much in Toby's life the last several years; it was more than time to leave Toby to settle his own life, his own marriage . . . his own kids. He had to keep hands off.

Meanwhile he had a small flood of messages answering the morning's mail, answers from the mainland, a note from the office asking on what priority they might be translating the transmission of what was, in effect, the archive, and *that* was a question that deserved an answer on better information than he had at the moment. He needed to compose a query to the University to see whether they might release what index they compiled.

Algini, meanwhile, was freed from his isolation, having had supper slipped in to his station. His security needed a briefing, and he provided it, a rapid, Ragi digest of what he had discussed with Kroger and Lund.

"Computer-operated machines," he said, but that was too cumbersome. *Roboti* sounded distressingly like a vulgar word for lunatic, which would never inspire atevi workers to trust them.

"Botiin." he said, which sounded like *guide* or *ruler*. "Like manufacturing machines, but capable of traveling out to the job, in the very dangerous regions. One sits back in safety and directs them."

"Air traffic control," Banichi said, which summed up a great deal of what atevi thought odd about Mospheiran ways, a system about which there was *still* fierce debate, regarding individual rights of way and historic precedences, *and* felicity of numbers.

He had to laugh, ruefully so, foreseeing a battle on his hands—but one he could win.

One he *would* win. "I have a letter to write to Tabini," he said to his earnest staff. "I want you to help me make it *sound* better than air traffic control."

They thought *that* was funny, and he went off to his evening shower with that good humor, undressed, preoccupied with the explanation of robots, entered the shower, preoccupied with the query about translation of an index for atevi access to the archive.

He scrubbed vigorously, happier than he'd been in years.

He expected a counteroffer tomorrow. He also expected *not* to get one. Possibly the captains were making an approach to Kroger's party, and certainly the captains were informed the guests had been putting their heads together in private discussions. There would be anxiousness on that score.

The water went cold. Bitter, burning cold. Pitch darkness. Silence.

"Damn!" he shouted, for a moment lost, then galvanized by the sense of emergency. He exited the shower, in the utter dark, feeling his way.

And saw a faint light, a hand torch, in the hallway.

Atevi shadows moved out there. One light source came in, bearing a hand torch, spotting him in the light. He flung his arms up and the light diverted, bounced off the walls in more subdued fashion.

"The power seems to have failed," Jago said.

"I'm all over lather," he said, still shaken. "Things were going entirely too well, I fear. Nadi-ji, please inform the staff. Power here is life and death. I trust the fuel cylinders in the galley will hold a while for warmth, but I understand warmth can go very quickly. Be moderate with them. Gather the staff near the galley."

"They should last a time," Jago said. "So should our equipment." Bindanda joined her, and moved in dismay to offer a robe.

He accepted it. "Warm water, if you please." Outrageous demands were not outrageous if it meant giving the staff something to do, and he was covered in soap. "I'll finish my bath."

"Immediately, nandi."

Immediately was not quite possible, and he had all too much time to listen to his staff bearing with the disaster, to attempt the communications panel, and to find it not working.

Warm water did arrive in reasonably short order, all the same, and Bindanda assisted him in rinsing off the soap, a hand torch posed like a candlestick on the counter.

"Very fine," Bren said with chattering teeth, trying not to think of a general power failure.

A large shadow appeared against the dim glow of the hall. "Bren-ji?"

Banichi.

"Any news?" He expected none. "If power has gone down, there *will* be the ship itself, trusting this isn't the alien attack."

"That would be very bad news," Banichi said in that vast calm of his.

But in that moment a sound came from the vents. The fans started up, failed.

"Well," Bren said. "They're trying to fix it. The air is trying to come through." He seized up the damp, still-soapy robe, with the notion of reaching C1 if there were moments of power, and Bindanda hastily snatched the robe away, substituting a dry coverlet. Bren gathered that about his shoulders and punched in C1.

There was no answer.

"The lock is electronic," Banichi said, "and we can access it, to the exterior of this section."

"We aren't completely sure there's air on the other side

of the door," Bren said, wishing they might supply power to the panel; but that did no good if no one was listening. "Do we have radio, Banichi-ji?"

"We have," Banichi said confidently. "We would rather not use it."

"Understood," Bren said. "Perfectly." He was comforted to think that, in extremity, they might have a means to contact the ship or the shuttle itself, hoping for some word of what was going on outside their section.

The lights came on. Fans resumed moving air.

He and Banichi looked at one another with all manner of speculations; and he heaved a great sigh.

"Well," he said to Banichi, "presumably it will go on working. Conserve, until we know what's happening."

"One will do so," Banichi said. "In the meantime . . . we'll attempt to learn."

"Wait," he said, and tried C1 again. "C1. What's going on? Do you hear me?"

"The emergency is over," C1 answered, not the main shift man, but a woman's voice. *"There's no need for alarm."*

"Does that happen often, C1? What *did* happen?"

"I believe a technical crew is attempting to rectify the problem, sir. It's a minor difficulty. Out, sir."

C1 punched out. C1 might have other problems on her hands. God knew what problems.

"It's not an alien invasion," he said to Banichi. "The central communications officer claims not to know the cause."

Banichi might have understood that much.

"One wonders how general it was," Banichi said. Jago had appeared, and there was some uncommon calling back and forth among the staff, confirming switches, in the hall.

"I've no idea," Bren said. "C1 certainly knew about it."

"One should rest, Bren-ji," Jago said. "One of us is always on watch."

He had no doubt. And he had no doubt of the rightness of the advice, no matter what was going on technically with the station.

There was not another alarm in the nighttime.

In the morning he was not utterly surprised to hear C1 say that Sabin had canceled their scheduled meeting; he was not utterly surprised to hear that there were no communications with Mogari-nai. The earthlink was down. Neither ship nor station was communicating with anyone.

"Is there still an emergency?" he asked. "Is the station intact?"

"Perfectly intact, sir," C1 answered, the regular, daytime C1, which reassured him. *"Sorry. I don't have the details. I have to shut down now."*

Disappointing, to say the least. He went to report the situation to his staff, that the day's schedule had changed.

"I don't know why," he said to the staff. "We felt no impact, as if there were explosion, or a piece of debris, but I don't know that we might, on so large a structure. I'll work in, today. Simply do what needs doing."

It was a slow day, in some regards, a frustrating, worrisome day, but power at least stayed rock-steady.

He made notes on the discussion with Kroger. He answered letters. He wrote letters . . . restrained himself from writing to Toby, and asked himself whether the link was going to be in operation.

There was a quiet supper. He had pronounced himself not particularly hungry, and perhaps a little overindulged from the day prior. "I get very little exercise here," he said to Narani, "I don't walk enough. Satisfy the staff, certainly. But I have no need for more than a bowl of soup."

He was primarily concerned, after his day's work, to have the earthlink function smoothly, and it seemed to.

But the messages were all from the mainland.

"Put me through to Jase Graham," he said, the ritual he and C1 had established.

"Sir, he's still in conference."

"I thought he might be rather less busy with the station's problems."

"I'm told he's still in meetings."

"Yolanda Mercheson?"

"Still in meetings."

"Captain Sabin."

"Still in meetings, sir, I'm sorry."

"Captain Ramirez."

"Sir, all the captains are in meetings."

One wondered if anything was getting done anywhere on

the ship or the station. He wanted to be cheerful for his servants' sake, but was glum at heart, surer and surer that Ramirez had not pulled off his majority, and that the meetings Jase and Yolanda were involved in likely involved sitting under guard, in isolation, and answering occasional questions from a deadlocked association of captains.

And that was the most optimistic view.

A shadow appeared by his bed, utterly silent—just *loomed*, utterly black, and his heart jumped in fright.

"Do you wish?" Jago's lowest voice. "Nadi?"

"Bren-ji," he corrected this slide toward formality. "Some aspects of this being a lord I don't like. Sit down." He made room for her on the narrow bed, realizing at the same time that she and he wouldn't fit it, or at least, not comfortably.

He shifted to give her room, her arms came about him. Deeper thought and glum mood both went sliding away, in favor of a thoroughly comfortable association and the easy, gentle comfort of her embrace. He heaved a sigh, not obliged even to carry his weight, not with Jago, who supported him without any thought. Her breath stirred his hair, ran like a breath of summer over his shoulder, and for the next while, and right down to the edge of sleep, he didn't think.

But he felt a certain uneasiness, a certain sense of embarrassment, the rooms were so small, the staff pressed so close. The bed required close maneuvering.

"You can't be comfortable here," he said. "Don't wake with a kink in your back, on my account."

"I have no difficulty," she said.

He was habitually cold; he wasn't, while she was in bed. But he truly didn't want the closeness of the quarters here to create a difficulty.

"Perhaps you should go for other reasons," he whispered to her. He always felt guilty for the relationship, the event, whatever she might call it. She had a partner. To this hour he had no idea whether her being here represented some allowed breach of that partnership, or what the relationship was between her and Banichi—which was a trust he had absolutely no willingness to betray. They had never been at such close quarters. She'd always assured him Banichi understood, understood, understood, but he was uneasy, tonight.

"What other reasons?"

"Getting some sleep, for one."

"I might sleep, if nand' paidhi weren't talking."

"That's not the point," he said, and felt the tension he created. "The whole staff must know, Jago-ji."

He felt, rather than heard, her laughter. "One is certain they do."

He couldn't bear the evasions any longer. He slid free and rested precariously on an arm near the edge where he could be absolutely face to face with her. "Jago-ji. I will not hurt Banichi. I have every regard for you, and I know *you* would never disregard him, but I worry, Jago-ji, I do worry what he thinks."

"He is amused."

"I know you say that, but a man is a man, and people are people, and they can say something, but it doesn't make it so, Jago-ji. I have no wish to offend him. I would be devastated to create a breach between you."

"There is none. There has never been one."

"Are you lovers, Jago-ji?" He'd chased that question all the years of their partnership. "Have you been, forgive me that I ask, but this causes me a great deal of guilt and worry—" He was under assault, and he fended it off, determined to get out what he had tried a dozen times to express. "—Guilt and worry, that I ever crossed any barrier that I might not have understood. . . ."

Jago's body heaved gently. After an instant he knew she was laughing. A callused, gentle hand moved slowly across his shoulder. "Bren-ji. No."

"What do you mean, no, nadi? Have you been lovers?"

"Bren-ji. He is my *father*."

He was stunned. He rolled back, fell back onto the pillow and stared at the ceiling. The whole universe shifted vector.

Then the thin mattress gave, and the general dim dark gave way to Jago's outline, her elbow posed on the other side of him, her fingers tracing their way down from his chin.

Amused, she said. Banichi was amused at their carrying-on.

Not disapproving.

But her *father?*

"Bren-ji. We do not make relationships public, in our Guild. I tell you as a confidence."

"I respect it."

"One knows without doubt the paidhi is discreet," Jago said, and found his ear, found his hands . . . outmaneuvering Jago was difficult, and he had no interest in trying that. For the first time he had a relatively clear conscience in her regard, and a joke to avenge. He pulled her close, dismissing the proximity of the servants as any concern to them.

They ran unexpectedly out of bed, on the edge, and nearly over it.

Jago simply rolled out of it, taking him and the sheets with her, and laughed.

18

Jago was gone before dawn, and he was in bed when he waked, in bed with the smell of breakfast wafting through the hall.

Bindanda and Kandana were a little reluctant to meet his eye. Had he and Jago embarrassed the whole staff, Bren wondered, chagrined. He found nothing to say, and thought he should ask Jago . . . he truly, urgently should ask someone what the staff was saying. It could hardly be Banichi; he couldn't envision that conversation. He knew he would blush. Jago might be the recipient of merciless amusement, and she was hardly the one to ask.

He thought perhaps he could speak to Tano . . . certainly to Tano, rather than staid, dignified Narani. He could manage to do that on the way to breakfast, which otherwise might be a very uncomfortable affair.

He had chosen less than formal wear for a day on which he had no schedule but deskwork: a sweater and a light pair of trousers with an outdoor jacket, about adequate for the chill of the air, after which he dismissed Bindanda and Kandana, opened up his computer, and went through the send-receive with C1, and through the usual litany of questions, refusing to give up on Jase or Yolanda or on direct contact with the captains, three of whom he was anxious to hear from.

No message from Toby, none from his mother, nothing this time even from Tabini, who was probably considering the last one, or who simply had things to do other than give the paidhi daily reassurances. Two advertisements had slipped into the packet, one for bed linens and the other for fishing gear, and he scrutinized them briefly for any content from the Foreign Office, any hint that someone had sent him something clandestine. It was a north shore fishing gear manufacturer, one Toby used.

But it was simply one of those hiccups of the communications filter. His mailbox on the island received such things, and he had no staff left there to filter them.

A message from the head of the Transport Committee reported on progress in the new spaceport. They were better than their schedule.

He half-zipped his jacket and went out into the hallway in a routine hurry for breakfast.

And ran chest-high into a stranger.

He recoiled, immediate in everything his security had dinned into him, achieved distance and was a muscle-twitch from diving backward into the door before his vision realized chagrin and offered respect on the other side of the encounter.

Atevi presence on the station was entirely limited, and more, he knew this man: the name escaped him, as his heart pounded, but it was one of the stewards from the shuttle.

"Nand' paidhi," the man said with a second bow. "Your pardon. Nojana, of the aiji's crew of *Shai-shan*."

"Of course you are," Bren exclaimed, taking a hasty breath. "How did *you* get here?"

He was no longer alone in the hallway. Almost as quickly as he had backed up, the noise of his move had attracted Tano and Algini and Jago out of the security station, and Bindanda from the dining room . . . which might say something about Bindanda's Guild associations: Bren noted *that* in the aftermath of adrenaline.

"Banichi sent me, nand' paidhi," Nojana said. "He wished to confer with the captain."

"Parijo. The shuttle captain." There were entirely too many captains in the broth.

"Even so, nand' paidhi." Nojana, in fact, was not wearing a steward's uniform, but the black of the Assassins' Guild . . . *security's* Guild, and by the height and breadth of the steward, it was Banichi's body type, Banichi's muscled arms and shoulders. This was not a man accustomed to passing out drinks and motion sickness pills, but it had not been so evident in his previous uniform.

"And is this *your* uniform, nadi?"

"No, nand' paidhi, it is not."

"And how long have you been here?"

"Since midnight, nandi."

Bren cast a look at his own security, and, with a feeling of mild indignation, directly at Jago, whose arrival in his quarters, whose determined distraction had left not a shred of attention to the fact the seal-door had opened and closed last night.

Jago, to her credit, met his gaze with a satisfied lift of her chin and the ghost of a smile.

It did beat drugging his drink, he said to himself, and he had no suspicion whatever that Jago had been dishonest in lovemaking, only that she'd had a considerable ulterior motive.

And he would not call down his senior staff in front of a stranger, or in front of the servants. He simply composed himself, smiled, nodded acknowledgment of a successful operation, namely deceiving the paidhi, and getting Banichi outside without consulting him—and directed his inquiry to Nojana.

"And have you had breakfast, nadi, and will you join us?"

"I had tea at my arrival, nandi, and I thank the paidhi for the kindness of his offer, nothing since. I would be very honored."

"Do join us, then," he said, and surrendered Nojana to the guidance of Tano and Algini, with a single glance.

Jago he stayed with a lowering of his brows.

"How in hell?" he said in a half-whisper. "How did he *get* there? Did they come after him . . ." He could envision that the shuttle crew might have some sense of the station: this was not their first trip. ". . . or did he use the map?" Even with that, it was a risk, not least of running afoul of the ship-captains and the likes of Kaplan. He was thoroughly appalled. Chilled by the very thought . . . and yet if Banichi had done anything of the sort, he trusted it was well-thought. "Jago, I know what you did. I'm not angry. But *what is he doing?*"

"He wishes to be sure the shuttle is on schedule."

"Have we established that?"

"Nojana says yes. There's been no difficulty at all. Nominal in all respects. It might leave early, except for small details."

"I've no need to have it leave early, or is there something going on I don't know?"

"One wishes to be certain. Banichi has been concerned about the behavior of the captains."

He was concerned, in that regard. But to go off across a trackless maze of corridors . . .

"What if he'd been stopped?"

"He would have been surveying for the station repairs, on his own initiative."

As a lie it was a decent one. "And what if he'd just gotten *lost?* They've done alterations since the charts we have, Jago-ji! How did *Nojana* get here? You surely didn't ask Kaplan."

"No," Jago said pleasantly, with a little shrug. "By no means Kaplan. They've not made signs, you think, so that the Mospheirans might lose their way."

"So that we would lose our way. You're saying you don't."

A second small shrug. "We *walked* from that area, Bren-ji."

It was rare these days that an atevi-human difference utterly took him blindside. He drew in a breath, replayed that statement, and it came up meaning what he thought. "You mean you don't lose count of the doorways."

"Yes," Jago said cheerfully, that disconcerting Ragi habit of agreeing with a negative. "Do you?"

When he thought about it, he thought he might have a fair notion how to reach Kroger's section: he *counted* things he saw; he'd trained for years to do that, from flash-screens at University to desperate sessions in real negotiations, real confrontations. He'd learned to have that perception, and yes, he saw how a mind that just natively saw in that way might have a better record than he did. The captains' precautions against invasion were simply useless against atevi memories for sets and structure. It was the same way atevi had taken one look at computer designs that had served humankind for centuries and critiqued their basic concept in terms of a wholly different way of looking at the universe.

"Amazing," was all he could say. "Really amazing. He shouldn't get himself in trouble, Jago-ji."

He didn't say a word about the diversion last night. He couldn't say whether if Banichi had come proposing an excursion to see whether the shuttle was safe, he might not have said no. He was very careful with Banichi and Jago in particular . . . as he supposed they were with him, and he couldn't deny that they had their reason, that he was a damned valuable commodity to have up here, and that in a certain sense it was folly to have him here.

But he couldn't become paralyzed by the notion of his own worth, either; he had to *do* his job to *be* valuable, and that was the bottom line.

Banichi sent him Nojana, and he meant to get the most out of the transaction.

"This is worth the walk, nand' paidhi." Nojana enjoyed the food: one could hardly blame him. "Very much worth it, and I am honored."

It wasn't quite proper to ask an ateva his Guild if it wasn't apparent or if the information wasn't offered, but Bren had his notions, looking at Nojana's athletic build. Arms completely filled out the borrowed uniform. There was a little slack across the chest, but hardly so. The height might be a little more: the sleeves were not quite adequate.

And Nojana was a member of the Assassins' Guild, members of his staff knew Nojana very well from before this: it was a small and very well-placed Guild, and generally supportive of the aiji, with rare and balanced exceptions. Into Guild politics the paidhi had no entry, and he thought it wise to seek none, as the aiji himself sought none.

He certainly had a healthy appetite.

"How long will you stay?" Bren asked, and reserved *What in hell is Banichi up to?* for a moment with his own staff.

"One isn't sure, nand' paidhi."

That was a fairly broad answer, warning the habituated that the ateva in question was hedging, and if pressed, would hedge more creatively . . . being too polite to lie unless cornered.

One took the answer and shut up, and asked Jago later, pulling her within his room.

"I don't know," was Jago's response.

"All right," he said. "But I don't know if I'm going down with the next flight. That's within my judgment." -

"One worries," Jago said. "Staff can manage this. Someone less valuable can manage this."

"Less valuable to the aiji because such a person might do less. If I can secure a meeting with the captains, I *should* secure it. If I can hold Ramirez to agreements personally, even if there's dissent, I should do it. If I can free Jase, I should free him. *In the meantime,* Jago-ji, I will prepare dispatches, if I have more than a few hours."

"One has more than a few hours. I should say quite a few hours, nadi."

"What is he doing?"

"One can't say."

"Well," he said distressedly, "well, show Nojana what he has to know and I'll prepare the dispatches. Give me at least an hour's warning when he leaves."

"I don't know that I can do that," Jago protested.

"I know you can work wonders," he said. "I believe that you will. —And you're not to risk yourself, Jago-ji! You're not to leave this place unless I say so."

"I can't take such orders," Jago said, but added quickly, "but I see no reason to go at the moment."

"An hour's warning," he insisted, and went off, precaution against surprises, to give the same instruction to Nojana, that he had dispatches that had to go to Tabini, and that Nojana should carry them.

That meant putting his notes in order and some sort of coherency, and more, committing them to an ephemeral card, which he habitually carried since the bad old days of Jase's descent and Deana Hanks' attempt to land on the mainland. It had a button that simply, physically, with a caustic element, destroyed the media beyond reading, not something he liked using—he had a dire image of the thing going off while he was producing it; and his scenario for needing it involved a situation in which he might want to destroy his whole computer storage, but this was a good deal less dire, simply to hand Nojana the record and to instruct him to give it personally to the head of the aiji's security.

"Only to him," Bren said emphatically. "This tab, do you see, must remain intact *unless* you think there's a danger of it falling into other hands. Once you tear it off, this record will be destroyed. If an unauthorized machine attempts to read it, the result will be bad for both."

"One understands," Nojana said fervently. "The record will reach the aiji's guard."

"Very good," Bren said. "There'll be another if we have time. These are the essentials."

"Does the paidhi have concerns for security here, or on the ground?" Nojana dared ask.

"Here, primarily. But take care, and ask for immediate escort once you land; I don't fancy you'll have to ask twice." He said that and asked, sensing a man who might have secrets, "Do *you* have concerns about which my security should know?"

"I have informed them of essentials, nadi."

"Inform us all," he said. "I want to hear it directly, and ask questions."

"Yes, nandi," Nojana said, and over at least three cups of tea which Algini made himself, not asking the servant staff, and within the security post, Nojana informed them of what he knew.

"Certain of the crew have become familiar with us," Nojana said, "and we do speak outside the bounds of our duty. We share food with them, some small extra sweets which they greatly favor, and we gain their goodwill. They mention their recreation and their associations, which we know, and which I can tell you."

"Do so," Jago said, and Narana did, mapping out all those individuals whose names or work they knew, and every name associated with them, and where they had complained or praised someone: Narana had a very good memory of such things, second nature to atevi . . . significant among humans, but not by patterns Narana might suspect.

"Very, very good," Bren said, having a clear picture from that and from Jase, a tendency to form families of sorts, even lineages and households, all with the tradition of marriage, but without its frequent practice. "You know Jasi-ji. You met him."

"Yes, nadi, I had that honor."

"His mother is resident here, perhaps other associates. We've been unable to contact him: the captains have given orders to the contrary. If I send word, might you use one of your more innocent contacts to slip a message to her to contact us? I think it might come much more easily from the other direction. They're routing all our communications through a single channel; we don't seem to have general access to communications as I suspect others might." An idea came to him, and he asked the question. *"How* do you reach the authorities?"

"C1 for communications and Q1 for dock communications; but we know a few more numbers."

"You've had no difficulty reaching them."

"None that I know. I speak enough Mosphei', nandi, that if a worker needs to reach us, I often receive the call, and if one might be late he calls, and on occasion we provide them small excuse, as if they were at work, but not so."

"You mean they ask you to conceal their tardiness and absences."

"They make up deficits quite willingly. We've never found it a detriment, nandi. Are we wrong?"

"Not at all," Bren said. "By no means." That the crew found occasion to play off on duty was within human pattern; that they made up the work was the pattern of a crew that understood the schedule and would meet it, all of which the atevi working with them had learned. And it might be unwise to use that route to reach Jase's mother . . . yet. It might trigger suspicion of malevolent intent, the contact might be rejected at the other end, and there was not quite the urgent need to do it. "But which human would you ask to contact someone outside your area if you had to do it?"

"Kelly. A young woman." Nojana had no hesitation. "She has a lover. She meets him at times. She knows Jase very well."

"Has the subject arisen? We've been unable to establish

contact with Jase; I'm somewhat worried, nadi. Has she expressed concern?"

"She has tried to tell me something regarding Jase, but the words elude me. She seems to express that Jase is associated with Ramirez-aiji."

"He is. That much is true. Ramirez functions as *his* aiji, or his father."

"Indeed. Kelly has said Jase-nandi is *with* Ramirez."

Nojana had used the Mospheiran word.

"With means very many things. Ask if Jase is in danger."

"I know this word. Shall I ask nadi Kelly?"

"If you can do so discreetly."

"One will attempt discretion."

"Report the result of that inquiry to Tabini-aiji when you take him the dispatch. I doubt it would be safe to send word to me, unless I make the flight . . . as my staff seems to believe I should. I remain doubtful."

"I shall," Nojana said. "Indeed I shall, nand' paidhi."

They conversed; Nojana slept and waked with the servants, another day, received more files, enjoyed meals with them.

"How long will he stay?" Bren asked Jago directly.

"Not long," was Jago's answer. "Tonight perhaps."

"How did he know his way in the first place?" Bren wondered, because that thought had begun to nag him.

"Banichi sent him with that instruction," Jago said. "I'm very sure. And Banichi won't have missed a thing."

"What in hell do you do if you meet guards?"

"One will endeavor not to meet guards," Jago said.

Some things there was just no disputing; and in some arguments there was simply nothing left to say. Banichi would come back. He believed that implicitly. Banichi would come back.

And true to his instruction, Nojana reported his intention to depart at midnight, enjoyed a cup of tea with him and the security staff, thanked the servants for their attentions, and stood ready to walk back down the corridors to take a lift to the core, with no more baggage than he'd arrived with . . . to the outward eye.

And could a human observer *miss* a tall shadow of an

atevi in a pale yellow corridor, where there was no place to take cover?

Atevi hearing was good; but that good? He was doubtful. Banichi was armed, and needed no weapons against unarmed humans; but the very last thing he wanted was harm to the crew, even of a minor sort.

"I have all you've entrusted to me," Nojana said, "nand' paidhi."

"I have no doubt," Bren said. Nojana seemed to read his worry as a lack of confidence in him, and he had no wish to convey that at all. "I know Banichi has none."

"Nandi," Nojana said.

Then Tano quite deftly opened the door and let him out, one more time to trace his way through foreign corridors.

19

They expected Banichi to arrive sometime after midnight.
"Wake me," he said to Jago, who shared the bed with
him that night. He knew her hearing, and her light sleeping,
that she would in no wise sleep through Banichi's arrival.

"Don't be angry," she asked of him.

"I shan't be," he said, lying close beside her. When he
thought about it, he knew he was disturbed, and wished
Banichi had asked before he did such a thing; but anger
was too strong a word. Banichi was rarely wrong, never
wrong, that he could immediately recall.

"Has he ever made a mistake?" he asked her, and Jago
gave a soft laugh.

"Oh, a few," Jago said, Jago, who knew Banichi better,
he suspected, than anyone in the world or off it. "There
was the matter of a rooftop, in the south. There was the
matter of believing a certain human would take orders."

"A certain human has his own notions," Bren said. "And
one of them is not to have my staff wandering the halls
and me not knowing."

"In the aiji's service," Jago said, "we overrule the paidhi.
And the aiji's orders involve the paidhi's safe return."

"The aiji's orders also involve the paidhi's success in
his mission."

"Just so, but caution. Caution."

"Caution doesn't get the job done." She distracted him.
Jago was good at that. He outright lost track of his
argument.

Besides, he intended it for Banichi, when Banichi got
back, after midnight.

But he waked in the morning first aware that Jago was

not beside him, that the lights in the corridor were bright, and that breakfast was in the offing, all at one heartbeat.

Two heartbeats later he was sure it was past midnight and past dawn and Jago hadn't done as he'd asked her to.

Or things hadn't happened as they ought to have happened.

He rolled out of bed and seized up a robe, raking his hair out of his face on the way to the central hall, across it to the security station where Tano and Algini and Jago perched at their console . . . aware of him from the moment he'd come out the door.

"Where's Banichi?" he asked at once. "Did he get back?"

"No, nadi," Jago said, and it was clear she was worried. "We have no information."

"Did he express any belief he might be late?"

"He said it was a possibility," Jago said, "if he found no way to move discreetly."

"Discreetly down a bare synthetic hallway," Bren said in distress. "I'm worried, damn it."

"I think it well possible that he delayed with the shuttle crew," Jago said. "If something came to their attention or something changed, he might wait to know. In all his instruction there was no indication he considered the schedule rigid."

"So what did *Nojana* walk into? He went out there expecting an easy walk home."

"Nojana is of our Guild," Tano said, "and expects everything."

"I have no doubt of him, then," Bren said, "but all the same, nadiin-ji, what is either of them to do if they meet some crewman going about his business?"

"Doors will malfunction," Algini said.

"Doors will malfunction. I hope not to open onto vacuum, nadiin!"

"One knows the route that was safe," Tano said. "Banichi did consider the hazards, nandi, but he wishes very much to assure our line of retreat is open."

"I agree with his purpose, but the risk . . . "

"Bren-ji," Jago said, "something changed when the power failed. The patterns of activity that we monitor here have shifted, whether because part of this station is no longer usable, we have no idea."

"How do you know these things?" He understood how they monitored activity in the Bu-javid, where they had the entire apartment wired, including some very lethal devices, but here in a structure where they had no other installations . . .

They had . . . one other installation.

Shai-shan itself.

And if in fact there was already an Assassins' Guild presence on the station, at least a periodic one, with the comings and goings of the shuttle, then there might be equipment which came and went in Nojana's baggage.

"We monitor sounds and activities," Algini said. "Very faint ones. We know the pattern of the station from before; we know it now. The structure speaks to us. Now, and ever since the power outage, it speaks differently."

Being paidhi-aiji, having mediated the transfer of human technology to the mainland, as well as being within very high atevi councils, he knew of atevi innovations that bore no resemblance to technology he knew on Mospheira, and no few of those innovations were in surveillance.

He had had a certain amount to do with the galley specifications: in this collection of monitors and panels and instruments his security had brought aboard . . . he knew very little, asked very little, mindful of his allegiance these days, and only hoped never to walk into one of the traps that guarded his sleep.

"Can you show me?" he asked.

"Yes," Algini said.

It was not an encouraging image, knowing the little he did know regarding the station. It indicated a change since the power outage, at least, a change in where Algini estimated personnel were grouped, where they traveled. Everything pointed to a disruption of a region forcing detours.

"I've no idea what caused it," Bren said. "I can't ask Kaplan-nadi. It would give too much away. I refuse to ask C1 to be off talking to the captains if one of our people is lost."

"Yet one can't break pattern," Tano said quietly. "Nandi, it would seem wisest to do as you always do."

"Bedevil C1 and ask for Jase?" Bren muttered. "Do you see any shift of activity in the area of the shuttle?"

"Nothing out of previous pattern there," Algini said, "except activity that would be consistent with fueling."

"Very well done." He was astonished by his security, astonished by what information they *could* provide him.

But none of it said why Banichi was late.

"I think," he said slowly, "that I'd rather rely on the chance Banichi's chosen this delay, and that anything I could do might bring adverse consequences. Do you think so, nadiin-ji?"

"One believes so," Jago said, but he had the most uneasy notion that she might make a move after her partner—her father—without telling him in advance.

But that was the thought of a human heart. He reminded himself of a certain hillside, and mecheiti, and how angry they'd been when he ran the wrong direction, as if he'd suddenly, under fire, lost his wits.

He was the lord, and under fire they would rally to him instinctively, all but blindly, with that devotion with which humans would run for spouses and children and sacred objects. They would run through fire to reach him, and only the exertion of extreme discipline could deaden that instinct. If Banichi was not here, it was *against* that instinct for him. Banichi *wanted* to be here.

That was a terrible responsibility, to know that one's protectors had no choice but to feel that, and that a word from him could move them to utter, fatal effort. It was that precariously poised, and so hard, so morally hard to say: let Banichi solve his own problems.

But in that interspecies cross-wiring it was the wisest thing.

"He's moved during their night," he murmured. "Is there a reason for this? I would have expected equal distribution of the shifts. It's traditional."

"There also is a curious pattern," Algini said, "since before the outage, the traffic in the corridors was more or less evenly distributed in frequency, and now there seems a cluster of movement last night just after our second watch and their first, then a great falling off. This is a nightly occurrence, as if a group of people moved."

"Is it likely the ship-folk have this sort of surveillance?"

"We have no information," Tano said, "but Jasi-ji confided to us that he knew of very little surveillance in the corridors. We failed to press him on the matter: it was Banichi's judgment we exceeded our authority to ask him."

It was understandable that Tano had. Anything to do with security involved their Guild and interested their Guild, and Tano had doubtless passed that information to the head of Tabini's security, too. On one level, the human one, Bren found himself distressed that Tano had asked after such things secretly; on another, the atevi-acclimated one, he perfectly understood it was his security's job to know everything that touched on the national business.

"Was Jase angry that you asked?" he asked, a human question, seeking the human degree of truth.

"No," Tano said, who, of the security staff, was closest to Jase. "And he knew I would report it to the aiji's staff. But one felt it was dangerous to ask too closely, to make Jasi-ji aware of the capacities of the equipment we prepared."

"Yet we needed to know certain things," Algini said, "to know how to design this console, and how to take best advantage, and what we needed defend against. And Jasi-ji knew some things, but others he was simply unaware of. One believes, nandi, that the ship itself has some internal surveillance to defend operations centers but that the general corridors of the station and the general corridors of the ship have very little. There are portable units, to be sure, but to a certain extent one suspects inbuilt security is bound to be outmoded and worked around far too rapidly; one would be continually delving into the walls to make changes. We do suspect the light installations in the corridors, as readily available power taps, but thus far, in this section, we turn up nothing."

Algini spoke very little, except on his favorite topic, security technology. And what he said, and what his security had been finding out from Jase over the last several years, was far more extensive than he'd hoped.

"I suppose that encouraged Banichi to think he could take so long a walk," Bren said.

"He has the means to operate these doors," Jago admitted, "and might do so if spotted."

"But it's damned cold where the heat's off," Bren objected. "Damned cold! And there's no guarantee of air flow."

"We chill less readily," Jago said. "Air is a problem."

"Yes," Bren said, hoping his staff would restrain its operations. "Air is a problem. And I *don't* want you to go out there looking for him, and if they've caught him, I have some confidence I'll hear about it. But please, nadiin-ji, don't surprise me like this!"

He met an absolute, impervious wall of respectful stares.

"You'll do what you know to do," he said more quietly, in retreat, "but I beg you be careful."

"One will be careful," Jago said. "During certain hours there's less movement in the corridors. One expects my partner will use his excellent sense and wait."

"Concealed in some airless compartment!"

"He has some resources," Jago said. "Don't worry. It's not your job to worry."

He had to take himself to his own room and sit down with the computer, to lose himself in reports and letters. There was no other way to avoid thinking about Banichi and disasters.

There was still no word from Toby, there was nothing from his mother . . . a silence from the island, and nothing from Tabini, only a handful of committee letters acknowledging his previous letters, a dismal lot of mail, none of it informative, none of it engaging.

That his mother hadn't written back was in pattern, too: when she was offended, she didn't speak, didn't reason, didn't argue, didn't give anyone a handle to seize that might be any use at all.

I hope you're seeing your doctor, he wrote her, in a three-page missive. *I hope Barb's improving.*

It wasn't the most inspired of letters.

He wrote Toby, too. *I know you're not in any position to answer, and I don't expect an answer. Just touching base to let you know you're my brother and I'm concerned.* He started to write that he hadn't heard from their mother, but that was the way he and Toby had gotten into the situation they were in: that he'd used Toby for eyes and ears where it regarded their mother, and a pair of feet and hands, too. And if Toby and Jill had a chance, it meant just shutting that channel down and not using it anymore, not even if it put their mother in danger. It was at least a self-chosen danger.

He sent-and-received, and the second round of mail was sparser than the first.

"C1," he said. "Can you put me through to Kroger?" He was down to wishing for another human voice, but C1 answered:

"Kroger is not receiving at the moment. There's a communications problem in that area, sir. Sorry."

A *communications* problem.

He signed off and went to report *that* to his security.

"It's not on Banichi's route, is it?" he asked.

"No," Tano said. "It should not be."

"Do you suppose," Bren asked, "that there's nothing wrong where Banichi is, that *Nojana* ran into trouble and just hasn't gotten to him?"

"We have considered that possibility," Algini said. "But we have emergency notification, a very noisy transmitter. We have not heard it."

That was reassuring. Another small feature of his security that no one had told him.

"How many other surprises are there?" he asked.

"Not many," Jago said. It was clear she wished there were more surprises available. She was worried, and by now he suspected the man'chi that held her to Banichi and that man'chi which held her on duty here, with him, were in painful conflict.

"Come with me," he said to her, not wishing emotion to make his security's decisions, and they sat in his room, and he offered her a drink, which she declined in favor of a cup of tea, on duty and remaining alert. They shared a small, out-of-appetite supper, served by a silent, commiserating staff.

It passed midnight of their clock.

And very quietly, with the opening of a door, someone entered the section.

Jago leaped up, and he did. By the time they reached

the hall, the whole staff was converging from servants' quarters, Tano and Algini coming out of their station.

Banichi looked quite unruffled, not a hair out of place.

But to a practiced eye, Banichi had a worried look.

"I fear Ramirez-aiji has fallen," Banichi said first and foremost, and Bren took in a breath.

"Is anyone behind you?" Jago asked, before anything else.

"No," Banichi said. "One regrets the delay, paidhi-ji."

"Did Nojana reach safety?"

"Yes," Banichi said.

"Drinks in the security station," Bren said quickly, breaching all custom, but he wanted all his security knowing the same thing and the same time, and he dared not have the instruments in that station unmonitored at this time of all times. "Tea, as well." Half his security was on duty, and would decline alcohol.

Banichi, however, had earned a glass of something stronger. Fatigue rarely showed in Banichi's bearing, but it did now.

Ramirez gone? Fallen? And not a damned word from Ogun or Sabin, God knew, none from Pratap Tamun.

One could babble questions. But direct questions rarely improved on Banichi's sober, orderly report, if one's nerves could bear it.

"The copilot, Parano, while I was there, heard the technicians talk about the power outage, but the copilot's command of Mosphei' has notable gaps. The technicians in his hearing asked each other whether they'd had any news of Ramirez, and went on to discuss whether they thought he was dead or alive or where he might be, at least as far as Parano could interpret the words. They discovered then that Parano-nadi was within earshot, changed expressions, and addressed him about business. This Parano reported to his captain, Casirnabri, and Casirnabri to me. Thereafter we spoke together, Parano, Casirnabri, and I, hence my information, directly from Parano. We attempted to overhear other things, during the regular course of work. The shuttle crew and the human workers maintain a good relationship . . . they do speak to one another in a very limited way, comparison of the translated checklists, translation from the key words list to settle what the topic is, all very slow, with hand signals they've devised among themselves, using number codes for operations. Cas-nadi thought they might have asked about Ramirez, if I wished: they do have confidence in the goodwill of this crew. But I asked them not to do so. I place great importance, Bren-ji, in assuring your safety.''

"We've been quite unbothered here," Bren began to say, and to add that he by no means took that as absolute, but Banichi frowned.

"No. I mean to take you home, nand' paidhi. Having you here is far too great a danger. We should proceed as if we know nothing, make our plans to depart, and have you out of the reach of political upheaval."

"Ramirez is old. Parano might have misunderstood. The crew language is full of idiom."

Now he saw every single face set against him. Here was rebellion.

"You will go," Banichi said in that deep voice of his, "Bren-ji. I have the aiji's authority on this. I request you comply."

"My usefulness is my ability to negotiate and to settle terms."

"Your usefulness is very little if you become like Jase, unavailable to the aiji. I went to the shuttle because I had apprehensions and wished to know whether there was, even at this hour, a safe retreat. I believe that there is, and I insist you take it."

On the aiji's authority.

"Banichi is right," Jago said, "given all he says. You should go."

He didn't want it. He'd had his doubts about being up here, he'd wondered daily about his usefulness where the captains continually postponed their meetings, but the ground had changed on him, without warning. Now he had to rethink everything, every gesture made toward them, every intimation of cooperation, or noncooperation.

"I'm not sure I improve our position by my leaving," he said. "We've not been threatened. They've simply withheld meetings. We don't know the reason. If the senior captain is ill, or stepped down . . . we just don't know."

"And they mean we should not learn, nandi," Tano said. "Have they offered any goodwill at all? Have they apologized or admitted?"

"They have not," he agreed, and Jase's situation flashed across his mind like summer lightning, the landscape revised in a stroke. "But if we leave, we leave Jase."

"If they have both you and Jase," Banichi said, "our negotiating position is not improved. If you stay here, they may attempt some move against our presence here. If our presence grows quieter, they may neglect that measure and leave us a stronghold."

"If you miss the shuttle," Jago said, "there's no chance for a very long time."

"It's the eleventh," he said. "The shuttle leaves on the fifteenth. We have four days."

"We can do nothing in these days," Banichi said. "And, Bren-ji, your security very strongly advises you not to make it clear to this Guild that you know something's amiss. We know humans do very odd things, but embarrassing them would seem provocative. We *cannot* predict this situation or their behavior, but reversal of expectations does not seem to please humans more than it pleases atevi."

"You're quite correct."

"Then a surprise would not be a good thing."

"No," he agreed. "It would not, Banichi-ji. Thank you. Thank you for taking precautions."

"We cannot take precautions enough," Banichi said, "to secure your safety for the next few nights. We hope the shuttle will leave on schedule. Preparations are on time. There's been no cessation of work there. I met no evidence of monitoring in the corridors, beyond what Kaplan carries on his person. I found nothing of the sort in the diagrams, and indeed, there seems none now. But there remains the possibility that they merely observed the movement and did nothing."

"Likely enough there never was surveillance," Bren said, "except in administrative areas. These areas were residential, and people would have resented it bitterly, as an intrusion, not as safety. The lack of signs seems their chief precaution. They couldn't navigate the halls without a map.

They don't think it's possible. They don't imagine it. So there's nothing to watch against."

"A blind spot," Algini said.

"A blind spot," Bren agreed. "Humans aren't the only species to have made such mistakes. I don't wish to tell them, not at this point."

"One has no wish to tell them," Banichi said. "But were I stopped, I would have been Nojana. One doubts they would know the difference."

"There are advanced technical means," Bren said, "even granted they don't recognize individuals that accurately. We mustn't risk it again, Banichi-ji. I thank you very much for doing it, but I ask restraint. I understand your concern." He saw his security poised to object to his objection, and held up a hand. "I will hear you. But give me today until the fifteenth to come to some resolution with the captains—not saying a word of what we know."

"Until the fourteenth," Banichi said. "The mission may stay. You, Bren-ji, with no baggage at all, will simply go to the shuttle early, and board, and Jago and I will go with you. The rest will stay."

There was no question Banichi had just come to this conclusion, that he had had no time since walking through the door to consult with the rest of the team, but there was no schism in the company, that was very certain. Banichi declared his plan and the others said not a word.

It was, beyond that, a plan that made sense, not to advise the captains in advance, to be just a little ahead of any move the captains might make to restrain him from leaving. It left the majority of the staff, left Tano and Algini in charge of the mission, the servants to support them, and someone here in case Jase found a chance to reach them.

But another thought struck him with numbing force. If they left, God, if *he* left, Kroger could only think the worst. If the human delegation had no warning of what Banichi suspected and it proved true, then he could by no means afford to leave them behind . . . Kroger left on a limb and feeling betrayed was beyond dangerous. They had had several centuries of bitter division, had just patched things into a workable agreement, and dared not leave Kroger alone with whatever mischief was shaping up on the station.

Particularly . . . another dark thought . . . since if something had gone wrong among the captains, the division might be a factional one as well as a personal power grab.

"We have to advise the Mospheirans," Bren said. "For diplomatic reasons, for courtesy if nothing more. If they think we've double-crossed them, they'll deal with the other side. They'll conclude they can't trust us. They have to have the same chance to get out of here. They have to know we're on their side."

"One can hardly speak securely on the intercom with them," Banichi said.

"One can't," he agreed, trying to think what to do.

"It's not that far," Banichi said. "I can walk there, too, and talk to Ben."

"You've had a drink. You're not on duty. No!"

"I might have another. If I'm walking the halls, I am doubtless an inebriate having strayed from duty, and will say I require Kaplan to guide me home. Humans understand inebriation. I recall your machimi. They consider it quite amusing."

"Not when you're damned guilty and in the wrong corridor. We're not supposed to be able to open these doors."

"One would certainly have to admit to that."

"And there's the problem of making the Mospheirans believe you when you get there."

"Give me a token for them. Is this not machimi?"

"One will be prostrate with nerves the whole damned time," Bren muttered, seeing less and less chance of dealing with a situation run amok. "One has not the least idea what Kroger may do. The woman distrusts me very easily. We simply can't—"

"A banner is traditional."

"Not among humans. Rings. Letters." It was preposterous. "It's a damned comedy, is what it is." Banichi wasn't one to propose lunacy. He had the feeling of being maneuvered, backed toward an ultimatum.

"We can hardly do this by intercom," Banichi said, silken-smooth and one drink down.

"I can simply invite them to dinner and tell them face-to-face. No more wandering about the halls. By no means."

Banichi sighed. "One did look forward to it."

And not for the simple pleasure of risking his neck, Bren was suddenly sure; if Banichi had ever been serious, Banichi had his own reasons for wanting to undertake that walk. But the more likely answer was Banichi simply nudging him to come up with a plan. "Damn the whole idea! No. I'll *invite* them back. Narani will arrange something. An entertainment."

"Machimi," Jago said.

He looked at her, looked at Banichi, saw conspiracy and an adamant intent.

More—a third sinking thought—there was always the remotest chance, while he was trying to shore up Kroger's doubts of him, that Kroger did know, and hadn't leveled with *him* regarding Ramirez and some scheme on the part of Sabin and those who dealt far more with the Mospheirans.

That was an utterly unwelcome thought. He was bounced out of bed past midnight, forced to think of abandoning everything he'd been doing here, informed that every agreement they'd hammered out was in jeopardy if not completely abrogated, and he found himself maneuvered into asking Kroger here to be read the conditions of a retreat.

And what would Kroger say? Wait for us, we're leaving? Or, You go ahead, dear allies, and we'll arrange things.

"I don't think, given the food here, we'll have any difficulty getting them to come," he said to Banichi, "granted only I get a message through. But, dammit, Kroger can mess things up. And she may have a mind to do it."

"Has there been difficulty with communications?" Banichi asked.

"Nothing worthwhile came through Mogari-nai," Bren said, recalling that fact in present context, too. "They keep having outages, malfunctions, which might discourage anyone from sending critical messages, such as must not be half-received, or meddled with. I did tend to believe them about the outages. Now I don't. It may well be an excuse to cut us off from communication. I haven't gotten anything worthwhile from the aiji; I don't know that he's gotten my transmissions: I've had no acknowlegments. And that, nadiin-ji, is a critical point: if we can't be sure our messages are going through, indeed . . . if they're lying to us, we can't do our jobs here. But if we give up our foothold here, we can't be assured of getting it back, either. If we *can't* rely on Kroger, if something's going through in secret, only to Mospheira, we have a grievous problem."

"One would agree to that," Banichi said, and solemnly accepted his second drink, having won everything he had come to get. "But the paidhi will not be the presence to test their intentions."

"Who can? There's a reason Tabini sent me. There's a reason I'm sitting here and not uncle Tatiseigi, Banichi-ji, and I can't contravene that simple fact. If I don't do this job, yes, you're right, there's no one else who can do it, but the simple fact is, if I don't do this job, indeed, there's no one else who can do it!"

The glass stopped on the way to Banichi's lips. Banichi set it down and regarded him solemnly.

"A dilemma, is it not?"

"One I can't solve."

"One we daren't lose," Banichi said. "This I have from the aiji, that you must return safely. Do what you can. Take what advantage these days offer. Go down, and if things seem in order, come back in thirty days on the next flight."

"And if things go wrong, I've left my staff in a hell of a position."

"We simply lock the doors," Tano said, "and hold out."

"Against people who control the light and heat, Tano-ji!"

"Do you consider it likely we would be killed?" Tano asked. "It would be very foolish of them if they wish anything from the aiji."

And Kroger had flatly said what he already knew, himself, that very few Mospheirans were willing to enter work for the ship under the old terms. Robotics, that missing part of the equation, might be Kroger's specialty, but to design and build those machines in space, where they must be built, still required risks in an environment which had proven a killer before now.

He had to talk to them. That was a given. He had to get a notion how Kroger might react once she did know, and once she did know he knew that Ramirez had met with some sort of difficulty. Jase was another concern, one he knew hadn't left his staff's minds, but one which none of them could afford to pursue.

Damn, this was inconvenient. And what *had* happened to Ramirez, and where *was* Jase, and why, if Jase had a mother aboard, was there absolutely no contact?

He didn't like the shape of it. Clearly, Banichi hadn't liked it, and had seen in the outage something that might not be an accident.

That hadn't been an accident, he was now certain. Something that had happened along with some struggle on the station, perhaps even a schism in the crew, or something designed to put the fear in them and justify both Sabin's reluctance to meet with him—God knew whether she was secretly meeting with Kroger—and the communications problems that cut him off from advice and information from the planet.

He had to work around it. Had to get *something* through to advise the planet there was something not right up here.

Mother, he wrote, in language he was very sure station spies could read, *I'm sorry to have been out of touch. They've been experiencing communications difficulties here. I love you. Be assured of that. I hope things are working out for everyone. I wish I'd brought my camera up here. One thing I do miss beyond all else is pictures of home. You know that one of you in the red suit? I think of that, and the snow, up on Mt. Adams. Sunset and snow. Fire and ice. You*
    Did you find a cufflink? I think I left it in my room.
    I hope Barb is better. Tell her I think of her and wish her a speedy recovery.
    Your son, Bren

There was no red suit. His mother never wore that color, swore it was her worst; that was why they had agreed on it as an emergency notice. Red suit: emergency; contact Shawn; watch yourself. It was the only code he had now that might get through the security blackout . . . if the authorities chose to let him go on receiving small messages, while they knew Tabini's signature and blacked those out. If they were at all wary, they wouldn't let it through. If they'd ever noticed Banichi's trip to the shuttle, they wouldn't let it through.

Trust me, he wished the captains still in power. Believe me.

God, he hoped no one had spotted Banichi's move.

"C1," he said, "we'd like Kaplan to escort the Mospheiran delegation here, if I can arrange a dinner meeting at 1800 hours." He held his breath. "Will that be a problem?"

C1 answered somewhat abstractedly, *"Kaplan, sir. Shouldn't be."*

"I don't suppose Jase can join us." It was part of the long-established pattern. He never let it up.

"No, sir, Jase Graham is still committed to meetings."

"What about Captain Sabin? Any chance of resuming that appointment? We could perfectly well set a place for the captain, if she wishes."

"I'll relay that, sir," C1 said, and a few minutes later replied, *"The captains are all in meetings, sir. She did relay regrets and asks for the 18th."*

The day of the shuttle launch, ship-calendar. It was an outright question.

"Tell her I'd be delighted. We'll arrange a special dinner."

Sabin wasn't the only one who could miss an appointment. He had no hesitation in that small lie, and was only minimally tempted to believe Sabin was oblivious to that date.

Was he leaving? Would he be aboard? Sabin very much wanted to know that, in her relayed question.

And dared he tell the truth to Kroger in time to let Kroger get aboard?

Certainly it would not be prudent to tell Kroger everything he knew.

20

"I propose to go down to the planet for a few days,"
Bren said, over the main course, and after a rambling
appetizer conversation that had taken them from skiing on
Mt. Adams to the better bars on the north shore. "I'm
disappointed in the degree of cooperation we've gotten.
Either we meet with the captains, or we don't. I suppose
that I'm coming back on the next flight, but I might not.
We've got to fly that test cargo sooner or later."

That occasioned raised brows. It was the same arrangement as last time, Kroger and Lund at the formal table,
Kaplan and Ben with Tano to keep them distracted, and
to get out of them whatever information Tano could obtain.

"You're breaking off negotiations?" Kroger asked. "Or
retiring to consult."

"Retiring to consult. I fully plan to be back. It's quite
open, as to whether we return on this shuttle rotation or
not. I have administrative duties back on the mainland . . .
and a family crisis on the island." He used that fact shame-
lessly to convey personal reasons which ought not to make
a difference, but which reasonably could. "I think a
month's stand down to let the captains think and analyze
might not be a bad thing."

Kroger had not quite ceased eating, but the utensils
moved more slowly for a moment. "We came prepared to
stay longer."

"My staff will remain here to work. If the cuisine on the
station is as bad as I hear, you're perfectly welcome to dine
here while I'm gone. My staff will by no means be sorry to
have guests to exercise their talents. And Ben and Kate of
course can practice their skills."

There was a small moment of silence, and the utensils came to a slow stop as Kroger tried to consider the possibilities . . . even the chance, perhaps, that the staff might know enough Mosphei' to be a problem to them.

And the reality, too, it might be, that atevi were here to stay.

"The aiji could waive the cost of a ticket down and back," Bren said, "if you wished to come down and make your own representations to him."

"I haven't that authority," Kroger said, clearly disturbed. "You have to talk to the State Department for that."

Interesting choice of words. Very interesting, to an ear attuned to language. The insiders to the various departments tended, though not infallibly, to shorten that down to State . . . *you have to talk to State. You have to talk to Science.* It gave Kroger credibility as an outsider, that expression, someone chosen for a mission, but not an insider, not ordinarily a negotiator: a robotics expert, chosen to come up here and see what the state of the machinery or the science might be.

Because *that* would govern how willing human beings might be to undertake the work.

The mind went zipping from point to point in mid-smile. "I will seek someone to do that," he said. "I think we ought to firm up the agreements we have."

"Sounds like a good idea," Lund said. Lund had stopped eating, and paid thorough attention. "I, on the other hand, wouldn't mind the trip. I've been curious about the mainland. And I might have something to say to the aiji, if I can get you to translate."

Kroger's brows knit, but she didn't say a word in objection.

Interesting power structure in this Mospheiran committee. One could discount Lund, but he *was* Commerce, and he did have, Bren suspected off and on, a certain authority in his own realm: trade, commerce, and business representations.

And indeed, it made a certain sense, as he'd set the matter forth to them. It was a good solution to the dilemma of how much to tell the Mospheirans about what could become a dicey situation, particularly for his own delegation.

At least he wouldn't have failed to advise them he was leaving. He could get his hands on Lund, figure him out within the context of Tabini's court, get on his good side.

"I'd advise you don't need to dismantle the mission," Bren said. "Just pack a bag, clothes, that sort of thing. The aiji can arrange flights to the island if you like, strongly supposing you'll need to consult while you're down there. The shuttle goes up again in a month, and you're guaranteed space."

"Two days," Kroger mused, the very short interval for preparation. "I don't know, Tom."

"You can always make it a last-minute decision," Bren said. "Unfortunately the shuttle goes down unloaded. Which is a situation we should fix. It's terribly expensive to do that."

"Get some manufacturing going up here," Tom said. "There's an archive full of things we could be manufacturing; there are dozens of abandoned facilities up at the core, in microgravity. Medicines, for God's sake. Metals. Ceramics."

"First we need to get enough atevi crew up here working to establish these areas as safe," Bren said. "I plan to bring a few technical people myself on the next trip up." Not to mention increased security, but a few atevi manufacturing experts, who understood the machines that built the vehicles and stamped and pressed and drilled. Robots. That new word, for a class of machines that had never been perceived to verge on intelligence.

The ones Kroger proposed were far more independent, capable of decision-making, and required, he suspected, more computer science than Science had ever admitted existed.

And it must, by what he suspected. Science hadn't told State, not at his level, but it must; and now atevi had to become privy to that knowledge as well, in computers, an area where atevi innovations had scared hell out of human planners . . . the one area of human endeavor besides security technology where atevi had simply taken the information provided, gone off on their own and come back with major new developments.

Humans had become very nervous about atevi and computers.

"Might we arrange the same?" Kroger asked. "Free passage?"

"I think I can arrange a suspension of the charges," Bren said. "On a one-time basis. This is to the benefit of both."

"Two days," Kroger lamented a second time. "Damned short notice."

"Busy month," Bren said, "on the ground. But every trip, the shuttle should bring a few people. We can arrange to carry a certain number free of charge, where they're filling up space."

"You can do that," Kroger said.

"At least for the present mission," Bren said, and took a fork to his dinner, very much relieved to have settled the human mission problem, still asking himself whether he ought to level with Kroger, and finally took the plunge. "We've received indications that there might be some disturbance within the local administration. That Ramirez might have a health problem. That the delays might be due to that."

"Are you serious?" Kroger asked, aghast.

"That's another reason for our timing in going down right now." He was very glad to see that she was surprised. "I think they're trying to sort something out; I don't think we're going to get damned much done until they do, and I think it's a good interval to go consult."

Clearly Kroger was dismayed. "That puts things in a different light."

"Not much. A delay." He chose the light to have on it, a bland one. "Captains will come and go. That matters very little to us. They settle their affairs, we settle ours."

"How do you *know* this?"

"We have our ways," he said. "It's an interpretation of what we see, not an observed fact, but I'd bet on it."

"You mean you're guessing."

"I mean observations lead us to this conclusion," he said, deliberately obscure. "That's different from a guess. How much credence you put in it . . . that's a matter of judgment, but I take it very seriously, seriously enough that if the captains are taking a great many pains to keep us from finding out, indeed, I'm not going to upset them by telling them what I guess. I'm simply going to take the pressure off them, allow them to solve what is their business, and give myself time to solve some of the other problems that are piling up on my desk at home. I just think this is going to be a hiatus in constructive work, after which we can get back to business."

It was a fairly complex lie in the center, with truth in the operational sense in that it wasn't quite a lie, in that it was honestly his best attempt to signal Kroger without spilling everything: *excuse me, Ms. Kroger, but we may be in the center of a local war; best keep a low profile . . . at the very least, don't stand up and wave for attention.*

Certainly she paid him strong attention. She had gray, cold eyes, one of her most disconcerting attributes, and all that concentration was on him.

"Are you saying there's danger, Bren?"

"There's danger inherent in our situation, but less if we mind our own business, which one can do simply by staying in one's quarters and waiting for them to sort it out. I just have too damned much business down on the planet, and there are constructive things I can do by relaying this to the aiji in person. It's far easier to persuade him, frankly, where there's give and take and where I don't have to worry about some faction getting wind of it. Tabini-aiji and I can do more over tea in one hour than in forty pages of reports on his desk. Much as we do here. If you feel uneasy and want to go, I think we can contrive an excuse, but if you're comfortable with remaining here and dealing with my staff, we could certainly use the on-station presence."

The ice in the stare melted somewhat, and Kroger rested her chin on a crooked finger. "There's more to this than you're saying."

"I haven't been able to get hold of Jase Graham since we got here. I'm worried about him and have been, and, frankly, yes, there could be danger of some sort. But if they want anything from the planet and I think they do—they'd be fools to do anything to us. We *aren't* members of their crew. Jase, unfortunately, is, and I think they're asking him very close questions about us, or preventing him spilling to us what's going on inside their power structure. That's my honest thought on the matter. It's possible the captain most favorable to us is dead. But we can't do anything about that. We don't corner them and they don't corner us. I don't say we have to like them or agree with them, but for the mission's sake we ultimately have to work with them, and to work with them we have to trust them just as far as we're sure is in their interest. That's why we don't mention this to them. They've constructed a fiction for us to believe, and it's our job to take our cues and not bother them, and do our job at the same time in a way that lets us go on working with them."

"Maintain the fiction."

"That's the job. For at least a month, until we get the shuttle up again, at which time we can arrange for you to give me a verbal signal, say, a message to Tom, here, that you think it's profitable for us both to come ahead, or we can work with you in charge up here and us on the ground. The main thing is that we have to maintain our agreement and reduce the number of parties here. There's too much chance of a divide and conquer move, and if they do it to us, they'll behave just as long as it takes to get all the advantage they get, then dig in their heels and become a majority with the other half of us. Let's not let them work that strategy. It's not in our interest. Not in yours."

Kroger considered it. The eyes windowed a factory of thoughts. The mouth gave not a thing away.

"Interesting," she said after a moment.

"He has a point," Lund said. "We can deal."

"Good," he said, feeling as if insects were crawling on every inch of his skin. He'd not put his apprehensions into words before, but laying them out, even in slightly deceptive fashion, focused the threat, even to such an extent that he considered advising Tom to move early, as he was doing, to reach the shuttle.

There were two days in which to make that decision, with Banichi's help, among others. Protecting their retreat had become a priority, one in which, if he had a regret, it was overwhelming worry for Jase. If he was right, his leaving might actually gain Jase more freedom.

There was certainly nothing else he could do to help him, except gain more power than he had now.

They spoke of details, in the security of the dining room, monitored down to the last tick and wave pattern from next door; they concluded their meal in a quiet exchange of promises and well-wishes and he escorted them to the hall and outside.

Ben and Tano had set up a table there, and Kaplan was seated with them when the door whisked open. Kaplan scrambled up, snatching his helmet and putting it on, very official. God knew what view their monitoring security had with the thing on the table, as it had been angled . . . or whether anyone was currently watching. It had been in a position to keep watch on the door.

"No need to be stiff-backed, Kaplan."

"No, sir." Kaplan had something in his mouth. Had pockets stuffed.

"Enjoy the candy?"

"Very much, sir."

"I like the orange ones, myself."

"I haven't had the orange ones. Just the red."

"Nadi-ji," Bren said, turning to Narani, "kindly find this young man a variety of the sweets, including damighindi ones, if you will."

Of all people on the station, he wanted to keep Kaplan well-disposed, for one thing because they might owe the young man an apology, one of these days; for another, because Kaplan's was the finger on the trigger, most locally, most likely, and he wanted Kaplan to have just that instant of remorse and regret that would give his own security a chance. *They* would have no remorse, but they wouldn't kill the young man, either, if there was a chance to avoid it: such were their standing orders.

He'd had time for Banichi's warning to sink in, with all its implications. He knew to what extent he was valuable, and knew that in the same way he'd resisted coming here, Tabini had dreaded sending him: Tabini had given Banichi and Jago direct orders, and here they were.

He'd told Kroger as much as he dared say. The rest . . . the rest depended on getting to the shuttle and getting it safely away. The captains had declined to stay abreast of their plans.

They shouldn't be surprised if those plans shifted around their own, and shifted in a major way.

Narani came back with a brimming double handful, which Kaplan took and stuffed into any pocket that had any room at all. The man blushed with embarrassment, thanked them, and filled every pocket to the top, until cellophane was clearly visible.

"Have to eat a few," Bren said cheerfully. "Obviously, or you'll shed them on your way."

"Yes, sir. Thank you, sir."

He wondered if Kaplan was sleeping at all on so strong a sugar intake. Jase had found it quite stimulating, in more ways than one, and addictive. *Spread them around,* he wished Kaplan without saying a word. *Let the rest of the crew share.*

They had to include a few crates of sweets and fruit juice on the next shuttle flight.

21

Another day, and the next, his last day, and not a word from his mother. Not a word from Toby. C1 claimed intermittent troubles, and said that Mogari-nai might have gotten the notion they weren't transmitting, they'd had so many equipment failures.

"I don't believe it," Bren said to Jago. "The message I have from Tabini-aiji is the most bland thing possible. *Felicitations,* in the plural for a population."

"It's faked," Jago said quietly. "They have text from the aiji's messages to them."

"But don't know one plural from another," Bren said. "Damned right it's faked."

"An indignity," Jago said.

"Hardly one we can take exception to at the moment." It was a death sentence, on the planet, inside the aishidi'tat. "One just has to be patient. They have no idea of the seriousness of the act. Tolerance, tolerance."

"One is tolerant," Jago said, with a grim and determined look. "But where is Jase, Bren-ji? Is this tolerance?"

"Good question," he said. And then had a horrid thought, considering Banichi's foray to the shuttle dock. "One I absolutely forbid you to try to solve, Jago-ji. You and Banichi, and Tano, and Algini. You stay here."

"We take no chances with your safety, Bren-ji," Jago assured him. "One wishes the paidhi simply pack those very few essentials, and we will go early, without Kaplan-nadi."

"I *am* packed," he said, "whenever I fold up the computer case and have it in my hand."

"You will not wish to leave it here, under Tano's guard."

"Much as I trust *him,* I daren't tempt trouble on him.

They might attempt him, if they thought that prize was here; they're less likely to attack me, no matter how I affront them."

"Nevertheless," Jago said, and went to a drawer in his sparsely furnished room and took out a small packet of cloth. She brought it to him, and began to unroll it, and by its size and shape he had a sinking feeling what it was.

"Jago-ji, it's hardly that great a threat . . ."

"Nevertheless," she repeated, and gave him the gun which had followed him, in his baggage, from one place to the other throughout his career with them. "Put this in the computer case."

"I shall," he said. "Or have it somewhere about me. I understand completely. I have no wish to endanger you and Banichi by having no defense, but I say again that my rank and their needs are my best defense."

"Nevertheless," she said for the third time.

"I agree," he said, and put it into the case's outer pocket, hoping the shape didn't show too much. "There. Trust that I'll use good sense." A thought occurred to him. "Trust that I have no more compunction shooting at humans than I do shooting at atevi."

"Which is to say, far too much compunction," Jago said. "But we agree with you that we wish a peaceful passage, and a completely uneventful flight."

"I'll be missing supper with the captain," he said.

"Is the paidhi concerned about that?"

"It's not the same as declining supper with the aiji. She knew when she asked me. She won't be that surprised. She won't take it personally, at least. There's very little personal in it. That's the problem."

"In what way is it a problem?" she asked.

"If it were personal, she and I would have been talking before now. But we aren't, and it isn't, and I don't think she plans to keep that appointment any more than the last. It was only a means to ask me if I was going to leave. That she didn't choose to ask me directly what should have been a plain question indicates something to me about the minds of the captains, that everything, no matter how simple, is complicated and clandestine; that, as Jase told me, no one ever states a plain intention unless it's an order, and the captains don't give one another orders."

"Do they do this setting the course of the ship?"

He laughed. "I don't think it goes that far."

"Then one of them can make decisions."

One had to think about that, one had to think very carefully on that point. If the rumor was so, Ramirez had ceased to be that person.

"Whenever you and Banichi think good," he said, "I'm ready to leave."

A presence hovered at the door, in the tail of his eye. He gave it a full look, and saw Narani, with, of all things, the silver message tray from the hall table.

That was the very last thing he had ever thought to see in use. He thought it must be some parting courtesy from the staff, a wish for his safe flight, a promise of their performance of duty.

"'Rani-ji," he said, summoning him forward, and Narani offered the silver tray.

"From a woman," Narani said.

From outside? A written message, rolled up, atevi-style? He opened it with trepidation.

It said, in bad courtly Ragi,

> *This message risks our lives, but we need your help, we need it extremely despairingly. If hostile person finds us we all die. Your lordship must not trust any of the leaders in charge of the boat. If you can make unlocked your doorway in the night I have attempted to visit, with all trepidations regarding security.*

"It's *Jase,*" he said, his voice hushed, even in this secure place. "It's his handwriting." The written language of court documents challenged even educated atevi, but Jase had rendered a gallant effort. "Not a damned melon in the document."

Jase had his problems with homonyms. But no one else on the station *could* have written it in just that degree of semi-competency.

"Narani-ji," he said, handing the document to Jago to read for herself. "Was it Kate?"

"No, nandi," Narani said. "A woman of years, if I can judge, and very anxious to be away."

Jase's mother was on the station. Friends. Cousins. God knew who it had been; their own hall surveillance might give him the image, but in that sense it made no difference who had gotten it to them. The fact was, it *was* from Jase, and the only scarier knowledge was, if it had been Jase's mother, *she* might be in some danger.

"He intends to try to join us," Jago said. "Tonight. Is there any means they might forge this document, Bren-ji? Is it at all possible?"

"Not as far as I know. Even a computer . . . even the most advanced computer . . . there are the impresses of the pen on the other side, and the paper . . . the ship *has* no paper, Jago-ji. It's not something they manufacture. Jase when he came had never written on paper, only on a slate. Never used a pen, only a pointed stick of a thing."

"One recalls so," Jago said, and added, "Jase did take a notebook with him."

"You inspected his packing?"

"He had few clothes, things which I know the ship to lack: sweets, a thick notebook, a packet of pens, a bottle of perfume. He went through no personal scan." Jago looked entirely uncomfortable, rare for her. "This may have been very remiss of us. But no more did we search you, nandi."

Weapons were in one sense the thing his security noticed most—on the person of an outsider; in another sense, they were so ordinary as to be transparent, if an ally had them in plain sight.

"God," Bren said quietly, then answered his own question, even considering Jase exercising his dislike of his captains. "No, he wouldn't. He would not, Jago-ji. Never in the world would he destabilize our situation up here. He can't have. They keep saying he's in a meeting."

"Which you say is a lie."

"I know it is. But I think they believe he can't contact us, and that means under their watch or under their control. If he brought something through and they searched his baggage, as he surely knew they might—but he can't have lived under your guidance for three years and have done something so rash."

"One would hope at least he would not be caught," Jago said fervently. "He does most clearly have the notebook."

"And a *hell* of a sense of timing! God! What do I do with this?"

"What is wise to do, nandi?" Jago asked. "What must be done, for this mission?"

It was surely a Guild question, *her* Guild's question: the dispassionate, the thoroughly professional question. What is wise to do?

Fail an appointment with Jase? Leave him vulnerable?

Or interfere in the inner workings of the Pilots' Guild, which was an endlessly proliferating problem?

It was a problem they were bound to meet, in long years of working with the Pilots' Guild. Tabini considered Jase his own, now. *He* did. There was no question of support for Jase's position on their side, no question what he *wanted* to do.

His arrangements at present didn't leave a station without representatives from the planet. It wasn't an inert, changeless situation, rather one in which Jase, if he was somehow involved in Ramirez' troubles, could become involved, changing everything.

Creating God-knew-what while he was back on the planet, unable to investigate what was happening.

"If he wants off this station, we're the only ticket," he said to Jago. "He knows the shuttle's going. He's taken the chance and made his break for our side."

"Man'chi," Jago said, though she well knew she was dealing with humans who felt it erratically, that overwhelming drive to reach one's own side, one's own aiji, in a crisis.

"Something like that," he said. "But he's not helpless against it. He knows what he's asking us to risk. He knows I can't act for my own welfare, or his, when it jeopardizes the whole damned planet. He can't ask that. I won't give that to my own mother, Jago! How can I give it to him?"

"Is he asking that?" Jago asked sensibly, and he had to draw a less panicked breath.

"No. He doesn't know we're going, and he doesn't know we're going early, but he knows the way you work. He doesn't even know we can get that door open, but he suspects you can do it. This is not a confident expedition, Jago-ji. He's desperate. I think he's completely desperate. But, damn! Damn it all!"

"I should tell Banichi."

"We should tell Banichi," he agreed. "We should establish some sort of watch in the corridor. I don't know what they can spot on their security boards, but I wouldn't have that door unlocked longer than need be."

"We know when something moves out there," Jago said. "Have no fear of that, Bren-ji. But when he comes, we may go to the shuttle in a great hurry. One should be ready."

One should be ready. One sat ready, waiting, for hours, talking companionably with Tano and Algini, who would be in charge here, with Narani and the others, who would be dealing with Kroger once they left.

They should be moving now. They should have reached the shuttle by now. It was technically night, and past midnight, that less active hour on the station. The computer was packed, he had his coat on, Banichi and Jago had their coats on.

They waited, having brought chairs into the corridor, just outside the security post, so that he could talk simultaneously to Tano and Algini and the staff, and he declined a cup of tea when the hours dragged on. There was a chance of long waits at the other end of their journey tonight, a chance of having to wait out of view, and he wanted not to have his eyes floating while waiting. He had tucked a few of Kaplan's sweets in his pockets: the slightly sour ones helped relieve a dry mouth, and dry and ice cold was the condition of the air in the core. He had good gloves in his pocket.

And they waited for a visitation.

All at once Tano and Algini paid sharp attention to their boards and passed a signal to Banichi.

Banichi rose; they all rose as Banichi attached a small device above the switch, and opened the door.

Jase was there, Jase in that wretched fishing jacket, Jase pale, sweating and out of breath, and with a hell of a bruise on his cheek.

Bren welcomed him, flung arms about him, making his security very anxious, considering the circumstances, but Jase hugged him hard as Banichi shut the door.

"Where have you been?" Bren asked, first question, at

arm's length and searching a familiar face for answers. "What in hell's going on?"

"They shot Ramirez. He's *alive*. Bren, I need your help!"

The one thing he wanted to avoid was entanglement *inside* the Pilots' Guild. Anything but that.

And Jase delivered it on his doorstep.

"Who hit you?"

"Getting Ramirez away," Jase said, still out of breath—scared: that was logical, but completely done in, into the bargain. "Been hiding. Had to trust. Had to prevent you going."

He'd spoken in his own language, had had nothing else to deal in but his childhood language for the last ten days, and probably couldn't think in Ragi at the moment, but it was important the staff understand all the nuances. "Ragi," Bren said, in that language. "This is the aiji's territory. We aren't giving it up, nadi-ji. You're safe here."

"Not safe," Jase said on a shaky breath, holding to his sleeves. "Bren, Bren, —I can't think. No words. Drink of water."

"He asks for water, Rani-ji. —Where have you been?"

"Hiding. Cold. No food. No water. Ramirez, we gave to him—but not much left."

"Get in here and sit down." Bren steered him to the nearest door, to the security station, and a chair by Tano, who offered a guiding hand. "Where have you been?" Bren pursued him. "Jase, make sense. Is anyone after you? Is the whole station in this condition? What's going on?"

"Don't think anyone's followed. Becky, my mother, few people, got us food and water, not much. It freezes, there. Blankets. I didn't know—didn't know whether he'd make it; tried to get here once. Couldn't. Becky's with him. With Ramirez. Crew doesn't know. They don't want it known."

"We can deal with that," Bren said.

"They're smart. They'll get ahead of us. They'll lie."

"Who'll lie?"

"Tamun. Tamun and his crew. I can't stay here. I've got to get back to him. Bren, have you got medicines? We don't have any medicines. Containers for water."

"You can't go back through the corridors loaded like a

mecheita at market, nadi. If they're after you, you can't take a damned picnic lunch."

"I know. I know. What I can put in my jacket. I can't leave him. Can't stay here."

"We're supposed to be leaving on this shuttle, tomorrow!"

"I thought you might." He reached out for the water Narani offered him, and had a sip, and a second. "Oh, that's good."

"I have the aiji's business to do! You know I can't divert myself on personal privilege!"

"I know you won't," Jase said hoarsely, rolling a look at him, and taking a third, a long, reckless gulp.

"God, you've handed me a mess!"

"I got him away!" Jase fired back at him. "I have him alive!"

"Banichi-ji," Bren said, "we have a rather serious problem."

"One gathers enough of this to believe so," Banichi said.

"What do you want us to do?" Bren asked of Jase.

"I don't know. If I knew I'd do it. Bren. *Bren!"* Jase made a strong bid for his attention as Bren looked momentarily toward Banichi. "Bren, they've given out among the crew that Ramirez was shot when I tried to take him hostage. That's the story. That's what they're saying. It's an atevi plot to have their way, and I'm in on it."

"Can Ramirez refute it?"

"He won't last ten minutes in their hands."

"Then bring him here."

"We can't. We aren't where we can get through the halls carrying him. We're in a service corridor, where they were working, where they haven't powered up yet, but there's a few . . ." Jase drew a breath. "This didn't take everybody by surprise. They're not working there now, but those who were, they know how to set up, and they did, and they warned me Ramirez was in danger, but I didn't know how much. And now we're there, and there's not damn much heat and there's no water because it won't flow through the pipes, but there's air pressure, because it's an air lock, and we can get it."

"You're living in an air lock?"

"A work area airlock. It's large. There's six of us." Jase's teeth began to chatter and he fought to control it. "I knew it would be hard, Bren. I didn't know it would be like this. I thought I could reason with Ramirez. I thought he could control the rest. I didn't know they'd go this far."

"We have made every arrangement," Banichi said, "to remove Bren from the station, Jasi-ji. In all high regard for you, the aiji's interests are best served if Bren is removed from this venue as soon as possible."

"I can't go," Bren said. "I can't go now." Very clearly his security was ready to hit him over the head and carry him to the shuttle, no idle threat, and he could not permit that. "We *are* involved. I didn't want this, but Jase is here, and whatever we do next, it can't be to leave him stranded."

"We can take him with us," Banichi said, "we can hold him here within this section and defy the captains to remove him. There are alternatives."

"The situation aboard is in flux," Bren said. "Baji-naji. If we take Jase away, Ramirez' interests will fall entirely or the station will enter a period of factional warfare that the aishidi'tat can ill afford."

"Nor can the aishidi'tat afford to lose you, nadi. You cannot run this risk."

"I'm valueless if I sit idle, Banichi."

"This is not a fifteen-day decision," Banichi said. "It's thirty days. Twice that, that the shuttle will remain on the ground."

"Then it can return with additional security," Bren said. "How likely, Jasi-ji, is Ramirez to survive his injuries?"

"With medicines, he may," Jase said. "Fever is setting in. We daren't take him anywhere. I have to get back to him, Banichi." He had recovered some of his fluency in Ragi. "It's not only man'chi, which I do feel, but logic. Without this man, my people will fall under Tamun's control and use only the Mospheirans, and destabilize them by doing so, and destabilize the aishidi'tat, perhaps, too, if things go badly."

"He's right," Bren said. "If Tamun deals with the likes of Gaylord Hanks, we're in trouble. The Mospheirans are back under the hand of the Guild, they're in civil war over that, and we in the aishidi'tat are in for a very rough ride being the only source of earth-to-orbit transport, with weapons orbiting over our heads, nadiin-ji. Remember, the ship is heavily armed. Under ill-disposed leadership, it might issue threats against the aishidi'tat, completely ignorant of the realities on the planet, completely foolish, completely unable to make peace after it has made a war greater than the War of the Landing. Bad as the situation is, Banichi-ji, I can *be* in no better position than I am now. We have Jase. We have a warning. The crew hasn't fallen all the way into Tamun's hands. There remains something we can do."

"There remains something the paidhi can do on the ground, too," Banichi said, "in safety. One can cut them off from labor and supplies and sit and wait. That is the more prudent course, nand' paidhi. We can rescue Jase, who can attest the truth of what happened, which they must deal with if they wish supply. The Mospheirans cannot build a shuttle. They have no materials. Above all else we must remove the shuttle from their reach until we have some resolution. We *cannot* allow them to have it."

Banichi's argument was a telling one, victory the slow way, starving the Guild of labor and supplies, possibly entailing the fall of the rebel captains.

"Yet if they know we have boarded with Jase and that we're taking that shuttle down to the mainland, not to return," Bren said, "they may move against us, and we may end with a damaged shuttle or a shuttle held by force."

"We have the other shuttles, not yet complete, but approaching it."

"And no destination for them without the station, and without the ship," Jase said. "Nadiin-ji, I can't leave Ramirez to die. I have to go back to him, now. He has to have the medicines. That's the answer to all of this. He can't die. I agree we have to get him here. We have to get him help. But right now, he needs help where he is, and every moment I stay here, the condition in the corridors could change."

"Thirty days' wait," Jago said. "Thirty days and an unpredictable situation."

"What situation? We've never received this information," Bren said in a tone of mock indignation. "We've had no visitor. We know nothing. They're cutting us off from Tabini's messages and no knowing what else, but we know nothing of that; we're completely ignorant and suppose Tabini simply has nothing to say. We carry on for thirty days, and wait for our messages to get down with the crew."

"We might trade one steward for one servant," Banichi said. "Nojana would be an asset. The shuttle can spare him."

"Dangerous," Bren said.

"We have to get them word, at any event," Banichi said. "If they see nothing of us, the shuttle will have a mechanical hold, some small problem, until they do hear."

How could he not foresee Banichi would have some such arrangement? He was appalled. "So we must contact them . . . and we have Kroger to deal with, too. We can't let them blithely proceed while we change our plans. They'll be outraged."

"One has one's tasks to do," Banichi said.

Bren cast him an unhappy look.

"First I must find where Jase is lodged," Banichi said, "and safeguard his return. Then Kroger. But Kandana can go to the shuttle, and exchange very easily with Nojana. If Nojana arrives, we shall know the message reached them."

"Be *careful*," Bren said.

"I mean to be," Banichi said. "Shall we find the medications, Bren-ji?"

"Do," Bren said, and laid a hand on Jase's shoulder. "If the place you're hiding has you in this condition, it can't be helping Ramirez. We have to get him *here*, into warmth, and care."

"He won't," Jase said, down to the honest truth. "He won't agree. I tried to persuade him. He's off his head, maybe, but I don't think so. While he's on his own, he's still in command. He hasn't appealed to anyone else, any outsider. He'll order the crew when he's strong enough."

"What's the damage?" Bren asked. "What help has he got? What care?"

"There's a medic with us," Jase said. "Or he might have died. We've gotten supplies in. We've got a blanket for him. We're just kind of short."

"He needs warmth," Bren translated. "Jase, *think in Ragi.*"

Jase made an obvious, physical effort. "I'm trying," he said in that language. "I'm just tired. Questions. A lot of questions. No sleep. Hiding. I'm not thinking at my best."

"One of my sweaters," Bren said. "I know we brought a couple. Whatever we can fit you up with. Is cold all you're contending with?"

"Cold, dark, there's just not much . . ." Jase looked for

a moment as if he'd fall on his face, and Bren brought him up with a hand on his shoulder.

"The hell you're fit to go back!"

"Have to," Jase said. "Not a choice."

"Banichi, if you can assess the conditions, determine whether we have anything that might assist."

"We have an emergency supply, condensates, warming cylinders, oxygen, water."

"We don't have liquid water," Jase said, "but we take ice. All of that, all of that would help."

"Easily done," Banichi said. "We should move soon. Jasi-ji is right. This is a period of little activity in the corridors; it will increase in another half hour. Jago will go to Kroger, Kandana to Nojana, and I will find where Jase is hiding."

"Can Kandana do it? Will he know his way?"

"There, quite well, I'm sure," Banichi said. "And Nojana needs no instruction."

"Then do it," Bren said. At certain times a prudent, reasonable man simply had to trust his security was right and dismiss the alarms clenching up his own stomach as far less important, not deserving of panic.

He was afraid, nonetheless. He was altogether afraid, and it was as hard to send Banichi and Jago out on their risky ventures as it was to send Jase off to his hiding place.

"You tell them," he said last to Jase, "that if they harm you, the aiji will take a very hard line with them, and that the aiji has a firm alliance with Mospheira, no matter what they think; tell them you're highly regarded in the Mospheiran government as well, and if they harm a hair on your head they'll have no cooperation."

"I never was as convincing as you," Jase said, in a laugh a little short of desperate.

"If they harm you," Bren said, "in any way, *I'll* file Intent. I'm not joking. I'll take them down, personally, under the legitimate provisions of atevi law."

Jase had started to laugh, obedient good will, but then he seemed to understand that it was indeed serious. Jase understood Banichi's Guild very well, by all his experience on the planet.

"I'm not worth that," Jase said.

"If they deal badly with one of their own, who wishes them

nothing but good," Bren said, "then damn them to hell, and *we'll* govern, the aiji will govern this whole solar system, by atevi law. The aiji will tolerate all sorts of provocations, but you think about it, Jase. Chaos is the absolute enemy of the aishidi'tat, and he won't have it, he won't have the abuse of his own associates up here. I told you that you have power. Use it!" He took Jase by both arms and lightened his grip on the left as Jase winced. "You get back here, hear me? Make it unnecessary for me to do anything so rash. I set that on your shoulders, because if anything happens to you, I'll take this place apart. Hear me?"

"I do," Jase said. "I'll be careful."

"Fishing trip," Bren said. "Promise."

"Deal," Jase said. "I've got to go. I've got to go now."

"Get out of here," Bren said. "Banichi."

"I am with nand' Jase," Banichi said. "Jago-ji, instruct Kandana."

"Yes," Jago said, and on that, Banichi hurried Jase out the supposedly locked door, with no fuss or delay at all.

"It's not supposed to do that," Bren said, feeling that things were not at all going according to his preferences. Half an hour ago he'd thought he was bound down to the planet where he could present Tabini apologetically with a negotiation gone to hell and ask his brother whether he'd been able to find his wife and children.

That was not the state of affairs he had. He had just been coopted into the very thing he least wanted, and the very thing that might *give* Tabini what he demanded, if they could keep Ramirez alive . . . if he could get his security team back alive, and Jase back alive.

Someone was in deadly earnest, some eruption of factional violence within the crew, and he could only look to their defenses and hope his security had foreseen the control of heat, light, and air being in hostile hands up here.

He could not permit the situation to degenerate. He had his meeting scheduled with Sabin, sure as he was she would break the appointment. He had Ramirez within reach, and the means, perhaps, perhaps, to get word to the crew—if he could get to the one almost-friendly officer in C1 . . .

He sat down with his computer and drafted an announcement:

Captain Ramirez, having suffered an attempt on his life, has taken shelter . . .

Sometimes one could see things more clearly in draft. And if that message went out, the immediate counter-rumor would be that outsiders had done it; if Ramirez died, they would be left with that accusation hanging over them.

But if Ramirez died, Jase would be the scapegoat, Jase who had *ties* to the foreign power, Jase who could no longer be trusted.

He saw the net drawing about them. He saw absolute chaos developing in the prospect of Kroger going down and him staying and his crew running about the corridors in various small teams.

He really wanted an antacid.

He wrote: *A dissident faction on the Guild Council has attacked and wounded Captain Ramirez. He appeals for support among the crew. The crew must demand the return of Ramirez and the support of his agreements . . .*

Who? he asked himself in despair. Who would support those programs?

And he remembered Ogun's face, Ogun's handshake, the fact that Ramirez had chosen Ogun to sit with him, the whole changing body language of that meeting that indicated to him that Ogun, too, had reached a like decision.

He cleared that draft and wrote, a third time:

Captain Ogun, Captain Ramirez needs your help. Jase Graham saved his life from an attack from someone who wanted the agreements nullified. I think you know better than I who that would be. We will stand by you and Ramirez and the agreements, and we have rejected the chance to go down to the planet. During this crisis, we offer whatever support you may need, including secure quarters.

He opted not to rouse help from C1 just yet. But he wrote:

Aiji-ma, things are going as optimally as in any mach-imi of homecoming.

And in Mosphei', to his mother:

Please let me know how things are going.

He wanted to write: *I've not been sure my messages are reaching you,* but he dared not give so strong a hint that he suspected the majority of his messages were going straight into a black hole, and that the ones he had been getting were old messages recycled.

Instead he wrote: I've had a great deal of time to think how very much the family has arranged its affairs and its expectations around me, and I think this has always been a strain on everyone. Trust that I'm well, Mum, and that I'm happy where I am. My brother's grown up into a remarkable man, and I hope you see that and give those great kids of his a hug for me. We're both your successes. I just turned out a little different, that's all, and I'm very content with that difference and with the choices I've made. I'll never stop loving you and Toby, and no matter where I am, I'll always be with you in mind and heart.

It was one of his better letters. He hoped it survived to get to her.

He wrote to a few of the councillors as well, the usual assurances that he remembered them. He did. He wrote to his staff, bidding them take privilege as they could and rest, since more work seemed imminent.

He hoped that would be the case.

He waited until near stationside dawn, and was still waiting when Nojana turned up, quietly.

"Nadi," Narani said, "Nojana has arrived safely. What place shall I assign him?"

"Kandana's, for now," Bren said, and heaved a breath of relief, hoping now that the shuttle made schedule. "Thank him. I'll speak to him after breakfast."

In a very little more, Jago slipped into the section.

"How did they take it?" Bren asked her first of all. "How was it out there?"

Jago gave a delicate shrug. "Banichi isn't back yet?"

"Not yet."

"There was a close pass of their security," Jago said. "I

heard them, and feared they might come my way. I took a lift up, then down again when I hoped they had gone."

Hearing. *There* was an atevi advantage he generally forgot to reckon.

"I hope Banichi hurries," he said. "The Mospheirans weren't pleased, I'll imagine."

"Not pleased. Tom-nadi is still going down, to fly to Mospheira to report; he hopes to come back on the next shuttle. Gin-nadi is remaining. She thanks you for your advisement and wishes to meet with you."

"You told her about Ramirez."

"Yes, nadi." Jago was very clear on that. "I told Kate-nadi to be sure the message was accurate, and asked Kate-nadi not to speak the news aloud, but to write it for her very small and to beg her not to speak this information aloud even among themselves. I indicated also we believe they are monitored. She replied by writing, and I memorized it and destroyed the note: namely this." Jago took a breath. " 'The hardliners have taken control. They want to deal only with us, using only Mospheiran help, no atevi in orbit. They want to fill out the crew by training Mospheirans. I've told them we can't produce the resources and can't manufacture what they need. They talk about surmounting that problem. The ship is armed, but I don't know what they can do. I believe we are potentially in trouble.' That is word for word her answer. Tom-nadi is going down to warn the President."

"It's not good news."

"Do they think to start another war?" Jago asked him. "Does this reference to weapons mean weapons turned against the mainland?"

"I don't discount the possibility. I rather think they mean that they can get the Mospheirans up here. *That* means getting their hands on a shuttle and being able to fly it."

"The shuttle has no accessible autopilot," Jago reminded him.

The autopilot required a complex code which atevi pilots would not surrender. "I'll feel better when I know it's away clear," Bren said, and thought to himself, *And when Banichi's back.*

22

"C1," Bren said, "send-receive to Mogari-nai."

"Yes, sir."

There was no question to him about the shuttle, which was due to depart. Nojana had informed them that the captain's instructions were clear and that the shuttle was continuing a normal preparation for launch. Kandana would be aboard by now; Lund would be headed in that direction at any moment, for a launch at local 0900, and there was still no Banichi, still no word from Jase, no word, as Bren expected at any moment, that the meeting with Sabin was canceled.

Come on, he wished Banichi, as everyone on staff tried to pretend cheerfulness in spite of the situation. Jago was brisk, cheerful in her comings and goings.

Bren thought of the fact of Banichi's absence in every other breath, telling himself that if anything should happen to Banichi for his sake he would never forgive himself. He could hardly look at Jago. He had no cheerfulness to spare.

The upload was felicitations for the safe shuttle flight from numerous agencies, and from his mother . . .

From his mother, an honest-to-God letter.

They say you're on the space station, and that's why you couldn't return my calls. I shouldn't be surprised ever at anything, I suppose. I know you must be worried about Barb. I sent her flowers in your name. She came through the surgery. She's very strong. She's gotten rid of a couple of the tubes, which she says is about time. I haven't told her where you are. She doesn't remember anything about the accident. She asks whether she fell on the escalators or whether she was shot or something. And you tell her, but she forgets. They still have her sedated, and she wanders in and out. She talked about going up to Mt. Adams with you, to the lodge. She said you'd promised that. I haven't told her anything to the contrary. You can't reason with sick people and this isn't the time for it.

I had a disturbing call from Toby. He's having trouble with Jill. He says she objects to his coming here, as if she didn't visit her family two and three times a year, not to mention dropping those kids on Louise. I think Toby should put his foot down about that. The children run around at all hours, and I know they've slipped out of the house at night. Louise can't keep up with them, and if Jill doesn't take a strong hand with those kids, they're going to be a problem in another couple of years. Toby just thinks anything Jill wants is fine and the kids are spoiled the same way. Too many material things, not enough family time, and by my opinion, too much running about on that boat. I never approved of exposing the children to the mainland. I know certain things are all right for you. But the children shouldn't see them.

At any rate, things are quieter here. I wish you were here.

Why did he let things like this bother him? *Why,* amid every other world-threatening worry he had, did this one letter send his blood pressure soaring, and how could it persuade him he was derelict not to drop everything and run home and talk sense to his mother?

There was no logic. She was his mother.

He wished she hadn't written today. He honestly wished that. And felt guilty about it. He felt *angry* about Barb lying there with a damned batch of flowers his mother had signed his name to.

How *dare* she? Easily. She just did, that was all. She knew best. Ask her.

"Bren-ji." It was Jago who leaned in the door, supporting her weight in transit on the door frame. "Four men outside."

The knell of doom, it might be. His mind leaped into a completely different track: Banichi might have run into serious trouble. Talking them out of it might be an option, but not with a handful of armed men.

And there was a *reason* atevi residences were constructed as they were. *"Mantos an,"* he said, for which there was no translation, nor any more order needed. Jago relayed the order, *mantos an,* and every door they owned whisked shut, within the same ten seconds.

Jago stayed on his side of the door. He was certain that Tano and Algini were in the security post, and that that door was shut, and in his mind's eye he could all but see Narani, alone, walking to the door.

The station might have opened that outer door and secured a tactical advantage. Whatever was up, they had opted not to do that.

Bren rose, having taken the gun from his computer case, wondering if the captains' men might cut down Narani and use some electronic key to the door locks, defeating all but armed resistence; and for some moments he waited, quiet, straining to hear any activity at all outside.

Then came a light, muted tap at the door, and Jago opened it, on her guard: he stood with gun leveled.

Narani was there, alone, with the silver tray, bearing an odd wisp of pink cellophane. A candy wrapper, and a card.

"They have no message cylinders, as it seems," Narani said. "They are John-son-nadi and his associates, the ones displaced by our residency."

Bren cast Jago half a glance, confused, but it was most certainly a candy wrapper, and somehow it had ended up in the transaction with Johnson and associates. "Kaplan," was his instant guess, the only route by which it might have happened, and he set his gun carefully on the counter and went out into the hall, with Narani.

Their front door, as it were, stood open, and Johnson, Andresson, Pressman, and Polano waited quite respectfully in the corridor.

"Mr. Cameron?" Johnson said. "We came to name our favor." And when he said nothing to that remarkable statement: "You're passing out those sweets for favors. Have you got any more?"

His security was on highest alert, Banichi was missing, and he wasn't without suspicions it was a reconnoitering mission; but he solemnly translated for Narani, who bowed and went off to find the requisite stores.

"My head of staff is looking for them," he said. "Friends of Kaplan?"

"Cousin," Andresson said.

"Ah. Would you like to come in and have tea?"

"Don't know tea, sir."

"Well, probably I shouldn't. It kept Jase awake all night the first time he had it. But I can see imports will be very popular."

"Like the sweets, sir."

"I favor them myself." He heard Narani coming back, but did not turn his head, having had Banichi and Jago for teachers. He received the small box, a common tin box, and presented it to Johnson. "Very happy to oblige."

"You want this back, sir?"

"The box? It's yours, if you like it."

"It's got pictures," Johnson protested.

It was printed with flowers and fruits, as it happened, and had an oval with the inset of a sea. Indeed it was a fine little box, where paper was unknown.

"I hope you enjoy them. We're very comfortable here, thanks to you. If you'd like to come back when you're truly off-duty . . . we could show you some of Jase's favorites. I wonder if you aren't that Johnson he mentioned."

"There's thirty of us Johnsons aboard," Johnson said. "And he's captains' level, which we don't get to, much."

Sometimes a devil took him. There was no other way he found to describe it. He had wanted to get word out to the crew, and in that small personal confidence, he saw an opening and went for it. "I heard the rumor. Have they caught the person responsible?"

"What rumor, sir?"

"That Ramirez was shot. You *haven't* heard? Maybe it's not true."

"Shot, sir? *What's* this?"

"I don't know. I heard something. You're Kaplan's cousin, are you?" The business of the request for candies had made complete sense to him now. Kaplan had had some to repay a personal favor; they were promised a favor; they wanted theirs in candy, and God knew what the sugar hits were selling for within the crew. "They're trying to blame Jase Graham, and that's a damned lie. Jase likes

Ramirez. I know damned well Jase would never shoot him—and where'd he get a gun, when he'd just been through a security check? But others hadn't. I'm damned upset. We had an agreement that was going to get the ship fueled, and now there's somebody trying to kill Ramirez, who for all I know is locked up in fear for his life."

"You're jessing us."

"I'm worried, is what. You're the only ones I've talked to in days. I don't like what I'm hearing, and I think maybe there's something damned underhanded going on. You want to come back here and talk to me, I'll be glad to tell you and anybody else in the crew what I know, which is that there's something damned messy in the works that's somebody's notion of getting the Mospheirans to work with them, but the Mospheirans won't, they don't want it, and some folk on this station are just scared to death of the atevi, who're doing their damndest to help . . . Narani, attend me closely. Smile . . . Does this look like an enemy? He's a perfectly upright, peaceful man with grandchildren."

"Yes, sir," Johnson murmured. "But we're security and we're supposed to know if there's something going on."

Security, was it? Naïve as children, and looking for a bribe, however fierce they might be if they were set off. "Look for yourselves, have a good look. We've got a table that violates a code, as I understand, a grandfather who's doing his own job the best he can, and my room, all my secret goings-on, right here, perfectly in the open . . . Jago, put the gun up and come smile at these gentlemen."

Jago came out and smiled and bowed very nicely, despite the sidearm neatly in its holster.

"Nadiin," she said, and said, in Ragi, "Be careful of these men, nandi."

"One certainly is," he said, and in his best approximation of Jase's dialect, "Damned mess, is what. My staff is concerned."

"Where'd you hear this?" Johnson asked bluntly. "Who told you?"

"I got it from the Mospheirans," he said, total fabrication. "I think they heard it in the bar in their area. It's a rumor. But it is sure we were supposed to meet with Ramirez days ago and it keeps being put off and put off, and no one ever meets. Tell *Ogun* what I've told you."

"We'd better get out of here," Polano said, and the others thought so, too. They retreated to the door, still with their box of candy.

"You tell whoever you report to that we're damned tired of waiting," Bren said, "and we don't care who we deal with, but we're here to deal and get this place operational. Tell Kaplan . . . tell him, too. I owe him an explanation. Tell him to get here."

"Yes, sir," Johnson said, and the door shut.

Bren heaved a deep, shaky breath, regretting twice over that Banichi hadn't shown up, and likely wouldn't, now, until the down cycle of the activity in the corridors. Banichi was lying up somewhere, surely, surely that was what had happened. It had just gotten hot wherever Jase was, and Banichi hadn't thought it safe.

Or Banichi was playing medic, in which Banichi had some small skill. Banichi would have used his own sense about that.

"You mentioned Ramirez to them," Jago remarked when the door was shut.

"I more than mentioned him," he said. "I told them the truth. They're security, but they're also part of the crew, and they're not happy about this, never mind the damn box of candy. Have we more of that coming, Rani-ji?"

"Of the candy, nandi? Yes. Kandana made a special note of it."

"Good." He rapped a code on the security post door, and was not surprised to see guns on the other side of it as it opened. "It's all right," he said, but he didn't know how more to reassure the staff. "I've broken our silence with the crew, baji-naji. Having Banichi gone and not knowing . . . I don't know whether I was wise, nadiin-ji, but we have limited means to make known what we do know. I'd rather have told Kaplan, but I made a choice. We don't know how long we have. We *assume* the shuttle will depart on schedule. Maintain watch. Anticipate a shutdown of lights and air."

"We remain prepared," Tano said.

"Could I doubt?" he answered. He didn't, not them.

Himself, and his own breakneck course through a field of rocks, oh, he had numerous doubts.

He could have waited until the shuttle left before doing something so rash.

He hadn't.

And he sweated the hours until, quite predictably, C1 read him a note from Sabin giving her regrets, her apologies for missing the meeting with him, and resetting it for the 16th at 1300 hours.

"Of course," he said quietly. "I suppose the shuttle got off safely."

It was after time. There was nothing to tell them, one way or the other.

"Right on time, sir. Nominal."

"That's very good," he said. "Thank you, thank you very much, C1."

Jago happened to be in the room, reviewing a section of the station maps.

"The shuttle has departed," she restated in Ragi.

"Just so," he said. "Reportedly without incident." He added, because it was the truth: "We now wait, Jago-ji. We have to wait very artfully, very cleverly, and hope what I did today doesn't cause us difficulties."

"One doubts we might supply ourselves so long," Jago said. "But we have identified valves which make it unlikely they would subject this entire section to harsh measures. We seem to share common conduits with quite an extensive occupied area. We measure considerable flow. To deprive us would deprive them."

"That's very good news," he said.

"On the other hand," she said, "we might disrupt that flow to create inconvenience. We believe there are redundancies. But the flow of water in particular is not wholly dependent on the spinning of the station. It's aided by pumps, and valved against unanticipated leakage; the movement of air is forced by fans. These are vulnerable systems. We believe we can set up alternate controls, which may allow us to seize control of them. We simply have to observe their normal operation. We know we can secure water and operate doors; we believe that we can control the gates of the air supply as well."

He was very pleasantly surprised. "Extremely good work, nadi-ji."

"Algini's work," she said cheerfully. "He's very good at what he does."

"I will bear those facts in mind," he said, "in my own work. I don't intend to wait passively for a month, Jago-ji, while the faction I judge opposed to us has its way. I *want* our missing captain. I want him alive. Then I intend to seize, oh, say, territory down to the central corridor, if you can set up to lay claim to it . . . but only as soon as it's auspicious to take it. We can make territorial claims all the way to the Mospheirans, just join up and claim the corridors between."

Jago lifted brows, quite blithely accepting his insane proposal. "Shall we not wait for Banichi, nadi? I expect him to have news of some sort. The captain's condition may have changed, one hopes not for the worst."

"I think that we should wait to know," he agreed, and added:. "I earnestly hope he has Ramirez."

"He knows you wish it," Jago said, though there had never been a direct request for him to bring Ramirez, only a suggestion to Jase. What Banichi would do if asked and what Banichi considered safe to do in a moment of opportunity, might be two different things, and, as little informed in the situation as he was, he didn't ask.

He settled to work with his notes, resolved not to pace the floor until they did hear from Banichi.

Most of all he kept telling himself there was no longer any shortage of time. Banichi had not acted, in going with Jase, as if he expected the meeting with the captain to go forward; he might not act, either, as if he believed he had to move today or the next day. When the Assassins' Guild operated, *patience* was one of the cardinal virtues. Subtlety. Finesse had its atevi counterpart.

And, thanks to Algini, it seemed that they didn't have to sit and let the station push buttons to inconvenience them.

In her study of that construction diagram, part of his own information, Jago was surely adding to Algini's schematic, his set of choke points for the station's choke hold on them.

Thirty days to wait.

Thirty days in which all hell might break loose, and in

which he might either want to maintain Kroger's territory as an outpost of their own, in a district next to human habitations; or draw Kroger and her team in with them, for safety. He did *not* think the ship wanted to offend the Mospheirans, not if they wanted something beyond fifteen hundred souls up here.

No Banichi after midnight. No Banichi on the following day.

And no word all day. None. Jago began to grow impatient, never to fidget, no such thing, but she gazed off at nothing, and listened to every sound, and at last, late after supper, came to him officially.

"I think I should go look for Banichi, Bren-ji." she said. "This is long enough. And I think I have a notion where he is."

"Where Jase is?"

"A certain corridor. We dare not track him too far, but we don't think he *is* far, nadi."

"You mean he's emitting some sort of signal? He's *radioed?*" He was mildly appalled.

"Not radioed. He hasn't transmitted for some time. But he wouldn't, if he thought it might compromise his position. One becomes concerned, however."

"I'm concerned, too. But we can't be running about the corridors. We can't risk another of us. No."

She evidenced no resentment. She had asked. There might be a time she might go without asking, but it was a rift in man'chi, an ateva stretched in two directions.

"Nojana might go," she said. "He knows the corridors. He speaks a little."

"No," he said, less and less sure he was right.

Jill and I are going up to the mountains, Toby wrote him.

> *We had a long talk. We're leaving the kids with Louise. I'm sorry about the timing, sorry as I know how to be, but I'm signing off with Mum, can't do it anymore.*
>
> *I think I'm going to quit my job. Jill wants to set up a tourist cottage on the north shore. I'm going to sell the boat, get a loan on one a little larger, take tourists out on day trips.*

I could help him, was the immediate thought. Finance was

never a problem for him, of all else that was. A tour boat?
It was a way to go broke. The repairs, the liability . . .

*I know you'll say let me help, but not this time. This
is all if I can talk Jill into it, and if the two of us can
remember who we are, and get the world and your security people out of our bedroom. This is my trump card.
It's what we've always talked about.*

What in hell are you going to do with the kids? he wondered. Toby, have you lost your mind? You opted for a
family, the house with the garden.

*About the kids, I don't know. They're old enough to
help. Maybe take radio school. They could do that. It
might be good for them.*

Living on a boat? It would cut them off for good and all
from normal society, he thought, right when kids were
learning to think of romance and other kids, and *these* kids
sliding toward rebellion. They'd pitch a fair fit when they
heard the plan.

And the danger, and the weather, in seas never reliable,
not on a calm day with the wind fair . . . and those kids
aboard? Their mum would pitch her own fit.

But Toby had a dream, Toby had a plan. It was safer
than what his brother did for a living.

And if Toby could convince Jill to trust him, if they could
manufacture some romance and honest love around those
kids and give them a dose of parental romance instead of
intergenerational recriminations, maybe there was a chance
for the kids, too.

He didn't know what more he could say. He wrote back:
*Good for you. You've got my whole-hearted good wishes,
brother.*

From Tabini, he had no word at all. He sent messages
and they dropped into a black hole.

After a couple of tries at faking Tabini's formal saluta-
tions, the captains seemed to have given up.

But given the shuttle landing, hoping to God it *had*
landed safely, trust that Tabini was hearing from Kandana

and possibly even from Lund, before Tom Lund boarded a plane to tell Hampton Durant and Shawn that things weren't optimum here.

And Banichi still wasn't back.

"Well, we've supplied you with supper," he called Kroger to say. "We're entirely bored. Not a thing moving on this forsaken station. I don't suppose we might arrange an invitation for us to join you at your local dinery. I'm tired of the local walls."

"Come over here," she said, just that abruptly, not fool enough to talk in detail, nor was he; but they managed to convey, each to the other, that things weren't just right.

Ginny Kroger punched out.

"C1," he said to that entity. "Send Kaplan at 1700. I'm taking a walk to the Mospheirans for a supper meeting."

"I'll put through that request," C1 said, but by an hour later: *"Sir, we haven't any personnel available for escort at that hour."*

"And earlier or later?"

"We don't have any personnel available for escort."

"Maybe I'll just wander around and see if I can find the place."

"We can't allow that, sir. Please stay in your section."

"This is annoying," he said. "I want Kaplan, and I want him or someone at 1700 hours."

"Let me see what I can do," C1 said, and an hour later reported: *"You'll have an escort, sir. I don't know who, but someone."*

It was a stranger who turned up at their door at 1700 hours, an elder crewman, white-haired and one-handed, who gave him and Jago and Tano sullen and suspicious looks from the one eye that seemed sharp.

"Nice day," Bren remarked midway to the Mospheirans' section. "Fine day. Don't you think?"

"Don't know," the crewman replied, with a surly glance at Tano and Jago . . . not knowing whether anyone aboard could tell Tano from Banichi without standing them side by side. It was what they hoped, at least. "They understand real language?"

"They don't speak to strangers," Bren said, knowing a hard case when he had one. He thought of adding, *Or servants,* but decided not to push it that far.

Algini was battened down tight in the home section with Nojana. It was their chance to familiarize Tano with the route, and he took it, with a sharp eye to either hand as they went, wondering if there might be at any point, down any corridor, some signal from Banichi.

There was not.

And Kroger was not encouraging. "We're not getting a damned bit of cooperation out of the administration," she said, she and he and Feldman walking, with the old man's guidance, to the mess hall, down an utterly deserted corridor, into an utterly deserted establishment.

Not a single crew member in the place.

"Is the bar this lively?" he asked.

"The bar's closed," she said with a lift of the brows. "I don't suppose you have a spare shot of vodka."

"I think we do," he said. "Unwarranted hardship, isn't it? What's that poem, Feldman?" He lapsed into Ragi doggerel:

> *"They would not send the ordinary guide tonight,*
> *They fake the aiji's messages for days.*
> *If you find your safety no longer right,*
> *Come visit us and plan to stay."*

"Yes, sir," Feldman said, and faked a nervous laugh.

Bad impromptu poetry and a young man trained enough in diplomacy and subterfuge to keep from blurting anything out. Feldman even managed a doggerel answer, half in meter:

> *"No people now, no one talks.*
> *No one we see, new guide not talk."*

"That's very good," Bren said with a laugh. It was amazing, for a novice. And informative. "We ought to let him practice with Jago and Banichi," he said to Kroger. "You and I need to talk."

They picked up their supper out of a bin, a container of something gray and something orange, and another container that held liquid.

"This is it," Kroger said as they sat down and opened their containers. "Don't even ask what it is. I don't want to know."

"I've sent for food," he said. "In thirty days we should have your mission something edible." He took a small taste, and it was bland, incredibly so. "I can send over some hot sauce. It might improve it."

"It's just pretty damned bad," Kroger said. "And it generates, pardon me, physiological upset."

"Dare I guess." He was afraid to eat much of it, and pushed it around with his plastic spoon. "You've got to come over to our place. We'll feed you."

"If you have enough to ship us some meals, we'll be in your debt."

"This is inhumane," he said. The orange had flavor, to be sure. It tasted like fish liver oil.

"I'm told you eat one and then the other. It does help. They're supposed to have every necessary nutrient."

"God, this is awful."

"Oh, there's better. But there's been *just* this stuff since Tom left."

The Feldman-Jago-Tano conference was going on next to them at the table, with some laughter over phrases like, "We distrust extremely the least senior authority; we believe lives are in danger," and "Have you heard anything from your offices?"

"No," Feldman said in reply to Jago. "We are concerned, nadi."

"What would you like?" Bren asked Kroger. "Fish? We've plenty of fish. Bread."

"We'll take absolutely anything," Kroger said, and she surely knew as well as he did that the real information was passing in the chatter she couldn't understand at all, that of Feldman with his security. "Our stomachs can't take much more of this. Neither can our guts."

"Glad to help," he said, and wandered on to a discussion of imports, franchises and economics, enough to lull listening spies to sleep, while Feldman limped through several mistaken nouns and some half-heard assertion that green vegetables were alarmed.

No, Feldman indicated, Kroger had not been able to get messages through. They had heard nothing. They had received no indication that the shuttle had met with any difficulty.

It made some sense. The captains that had seized power dared not prevent them sending word down, but it limited the instruction they could get from the ground.

That silence meant thirty days for the captains in power to gain control of the situation, trusting *they* wouldn't act without that instruction getting through to instruct them. He himself was the most dangerous presence aboard, because he could act without orders.

And intended to, at this point.

God knew where Banichi might be. The first thing the dissident captains certainly had to assure was Ramirez' death and a lack of knowledgeable witnesses. And he had bet heavily that Ogun might not be as committed to the plot.

God knew what the rumor he had spread via Johnson and Andressson had done, whether it was still spreading or whether the candy-loving so-called security personnel had gone straight to the captains who'd attacked Ramirez and suggested they had to be silenced quickly.

He couldn't tell Kroger all of it, not in this venue. He left that to Jago's cleverness, not mentioning a single name, struggling for nouns the novice translator might comprehend.

And all the while there was such gentle, good-natured laughter from that table, just the very picture of the beginner practicing his understanding . . . if anyone in this insular community could comprehend the pretense of that art at all.

At least it might confuse them. Feldman spoke a fairly good code himself, for anyone who knew from infancy that it was easy to mistake the word for green vegetables for that for one's superior.

Malapropisms and all, they endured the meal.

"Want to come to our place for a drink?" Bren asked then. Kroger had gathered up some of the disgusting supper for Shugart, on watch in the apartment.

"No," Kroger said. "Kate would worry."

Read that she was worried about Kate Shugart's safety, and wouldn't leave one of her own where at any moment the ship might close off access and she might not be able to get back. Either Kroger had grown with the job or he had been mistaken in the woman's native good sense, Bren thought: likely both.

He accepted that declaration with respect, and after a

walk back with the old man's glowering accompaniment, paid his respects at the door.

"Take care," he said to Kroger and Shugart, with more than social meaning.

It was back to their own quarters, then, very little better informed, except that the Mospheirans were worse off than they were, and trying as they were to carry on the pretense that nothing was wrong, or at least that they were completely oblivious to the failure of their government's messages to get through.

"Did you learn anything?" he asked Jago when they were all back in their own section.

"No," Jago said, and she had a far more worried look, her true feelings there for him to see. "They know nothing. I informed them of what we know. Ben-nadi will accordingly inform her. —Bren-ji, let me go out in this next slow watch. Let me see what I can learn."

"No," he said. He was never so nervous as when he had to give orders to his security about their business. "What would he say, Jago-ji? What would Banichi say if he heard this?"

"He would still say sit still," Jago admitted, the telling argument. "But, Bren-ji, he has been wrong, now and again."

"So we daren't be. There's been absolutely no sign of him. That's very likely by his choosing. He may have stayed to administer aid to the captain; or even have found a better place for them: he might not even *be* where you think he is."

"That might be," Jago conceded. "But, nadi, he would leave me word."

"One more day," he said. "Jago-ji, I request it. I believe that's what he wishes."

"One more day," she said. "Then. Then I will advise you send me to search for him, nandi."

Tano and Algini, standing near, said nothing, nor did Jago look at them.

Nojana, separated from his own partner, who had left on a shuttle about which they had heard nothing, likewise bore a somber look.

The lack of information was hell on all of them.

23

Jago did not come to bed, rather hovered gloomily about the security station, watching every tick of the instruments that he knew now monitored the smallest sounds, even the flow of water through the pipes: she listened to everything.

Bren tried to sleep, hovered near it a long while.

Then the outer door did open, and he leaped up, snatched a robe . . .

And confronted a shut door, utterly in dark.

He groped for the lights. Either the station had sealed him in by remote control or his own security had. He found the wall panel.

The door opened by remote, as it had shut, and he heard voices outside, his security, and a human voice: Kaplan's.

He went out to confront the scene, his armed and nervous security, Kaplan . . . and Narani and Bindanda. *Everyone* was out, *everyone* had pounced on Kaplan, who looked scared, small wonder.

"Sir," Kaplan said. "Sir!"

"Allow him, nadiin," Bren said, and his security let Kaplan come closer, Kaplan looking anxiously over his shoulder, down a stretch of hallway with numerous doors, any one of which might house monitoring equipment. *We need to take that,* Bren said to himself, and shortened his vision to Kaplan, who was without his usual gear, in nothing but a coat.

"I heard what you said," Kaplan began shakily, "and a friend of yours said the situation's better, and he wants to move it here, if he can, if he can get through, which is

scary. I don't think he ought to try, but he's going to, an
he needs help."

"Is Banichi with him?"

"The big guy. I don't know. I can't stay here. I've got t
go. I can take you there, and I've got to get back where
belong or I'm cooked."

"Jago," Bren said, and had a dilemma on his hand:
Jago's imperfect command of Mosphei, Kaplan's accen
and Jase's and Banichi's safety. He couldn't take protectio
from the place, not with all their chance of holding ou
until the shuttle got back vested in these few rooms. "Jag
and I will go. Now."

"Bren-ji," Tano protested. "At least take one more."

"Jago," Bren said for good or for ill. It was Banichi the
were looking for as much as Jase and Ramirez, and Jag
knew the halls best. "Two seconds," he said, and ducke
into his room and took his gun from his computer case.

Bindanda followed him, dressed in frantic haste, assiste
and gave him a small packet tied up with cord. "Food,
Bindanda said. "Medicines."

Was there *nothing* his staff failed to anticipate? "You ar
amazing, nadi-ji," he said, and hurried out into the hal
where, second wonder from the same source, Kaplan ha
come into possession of a gilt-and-flowered box, which h
clutched anxiously. Keep the fellow bribed, Bren though
and hoped the supply held out.

Jago was ready; Jago had been ready for days.

"Let's go," he said to Kaplan, and they moved ou
quickly down the hall. "What chance we're monitored?"

"Don't think so, sir. They keep putting it in and you
guys keep taking it out."

Whether or not she understood, Jago didn't say a thing
and he was alarmed to think Banichi had been quietly dis
posing of station monitoring where he found it. Warfar
had been going on, unannounced, things the station faile
to say, things Banichi failed to say . . . even to him.

Now Banichi was off on his own recognizance, and h
knew Banichi received some instructions not from him, bu
from Tabini, and likewise from his Guild.

"He says Banichi has removed station surveillance," h
said to Jago. "Is this so?"

"Occasionally," Jago admitted.

"And didn't tell me? This might affect negotiations!"

"So might its presence, nandi," Jago said as they walked, and that was the plain truth, one he couldn't deny. What were the spies on the other side to say? You destroyed our bugs?

No, they attempted to replant them, and to assure . . .

God, what might Banichi have planted in the rest of the station?

Was *that* how Jago claimed to know where Banichi was? It couldn't be clear radio transmission. Surely they'd locate that. But something was going on.

Were they tapping on the damned water pipes? Knocking on the walls?

Kaplan had stuffed a candy in his mouth and hastened along with a bulge in his cheek, the box tucked in his jacket.

And now Kaplan led them down one corridor and through one and the other doors, and, with fearful looks, led them into a recess and a dogged-down door.

"It's cold," Kaplan said around the candy, "but it's pressurized. Next level down. You want to tuck your hands in your sleeves."

It was a fast climb, the cold all but numbing the lungs and face and hands. And damned right he wanted to tuck hands into his sleeves to hold onto the ladder. He descended above Jago, Kaplan last above him, and Kaplan shut the door again before coming down in a darkness absolute except for a light Jago produced. There was another door in this tube, and a small platform, and Jago stood astride the ladder and platform to open it into light, onto another level.

The passage went on and on into depth.

"How far?" he asked. "All over?"

"'Case the lifts fail," Kaplan said. "There's pressure seals below. You don't open a pressure seal. Blow the whole damn section. Tell her that."

"He says there are pressure seals below and if we open them we will have a fatal decompression, Jago-ji."

"One understands," Jago said.

And seized her gun, and scrambled up the rungs as i
stung.

"One damned well does," Banichi's voice said out of the
dark below them. "Nadiin-ji. One is very glad to see you."

"See," Bren scoffed, in near dark, and addressing the
darkness itself. His heart was beating so he had trouble
holding his grip, and Kaplan had let out a yelp that stil
seemed to echo through the tunnels.

"We have Ramirez safe, and improved," Banichi said
"Where we have him, we don't wish known. So we make
noise within the system. Oblige us all by going back by the
next passage, nadiin. We are safe. How do you fare?"

"Well," he said, "though as yet we've had no knowledge
of the shuttle."

"It landed safely," Banichi said, a fact which, indeed
Kaplan might have told them, Bren was chagrined to real
ize. "Have you brought medicines?"

"I have them," Bren said, and passed them to Jago, who
climbed down on the ladder and passed the packet down.

Banichi took them.

"I'm losing my grip," Bren was forced to say. "The cold's
numbed my fingers."

Jago moved upward at once and took a grip on his arm
That Jago could climb hauling him up he halfway believed

"Take him to safety," Banichi said. "Rely on us."

"Yes," Jago said, and shoved him upward.

He moved, Jago moved, Kaplan moved . . . whether
Kaplan had gloves or whether Kaplan's coat was better
insulated, he had no idea, but he literally could not maintain his grip much longer. He shoved himself upward with
his legs and tried to give Kaplan relief the same way Jago
supported him, but it was a damned dangerous maneuver
he was all too aware.

Kaplan managed to get them into the upper corridor
and they startled one stray odd-hours walker, but Kaplan
high-signed that woman, who stood stark still. "Ramirez!"
Kaplan hissed at her.

The woman just stared and backed away a step, and a
second, and ran. Jago had a gun out, but Kaplan put himself in the way, wide-eyed and horrified.

"Cousin," Kaplan said, as if that explained everything.

"How many cousins do you have?" Bren asked, and himself restrained Jago with a signal.

"Never counted," Kaplan said, and tugged at his sleeve, taking them in the opposite direction, and then into a doorway they hadn't used before.

It led to another corridor, another route. The feeling was coming back to Bren's hands, and they burned. His face burned from the recent cold, and his lungs felt seared. He'd never breathed such air, not even on Mt. Adams' snowy slopes, and he heaved a dry cough, trying to smother it.

The next section door and two more had them turned about again, and the fourth set them out in a transverse corridor.

"That's it," Kaplan said, "that's yours, got to go."

"You wait a second," Bren said, and caught him by the sleeve. "Is that our door, Jago?"

"Yes," she said, and in a moment more it opened, their own team having spotted them by some means he had no knowledge of. He let Kaplan go, gave him a pat on the shoulder, and Kaplan hurried back the way they'd come.

The door sealed them in, safe, and Jago a damned lot happier.

"We survived," Bren said, the images of the whole chaotic trip jostling each other in his mind. It was incredible that that dark cold interior existed, but they had been there, and now were here, and Ramirez was alive and the word was spreading.

It wasn't the candies that kept Kaplan on their side, he strongly suspected that. It wasn't only the candies that might seduce the likes of Johnson and his friends. He wasn't sure, in a human way, whether Kaplan and Johnson and the rest wanted to follow the logic of what they were doing all the way: he'd had Jase's word for the mind-set of the ship-folk, that rebellion wasn't in their vocabulary. But rebellion by indirection, rebellion by doing uncooperative things, a passive rebellion against the powers that literally regulated their breath and sustenance . . . there might be a will to do slightly illicit things against a slightly illicit authority.

Damned right.

No alarm had rung when that crewwoman had reached

her destination. She hadn't reported her cousin. Humans on the ship did understand a sort of man'chi not unlike that on the island.

It was the first time he'd truly warmed to these folk. It was the first window of understanding he'd had.

"What's in the adjacent rooms?" he asked Jago that evening.

"These have been vacated," Jago said, "so we believe, when Johnson-nadi and the others left. They set up a bug next door. Banichi removed it, among his first actions. No one else has come there."

A buffer zone, then. He sat down with his computer and called up the map, and tried to figure for himself what area they might take for themselves if they pulled Kroger and her team in.

"There are a good many of Jase's associates we have never heard from," he said to his security team later. "And Mercheson-paidhi. I believe that the Ramirez matter is spreading through the crew quietly. We haven't ever heard from Jase's mother or from Mercheson or her mother or any relatives. One can't predict among humans, but the man'chi is strong in such associations, and this silence in itself indicates trouble."

"Restraint, nadi Bren?" Tano asked.

"Kaplan-nadi has many cousins. We met one such in the corridor, whom you wisely did not shoot, Jago-ji. I think these are all potential allies. The captains who attacked Ramirez must surely hesitate to harm all these people. They cannot simply go shooting every crew member who opposes them. Man'chi binds the crew to obey the captains, for one thing because they have no technical knowledge how to manage the systems without the high officers, and have no productive choice but to let the officers settle their disputes and pretend not to see them. The crew dares not look to us for a solution. But Jase said they had a custom of ignoring high command disputes."

"Man'chi, and practicality?" Algini asked.

"Deep practicality. Common sense around an environment that has no compromises and takes no votes. I believe I'm beginning to understand Kaplan, even his fondness for sweets. I think he's allowing us to buy him; I think Johnson outright coming and telling us they're security is another bid for our attention, and our purchase. They don't know how to approach us, without some excuse. And I think they plan to plead naïve stupidity if caught."

His atevi hearers were both amused and aghast. "Truly, nand' paidhi?" Nojana asked diffidently.

"I do think it. I think they have to have an excuse. More, I think they have to have an excuse in order to persuade themselves they're not doing something bad."

"They wish to be bribed?"

"I think they do. I think I understand. They want, individually, to see us, to assess our behavior, our patience, our tolerance of them . . . in short, they've never seen atevi up close, they're scared, but they're letting themselves grow familiar. At any given wrong move, they could turn on us and draw weapons, but right now I think they're edging toward believing we're not that scary, that they might deal with us. In a certain way I think they're trying to figure out whether Ramirez is, after all, right about dealing with us, and one must respect their courage and common sense in trying to make that assessment. I'm not sure *they've* thought it all out. But I think there's a real curiosity about the candy . . . about the planetary resources . . . and about us. In a certain sense, food is a very basic, very instinctive gift of goodwill. And they're taking it. They're approaching us. They're supporting Ramirez."

His security looked at him as if he and his entire species had run mad in the streets.

"They test whether they maintain man'chi to Ramirez?" Jago asked, always the cleverest of his staff at seeing through human behavior. "They test feelings?"

"Something very close to that," Bren said. "In this case there's less intellectual about it than usual. This is far more instinctive . . . far more simple, in many regards. These people have been left no way to choose their leaders, but they *are* choosing, I'm relatively sure of it. And every one of them is taking a chance."

"Of harm?"

"Of harm to the entire ship. The power structure isn't instinctive, not wholly; it's pragmatic. And it's functioned

against their will. I believe a good many of the crew hope
Ramirez will survive, but they have no confidence in his
state of health; they act as if it's a doomed cause, but not
one they've utterly given up. Banichi didn't say, but I think
some of them are sheltering him, and I would not in the least
be surprised to learn that Jase and Mercheson and various
others related to them by kinship are in on it. Subterfuge and
indirection, it well may be mediated by kinship. The *captaincy*
seems to pass down by kinship instead of merit."

"Who are Ramirez' kin?" Jago asked, straight to the
point. "Is it not Jase? Do I not recall Ramirez has no
descendants?"

"Jase. Jase and Yolanda. Ramirez's wife died long ago.
Her network remains attached to him, one gathers. Jase
tried to lay out the relationships for me. Until Kaplan and
his cousins, I confess I didn't understand all he might have
been saying."

Jase and his family chart, he began to think, might be
more important to them than their map of the station and
its workings.

"The crew has no weapons," Algini said.

"None." They had been over that with Jase, and as far as
he had ever learned, it was the truth. The crew had no access
to hand weapons. Those existed, but the officers had the keys,
and the resistance to shooting one's cousins and officers, one
could only guess. "But *we* have Ramirez, if we can keep him
alive. I think there's good reason not to bring him here. The
crew has to believe he still has authority, not our authority:
his authority. If he dies, any hope they have of a captain of
his disposition dies with him. And the fourth captain, the one
we've not met or dealt with, *that* captain is our problem."

"Tamun."

"Just so. I rather think Ogun might stand with Ramirez
if he had the chance. He may be doing so, for all I know.
For all I know he's barricaded in some safe place trying to
keep himself alive."

"Tamun must fall," Jago said.

"But *we* mustn't do it," he said.

"Are they not pragmatists?"

"Emotional creatures, as well. We should not do it if
we can possibly avoid it. The captains are reservoirs of an

expertise in operating this ship that we can't pull out of the archive: it's the same business as the starship crew not being able to fly the shuttle. We can't just take over the ship and hope to operate it. And without it, if the aliens are real, we have no defense. We *have* to get Ramirez back in power, but at worst, we may have to make peace with Tamun, if only for the sake of what he knows."

"This would not be an agreeable outcome," Jago said.

"No," he said, "it would not be. But we are limited in what we can do, besides try to maintain an alternative, and not frighten the crew. If we run out of candy, we pass out dried fruit and offer them shots of vodka, and promises, and we hope Banichi stays safe. He's doing the right thing in trying to keep Ramirez alive and away from assassins: I think *Jase* is advising him how important that is, and we need to support him. Take inventory of supplies we do have. We need to get decent food to Kroger's rooms and advise *them* of the situation."

"Do we trust her, Bren-ji?"

"Against the likelihood of a conflict in the crew and an unknown rising to authority?" There was one thing Mospheira detested even more than change and that was uncertainty. "There's all the history of the Pilots' Guild and the colonists in our favor. In this, I think quite likely they'll work with us."

That the shuttle had landed safely was the most welcome news.

There was not one damned letter from any of the committee heads, and while it was remotely possible that Tabini hadn't written, it was by no means possible that felicitations from the mainland would not pour to Mogari-nai, and onto his staff, who likewise sent no word.

Infuriating. Troubling. Bren found multiple words for the situation.

From his brother there was not a word. None from his mother. *There* was a disturbing situation. If she'd mentioned the shuttle landing, that alone might have caused the captains to censor her letter—which she would hardly understand, when her son failed to write, when Toby was trying to hold his marriage together, and couldn't take time out to go solve another crisis that was the cause of the difficulty in the first place.

Bren took his computer back to his desk and carefully, patiently, constructed a positive mood . . . an hour's worth of construction, which led to a day's constructive work in another set of missives for Tabini.

His last ones had gotten through. He was relatively sure Tabini had a clear notion that not everything was as well as the first letters indicated.

At the mid point of the night the outer door opened, and shut; and Bren rolled out of bed, looking for the gun.

His door shut. Immediately. He waited in the dark, shivering in the chill, listening with trepidation as the door opened and shut a second time.

The door of his quarters opened; and Jago stood in silhouette against the muted corridor light.

"A message," Jago said. "Nothing of concern, Bren-ji. Banichi says a hunt is going through the tunnels and that we should not affect to hear it."

"They're hunting Ramirez."

"They have begun a door-to-door search, claiming we have secreted some personnel aboard, nadi. Banichi will not be caught by their nets. Go to sleep."

"On that?" he asked. "Jago-ji, he can't stay out there forever. If you're communicating with him, tell him the hell with independence: bring Ramirez here. Let's raise the wager. Let them take him from us, damn them!"

"I believe he would be willing," Jago said. "The humans may be reluctant."

More than likely, he thought, trying in vain to recover any urge toward sleep. More than likely there was considerable resistance in the crew, all the reasons he himself had already thought of, but what they were risking, keeping a wounded man on the run, was everything, everything humanity owned in this end of space.

Come in, he wished Banichi, staring into the dark. Don't listen to human reasons. Talk sense into Jase. Say no to him and get back here. Get *him* back before someone gets killed. There's still a way to patch this.

*   *   *

Wishes did no good.

Sandwiches did, at least improving Kroger's rations, a strike back in a war of nerves.

The lights went out for fifteen minutes or so in the evening; came on; and went out again an hour later.

A candle in the hallway provided sufficient light for atevi, and the household proceeded with supper.

"I fear they may be aware of our monitoring," Bren whispered to Tano after supper, in the utter, ghostly stillness of that dark. "Dare one think they might move up on us?"

"Significant monitoring is passive," Tano said, "and we listen, nadi Bren, we do listen for any such. They make noise in the tunnels now and again, but nothing near us."

"It makes no difference that we have no idea where Ramirez is. Certain authorities might *think* he's taken refuge with us."

"We watch, nadi Bren. We watch."

"One knows so," he said. He wanted Banichi back. Immediately.

But he did no good pacing the floor or making his security nervous. There was always the chance that the lights might not come on again. There was the chance they would freeze in the dark, though he doubted that his security would allow that without a blow struck.

He *wanted* the adjacent rooms in their hands.

And then he had the most uncomfortable notion where Banichi might be, and where Ramirez might be, and how the fugitive captain was receiving food, water, and care. He cast Tano an uneasy look, and kept quiet about the idea.

He went back to bed, where it was warmer, and shortly after that all the lights came on and the fans started up.

"One doubts they will willingly freeze the water pipes," Jago said blithely the next morning. "One believes, nadi, these outages are connected with the search."

"With listening?"

"Likely," Jago said. "Likely they hope to hear movement."

He simply cast a look toward the door, by implication toward that section beyond it.

Jago shrugged, and said not a thing.

He made a gesture for *here!* Made it emphatically. *Bring him here!*

Jago gave a negative shrug: not wise, she meant, he was sure of it. His security would not jeopardize *him*, whatever else, and would not let the search lead here. He recalled what Banichi had indicated, of making noise in distracting directions.

A dangerous set of maneuvers.

Damned dangerous, he said to himself, but he doubted close questions served anyone's safety: if they were where he thought, they were as good as within their perimeter.

Day, and day, and night and night.

No messages came up from Mogari-nai, not a one. He ordered C1 to send-receive, and had no idea whether his messages went anywhere. He wrote to councillors, to department heads, to his staff, and to his mother, not daring to mention that he hadn't gotten any messages, not daring to admit he was worried.

"Any word from Jase Graham?" he asked daily, as if there were nothing wrong in the world.

Occasionally he called Kroger, and twice summoned Kaplan for uneventful escorts over and back.

He'd thought he'd found the limits of his nerves and passed them long ago. Shouting and argument he could deal with; silence was its own hell.

But withstanding that was as important. And Jago was happier, at times, even cheerful . . . interspersed with days of bleak worry, when he was relatively certain something was going on that his security opted not to tell him. There were more outages, and one that lasted until he was sure the pipes were in definite danger.

He sat by candlelight fully clothed and wrapped in a blanket from shoulders to feet, and with his hands tucked under his arms and his feet growing numb no matter the precautions. How general it was or whether Kroger was likewise suffering he had no idea. The silence without the air duct fans was eerie . . . one grew accustomed to that constant sound. The notion of air that no longer moved gave the place a tomblike feeling.

He wondered if Tabini had done what he urged and opened direct negotiations—such as the University on Mospheira could mediate, using more Bens and Kates—with Hampton Durant on the island. He hoped so. He hoped that by virtue of what he had sent down to the world that men of common sense could form a common purpose and not give the Guild what would damn them all: if it was the xenophobes in charge of the Guild now, minds that truly didn't want to deal with foreigners of any stamp, and they were determined to alienate the atevi before they took on aliens from far out in space, everything was in jeopardy. He'd made that clear to Tabini, and included a letter for Mospheira, and hoped Tom Lund had corroborated his report.

At times things seemed to be going very slowly to hell with his own position, and in the candlelit dark he asked himself whether he or any of his team might survive this, or whether fools were going to let this go on until the station was damaged, the ship remained unfueled, and the planet had to take its chances with whatever came, helpless to launch more than a shuttle.

He passed despair, achieved numb patience—and guilt for having drawn people he cared for into this mess. He reanalyzed the meeting he had had, when everything had gone too well, too fast, and wondered if he might have precipitated this reversal himself, simply because he was a negotiator and the captains weren't. Perhaps, he thought, he had pushed the opposition into desperate measures.

It might have happened. It might be that he had driven the opposition to desperation, or encouraged Ramirez to an aggressive posture that proved his downfall . . . if that was what had happened.

"Mr. Cameron," the intercom said, breaking its long silence. The lights stayed out.

He stayed seated. The intercom made several tries. He still stayed seated. If they were going to ask him if he had had enough, he wasn't going to make it convenient for them.

The lights and air came back on within the hour. His security had kept their watch, and reported no movement in their area.

He found himself tempted to order a seizure of the adjacent rooms and main corridor, down to the next security door, in the theory the blackouts might be local, and that he might command an area more difficult for them. But he had no desire to provoke anything until the shuttle was back.

"Mr. Cameron," the intercom nagged him. He refused to answer.

It went on intermittently for the next day. Narani and the servants ceased to regard the noise. He ceased his daily harassment of C1, preferring to let the captains worry about the silence from his side.

"Mr. Cameron," the intercom said finally. *"We know you hear us."*

He somewhat doubted they could guarantee that.

It interrupted his sleep during the night.

An alarm went off, flashing lights from the panel, a loud klaxon that sent them all from their beds.

Jago was in his, and he said, the two of them entangled beneath the sheets, "I honestly hope that's real and they're having a bad night."

"I should go to security," she said, and eased out of bed. She flung a robe about herself on the way out the door.

He lay and watched the ceiling in the flashing red light. The intercom said,

"Mr. Cameron. The captains are willing to meet with you now."

That worried him. But he stayed in bed.

The section door opened and shut outside. *That* brought him out of bed, wrapped in a sheet.

Banichi was back, and for an man who ordinarily suffered not a hair out of place, he looked exhausted.

"Bren-ji," Banichi said. "One apologizes for the inconveniences."

"What's going on?" he asked. "Be *careful* out there, nadi-ji, I earnestly request it."

Banichi found that ruefully amusing. Jago, who had turned out with all but Algini, did not laugh, nor did the rest.

"We have lost contact with the lower level," Banichi said then, not happy. "A number are cut off. I ask your leave, nandi, to deal with that."

He felt a chill that was far more than his bare feet on

the cold floor. This one went to the gut and advised him what Banichi was asking, political permission for lethal force.

"I don't know enough to decide, Banichi. Advise me. We have repeated requests from the captains for me to meet with them, since the last outage. I keep refusing."

Banichi did not seem to account that good news at all. He heaved a heavy sigh. "It is not from weakness," he said. "They may have taken Ramirez."

No, not good news. "I hoped he might be here."

"We tried to convince them he was at another place," Banichi said. "The rooms next to us are all vacant now. We had moved everyone back, fearing they might attack here, jeopardizing you, nandi, and we never convinced Ramirez to come to this level. For your safety, Bren-ji, permission to act."

"To protect this place, or yourself, or our people, Banichi. But if Ramirez is lost, we have no choice but deal with the successors."

"You must not go to their meeting," Jago said.

"No," Tano agreed. "You must not."

"We can't protect you," Banichi said. "It would not be wise, Bren-ji. Your security strongly requests you not take such a chance."

"I'll talk with them," he said. "I won't agree to go there. But I'm worried about Kroger's safety."

"We cannot guarantee it," Banichi said.

"But the station has no reason at all to antagonize her," Bren said. "That's in her favor. If she just stays quiet."

"One fears Mercheson has contacted her," Banichi admitted.

"Then she is involved."

"Yolanda Mercheson believed she had credibility with the Mospheirans," Banichi said, "and one believes there was contact from Ramirez as well."

Worse news.

"Stay here," he said. "Narani, attend him. Banichi, at least an hour or two. Rest. Eat. Whatever suits. I'm going to talk to the captains."

"Agree to nothing that involves going to them, nadi-ji. I

most emphatically urge against it. No matter what they urge."

They had seven more days until the shuttle came back . . . let alone the fifteen until they could service it and give them another chance to get off this station. He had been known to lie, in the course of diplomacy, when it was absolutely necessary; but in this case . . . he had decided qualms about a lie to Banichi, and even greater qualms about a diplomatic failure.

"I'll do what I must," he said, knowing it was not what Banichi wanted to hear. "And trust my security will rest so they can deal with it. I have to deal with these people. If the threat they foresee materializes, we can't afford years of standoff. I have to find out what we're dealing with."

"Don't go *there*," Banichi said, as forcefully as Banichi had ever said anything, and that stopped him and made him think hard.

"I can't evidence fear of these people," Bren said. "And they have a certain obligation to respect a truce."

"These are not Mospheirans, Bren-ji."

"No," he agreed. "Nor would I risk my security; but, Banichi-ji, if we arrange a meeting and they attack, it will not please the crew. The captains have used up all the crew's patience with the attack on Ramirez. But I believe the crew has a limit, and I believe the captains are worried they may reach it."

"Bren-ji," Jago said. "We have the aiji's orders, as well."

"You'll have to follow them, nadiin-ji, as I must, and mine are to take this station. My way is by negotiation, and the aiji sent me to try that to the limit of my ability. I believe I read this correctly, and I will not lie to you. I intend to go and to confront them in their territory and to demand they honor agreements."

"If they were atevi," Banichi said directly, "you would not be right."

"I may not be right as it stands," he said, "but if I'm not, I give you leave to remove the captains and their security on the spot."

"That," Banichi said, "we find satisfactory."

24

It was not Kaplan who guided them. It was the old man, whose name-badge said Carter; and it was a long, glum-faced progress into the administrative section, into the region of potted plants and better-looking walls.

It was the same chamber, at the end of the hall, and the old man opened the door and let them in.

Ogun was there. So was Sabin, so was Tamun, and a fourth man, a gray-haired man, who was not Ramirez, all seated at the table, with armed security standing behind, and next to the interior door.

Bren stood at the end of the conference table, waved Jago and Banichi to the sides of the room . . . one each, hair-triggered, and expecting trouble, but not by the stance they took. Banichi adopted an off-guard informality he never would have used in the aiji's court, a folded-arm posture that verged on disrespect.

Jago became his mirror image.

"Mr. Cameron," Sabin said reasonably. "We won't mention your incursions into the station. We understand your security precautions. We advise you we have our own."

Interesting, Bren thought. Ogun sat silent. Sabin, now second-ranking, spoke, and Tamun still said nothing. The new man sat silent as Ogun. "I'm glad you understand. I see you've rearranged your ranks. This is no particular concern of ours."

"It shouldn't be," Sabin said harshly.

"We can salvage agreements," Ogun said, "if you'll observe that principle."

Ogun had difficulty meeting his eyes, and then did, and on no logical grounds he read that body language as a man who took no particular joy in the present situation, a man who might be next.

"Captain Dresh," the fourth man said. "Taking Ramirez's place. We will not *tolerate* any interference in our command of the ship."

"What you do with the station—" Tamun spoke for the first time. "—is your affair. Yours and the Mospheirans. You don't interfere with command, you don't interfere with the ship, her officers, or her operations."

He cocked his head slightly, cheerful in the face of what was surely an attempt to shake his nerve. He had Banichi and Jago on his side, and the security standing at the captains' back had no idea, he said to himself. He failed to give a damn for the threats, did hear the proffer of an understanding, and refused to proffer anything in return.

"Mr. Cameron," Sabin said. "Do you understand?"

"I'll relay your sentiments."

"We have messages," Ogun said, "representing our position. We'll transmit them when you take the next flight down. They'll be extensive, and detailed. We include the agreements as we see them, our requirements, our commitments to the aiji and to the President of Mospheira."

They hadn't gotten a separate offer. Durant and Shawn had been too canny for that; so had Tabini.

And *next shuttle flight* had seemed attractive until *they* offered it, and thought it to their advantage.

"My clerical staff can begin work," he said.

"You begin work," Sabin said. "And you take that flight, Mr. Cameron. We've done all the negotiating we're prepared to do."

"An incentive." Tamun tossed a signal at the guards behind him, and the man nearest the door opened it, not without Banichi's and Jago's attention.

The guards brought out a man in filthy coveralls.

Jase.

Clearly he was meant to react. He did, internally, and thought of options at his disposal to remove Tamun from among the living.

"Take him with you," Tamun said. "Take him, take Mercheson, and their adherents. They've refused to live under the rules of this ship. You repeatedly claim you need their assistance in translation. You have it."

"Jase," Bren said calmly. He was rumpled and scraped and had a bloodstain on his sleeve; he might be unsteady on his feet, but he saw a signal to join him. The guards brought Mercheson out, similarly bedraggled; two older women, and a younger . . . Jase's mother, Bren thought. He'd seen her in image.

All of them, exiled. All of them, turned over for shipment down on the next flight.

"Chances for dissent are few," Tamun said, "except at stations. Our last port of call took away no few dissenters, but they had no luck. Let's hope, Mr. Cameron, that this one fares better."

"Let's hope that my mail starts coming through," Bren said. "Let's hope that the power stays stable. Let's hope I take this gift as an expression of your future will to have a working agreement and get our business underway. Where do the Mospheirans fit in this?"

Sore point. He'd thought so.

"You raise that question with Ms. Kroger," Tamun said. "Next time let them send someone with power to negotiate."

"Probably myself," Bren said equably. "I'm a pragmatist, Captain Tamun. I deal where I have to, to my own advantage. I can use Jase; I'm sure I'll find a use for other help."

"You stay the hell out of our affairs!"

"You give me direct communication with the aiji and no damn censoring of my messages, Captain. Blocking out my messages won't make me any more reasonably disposed."

"Don't push us."

"The messages, and stable power to our section. We'll be taking the adjacent rooms. We *need* the space."

"The shuttle will be on schedule," Tamun said quietly, as quietly as he had been violent a moment before. "Be on it. Let's see no more than scientific packages for a while, Mr. Cameron. We'll honor agreements. This *is* the authority you'll be dealing with. Accept it, and go do your job, whatever that is."

"My mail."

"Damn your mail, sir! You don't make demands here!"

"You don't make them down *there*. If you want anything transported, I need access to mail I know hasn't been tampered with. You altered one of the aiji's messages! That's a *capital* matter in the aishidi'tat, sir, and you leave me to explain that to my government, which will be damned difficult, sir! If you want *any* cooperation out of me *or* the mainland *or* the island, you consider the mail flow sacrosanct! You're verging on no deal at all."

"Get out of here!"

There was the explosion point. "Jase. Yolanda. I take it these are your respective parents. Let's go."

He turned, gave a glance to Banichi, a signal, and Banichi moved with him, not without a harsh glance toward the captains, and Jago never budged from her position by the door until their whole party was out it, in company of the sullen old man who had guided them there.

Then she swung outside, hand on her sidearm.

"We'll return to our apartments," Bren said to their guide, and the old man led off.

There was a conspicuous presence of armed men down the hall as they walked, a presence that retreated down a side corridor when they came and that proved not to be in the side corridor when they passed.

Jase said not a word, seeming to have enough to do simply to keep himself on his feet, but doing it, walking with his hand on his mother's arm. Yolanda walked with the two others, and Jago brought up the rear, not taking anything for granted.

Not a word, all the way back, and to their own doorway, which opened to receive them.

Narani hurried out to offer Jase his support. Bindanda took Yolanda in charge, with small bows to the relatives.

The door shut, walling out their guide; and Jase slid right through Narani's grasp floorward, would have hit if Narani had not caught him a second time.

Bren offered his own arm, supported Jase's head, and he was cognizant, half-out, as his mother attempted to intervene from the other side. "Sorry," Jase said.

"Sorry, hell," Bren said. "Narani-ji. Use my bed. Jase, where are you hurt?"

"Ribs. Slid down the damn ladder."

"Damn. Damn. Don't pull on him, Rani-ji. Broken ribs. Banichi?"

"Bandaging," Banichi said, and gathered him up as if he were a child in arms.

"Ms. Graham," Bren said, laying a hand on her shoulder. "Yolanda. I take it this is your mother and sister."

"Yes." Yolanda was fighting reaction, vastly upset, but not letting go. "It's Tamun that's done this."

"I'm fairly sure," Bren said calmly. "Are you hurt?"

"I'll live," Yolanda said between her teeth. "My mother, my sister . . . This is Bren," she said suddenly, as if there were no knowing.

"Ms. Mercheson. Olanthe, is it?"

"Yes, sir," the girl said. She was in her early teens, thoroughly shaken, tear-tracks on her face. Eyes darted to the least movement of the atevi near her.

"These are *my* family," he said to reassure her. "You're completely safe with us. Come into the dining room, and we'll get you something to drink. Fruit juice, Bindanda, if you would. This smaller one is a child."

"One understands," Bindanda said. "Yolanda-nandi, will you bring these good persons and come? Come. We will find you whatever comfort you ask."

"I have a report to give!"

"You have them to settle," Bren said. "Easy. We have time. God knows, we have time. You can talk to Bindanda. They can't."

"See to Jase," she said, distracted, and went to direct Bindanda. Yolanda always tried to take charge. It was her way, but she worked, she tried with all that was in her. She'd refused to give up on the Mospheirans, and she'd helped Jase, that much he knew.

Tano and Algini were inside the security center, monitoring activity with fervent attention, learning what, he was not sure. Nojana had gone to help Banichi.

Jago was distressed and angry, and had nowhere to spend her temper.

"I do not consider this a reverse," he said. "Only an obstacle. I need the additional rooms, nadi. Get Nojana, and go take them."

"Yes," Jago said fiercely, and went on that errand, braid swinging.

"It hurts," Jase said, lying slightly propped. "I hit every rung for ten feet, and caught a platform edge."

Bren could only imagine. It gave him chills. "Banichi says the ribs aren't broken. Cracked, more than likely."

"I couldn't tell."

"They didn't hit you."

Jase shook his head slightly. "Not except when I laid into one who had it coming. Releasing us is what they had to do. They could shoot Ramirez. They can't hold a crew-wide bloodbath. Couldn't attack my mother. That was their downfall. Women . . . women are damned near sacred, remember?"

The necessity of child-bearing. Continuance of the species. The Guild had set that priority and the women had fought it; and kept their job rights, Jase said, even if risks set the Guild's teeth on edge. But you didn't attack one. You outright didn't attack one.

"Good job that's so," he said.

"Doesn't help us, with me here, and her here," Jase said morosely. "Getting rid of us and our next-ofs this way, nobody's going to challenge them for what they've done. Give it three years and people won't bring it up again. Maybe she could even come back, and she'd only be a nuisance."

"I understand that," Bren said, still doubly glad he'd taken the course he had, the lower-key, less confrontational course. It had left them with resources, the women not least. "But three years, the four years, *five* years that we may spend building their ship . . . they'll hear about it. They'll hear from us. They'll get damned tired of hearing about it."

"I think they know their situation's precarious." *Precarious* was a long word. It brought a wince, a grimace. "Damn! But it won't last. They'll settle in. Nobody questions what's set still long enough."

"This Dresh fellow."

"Uncle of Tamun's. Ramirez hates him."

Present tense.

"They didn't get Ramirez?"

"No," Jase said in Ragi.

"Do you know where he is?" Bren asked in the same language.

"I might," Jase said.

Trouble, Bren thought. He wasn't willing to have a confrontation over Ramirez, not until he'd gotten essential personnel to safety. Granted there'd been minimal bloodletting this far, that wasn't saying what would happen if guilty parties found their backs to the wall . . . even familial reservations about bloodletting might give way, not even mentioning the fate of aliens in their midst.

But he reached out and patted Jase's arm, gripped it with some consideration of the bruises. "We just appropriated the next rooms down the row. The station can't cut power to them except locally, without switching off the entire region, and we've got the switch. Everyone will have beds, room, heat, air, every comfort. No shortage of food. We packed the kitchen sink."

"Don't make me laugh. God, don't make me laugh."

"You're safe."

"I'm glad to have my mother out of their reach. You don't know all she did. Helped us with food, with running messages, gathering up Yolanda . . . I don't know who's in as deep trouble. Her. Yolanda. Yolanda's set. I think Tamun would have killed us."

"And still didn't dare?"

"Didn't dare. Because of them. Because of what Yolanda and I are. That stops them. But not now."

"Stopped them long enough," he said. "Made them turn you over to us."

"Flinging us onto a planet."

"How many can they fling down there? Is anybody else in danger of their lives?"

"I hope not. I hope not. Their story started to be that I killed Ramirez. That didn't work. Then that Ramirez had a mental breakdown. Shot himself. No one believes that, but they have to pretend to. You don't know what it's like."

"Yes, I do. I'm Mospheiran, remember? Denying what's in front of one's eyes is a social skill. I know that transaction very well."

"You have to live with them, that's all. They can run the ship. But they need the techs, techs need the crew . . . it's just the way it is. They're going to try to work with the rest. And the rest will give in. Nobody but me and Yolanda wants to leave the ship. My mother . . . she'd rather die, but she'll go with me. You have to understand. She's scared. I can live down there. I wouldn't mind living down there for the rest of my life. But this is so hard on her."

Jase was working himself into an emotional state. It resonated, with a man with a mother bent on indirect self-destruction, and no damned messages but, *You should write to her* . . .

"We'll get her back up here," he promised Jase. "We'll get this patched up. Tell her that. Tell her to give it some time, and we'll treat her like a princess; we'll get her back up here if we have to make her a court emissary."

"I appreciate that," Jase said shakily.

"Listen. Hear me in Ragi." Meaning, with the associational web in place. "If we have no choice but this set of captains, that's what we'll deal with. If things settle, they may take you back."

"I won't go," Jase said. "*I* won't go down there. I won't take Tamun's orders, no way in hell . . . "

"We do what we have to do in the short term to get results in the long term."

"Short term, Ramirez will die. Bren, I can't leave. Send *her* down, but I can't leave him here. They'll find him and they'll kill him. Get him some *help* up here."

"We'll talk about it," Bren said. "We're not abandoning this post. We're not giving up. Just get some rest."

"The hell. Don't patronize me." Jase had had a painkiller, a Mospheiran brand. He was running out of energy and voice. "I won't go."

"We'll talk," Bren said in that tone that meant, definitively, later. He and Jase had had their rounds in the last three years; they had their codes, to keep from arguments. He saw Jase's eyelids sink, flick up, sink again. The strength that had kept him on his feet to get here was ebbing low at the moment.

"Crew won't listen to you. To him, yes. To me. To my mother. Tamun wants to do this quietly. Won't work."

Awareness went out, bit by bit.

"Get some sleep," Bren said, elicited one more twitch of the eyelids, and that was all. That last had been the drugged, trusting, truth.

And Jase listened to him. Jase still worked with him. The captains had attempted to avoid a shoal they saw in their own affairs, and had handed him a weapon, one he had no compunction about using, as Jase had none about being used.

Jase was a weapon the value of which they might not yet appreciate. *Wouldn't dare* . . . Jase had said, *because of what Yolanda and I are* . . . Mystique: an indefinable, irreplaceable commodity.

And somewhere, either aboard ship or lost to that alien encounter, Jase had said there were eight others of Taylor's Children. Yolanda was one. He wondered if the other six held similar loyal feelings toward their father-by-authority, and whether or not Jase could contact them.

And it was a question why Jase had never, in three years, mentioned the whereabouts of those quasi-brothers and sisters, and slid aside from questions.

He and Jase had atevi owing man'chi to them; he had led his people into this volatile situation, and he had to use all his assets.

The women were an asset. A reassurance. The captains couldn't rule them . . . and wanted them off the station, out of mind, out of view, in a situation in which the captains could absolutely govern and censor the messages that reached a crew that didn't want to remember what led to familial violence.

So the captains thought.

If they had to print messages on candy wrappers for the next decade, they were going to keep the issue alive. They could push the matter back *into* the captains' laps, eventually, and maybe not have even much of a fight about it.

Give or take Ramirez, whose principal support he still bet was Ogun.

He hadn't given up. But all his assets seemed future ones, long-term ones. And his heaviest bet was that there wouldn't be an accident that took them all out.

"We are very vulnerable," he said to his security, "to

accidents, if not of air pressure, still, of dark or cold and scarcity of water, concentrated as we are in this section. One hopes that no such thing would happen, but if they could somehow silence us all at once, the disposition of all the crew would be to pretend ignorance. The captains' skill is irreplaceable, and they believe they may have lost one captain. The fear of losing the captains is the most important fear they have."

"We believe," Banichi said, "that we can operate any lock and open any corridor. The whole station seems of one style of operation."

"I have no doubt of you," he said, "nadiin-ji. Can we hold what we have? Should I pull in nand' Gin? Or have my ambitions even this far been excessive?"

"We can hold these rooms," Banichi said without a doubt. "And we can move to others, despite their resistance, at any hour."

It was remarkably reassuring to hear that.

There was, damn it all, *still* no word from Tabini.

It was possible that Tabini had not gotten his messages since the ones Kandana carried, and that that was the reason for the silence.

Bren resent all his prior messages to Tabini in a single gulp. He did have one from his mother, short and to the point: *Please write. I'm worried. This is no time for temper.*

She hadn't gotten his letters. He resent immediately, resent all his mail to everyone, and restrained the urge to dent the panel.

"C1. Voice contact with Mogari-nai."

"I'll try, sir." In a moment more he had it, and had, in Ragi, from the Messengers' Guild, confirmation that there had been no messages coming in, that the aiji had given orders to transmit no ordinary business with the station, either.

"Until one heard from you, nandi."

"You've now heard from me," he said. "Give my apologies to the aiji. Ramirez has met with adversity. They have appointed a new captain, Dresh, related to Tamun. Relay that information immediately."

"Yes, nand' paidhi."

He signed off, went out into a hall which had doubled in length, his domain.

Narani and Bindanda were quietly bringing harmony to the further rooms. The table with the message bowl was advanced to the center of the corridor, at the far end, and two more tables stood behind it, at intervals, each with a dish and a small arrangement of wood and stone.

The servants attended felicity, and assured good fortune. The paidhi's attempt at the same job, however, was unfinished.

Jase's mother had looked in on him, to reassure herself, then had fallen asleep in an atevi-sized chair in the dining hall, utterly exhausted. He went quietly to talk to Yolanda, where she sat with her mother and sister in the new sitting room, the first one across the section line. The temperature in the new rooms had reached something more livable. The decor was still considerably lacking, but they all had blankets and steaming cups of tea.

"Jase is fine," he said. "Just a little bruised. Nothing broken. We'll be getting you down to the planet at first opportunity. Don't think of it as permanent, but it's the safest place for you to be."

"It's not the crew that's done this," Yolanda's mother said. "It's Pratap Tamun."

"It may be," he said. "But still, the planet is safest for a few months. I don't doubt things will quiet down."

They weren't happy. The young sister was scared, and didn't want to leave her cousins.

He left them to a serving of sandwiches, which ought not to upset their stomachs, and another round of tea, and ordered them a few of their precious currency, the fruit candies, wondering if Kaplan was in trouble, too.

A family of this size and complexity, however, could not engage in a bloodbath without destroying itself. The captains had acknowledged that in turning Jason and Yolanda over to him with orders to leave.

But the very reasons that had saved these few had also dictated the crew simply had no mechanism to use to fight back. The captains were not elected. They were a life appointment, by the other captains . . . who else could judge competency?

He ventured into the security station to fill in his staff on what he'd learned, and Banichi was there, looking like death.

"You, nadi," he said to Banichi, "ought to be asleep."

"A superfluous habit," Banichi said. "Conducive to ignorance. What has Jasi-ji said?"

"That Ramirez is alive. Yolanda says that Ramirez may be alive. By all that's happened, I'm all but certain he is, and I'm certain Jase feels a profound man'chi to this man."

"Ah," Jago said. "Something we understand. This is old, even for machimi."

"Indeed," Bren said, and sank heavily into a chair. He *was* tired. He had not thought how completely atevi *that* ancient ploy was, machimi to the hilt, and transparent as glass. "Atevi, however, tend to think around the urge. Jase will want to go straight to Ramirez, when the painkillers wear off."

"He must not."

"Absolutely, he must not. But I'm relatively sure he'll listen, in that regard. He'll want us to do it."

"Possibly," Banichi said. "But after you leave."

"Not without you, nadi."

"Then Ramirez must fend for himself."

"We might be well advised to do something."

"And we to get the paidhiin off the station."

"I may remain," Bren said, "if we can get Jase down."

"No." That was Banichi, Jago, and Tano, all at one word.

"Jase *can* translate, nadiin-ji."

"Not well enough," Jago said. *"Melons."*

"That was three years ago."

"Flying fish."

"Such were said to exist, on the Earth of humans."

"Nevertheless," Banichi said. "Jasi-ji, as highly as we regard him, cannot do your work, he cannot deal with the aiji, he cannot deal as effectively with Mospheira, and we are instructed, besides all this, paidhi-ma, not to return without you, so if you stay, we stay."

"Good fortune attend our getting Jase onto the shuttle if we do nothing for Ramirez."

"Many days hence," Banichi said. "By then things may

well be different. If we see an opportunity, we may act. But not otherwise."

"The crew is forcing the captains' action. The captains fear to alienate the crew. They attempted to blame Ramirez' misfortune on Jase; that didn't work. But they dared not have Ramirez on the planet broadcasting messages to the station. If we might assure his safety, *here,* I think he might rouse the crew to action."

"He has not roused them to action where he is," Nojana said.

"Not as an ateva would," Bren said. "But he has roused them to action of a sort. Someone is hiding him. No few, likely, are participant in hiding him. These are obedient people, lawful and cautious, and having very few among them who actually know how to repair and run the machinery on which their lives depend. They *fear* to remove any person who has that knowledge. If he were the most reprehensible of men, they might protect him for the sake of that knowledge, and by all I know from Jase, he is not the most reprehensible of the captains. I think Ogun-aiji, too, the dark one of the captains, was not consulted in the overthrow of Ramirez. I think he rather well fears he may be next, and if he cares for his people, he may fear the consequences of a general bloodletting in the ranks of the captains. He can do good by moderating Tamun's influence, as I think he did in insisting they stand by agreements. I think Kroger also stood by them; I think Tamun thought he could deal with her to our detriment, and couldn't. I owe this woman a profound apology for all my suspicions: I think she's thrown him back to Ramirez's agreements with us, and between Kroger and Ogun he's had to moderate his position."

"Ogun did not look at Tamun, throughout," Jago observed.

"A fault line in the association of the captains. And I think one might even suspect Sabin might have been against dealing with us, and for dealing with the Mospheirans, but even she may be doubtful now, seeing Tamun's kin as the fourth captain. This *cannot* please Ogun or Sabin, who now may find they have something in common simply by not being Tamun's."

"They are *not* incomprehensible," Tano murmured.

"In some regards, more like the aiji's court than the Mospheirans are," Bren said. "Obscure connections, subterranean agreements—so to speak—placing the interest of their own small association of birth and convenience as paramount within a very large kinship. Threaten the kindred as a whole and that might unify them; but the planet and its offers are a potent force for change in their community; and where change happens—" He gave a shrug.

"Gold among thieves?" Jago suggested wickedly. It was a proverb: the impetus first to unite, then to dissociate bloodily in self-interest.

"Something of the sort. Although one might think . . . perhaps a slight bit more noble."

"Indeed," Jago said grimly. "Yet another angry faction—the just and noble."

He gave a rueful laugh. "True, I very much fear. Jase's faction, the very ones Tamun is sending into exile and the very ones the crew can least afford to lose. One wonders what they lost when they colonized the station, and what manner of folk died when it perished."

"Ramirez created Jase," Banichi said thoughtfully. "Created Jase as a man without man'chi, except to the ship. Ramirez created Yolanda. Now Tamun exiles them both. What does this mean to the crew?"

"Nothing good," Bren said. "Nothing good for them at all."

"We could shoot this Tamun-aiji," Algini suggested.

"It's very tempting," Bren said. It was even counted virtuous, among atevi, that leaders, and not the followers, should die in conflicts. "But to satisfy them and to have an agreement later, we have to deal with their law. We have to hope for other means."

Barb is showing improvement. Paul showed up and signed the necessary papers. He had very little to say. I haven't heard from Toby. Do you know where he is? I'm concerned about him and Jill, and I suspect Louise isn't telling me the whole story.

The security people are making a fuss about my being here. Ever since the news said you'd gone up to the station, they haven't let me answer my own phone. I hate this. They have guards on this floor, guards watching Barb's room. It's just crazy.

I phoned Shawn and phoned your office on the mainland and told them to tell Tabini you hadn't been in touch.

Barb is going to have another operation tomorrow. This is the third, but this time they have the bleeding stopped, and this one is to take out some of the tubes and such. She says thank you for the flowers. You could at least send her a hello. It's only polite.

He didn't react with temper. He composed a polite, concerned reply, wrote to Tabini:

We have Jase in our keeping, aiji-ma. An opposing association surrounding the fourth captain has seized enough power to insist on his banishment to the planet but not sufficient power to do him harm. The senior of the four has been the target of an assassination attempt.

To Shawn Tyers he wrote, in Ragi, via his office:

As best I can determine, the head of your operation here has valiantly resisted attempts to divide our interests. She persists through hardship, and we support her as best we can. I have not yet drawn her within our protection because having more than one vantage within the station affords us a certain operational flexibility. I urge you to consult with the mainland for more details.

More than that, he dared not write. There was too much chance of having communication cut off again, if it was in fact going through . . . and he had no proof of that until someone answered him with direct evidence of having read his letters.

"Put me through to Kroger," he asked C1.

"Kroger has given notice she is not receiving messages," C1 answered. *"This is a sleep period."*

"C1, put me through, or I go there."

"Let me consult," C1 answered him, and put him through, all the same.

That was interesting, he thought as Kroger answered.

"Bren Cameron," he identified himself. "We have Jase, we have Mercheson, we have the families, as best we can guess. Jase is moving slowly, but everyone seems in good health. Want to join us for supper?"

Jase roused himself out of bed, sore, upset, and in bad temper. At a certain point, Bren thought, one just let the anger slide off. He didn't blame Jase.

"You're not getting out of here," he said to Jase in Ragi. As Jase stood, in a bathrobe, it was not imminent, but Jase was pushing himself to ignore the pain. "That's exactly what they want you to do, and you're not going to do it."

"It doesn't mean—" Jase began.

He finished it: "You're out of the game, Jase. Figure it out. *Pride* be damned. Throwing yourself away and helping them find the man you don't want them to find isn't sensible. Shut up and sit down."

Jase reached a chair and sat. "A moment, nadi."

He gave Jase that moment, sat down, himself, and let Jase absorb the pain, and the facts of his situation, in peace. That Jase remembered Ragi, and the self-control of the aiji's court, was a wonder in itself, considering the circumstances.

Perhaps indicative of the direction of his thoughts, Jase pushed his hair back, straight back, as he'd worn it until he'd done such a wretched job cutting it.

"You've become part of *this* mission," Bren said.

"Clothes," Jase said.

"We have yours being cleaned and pressed. Even that jacket."

Jase managed a short, pain-clipped mirth. "Narani so wanted to do that."

"Desperately."

"You can borrow mine."

"Can't wear yours."

"Funny, you don't appear to have put on weight. I'd say, in fact, you'd have trouble filling them out at the moment."

"I need *ship* clothes."

"No, Jase, in point of fact, you don't."

"He's out there; he has no help. I have to do something, Bren!"

"Don't count that he has no help," Bren said. It was Rami-

ez they were talking about, in this coded mode of no-proper-
ames. "Conspiracy is spreading through the crew. The shut-
le's due back imminently. I'm going to talk to our fellow
delegates from the island, fifteen days to wait while they
heck out the shuttle . . . we have to get out of here. We
have no more reasonable, rational choice. I can't lose you. Do
ou hear? If everything's lost, there's *you*. That's his legacy."

"I'm not him!"

"No. You're his project, his program, his hands, and his
determination to have his way. *Don't* give up."

There were several moments' more silence while Jase
hought that over, and the court mask came over his face,
despite the pain.

"The aiji's favorites have a way of ending up in charge,"
Bren said, beyond that. "And atevi are coming to this
place. The ship has no choice."

Jase gazed at him, absorbing that thought, that idea,
hat proposition.

"He will have won," Bren said, "if you *don't* do the
hings the captains are prompting you to do. I think the
new senior may have great misgivings about all of this.
There's an ally, if you can convince him."

"I have to think about this," Jase said, and by midday he
was limping about the place, talking intensely to Yolanda in
private, and then to Banichi and Jago, filling them in, Bani-
hi said, on every detail of the tunnels, where they had
been, where they had been discovered, where they had run.

Bren came in on it, and sat and absorbed the information.

"The food has improved," Kroger said, "but they're delivering it. They're being very cooperative; we walk about.
There's no quibble about that. They arrange for us to go as
far as we want. One corridor they wouldn't let us into. They
said that was the end of the pressurized section. It may be."

"You're close to the boundary," Jase said.

The dining hall was at capacity. Banichi and Jago took
to having their meals with the security team and the staff,
with Kate Shugart, who was here for her own turn at
translation.

The Merchesons and the Grahams shared the table; it
wasn't until the after-dinner drink, alone with Ginny Kro-

ger, that serious talk went on, quiet discussion of treaty
and operational matters as if there were not a thing unusual
going on.

"They don't want us to leave," Ginny said. "I have had
that word. They're hopeful not to deal with atevi for a
month or so, and then maybe to have you back, but no,
Mr. Graham, I'm sorry to say. I think you might be in
some danger."

"The aiji will send whatever representative he pleases,"
Bren said in Ragi, with a clear notion it might well be Jase.
Tabini could be contrary as hell when he felt pushed. That
statement was to keep Jase on an even keel. But he smiled
and shrugged. "They'd be fools to lay a hand on him," he
said in Mosphei', all but certain there weren't listeners, but
almost hoping there were. "The aiji can be damned stubborn when someone pushes the right button, and this would
be one. Same with tomorrow. We're receiving cargo, I'm
very sure, and we plan to be there when the shuttle docks.
Tom may well be on it. Want to join us and lay claim to
what's yours?"

Ginny thought that one over. She was anxious about it,
that was sure.

"Can we do that?"

They didn't have Kaplan this evening. They had the old
man for a guide. They hadn't seen Kaplan, Andresson,
Johnson, or any of their former visitors, and Bren didn't
take it for coincidence that these people should all be
unavailable.

"I'm not going to have their security going over our
cargo," Bren said. "And I'm expecting a crate of candy.
And you're hoping for Tom. We have a vested interest."

"I can guide you," Jase said, the very last guide he
wanted.

"You have to stay here, nadi-ji," Bren said in Ragi.
"Those were the conditions."

It didn't make Jase happy, not in the least, but years in
the Ragi court had reshaped some of Jase's headlong rush
at things, redirected that hot temper, once intellect was in
the ascendant.

"As long as Yolanda and I are not along," Jase said, "I
imagine you'll have an easier time of it."

25

"C1," Bren said. "Progress on the shuttle?"

"Approaching dock," C1 reported. *"Nominal."*

He received such advisements, reckoned they had another hour or so of fussing about and fine adjustments before the hatch opened.

There was time for a hot shower before the event, to warm up against the cold.

"If the aiji has sent a reply," he said to his security, "I don't wish to see it disappear during any dispute over baggage. We shall escort Nojana back, and perhaps regain Kandana."

If not, he was certain, Nojana must stay with them until they could arrange an exchange. But that was Banichi's domain.

He took his hot shower, put on warm silk beneath his court finery, earnestly hoping Kandana had thought to bring gloves as well as fruit candies, and prepared as carefully and in the same ceremony as if he had been going to a court reception.

"C1," he said, "please send Kaplan." He always asked for Kaplan, and had not yet gotten him. "We intend to meet Mr. Lund at docking."

"I'll have to consult about that," C1 said.

Bren smiled at the faceless wall panel, having no intention in the world of waiting for C1 to consult and take an hour about delivering them an escort.

He adjusted the lace at his cuffs, last detail. "Jase," he said, "you're in charge."

Jase knew procedures, and having had his own education

in the aiji's court, clearly understood that they would no
voluntarily drag him past station security's noses.

"You be damned careful!" Jase said. "I can't get you ou
of their hands."

"I shall be careful, nadi." His mind was already searching
down the corridors, trying to remember what Banichi had
remembered effortlessly. "If anything should go wrong, stay
in the section."

"Yes," Jase said, that flat, Ragi *yes*. In spite of the others
present, he had slipped back into the mode, and even his
bearing had stiffened. Court precautions. Security con
sciousness, in every breath and attitude. "Just be safe."

"I very much intend to. If our escort does show up, don't
open the door. Talk only via C1. Get Kroger in here."

"Understood," Jase said. It was preparation against ex
treme disaster.

But they had advised C1 exactly what they were doing
so there would be no startlement. There was no question
of them seizing the shuttle. They owned it, and it was going
nowhere without service and refueling. It was simply an
excursion, one with several purposes.

"One thanks the paidhi for his very kind hospitality,"
Nojana said as their small party gathered for the venture.

"My gratitude," Bren said, "for resourcefulness as well.
I count you and your partner welcome guests at any time."

Welcome one, welcome the other of such a partnership.
That was obligatory in an invitation, and he offered not the
formal assurance, but an informal one. Nojana might be
excused without prejudice from any Filing against him in
the Guild he was sure Nojana belonged to; and likewise
Banichi might decline any proceedings against Nojana's
principals: but since the principal in question was very
likely the aiji, such contracts were very unlikely.

It provided a human a warm feeling, at least . . . to
an ateva perhaps a widening of his horizons. Both were
good emotions.

They were not, Bren decided, badly situated. Things *were*
settling out; there *was* a way off the station, or would be.
The Pilots' Guild would settle its internal affairs with or
without Ramirez. How that happened might be Jase's ago
nized concern, but it simply could not be his, and Jase had

become pragmatic enough to know that. Say that Jase himself might become a focus for crew dissent . . . and they would deal with that, but Banichi had persuaded him that getting out of here at the moment was a good idea, and assuring their line of retreat was a good idea.

Getting his hands directly on the aiji's reply was a good idea, even if that reply had nothing of great substance. Not receiving it would be an incident, and he had no desire to leave the station in the midst of an incident, issues unresolved.

"So," he said. "Banichi?"

Banichi opened the door for them, an immediate left turn, now, since they had appropriated everything up to the main corridor.

And they walked briskly on their way toward the lifts. How Banichi had done it once, how Nojana had done it . . . he had no idea, though it might have involved, likewise, walking straight down the middle of the hall, tall and dark and imposing enough to scare hell out of crew.

This time they did meet two walking toward them, crew who stopped dead in their tracks and stared.

"Hello there," Bren said cheerfully, and waved.

"Yes, sir," one said quietly, wide-eyed, as they walked by, and not a word else.

They reached the lift.

Was it a surprise that someone came running down the hall?

His security took a mildly defensive posture, hands near guns, as suddenly, breathlessly, a woman with Kaplan's sort of gear came pelting from a side corridor.

And slowed considerably on the approach, holding hands in sight. "Sir. You aren't supposed to be here."

"Just going down to the dock. Out to the dock. Up to the dock. Whatever you say."

"You can't just walk around, sir!"

"I'm not walking around. Just going to the dock. Want to come along? I've no objection. —This seems to be an escort, or a witness, nadiin-ji. Don't shoot her."

His escort understood a joke, and laughed, to the woman's consternation.

"Pauline Sato," she identified herself. "Tech chief. You can't be taking the lifts, sir."

"That's fine, but I don't see a way to walk down. Are you in contact with C1?"

"Yes, sir."

"Well, you're our escort, then. Just get us down to the docks. Out to the docks."

Sato seemed to hear voices. Doubtless she did hear one.

"Yes, sir," she said, and fell in with them, nervously so. She opened the lift door when they reached it. She kept a nervous eye on the atevi and their weapons as they entered, and eyed them with misgivings between button pushes as she gave the car its instructions.

"We haven't shot anyone since we've been on board," Bren said as the car glided into motion. "The only one who's been shot so far is Captain Ramirez, and we didn't do it."

"I can't talk about that," she said.

"Jase Graham didn't do it," he tossed after. "I rather suspect it was an internal dispute. —But we don't take sides."

"Yes, sir."

"How's the shuttle docking coming?"

She listened to voices which obviously didn't need a repetition of the question. "It's going fine, sir. They are docking right now."

"That's good. Lead on. We're doing just fine. Think of it as a holiday. A sacred custom among us, to welcome guests. We expect Tom Lund back. Who knows? Ginny Kroger may bring her own party."

"You can't be running about the station, sir!"

"I'm sure. But we're *running* the station for you, Ms. Sato, whether or not you've had that information officially. I'm sure it will come damned soon. And we, meaning the atevi, will be repairing your ship and doing other useful things, while Mospheira supplies your food, so I'd suggest it's a very good idea we explore this place and establish routines with the shuttle. Absolutely nothing to worry about. I *assure* you this whole operation will become routine. We're *not* fools."

"Yes, sir. Please take hold. We're going up."

"Take hold, nadiin-ji," he repeated in Ragi. "—Have you seen Kaplan, these last few days?"

"I don't think so, sir. That's Leo Kaplan. I haven't seen him."

They stuck to the floor by virtue of acceleration, but the illusion of gravity began to sink toward the waist, and toward the knees . . . a queasy sort of feeling. Bren drew in a deep breath and found the ambient air colder than it had been, rapidly so. The car went through a sudden set of gyrations, thumps, and bumps.

"You did push the right buttons, didn't you?" he asked Sato in all the jolting about of the car. "If you sent us somewhere you shouldn't, my security would be very upset. They're obliged to shoot anyone who threatens me. You understand that."

"It's the right place," their guide said staunchly, if anxiously. "Sometimes it just does this. And you can't be shooting people."

"I quite agree," he said, finding the acquaintance of his feet with the floor increasingly uncertain. "I notice you have a gun, amid that other—" He wagged fingers, indicating the heavy load of gear. "—equipment. Tell me, do you use it on other crew? Family members, perhaps? Or have you ever used it?"

"Don't threaten us!" Sato exclaimed, her eyes wide with fear, and he laughed.

"Don't worry. Just don't, under any circumstances. You really shouldn't carry that sort of thing about."

"Yes, sir." He'd deeply annoyed Sato. He thought he detected a blush under the stark lighting.

"Don't worry," he said. "We're friends."

"I have my orders."

"Here." He'd tucked a candy or two in his pocket in case Kaplan turned up. He offered it.

"I can't take it, sir."

"Oh, come on, no one's looking. Or are they?"

"I don't want it, sir!"

"That's fine. No obligation." He pocketed the candy. There was a silent interval.

What he took for a position indicator, a dotted line on a panel and a glowing light on the schematic that he took for their destination showed, at least a good guess, that arrival was imminent.

The car slowed. They began to float, and the car repositioned itself, simply turning them as they held on.

"Interesting device," Jago remarked.

The car stopped.

The door opened on the bitter cold of the dock, on a place they had indeed seen before, with the crew members drifting about in orange suits, following a web of handlines.

The hatch that had lately mated with the hatch of *Shai-shan* was right in front of them: the right destination, indeed. A light board said, in letters a Mospheiran could read, *Engaged.*

Shai-shan was almost certainly in dock.

A second lift, just next to theirs, opened a door.

And this one gave up a dozen floating crewmen with rifles, on handlines.

His own security produced guns at the first sight and in a heartbeat, all three were very well anchored and facing the others with no disadvantage.

"No!" Bren said, holding up a hand.

Everything stopped, save a handful of crew drifting on inertia and probably wishing to be less conspicuous targets.

"You'd be fools," Bren said, in Mosphei', to the rifle-bearing crewmen. His breath frosted copiously in the icy air. The chill and the fright together produced a damnable tendency for his voice to shake, and he determined not to let it. "Ms. Sato, kindly inform your listeners that there's absolutely no need to blow our negotiations to hell. This is a quiet visit to our own shuttle, official business, of which we're bound to see a tiresome lot, and a very tiresome lot if you insist on customs raking over our cargoes or armed fools standing over us. You've already begun one war with strangers! For God's sake, do you think you need a second?"

"Mr. Cameron," Sato began, and all of a sudden, bad timing, the air lock flashed a light and opened.

Atevi came drifting out, fairly briskly, disembarked, took a split second to realize guns were deployed, and immediately deployed their own.

"Hold!" Bren shouted, in one language and the other. "Hold still!"

There were twenty, thirty of the atevi, in the black of the Assassins' Guild, all armed, all at a standoff. More were coming out.

And amid all of it, a white-haired ateva floated out: Cenedi, he would swear.

And behind Cenedi, having hooked the line efficiently with her cane, Ilisidi sailed along, in all the fur-trimmed, long-coated winter finery of court tradition. Black furs, red brocade that glittered with gold thread.

"Don't fire!" Bren shouted out, and turned about to face his guide and the ship security personnel. "This is an atevi ruler! This is the aiji dowager, the aiji's *grandmother.* Angle up your damned rifles before you touch off more than you can ever in two lifetimes deal with!"

Rifles wavered, lifted. It was hard to tell with the holders of them in free fall, but there was uncertainty in those ranks.

There was no hesitation at all in Ilisidi. And now Tom Lund had disembarked, with four, five, six other humans to the rear of the atevi.

"Well!" the dowager said, with a wave of her free hand. "Nand' paidhi, and what nonsense is this? *Weapons?* Do we see weapons?"

"A mistake," Bren said. "Sato, she's very annoyed. This is not good. Inform your captains you have the most famous, most revered woman on the planet for a guest. She's not known for patience, and she'll expect to be out of the cold *with* her baggage in an official residence immediately—which we're prepared to oversee, if you'll get cargo unloaded."

"Sir," Sato protested.

"If you want your agreements to hold, this is the woman you have to convince. She's the worst possible enemy; and a damned powerful friend. You stand to lose everything, or win!"

"I'm receiving instructions," Sato said desperately. "This wasn't cleared!"

"The aiji dowager doesn't clear things with her grandson or the legislature, either. Put those damn guns away." ·He couldn't control the humans, but there was one instigation to violence he could command. "*Banichi!* Stand down!"

"*Yes*, nandi." Banichi made a great show of putting weapons away, by no means affecting the thirty-odd other atevi of Ilisidi's guard, but at least minutely reassuring the ship-folk.

Bren went out along the handlines to offer the dowager an extended hand which felt frozen through. Ilisidi took it in hers, floating along with remarkable dignity, and her hand lent his a burning, firelike warmth.

Tom Lund came forward, bravely mingling human targets in among the rest, and called out, with a wave of his arm, "Put the guns away! Put them away now!"

"Aiji-ma," Bren said anxiously. "Cenedi-ji. Be at greater ease. They are anxious house guard, not accustomed to armed guests."

Cenedi gave a signal, the back of his hand, and instantly the dowager's guard lifted weapons up and off target, so abrupt, so disciplined a move it seemed to shake the confidence of the handful of humans who kept their guns on target . . . a lingering threat of some alien-distrusting mind with a nervous trigger finger; but all the armed humans had gear like Sato's, they all were waiting for orders, and those orders seemed to come. Guns likewise lifted, uncertainly, apt to come back on target in a heartbeat.

"One must see the dowager to warmer places," Bren said to Cenedi. "Be cautious, nadi-ji! This is the midst of a dispute, one captain is wounded and in hiding, two scoundrels are in power, hearing every word of human language, and Jase is holding the residency we have made, where things are far more reasonable." He realized objectively he was terrified. The dowager had committed herself to the station for at least the fifteen days it would take to fit the shuttle for the return voyage. It was not just the threat of guns where they were, and Ilisidi and himself and Lund all in reach of bullets; it was far more than that, where the station and the ship were concerned. Real terrestrial authority had arrived, and the bid of Tamun and his ally for power up here in the heavens could run up against a power in their midst that simply would not bend. Species extinction was suddenly completely possible, given the scenario they were offered.

But Sato kept chattering away, a running account of what was going on, her interpretation of events mingled with pleas that no one start shooting, insistence that there was no threat. The humans in the home guard seemed thrown into confusion, and now Cenedi had ordered his guard to come out of the cover certain of them had secured behind structural beams. They came, taking the handlines, moving in surprisingly good order and self-assurance for men and women completely unaccustomed to ungravitied space . . . but their guild left no situation unplanned and devoted their lives to physical preparedness.

And they, foreign as they were, large as they were, numerous as they were, and armed to the teeth, hardly needed leveled weapons to scare the hell out of the human guard. A handful of weapons stayed leveled, and if anyone should fire, bullets might go anywhere, ricochets like swarms of deadly midges.

Sato hovered close, trying to tell him something about cargo.

"Hell with cargo . . . order those guns up!"

"They *are* ordered, sir."

"Have them order it again! They're not complying."

Sato did. A moment later the last guns lifted out of line, and Bren drew a whole breath.

"About the cargo, sir," Sato began.

"Ha!" Ilisidi waved the cane perilously near the lift panel. "Does one *float* up here, or is there sensible ground somewhere?"

"There is ground, aiji-ma. —She wishes to find a place with what she designates a sensible floor. She's very old, Ms. Sato. I can't reckon, myself, how old, but she's revered from one end of the aishidi'tat to the other. She'll have come with considerable baggage. We need more space. The other corridor will do."

"He says she's very important among atevi and very old and she has a lot of baggage, sir," Sato relayed that. "He wants more room." Sato winced, and Bren could hear that noise past her earphones. "I know, sir. But there's thirty,

thirty-six of them, sir, not counting the shuttle crew." Sato winced a second time.

"Tell the esteemed captain the rooms I last took were vacant, which shows there *is* vacant space on this station and the aiji dowager needs it. She has health conditions. If she were to die up here, I couldn't predict the consequences. We have to get her out of this chill, immediately. —Nand' dowager, please come into the car. Banichi, Jago. Come." He gave no orders to Nojana, who had moved somewhere, vanished, in the way the Assassins' Guild was notorious for doing. "Ms. Sato. *Immediately!*"

"Yes, sir." Sato was still talking to the captains, saying, "She really is *old,* sir. She's tiny for one of them and very wrinkled and grayed. Everybody treats her like royalty."

"She *is,*" Bren said. "No question. Ask the Mospheirans. Her security's hair-triggered and extremely dangerous."

"The captain says, sir, be damned to you."

"If I translate that, you may be at war."

"Don't translate that, sir." Sato flinched from a direct question from the dowager, which happened to be, "To whom does she speak?"

"To the captains," Bren said. "Nandi."

"Then tell them they have a damned cold reception hall! And a damned disorderly procedure!"

"I have registered that complaint, aiji-ma." The lift had started moving, and he quickly instructed their fellow passengers, the dowager, and about half her security, in managing the shift of floors.

Ilisidi set her stick against what proposed to be the floor and rode through the change with no evident distress, her eyes snapping and fierce, and her jaw set.

"Well, well," she asked when they weighed something again, "is this the dread transition? Are we now in the station proper? And are we soon to meet these troublesome captains?"

"She wishes a meeting with the captains," Bren said to Sato, and Sato relayed that.

"Tomorrow," Sato relayed back. "At—"

"At oh-one-hundred," Bren supplied.

"Yes, sir."

"Is that a local proverb for cold day in hell?"

"Sir, I don't—don't understand."

"Cold day in hell, Ms. Sato, as in *at no damn time!* This appointment is made, it is firm, and if you want cooperation, you will damned well make that meeting happen!"

"Is there a difficulty, paidhi-ji?" Ilisidi asked as the car went through a set of jolting intersections amongst the tubes, swaying all of them.

"One expresses determination the captains be punctual," Bren said. "Will tomorrow suit?"

"No," Ilisidi said. "The day after. My bones hurt. I wish to rest."

"Yes, aiji-ma." He turned a bland look on Sato. "Relay to them that she will meet with them on the following day."

"However!" Ilisidi said. "I shall see Ramirez-aiji in my quarters immediately."

"She says she will speak to Ramirez tonight."

Sato's eyes went wide, behind the lense she wore. "Captain, she says—" She broke that off. "You can't do that."

"She favors Ramirez. You'd better produce him."

"Sir, —sir, I'm to tell you that that's impossible. He's dead."

"No, he isn't. You produced Jase Graham, after trying to pin Ramirez's death on him, which was a lie. I happen to know he's alive, and he'd damned well better stay that way. Are you talking to Tamun?"

"To Captain Tamun, sir."

"Well, well, tell him that. Tell him whether Ramirez has retired from the post or whatever he's done, he's valuable as a mediator, and his health matters. Put me through to Captain Ogun."

"I can't do that, sir."

"Can't? What does Ogun have to say about it?"

"I mean, sir, I don't have that control. *Phoenix*comm does it."

"Well, then *Phoenix*comm can damned well find all the captains. Let's not play favorites. The aiji dowager wants to talk to the lot of them; she'll do *far* better if there are five captains instead of four. Atevi detest the number four. And two. They find all sorts of offense in it. *Five*, Ms. Sato. And I suggest you relay that quite seriously. —Banichi, nand' Cenedi, we'll be going to our own quarters. I trust you'll be pleased to sit there until we can secure more comfortable arrangements. Because the station is in such bad condition, not all of it is accessible."

"She will wish to sleep, Bren-nadi."

"Ah. *Mattresses!* That's the other point. —Ms. Sato, *mattresses,* in sufficient number. Atevi-sized mattresses, and beds. Or the makings of them. This is a very ingenious crew."

"Sir." Sato looked as if she were living the worst day of her year, and dutifully relayed to someone who seemed to be overhearing quite efficiently, as was. "The captain says this is outrageous and he won't put up with it."

"Who is this strange creature?" Ilisidi demanded, freeing her cane to take a poke at Sato, who looked horrified, and flinched, jammed in as they were, shoulder to shoulder, atevi and humans.

"This is a young woman, aiji-ma."

"A woman, is it? She looks like a television with *limbs!* Is this the fashion here?"

"The aiji remarks on your equipment and says you resemble a television, which she detests. —Aiji-ma, she is a dutiful member of the ship. She is speaking with her aijiin, who instruct her."

"Does she! A very odd arrangement. Are the captains afraid, and send this young girl?"

"She asks if the captains are hiding in fear."

Sato half-relayed that, in modified form, winced at the reply. "The captain says she has no business coming here without arrangements."

"I won't translate that. You'll have days straightening it out, and maybe a lifelong enemy. The atevi didn't arrange this. *Your captains* did, when the captains sent down an agreement. Atevi have *accepted* it, in the dowager's coming here. You'll get your station built; you'll get your ship; or you get the nastiest damned war on this front you can conceive of. *Phoenix* can choose which it would rather have."

There was a lengthy silence while Sato listened to something else from the captains.

She was still listening when the lift arrived at its destination and opened onto a corridor . . . not a deserted corridor, not a corridor with an official welcoming committee, but a corridor crowded with about twenty or so crew in blue coveralls, men and women and a scattering of young folk, all of whom stared at the strangeness that had arrived in their midst.

"Look at the floor!" Bren said, *feeling* the impropriety of the stares, and crew, accustomed to orders, did that, at least for a split second.

It prevented drawn guns.

"Thank you very much," Bren said, and in that unplanned-for, crew-level curiosity, he found brazen opportunity. "The aiji dowager, Ilisidi, grandmother of Tabini-aiji, ruler of nine tenths of the planet. She intends to meet with all the captains, and build you a working station and a second ship! She's as curious about you as you are about her; and if you value the comfort and ease of our future relationship, be polite, don't alarm her security, and *smile*, if you please!"

Ilisidi exited the car to survey this crowd, leaning on her cane, flanked by tall, armed security. She clearly found interest in the unprecedented encounter with curious humans, and diverted her gaze to a young boy who wriggled through the adult ranks to see. For a moment she stared as frankly, as curiously, then stamped the heel of the cane fiercely on the deck, prompting a startled intake of breath from the crowd. The child ducked back in fright.

"Well!" she said. "This is a village, is it not? And *where are* those in authority? Are they hiding?"

"She asks if the captains are hiding," Bren said, and in Ragi: "I think we must move along, nandi. They are all restricted in their society. These people have come without their aijiin ordering it, out of their own curiosity about this new association, but they have no authority except that of all people."

"Ah." Ilisidi drew basic sense out of that shorthand comparison to atevi affairs, instantly grasped the situation, and reached out a hand to touch the arm of a startled young girl, to caress a wide-eyed early-teener face. "Pretty child."

"She thinks you pretty," Bren said, and the girl broke into a nervous, very human giggle, blushing and ducking.

"Not a captain to be had," Lund said. "What's going on, Chindi?"

"Mr. Lund," a man said, from the side, and looked abashed.

"So what do they want?" someone called out. "What are they here for?"

"To build you a station," Bren said, and by now the second lift had arrived, bringing human security and about fifteen more of the dowager's security, uneasy package that *that* car must have been. It spilled out both sorts of passengers, armed, and confused at what they met.

"You all better break it up!" Sato lifted her voice. "We've got to get them to their quarters. You've all got jobs to do! You're to get back to work!"

"What's all the guns?" another asked. "What's all this with guns?"

Lund shouted out, "I've got four industry representatives freezing up on the dock, here to arrange imports, and trade, nothing to do with guns."

"The aiji dowager is here in response to negotiations," Bren said, "and she's establishing atevi presence on this station. You wanted help. You've got it. You can tell that through the crew. You're fifteen hundred people in deep trouble, and you came here wanting food, shelter, and supplies. You're in reach of them, if you can make this lady happy. She's the aiji's grandmother, and her good report will weigh very favorably with the aiji."

"Take her to her quarters!" a woman called out. "Get her whatever she wants!"

"Cheers for the aiji's grandmother!" someone yelled from the back, and the crowd shouted out alarmingly.

"A welcome," Bren said quickly. Clearly now the crowd wanted to make itself the dowager's escort, and Tom's, and for a moment the crowd and Cenedi's guard looked to be heading for difficulty, but Bren threw himself into the midst, physically pushed several too-familiar reaches aside, and waved his hands, clearing a space. "Easy, easy. Her guards are anxious. Back it up, there."

The crowd's enthusiasm was in no wise dampened. They kept to one side of the hall and marshaled themselves into a line. Sato and the human security tried to insinuate themselves between, but they were having little luck at it.

Cenedi's force simply moved in and stood their ground.

Bren ushered the dowager along where Sato tried to lead, the whole confused situation beginning to travel, now, as the lifts gave up still more humans and more atevi and a slightly disheveled few human guards who no longer had their weapons.

Keep it moving, was Bren's most urgent thought, and they walked, accompanied and pursued by crew, the dowager walking along at her own unhurried pace, observing the appalling infelicity of the dingy corridors.

"This is a very poor place," she said. "We can improve this, nadiin. We certainly can. A common vase and field flowers would improve this."

"One does think so, nand' dowager."

"And this!" Ilisidi gave Sato's leg a moderately gentle swat of her cane, startling Sato into a moment of stark fear. "What is this strange creature doing?"

"She is broadcasting to the captains."

"Aha!" Ilisidi stopped. Everyone stopped around her. The perilous crowd thickened, those near the rear bunching up. "And to Ramirez?"

"Ramirez is not likely receiving," Bren said, his heart beginning to pound. There was nothing he could do to restrain the dowager in public, no more than he could prevent an avalanche, and, besides, she was no fool. What she did she meant to do, ignorant as she might be of things never in her ken. "The present captains have attempted to kill Ramirez, aiji-ma. At least Tamun has. Ramirez is alleged to have escaped, but no one knows."

"Do they not know?" She turned, that dreadful cane clearing a hasty circle. She stood, a dowager empress of most of the world in black furs and red-and-black brocade, the hand that held the cane black-gloved, leather glittering with ruby insets, and she swept that cane about as if she owned the hall, the guards, the humans, all of them. "Ramirez, I say! *Ramirez!*"

"Ramirez isn't here!" someone yelled out, and every atevi nerve must have been twitching at that exchange, fingers must be itching to fire at the mere thought of someone addressing the dowager out of turn.

Bren held up a hand. "Ramirez was shot," he said, "but a guest of mine says he's alive and in hiding on this station."

"Mr. Cameron!" Sato protested, but the fear was in him, the adrenaline was running high in him and, as an official of the aiji's court, he did what he had to do. He backed the dowager's demand.

"Ramirez escaped," Bren said above the noise. "He's still in hiding from whoever tried to kill him . . . from whoever's *still* trying to kill him, and I'll swear to you it's not *us*. They tried to pin it on Jase Graham, and then they had to send Jase over to us when it turned out Jase Graham had been helping him hide." He saw the shocked faces, knew what Jase had told him about truths not being admitted in this crew, even among those who knew better. "So where is he? And why did they send Jase to us, if not in hopes he'd be fool enough to steer them straight to Ramirez?"

"Mr. Cameron!" Sato said, and a gun hit the floor from somewhere about her person, spun across the tile—and stopped dead under Jago's foot.

The crowd flinched.

Ilisidi's cane hit the tiles, right beside. "Unacceptable!" she snapped, and no translation would serve.

Jago merely bent, picked up the gun, spun it over butt-first and mutely handed it to Bren.

Bren handed it to a very chagrined Sato, while all the crowd watched. By now, more had gathered.

"Better not do *that* again," Tom Lund said. "You don't know how fast these people could nail you to the wall."

"There aren't to be any unauthorized weapons," Sato declared, but Bren didn't even bother with translation. More and more vividly the old devil obstinacy reared its head and said Go now, downhill, hellbent, and he saw his course.

"We'll set up to receive visitors," he said. "I'm sure one of you hearing me knows exactly where Ramirez is, and the aiji dowager quite reasonably wishes to meet him. The captains are listening to us, at least Tamun is, through Ms. Sato, here, who's a nice young woman. So from them, I'd like to hear the answer myself, where Ramirez is, and in what condition, and why in hell some member of this ship's crew tried to kill a man who's laid down the essential agreements that are going to protect this ship! I know the aiji wants to know! I'd promised it was your business and none of mine, but there's a lie being told to you, and to us, and there've been too many lies. Settle your internal disputes any way you like, but this one's become damned inconvenient. It's time you dealt with the truth. This atevi delegation is here to bring about everything you've expected in coming here this whole long voyage, and we're being badly treated!" It was Jase he spoke for, all Jase's frustrations. "Taylor's Children, Jase Graham and Yolanda Mercheson, have taken refuge with *us,* with strangers, because their own won't deal with them."

"That's not so!" someone shouted out, and suddenly there was a thump, a movement among the security ranks, two and three humans trying to go at one another, by what it seemed, and then five and ten and twenty, but atevi simply hauled the two sides apart.

"They've been lying!" one of the original two yelled, and atevi hands pried guns away from the combatants.

"We should get the dowager to safety," Banichi said, "very soon."

"One is quite willing," Cenedi said. "'Sidi-ma. Come. Come and let us establish a safe area."

"Badly run," was Ilisidi's damning judgment of all she saw. She waved her stick forward, and they walked, Jago marching Sato along, and the crowd tailed after them, with shouting and the constant threat of weapons in that crowd, a family fight, Bren said to himself, a factional spat. Ilisidi having stirred the pot, it boiled.

They took a turn. They passed security doors which the crowd behind prevented from closing, and they moved as briskly as they could persuade Ilisidi to walk, toward their own area. Lund was still with them. There was no question of separating. Everything remained volatile.

Another set of doors. They were in the main corridor, headed for their own, and suddenly, from that side passage, an armed presence entered, Tano, and Algini, and then Jase, and Becky Graham, and the Merchesons . . . they all had come, and had the door open for them.

"Easy," Bren shouted out in Ragi. "Be calm! We have 'Sidi-ji among us, and a crowd of the curious. No one fire!"

Ilisidi would not hurry. It was the longest few seconds in

his life until he reached that refuge and offered that doorway to Ilisidi and Tom and those who had come up with them.

But Ilisidi would not, however, retreat. She turned with no great haste, stood, and regarded the gathered crew with a calm demeanor, until the jostling stopped, and the voices fell silent.

Then she spoke, quietly, deliberately.

"We have welcomed your cousins to the world," she said in Ragi, "and the aiji of the aishidi'tat will welcome this new star into the heavens."

Bren rendered it into Mosphei', in quiet tones, that most basic of his jobs, the one he least often performed.

"We have agreed to accept your technology and to construct things which benefit you. We shall make this station a place for children, and for persons of creative and sensitive hearts. We shall make this new star enjoy harmonious sights, and comforts of living things; we shall build a ship, and defend this place as our own. We take up residency among you and look forward to wonders which we have not seen. We shall build in ways which neither of our peoples now know, and teach you as you teach us. Felicity on this great undertaking, this association in the heavens. Its numbers are three, you, and ourselves, and the Mospheirans. We have done away with the infelicity of two which once plagued us. Three is the number of us, and in that, we have very much to gain."

"The last," he added on his own, "is the most important change, and atevi know it and the Mospheirans understand. That you don't, yet, is *what* we have to give one another. The aiji dowager of the Ragi atevi and the aishidi'tat wishes you well."

"I *still* wish to see Ramirez," Ilisidi muttered irritably, and turned, and walked away inside, leaving her security to shut the doors.

"She asks for Ramirez," he said to the crowd, and stepped backward and followed the dowager himself; so with the rest of them, until Cenedi and Banichi shut the doors.

"Nand' dowager," Jase had said, and bowed; and so the

servants bowed, among the human guests; and Bren leaned
his back against the wall and heaved a breath.

"Jago-ji, did we shut Sato-nadi out?"

"She has electronics," Jago said, "and we did, nadi."

"Good," he said, and drew a second and a third breath.
"We survived. We're here."

"The felicity of these surroundings," Ilisidi said meanwhile, leaning on her cane and slowly surveying the premises, while the servants held their breath, "is without doubt.
Exquisite taste. —I am promised supper, and past time!"

The whole staff jumped. Human occupants stood aside,
while Banichi said solemnly, "Shall we take the corridor
across the hall, Bren-ji?"

"Do that," he said. He could only imagine the situation
he had helped provoke among the crew. The fight Ilisidi's
security had broken up was only the visible manifestation.
It was the dogged factionalism that had haunted *Phoenix*
from the outset, that had damned some to venture outside
without protection, as the robots failed, and others to sit
safe, directing it all.

His heritage. He'd always held apart from what he negotiated, never wholly Mospheiran in sympathy, never atevi
by birth, but this—this reached him, this thoroughgoing,
asinine insistence on the rightness of one's own cause; and
he found himself infected with it—more, suddenly questioning everything he'd just done, everything he'd ever
done. He found himself in a state of cultural recognition,
at great depth, right down to his family's spats and feuds
and his hellbent inclination to take a situation and decide
he was right. God, how could he?

His hands were shaking. He wiped sweat off his face and
confronted Jase, who looked as shocked.

"Did you know the dowager was coming?" It was a question spoiling for a fight, damned mad, and not quite over
the edge yet.

"No, I didn't know! This is her style of dealing; this is
how she's damned well survived a century of goings-on like
this, while the rest of us have heart attacks."

"There's a stack of messages," Jase said. "Almost since
you left."

"I'll damnwell bet there are. Jase, do you know where

Ramirez is? Can you remotely guess, that might be worth going after?"

"Isn't that what they want us to do?"

"I know it is. But knowing *where* he is might be the best thing, right now."

"I know they'd have moved him."

"And *where?*"

"I don't know. I swear I don't."

There was a slight commotion at the end of the corridor, where a handful of lingering humans attempted to protest the annexation of the matching section across the hall, and made no headway against thirty or so armed and determined atevi.

"This is the best we can do," Bren said anxiously. "We can't house *her* in what contents us. We have to establish an exterior guard, if we can't secure that intersection . . . which I presume they have to use."

Jase shook his head. "They can work around. They'll reroute. Take it. This is *not* the fanciest accommodation they could have managed."

"Captains get that, do they?"

"Captains and techs. Bren, we've got a potential problem . . ." Jase gave a nervous laugh, as if he'd only then heard himself. "A rather major problem. If they pull the ship off station . . . it's armed. And they can stand us off."

"No, they can't," Bren said, just as madly, just as irrationally as he'd argued the rest of his case, and he knew it. "They *need* us, remember?"

"Tamun's crazy. He's stark raving crazy."

"Well, thus far, he has company in that affliction, doesn't he? Dresh, Sabin, Ogun? They've all lost their minds."

"I'll still bet on Ogun," Jase said on a breath. "Bren, get to *him.*"

"We're not getting to anyone until after supper. The dowager wants dinner, didn't you hear her? And I've got that stack of messages. I trust some of them came with 'Sidi-ji. At least one of them. I *need* to hear from Tabini . . . I need that most of all."

26

Mattresses were going to be an issue: Bren very much feared so.

He very much feared they weren't the only issue.

"I fear they're rather put out with us," he said to Ilisidi, who awaited supper in what had been his room, the best they had, the warmest, and the most comfortable. Even she, however, had to rely on Jago's mattress, which Jago had gladly contributed, while Sabiso, assigned to the dowager's fearsome demands, had explained the workings of the shower. "I can by no means foretell what may happen to the cargo before we can free it."

"Our cargo," Ilisidi said, seated, hands bare now, both clasped on the head of her cane, "our most valuable *cargo* is still aboard the ship. Another fifty of the Guild, serving Lord Geigi."

He was not seated. He had a sudden impulse to sit down, and had no available chair. "Aiji-ma, are they *in* the shuttle? They'll surely freeze! They may have frozen already."

"Not so readily." Ilisidi waggled fingers atop the head of the cane, as if to say that was quite a negligible risk. "They're prepared. But so we must have rapid resolution of this matter, or there will be far harsher action than these ship-folk will like. I have a message from my rapscallion grandson. He says, *Bren-ji* . . . he did say *Bren-ji*, I distinctly recall it: these modern manners!"

"I am overwhelmed."

"He said, *'To Ramirez we cede rights to come and go at the station, which we regard as within our association, and to anyone Ramirez deems fit, so long as the aishidi'tat, in lesser association and cooperation with the government of*

*Mospheira, holds the earth of atevi and all that come within
its grip.*

'These are our reasonable conditions, as you have stated,
so we state; as you have promised, so we promise; as you
declare, so we declare, to which the hasdrawad and the tashrid set their approval . . .' The usual sort of thing," Ilisidi
concluded with another waggle of her fingers. "So! Paidhi.
Associate of my rascal grandson, that thief, that brigand,
my grandson. What do you propose we do to find
Ramirez?"

"I've asked the crew to find him," he said, "which I
believe certain ones well know how to do. Jase and his
mother have contacts."

"Allow four hours," Ilisidi said.

"Four hours."

Ilisidi reached to her coat, a far lighter one for the anticipated dinner, and drew out a watch, an old-fashioned sort
of elaborate design. The multiple cylinders were of gold,
beyond any doubt, and set with pale stones. "We certainly
have that long to unload before we need do anything unpleasant. My grandson has extraordinary confidence in your
powers of negotiation, Bren-ji, but allow me to say, if these
unpleasant people do not rise to a civilized level of welcome very soon, we are prepared to take what we justly
demand. I have not come on this extraordinary journey to
sit in a windowless room and dine in haste. I am too old
to sit on unreasonable furniture and to see my essential
baggage delayed by bureaucrats with absolutely nothing to
gain but inconvenience. I *detest* pointless obstruction. Do
you not, Bren-ji?"

"I do detest it myself, nand' dowager, but there are numerous innocent parties whose very air and warmth might
be adversely affected. . . ."

Another waggle of the fingers. "If I have cast myself
among utter fools, then let us wait no longer. But I rather
think that the paidhi who has served us so well is not the
only human with powers of reasoning. Use your ingenuity,
paidhi-aiji. In the meanwhile, send me Cenedi, and let us
see how to use the devices and the records and the maps
your security has so elegantly established."

He knew when he was being pushed to the wall. He

knew how and when to push back, and he went to his small parcel of belongings by the door and returned with a small mag storage.

"More than the maps they have made, nand' dowager. These are the charts the *makers* made. Here is every conduit and switch and component of the entire foreign star, if the dowager will accept this modest offering."

Ilisidi's aged lips twitched in restrained mirth. She reached for it with a flourish. "So! Am I ever mistaken?"

"I have yet, nandi, to observe an error of taste *or* judgment," Bren said. "Begging excuse from supper, I shall attempt what I can do."

It became a more sober smile, even a gentle one. "You are excused the supper, nadi. I shall entertain this uncommon set of guests. I cede you your security; mine is adequate for my needs, or nothing is."

" 'Sidi-ji," he said quietly, and bowed, and paused again on a second thought. "Take charge of this machine of mine. Tano and Algini know how to read it, and know the codes. They would be an asset, if they were not mine."

"They would indeed," Ilisidi said. "As any resource of mine is within your reach, paidhi-ji." A wave of the hand. "Go! Go, damn your flattery! Out, *out*, and kindly use your wits, nand' paidhi!"

"Geigi has sent men," he explained the situation to his staff, and to Jase, in close conference in what they now styled the *old* dining room, in Ragi. Cenedi sat in their midst, advisor; and Tano was with them, while Algini refused to leave the monitoring, the parameters of which he knew intimately, where Cenedi's men could not replace him. "There is force to be had, aboard the ship," Bren said. "But it won't be enough, either, to secure the entire station without destruction, not to mention the hazard to the shuttle. On such short notice, I have *not* involved Yolanda or Tom, though I regret it. She doesn't speak well enough to understand this situation, Tom doesn't speak at all, and I won't say what I have to say in Mosphei'. So here it is. We have a handful of hours to act before you, Cenedi-nandi, will act. Is that so?"

"It will not be finesse," Cenedi said with a downward, deprecating glance. "But it will be forceful."

In earlier days, Jase would have flared up, sure no one would consider his view, but at this hour, included in this conference, he had no doubts what he was to represent.

"Within that necessity," Jase said quietly, "if we could reach Ramirez, and have his support with us, then we might convince a number of the crew they are not threatened."

"Yet, forgive me, Jase, you say the crew will not admit a truth when it stares them in the face," Bren said in utter frankness. "And will do anything and suffer anything to preserve the captains. We will threaten Tamun, indisputably, we will threaten Tamun."

"Dresh is an improvement," Jase said somberly. "Save him. To *hell* with Tamun."

"Yet, finesse," Banichi said. "Finesse, nadiin-ji, amid such fragile equipment. We have the access tunnels. We *can* move and we *can* reach the captains, and various other places."

"They may have established surveillance in those accesses," Jase said. "Tamun has reason, and increasing reason. Let *us* go, myself, my mother, Yolanda, all of us that have been involved in this. We may be able to find where Ramirez is. If we could do it quietly, we could bring him here."

"Can we breach communications?" Tano asked, the sensible question.

"Can we avoid C1," Bren rephrased that, "and get to people directly without risking our necks?"

"Everything goes through *Phoenix*comm," Jase said. "We can't."

"Does that gear the guides carry?" Jago asked.

Jase blinked. "That goes differently," he said. "That reaches security on a direct link. We don't want security, nadi-ji. They're most likely to stay by the captains."

"Ogun," Bren said. "Captain Ogun. The new senior. He seems to me not participant with Tamun. He seems to me to have rammed the practicalities of the agreements down Tamun's throat, when without him, Tamun might have abrogated all the agreements."

"Ogun's a puzzle," Jase said. "He's hard to read. *Disciplinarian.*" Jase used a single word in Mosphei', to express what Ragi could not. "The crew does not favor him, for his harsh measures. Ramirez breaks customs for good reasons. Ogun is conservative as any lord of the west."

"Sabin?"

"Ogun's partisan. The two of them have made it difficult for Tamun to have his way completely."

"Do they favor Tamun?"

Jase frowned. "They have supported him. In his objections against Ramirez' ventures, they have supported him. Now they have power and Tamun is under them, and ambitious for power . . . one would wonder how they view him now."

It was a discouraging portrait, one in line with Jase's previous notes on the two. But he had a hope in Ogun, and gave it up only reluctantly. "Have they struck at Ramirez, nadi?" he asked Jase.

"Not directly," Jase said. "I don't think so."

"And might they be looking at Tamun anxiously?"

"Now? Sabin, I don't know."

"And Ogun?"

"Thinks he can manage Tamun."

"But supports the rules. Supports the agreements once made. Sat *beside* Ramirez when we had our negotiating session. At least appeared to be consenting to all we said."

Jase drew in a breath and leaned back, seeming to go into himself for a moment. Then he let out the breath. "I can imagine him doing that," Jase said. "And likewise supporting the agreements."

"So dare I go to him?" Bren asked. "Dare he come *here?*"

"Ogun would dare what suited him," Jase said. "This man is an aiji, in a way Ramirez is not, if he could gain the man'chi of the crew. Humans prefer to *like* their aijiin, nadiin-ji." The word ineluctably drew amusement from Banichi and Jago and Tano—who understood the relationship between salads and human emotions—and bewilderment from Cenedi. "But failing to *like* him, we still know he deserves man'chi, while Tamun . . . Tamun only *desires* man'chi, and promotes fear of aliens, fear of weakness, fear of everything, all to gain his followers."

"We know this man," Cenedi murmured in a low voice. "This machimi we do well understand."

"So do I," Bren said, fervent in hope of a path through their situation. "Machimi indeed. Confront Ogun with Ramirez, with wrongs done *him* by Tamun's spite."

"If you can reach him," Jase said, "on *his* shift. Which ought to be in a few hours."

"We have no leisure to wait," Cenedi said, "nadiin-ji, except as the shuttle crew can maintain excuses to delay. They are to move, either at our order, or reaching a point where they can no longer sustain themselves in the shuttle."

"Is there *any* way to get to him?" Bren asked. "Do you know where he lodges?"

"I don't know if he's taken Ramirez' cabin," Jase said. "He might. He would take it to make the authority clear to the others—but to get there . . ."

"They guard against one another," Bren asked, "to that extent, in a population of fifteen hundred human beings?"

"They didn't," Jase said, "but we didn't shoot each other, either. I don't know what he'll do. I don't know what I thought I knew about these people, and I was born here. But if you wish to reach Ogun, if you think he might do something . . . *I'd* risk it, I, personally, *I'll* make a try at it."

"You find Ramirez. You're more able at that, if you can climb a ladder with those ribs."

"I can do it."

"Not a question of wish. Can you do it, without breaking something? Maybe Yolanda."

"No. She gets disoriented in heights and the tunnels spook her. Better if I go."

"I shall go with him," Tano said. "I can carry you if need be. How far need we climb?"

"Only one level. Maybe a transverse. I know, at least, where to start looking, as I don't think Yolanda does. —I also know where Ogun sleeps and where his office and Ramirez's offices are, but I'm afraid there's no access near there."

Bren shrugged. "An access takes too long. I shall walk, nadiin, down the middle of the corridor. *I* have an appointment."

"With the crew below, tomorrow is too late," Banichi said.

"I *lie*," he said. "I *lie* to the guards and claim a misunderstanding. I see no other course. If we run out of time and Geigi's men break out, we three can deal with that distraction. It will create a few moments of confusion, will it not?"

"The guards will not likely believe you are there by error, nadi-ji."

"They have to ask before acting. Can you deal with them without killing?"

"One will do one's best," Banichi said, and still had a worried look. "*You* will take the gun, nadi."

"I'll take the gun," Bren conceded. He planned not to use it. Carrying it into a meeting after one assassination attempt on the ship was in itself a guarantee of trouble, if someone noticed the fact. At the very least, it would rouse distracting objections and put one token on Ogun's side of the table in any negotiations. It didn't make *him* feel safer.

But conceding that made his security far happier.

The ship-folk had never yet questioned how his security breached doors and walked about as they pleased, and one did rather think the ship-folk had noticed. Probably the ship-folk very well guessed *how* they routinely activated the locks, but found no percentage in doing anything about it.

So they went, brazenly, right down the main corridor, into the more trafficked area. There a handful of curious young women, who seemed ordinary crew, simply stared at them, wide-eyed; and a pair of guards in Kaplan's style of gear, the sight of whom sent Bren's heart rate up a notch, let them pass down the hall and through the intersection with only a close look and a consultation, perhaps, with C1.

Turning their backs on that potential threat was hard. Bren kept thinking of shots coming at them, of a solid wall of guards turning up to cut them off . . . a situation he would have to talk their way out of.

But they kept walking, unchallenged, as if the guards who observed assumed they had orders. They reached the corner, turned, finding a bare corridor. No one followed. Banichi and Jago were listening all the while, Bren was sure, to every slight sound, much of it below his level of sensitivity.

They walked that corridor unmolested.

Jase and Tano meant to dive into an access . . . might

be below their feet at this very moment, for all they could know.

One hall and the next, no one challenged them.

At the third, an ordinary woman stood to the side to let them pass, and said quietly as they did so, "Good luck."

"Thank you," he said, and kept walking, heart beating hard. Good luck? What in hell did the crew want? Or how much did they know?

Or what were they walking into?

"She wished us luck," he said, in the unlikely chance his security hadn't understood that remark.

"Baji-naji," Jago said, the reciprocal atevi expression. The world upside-down, pieces landing as their inherent numbers let them . . . which led to the new and more flexible order, once things had gotten bound up and stressed to the limit.

It didn't guarantee the survival of the pieces.

Another turn.

They took the lift, alone, no one stopping the car. They had time to exchange silent glances, to express with the eyes what was imprudent to express in words: it was the diceiest of situations. They hoped. They didn't know. They couldn't guess the eccentricity of the crew's behavior, except, Bren said to himself, in a population who feared its leaders. In this case, they feared *for* their leaders.

Or maybe it was both.

They exited, reached the region of better-designed corridors, the spongy, sound-deadening flooring, that row of glossy-leaved potted plants.

Even a numbers-blind human recognized the landmarks here: the tendriled green-and-white plant, the large-leafed one.

Turn right at the green-and-white one.

"Third door," he remembered, all on his own, from Jase's description. That was Ramirez's cabin. If Ogun wasn't in it, at least no one else should be, that was how he reckoned it. What could they access with least chance of touching off a general alarm.

He pressed the button to signal the occupant there was a visitor. Banichi and Jago waited just behind him, whether ready to fire he did not count it his business to see.

The door stayed shut.

"No one home," he said with a deep sigh. That had been their best hope: that Ogun might answer, hear his concern for the ship, immediately agree to rescue Ramirez, arrest Tamun, and honor the agreements.

That proved a dead end. He counted doorways from that, two, and moved down to what was Ogun's office: no help there.

Then Ramirez's old office, where Ogun, acting as senior captain, might be trying to find loose bits of business.

No answer there, either.

"I fear Ogun knows we're here," he said. "Or maybe Ogun himself has met misfortune." It was one of those moments of not-quite-logic, one of those moments that had to do with estimating human beings, but it was a rational hypothesis.

Banichi and Jago said not a word, only maintained a wary watch on their surroundings, trusting absolutely nothing.

He *wanted* to take to his heels and put distance between himself and this slowly sealing trap. But they had a shipload of atevi whose choice was to freeze to death, surrender, or come out shooting.

And for good or for ill, they had the dowager on their hands. Baji-naji. There *was* no way to unravel that design. Pieces were going to shift and settle, or break.

"We're down to Ogun's cabin," he said quietly, and moved to that one and buzzed it.

No answer.

"Sabin's our next hope," he said, counting doors. "If they haven't retreated to the ship, which is far less comfortable lodging."

No answer, at either Sabin's office or her cabin. The hour it was now had been Tamun's watch, according to the schedule Jase had given him; but now that ought to have shifted to Dresh, the new man, if nothing else had changed. The higher the captain, the more mainstream the watch that captain took. It was status . . . and he read Tamun as likely to grab it with both hands.

If anyone was alone in the conference room, it would

likely, at this hour, then, be Dresh, who would not be good news.

"Why do they not investigate, nadi?" Jago asked. His security was growing more and more anxious.

"Perhaps because they don't need to investigate," he said. "My guess is, they know we're here. They very likely are armed, they very likely have already gathered security about them." The second risk was the worse, and he spelled it out for nonhuman minds. "They greatly fear losing all skilled pilots and captains at once. They may have separated. One captain may stay and serve as bait for adverse action, or we may simply walk into a trap consisting solely of security."

"Then shall we trip it?" Banichi suggested. "The conference room seems likely."

It was an outrageous action, and yet they were running out of time. They might walk in on an odd-hours meeting of all the captains, for what they knew. Or an ambush.

It was the last door that might possibly lodge someone sympathetic. The very last chance of a peaceful outcome to their effort.

He reached for the button. Jago prevented his hand, drew them both aside from the door opening, and pushed it with a piece of flat plastic.

The door opened. Ogun stood behind the conference table. Four armed security, in eyepieces and backpacks, arrayed two in a corner, held rifles aimed at them. There were likely two apiece in the corners they couldn't see, those nearest them.

But in for a little, in for the whole pot, he said to himself. He walked in, heedless of the display of threat from the man they'd come to see, and he bowed just the same as he would in Tabini's court, with far more lethal, less equipped security . . . bowed as if there were nothing particularly unusual in the leveled rifles. "Captain Ogun," he said calmly. "Just the man I hoped to find. Call them off, if you please. We're not here to cause trouble. I hope you'll be glad to know Ramirez is alive."

Ogun's expression, forbidding by habit, varied not at all at that news. Still, he lifted a hand, waved it, and rifles lifted just slightly out of line.

"Where is he?" Ogun asked.

"I don't know. I know those who know those who may."

Ogun stared at him in glowering silence for a moment. Banichi and Jago had not come in, and remained a potent threat, one Ogun could not ignore.

"Jase is very much his partisan," Ogun said. "Some say he shot Ramirez. I don't happen to believe it. But my priority is the safety of the ship. We all have to be pragmatists. Go back and pretend you didn't come here. If Ramirez is alive, leave him to crew and leave our matters to us. We don't need your help."

"I wish it were still that simple," Bren said, "but now the aiji-dowager has come up. She's old, she's infirm, she has a temper as well as a soft spot, and she's immensely influential. If she doesn't like what she sees, all we've talked about is undone and all to do over. On the other hand, he's agreed to meet with you, personally . . . a considerable concession. I might arrange a personal meeting over drinks, in our section, right now. You'll be perfectly safe and free to leave. And if Ramirez should by some incredible chance decide to show up sometime during this meeting, you might even have a chance to talk to him, and find out what *he* may know. I'll just about bet you *don't* know what happened. And he does."

"No games. Go back to your zone. If Ramirez were here, he'd have simply called in from your section."

"*If* he should attend, I said. You have the power to command security. If we had assurance of his safety, we might arrange for him to be there. If I'm right about your place in all this, you didn't consent to Tamun's move against him, but Tamun can't do away with everyone at once. Yet. The ship and the station are in danger, you are, the whole agreement is. I know it takes a degree of trust to walk back with us and *protect* your chief ally on the Council of Captains. You're wondering if we have the resources to keep you alive so much as an hour, and I'll assure you your guard can be right outside, armed, no problems. Tamun hasn't come at us. He won't, if he's wise. Come with us. Take the chance."

Ogun's expression never altered, not even at those provocations. "I stand with the ship," Ogun said. "Go back to your zone, Mr. Cameron. I'll advise you now the meeting with this woman is likely to be moved back, perhaps in definitely, for her safety, and I'm not about to commit myself to your guard. If she's all that valuable, which I think she may be, I suggest she stay in her station and keep her head down, because your aiji of all the atevi can't do a damned thing up here. You have fifteen days until the shuttle's ready to go down. Safer for you *and* her to be on it. Safer, too, for you not to be in the corridors until then. We have our internal differences. You've come up here without invitation, at an embarrassing time. I understand why you did it. I don't particularly care. What you have to do now is to leave."

"By what I've seen, any moment we arrived would have precipitated this fight. Any moment Ramirez invited us up here would have precipitated it. Any moment there seemed to be a deal would have done it, because Tamun doesn't give a damn whether what we offer is good for the ship, he knows the fact we can deliver power to Ramirez is bad for him, bad for his ideas about getting the Mospheirans back, bad for his ideas of running things to his liking. Your ability to do anything about him is eroding. When we were on our way, people in the corridors wished *us* luck. You sent us Jase Graham, which I take for a bid to protect him from Tamun, and we thank you for that. But you won't walk out into the corridors, take a handful of these fine gentlemen with their supposedly functional rifles, and get the crew's help while they're still able to give it. I know Jase's version of this. He reports you as an honest man, and what I see confirms it. Use the help you've got at hand."

"Take my advice," Ogun said. "Don't tell me how to manage my responsibilities. Take care of your own, and protect your high official before she gets killed. I won't ask you a third time. Leave."

"You'll let Ramirez die. You'll go on trying to finesse this, and Tamun's not playing that game. Ramirez dies, and that's one ally down."

"I'm not his keeper. I have the ship's interests to look out for. Contact me from the planet, when you get there. We'll talk at that safe distance, when I'm not having to protect your lives. Not otherwise."

"Very good," Bren said. "I've made the offer. You've made your choice. We'll go back now."

"I'll send an escort with you. —Frank, walk them back."

There was just a little hesitation, a little worry in the glance the man named Frank exchanged with his captain, but there was no disobedience.

His own estimate of Ogun was dead-on right, Bren thought; these men were worried about Ogun; these men protected their captain as the only force likely to keep a very bad choice out of power, and Ogun meanwhile thought there was some danger to them in walking the corridors, a danger that one man walking with them might abate or shame into good behavior.

And by all he'd seen of the crew's attitude, it wasn't any danger from the crew in general. That meant Tamun. That meant a very good likelihood of Tamun growing much less secretive about his actions.

What was it Jase had said, that the crew would know things and not mention them or do anything about them until there was just absolutely no choice about it?

"Nadiin-ji," he said quietly to Banichi and Jago, who had remained somewhat behind him, just outside the door: and yes, there were four more men at the rear of the room, at either side. "Nadiin-ji, these reliable men have man'chi to Ogun, he relies on them, and he sends one man to protect us walking back. Whatever the threat to us in the halls, Ogun believes this one man can avert it by his presence and the threat of Ogun's displeasure. Ogun-aiji will not join us, apprehends he is himself in danger, but insists his man'chi is only to his ship, so he will not compromise his authority even by visiting us. Our arrival here touched off action against Ramirez. It remains a point of contention."

It was useful to Banichi and Jago to know the situation as fully as possible, predigested for atevi comprehension: he did what he could to make it understood in shorthand, and he gave a second, reflexive bow of respect to a man of pragmatic combativeness and considerable virtue.

One who wasn't prepared, however, to cast his people's fortunes on strangers or turn loose of his power to do something yet on his own terms.

He backed out the door, surer and surer that he had

read Ogun right, and that Ogun was equally sure he was himself the next target on Tamun's list.

The guard who joined them outside also knew the score and had no wish to leave his captain, not for a minute.

"Ogun is in danger," Bren said to that man as they walked down that aisle of potted plants. Then he asked the most critical question: "Do you trust Sabin?"

"Can't say, sir."

"Well, it's damned certain Tamun will lead you to disaster if anything happens to Ogun," Bren said. "Tamun will get you no repairs, no help. He's about to offend the aiji's grandmother, which is a bad mistake. But I don't have to tell you that. You're Ogun's man."

"Can't discuss that, sir."

"Cousin of his?"

"Can't discuss it, sir."

"From what I see, the crew in general isn't happy with this situation, are they? Ramirez was already head-to-head fighting Tamun when we came up here. And rather than let Ramirez win that argument and take what he wanted to take from the aiji in Shejidan, Tamun shot him."

"Can't say that for sure, either, sir."

"So now Tamun's got a small but pretty damned well armed set of helpers, probably cousins, who've all gone just one step too far, and probably are just a little dismayed at what's developed, but they know there isn't a way back to good grace for them now. They can't pin it on Jase Graham, their lie is leaking out faster by the hour, everybody knows exactly what they did, and it's getting hotter and hotter, isn't it?"

There was no more denial, only a silence, and he hoped Banichi and Jago were following this, at least marginally.

"So the only reason Ogun hasn't shot Tamun is because you resourceful fellows can't get to Tamun to blow him full of holes."

"I honestly couldn't say that, sir."

"So what *is* the reason against it?"

They reached the intersection; reached a point where to his immediate attention movement showed in the distance.

Two crew walked the curvature of the hall toward them. And they carried rifles.

"Those are Tamun's cousins," their guide said as they walked. "Keep behind me."

That deserved translation. "Tamun's father's sons, nadiin-ji. Our guide proposes to go first and to watch them carefully." It occurred to him that if all his running hypothesis was correct, he might remove a significant portion of Tamun's support simply by targeting those two men and telling Banichi and Jago to take them down on the spot.

But the fragile relations of crew to crew were strained to the breaking point: fracture had already happened. Worse could yet happen. His flitting mind ran beyond his own arguments to the reasons *why* Ogun remained reluctant to act, why nine tenths of the crew walked in fear of upsetting the balance. Knowledge of how to run the machinery was stretched so, so thin, the Pilots' Guild for centuries had restricted knowledge, not disseminated it. The old policy that had so alienated the colonists had come to this, an aristocracy as absolute as that in the hinterlands of the mainland.

Their guide went just before them, stopped and swung to keep an eye on the two as they passed, and still watched them as Banichi and Jago passed, wary, every line a threat.

"Don't—" their guide began to say, and the next instant Bren felt himself yanked backward into a fall. An explosion and an electric crackle brought a grunt from someone, but Jago had his arm, jerked him toward his feet before he could form a notion what had hit him. She and Banichi both fired, the two attackers went down, but so had their guide gone down, in a corridor otherwise void of cover.

Jago steered him and Banichi scooped up their guide, slung him over his shoulder, as all of a sudden more shots crackled after them, small devices that embedded in the wall and gave off electricity.

Jago let off covering fire and the shooting stopped, more men ducking back around a corner.

Communications was working, all right: it was working far too efficiently in Tamun's favor; and the next ten minutes could see Ogun dead, those men simply breaking through the door to the conference room and mowing down everyone in the room.

"Ogun," Bren said breathlessly, being dragged along.

"This entire quarrel has broken wide open. Ogun's in immediate danger."

"So are you, nadi," Banichi said, heaving his hapless burden over his left shoulder, his sidearm in his other hand. "And you are far more valuable to *us*. Into the next access. Go!"

"I need you! Do you hear? Don't risk yourself, Banichi!"

Jago hauled him violently down the corridor and toward that nearest service access, and time now was everything. Every moment he held these two separated, they were all at greater risk. She opened a refuge, and he went in as rapidly as he could, climbed up, knowing the next level was safer than this one and at least closer to home, and knowing by the continuance of light that the door below was still open.

He trusted everything to the belief they would both follow him more rapidly than he could race this climb, and in truth, in the very moment he thought it, the ladder began to shake with atevi presence. All light went out in one section. A small, intense light stabbed upward in the next second, a hand torch of some sort, and he knew who was on the ladder and who had shut the door as clearly as if he could see them both.

He climbed at breakneck pace, heedless of the pain of cold metal on his hands. He reached the next level, sweating in the icy dark, and feverishly opened that next access door at the risk of frostbite. Light and warmth met him, heat like a wall, air that didn't burn, but that flowed like syrup into the lungs. He couldn't get enough of it.

Jago arrived. He had no idea where he was within the level, had no grasp of the relationship of the cabins: the grids jumbled in his brain, a webwork of intersections and major and minor cross-corridors. He trusted she knew.

Banichi came out, still carrying their guide, shut the door, and without any hesitation, Jago broke into a run ahead and looked down the cross-corridor, then raced farther and opened another access, while at any moment Tamun's men or innocent passersby could come around the corner and they couldn't know which was which.

He ran, with Banichi behind him, ducked into that next access after Jago, as Banichi followed, and they climbed again, then walked a traverse grid, and climbed farther, by Jago's small light. They climbed until his hands were utterly burned and then numb. At the last, telling himself he couldn't fail, he couldn't be the weak and fatal link in the world's plans, he gripped the rail with his elbows, shoved with his legs, and reached a platform, cold air stabbing into his lungs, racking him with coughs. He tottered. It was beyond him to open the next door. Jago both steadied him and opened it, then shoved him through into blinding and ordinary light.

Another coughing fit overtook him, affronting lungs and a cold-stung throat. He heard the door slam shut, a frightening noise. He knew there was every chance of someone hearing it, but for a moment he could scarcely breathe past the coughing. He tried to run, and Jago hauled him a long noisy sprint down a side corridor, around a corner.

Another climb, he thought. He couldn't do it. They'd have to carry him.

Banichi's heavier footsteps overtook them, and his tearing eyes showed him not an access panel, but a door, a section door Jago was attempting to open. He bent over, coughing, and was still coughing when he straightened and realized where he was.

Inside the Mospheiran section.

With Kaplan, of all people, standing in the middle of the hall looking scared, and holding a rifle on them.

Behind Kaplan were Andresson and Polano.

And five others he didn't know.

Kate put her head out of a room. "It's Mr. Cameron," she exclaimed, as if there weren't two very tall and conspicuous atevi holding him on his feet.

Rifles lowered as Bren stood there trying to control the coughing fit and ask what was going on. Banichi let their unfortunate guide to his feet and slowly to the floor. Polano edged forward, cast an anxious glance at Banichi and dropped to his knees, trying to care for the man while the rest maintained an armed, anxious stance.

"It's Frank," Polano said. "He's alive. He's alive. —His rig's shot all to hell."

"Too bad for that part," Andresson said. "We could sure have used that."

Frank, their guide, tried to speak, managed a handful of words, "Ogun" among them, nothing that made sense. Polano wadded up his coat and put it under his head. "Yeah, yeah," Polano said. "Leave Ogun to Ogun. Damn, we need some meds here. His heart's jumping."

The electrical shock. Frank's sleeve was burned through. His face was white.

"Nothing in our kit," Kate said. No one asked the sensible things: why was there shooting? where did you come from? none of those critical questions . . . as they hadn't asked Kate why Kaplan was on armed guard here, looking for atevi.

He only thought about doing that, when suddenly the lights went out.

Jago's small light immediately went on, spotting Frank and Polano. The bounce of luminance off the ceiling picked out the details of Kaplan and the rest in the hall . . . as Ginny Kroger came hurrying out of her cabin, gray hair in less than its accustomed order.

Clearly she hadn't expected to see him, in the middle of the blackout, and with atevi eyes picking up reflected light in a way that inevitably touched off primal human fears.

"Mr. Cameron," Kroger said in a reasonable, if strained, voice. "*We* seem to be in another outage. Do you know anything about this? —Or did you do it?"

"We've just had a little set-to with Tamun's friends," Bren said. "One of Ogun's security is hurt. It's pretty damned certain Ogun knows he's in danger, if he's still alive. What's going on here?"

"Get a blanket." That was Kaplan, no longer threatening with his rifle, showing a sign of peace, a simple outheld hand. "Let us wrap Frank up and get him warm. He's shocked. He isn't doing well. Needs to be as warm as we can manage. Shock takes it out of you. Keep 'im in the light if we can."

"No question," Bren said. "Kaplan, what in hell are you doing here?"

"Best we can," Kaplan said. "Best we can, sir. Wish that rig was in better condition."

"How much trouble are we in?" Ginny Kroger wanted

o know, insistent and on the edge of her nerves. "Where's Tom? Did he come up with the shuttle? Who's out there?"

"Tom Lund *is* here," Bren said. "More, the aiji dowager s here, with thirty of her guard in our quarters and half a undred of her guard and Lord Geigi's stuck on the shuttle, which they have to get out of, before they freeze. They *will* et out of there in their own way in short order, if we don't et clearance for them to leave and join us."

"Shit," Kaplan said. "What *is* this?"

"There's going to be atevi, Kaplan. If you want this sta- ion fixed, you're going to be outnumbered up here. Or was that ever the plan?"

"I'm not saying it wasn't, sir, only . . ." Kaplan gave a nervous glance at Jago, whose eyes probably shone in the reflected light. "It's perfectly fine, sir, except there's a lot ll of a sudden, and we've got problems right now."

"They're not here to take the ship. They *are* here to run he station, which certain people aren't happy about, as t seems."

"So what are they going to do?" Kroger asked. "We can't be firing guns up and down the corridors! This is a fragile environment!"

"I'm aware of that," Bren said. "Believe me, I'm aware of it, and the atevi are just as aware of it. The shuttle crew s with those men. Damned right they know the danger."

"Are we at war?" Kroger asked.

"I don't know. I tried for help from Ogun. We're not getting any help there. Ogun won't come to our section; but at least he's not with Tamun. He's protecting all his alternatives."

"Bren?"

There was a familiar voice in the dark of the blackout, n Kaplan's fears and Kroger's anxiety . . . one sane human voice.

"Jase?" Jase had arrived from somewhere back in the section hallway, drawn and pale in the light, a little the worse for the mission he'd been on, and, God, he was re- lieved to see him.

"We have Ramirez here," Jase said in a slightly shaky voice. "Alive but very weak. Leo was with him, protecting him. Paul Andresson heard Tamun was tracking you, got

to Leo when I'd gotten to them. We tried to send a man
up to warn you."

Leo Kaplan. Kaplan and his band of sugar addicts, com
ing and going with, at last, a comprehensible purpose al
along.

And Kaplan and his men turned out to be welcome news
too. They had firepower here: rifles. At least that.

"Is Tano with you?" he asked Jase next, unthinkingly
in Ragi.

"I am here, nandi," an atevi voice said out of the dark.

"One is extremely glad, Tano-ji." Tano; themselves, a
number of armed crew. Better and better. They were no
hopeless here. And beyond all other assets in this succes
sion war, *they* had Ramirez.

"This isn't at all what I envisioned for this mission," Kro
ger said in a thin-edged voice. "*Bren,* our esteemed friend
what do you propose to do at this point?"

"We have this place, we have our section, we have the
shuttle dock, in effect, or will have, and we have Ramirez
That's not an inconsiderable hand. —Jase. Can Ramirez
get through C1?"

"He might," Jase said. "If one of Tamun's men isn'
sitting the post. But Tamun may well go there, up to the
ship, if he's threatened. That's the trump card of all other
cards, the ship—if he has that . . ."

"He's certainly being threatened," Bren said, and
coughed. The throat was raw, proof what five minutes in
the less friendly environment outside the corridors could
do. "What can he do from the ship?"

"I don't entirely know," Jase said. "I don't know all the
resources. I do know he can shut down communications
He might even hole the station with its weapons, but I
don't think he'd go that far; he wouldn't kill crew . . . not
that many of us, at least."

"That's an extravagantly hopeful statement. He's shot a
brother captain." Bren ran a rapid translation of that reck
oning for their security, the lot of them standing in the
dark, in rapidly increasing cold, in a section in which they
had no independent power, water, air movement, or light
excepting Jago's pocket torch. They had high cards, indeed
but Tamun might have his finger on the button to shut

down the whole table. "Tamun can possibly cut off all our resources—may possibly expose sections to vacuum if he grows desperate and unstable. We dare not wait until he grows that desperate."

"Indeed," Banichi said. "This dark extends all over the station?"

"As best we figure."

"Innocent persons in the dark, armed, and fearful of us. And an unstable man. One never likes to consolidate one-self as a target, and I dislike to put all our resources back into our section, but clearly we have vulnerable points here. I can carry Ramirez. We can move him to an area where we can supply oxygen."

"He may die," Jase protested. "If he does . . ."

"If he does, we still may have Ogun," Bren said, the harsh, blunt truth with a friend with whom he had ex-changed a long series of blunt truths, and received them. "One assumes Ogun, if he has survived, has access to the ship. If not Ogun, then Sabin may have moved. I make a structure of assumptions, but it seems to me Ogun has re-sisted Tamun at every turn and Sabin has stood between."

"Ogun would fight to hold the ship from Tamun," Jase said in Ragi, the *fight* that also meant *as for one's man'chi.* "Crew would join him. But we cannot move Ramirez to our region of control. We have to keep Ramirez in reach of the crew, among his own. It's a question of man'chi."

"A dead leader has no followers," Banichi said. "If he dies, it all falls apart."

"These are humans," Bren said. "If he dies for the crew, then, *then* a man'chi exists, and has to be reckoned with."

"Even if he dies."

"Especially if he dies. Little as I like it, Jase is right."

"One hardly sees how this works in strictly practical terms," Banichi said, "but this is clearly not *our* machimi, nandiin-ji. Lead. Your security takes orders, in this matter. What shall we do?"

Thinking from the outside: seeing objectively what was subjective to others. Perspective had been a tool of the trade for the paidhiin, but Bren had never reached so far outside himself as to try to shed two cultures, his own, and the atevi one, at once, and think in a third.

"Can we get word to Algini, Banichi? Can we at leas advise him we're alive?"

Banichi bit his lip and seemed to think for a moment staring into nothing. "It is done," Banichi said, and as t how, or whether, scarcely making a move, Banichi had sen some signal, Bren asked no questions, thinking of Algin back in their security station, of Cenedi, the dowager, an all that equipment.

"Second question: Jasi-ji, we need Ramirez to order C to broadcast. But the wall units have no power."

"Those suit communications," Jase said, "can get int C1, no question, if we could lay hands on one of thos units that's working. Kaplan has lost access. Everyone wh would support Ramirez has been quietly cut out of th system. The men with Ramirez couldn't get to thei equipment."

"We *have* that one unit," Bren said. "Our guide's. Whicl they think is out of commission. But if we could get it t work, if we could get one pronouncement from Ramirez one order through that system . . ."

Jago unzipped her jacket and took out a small black plas tic box. "A recorder, Bren-ji, may be of service. If h should die, Jase would have a record."

"A recorder."

"But mind, Jasi-ji, we have not secured this area for com munications, not in the grossest regard. We may be moni tored whenever you speak Mosphei'."

"Meanwhile," Tano said, "let me see whether we car repair the communications function in this equipment."

"Let me talk to Leo," Jase said, and Jase pulled Kaplar close, urgently to translate all of that, and immediatel Kaplan and Andresson put their heads together with Jase all for a brief, jargon-laden discussion in the near-dark three men hunkered down to keep the conversation as low as possible.

"This is a discussion of resources," Bren said in Ragi "These few men know this equipment. He dropped dowr to crouch by them, invading the conversation with one sim ple question: "Can you do it? If you can get through t(anyone who can restrain Tamun's communications—"

"We need the captain's order," Kaplan said.

Bren restrained what he thought. "Then I suggest we try to get it," he said. "Urgently. Can we talk to him?"

"I'll talk with him," Jase said. "I'll get the order, if I can. I don't know if he will."

"There's no alternative, Jase. There's just no damned alternative." They were on the verge of losing everything, and ship mentality didn't want to trouble a wounded, perhaps dying officer to get a critical order.

But Jase mentality, that he had lived with these several years, said that if there was a member of the crew that understood there was no luxury of time and second chances, it was Jase, who had the recorder, who knew the right questions; and Kaplan and his friends at least had had the will to hide Ramirez these last dangerous days, play the charade, finally cast their lots for good and all with a captain who wasn't doing all that well . . . they might live rejecting the obvious, but rejecting the obvious gave them a certain blind strength of purpose, if nothing else.

"Jago-ji." He stood up, silently reached for the light to find his way wherever Jase had to go. Jago gave it to him, all the light there was, and as he took it, his section of immediate hallway showed him Kroger and Ben Feldman, grim and worried.

Jase went to what had been Kroger's room at last knowledge, and vanished into the dark of that open door.

Bren followed. Kaplan did. Kaplan went in, followed Jase to the bed and the man lying in it, and the two of them bent down and tenderly gained the captain's attention . . . the captain, whose fingertips, on the coverlet, were darkened with exposure and who otherwise seemed half alive, at least responded to the arrival of light. They had wanted to keep Frank in the light, not to take him off into the absolute dark, even for warmth. It struck him that for a man near death, it would be that much chancier, that much easier to slip right over the edge into dying, in that awful, absolute darkness. It was no condition in which to abandon a man.

He ventured closer, not to intrude a foreign presence, but to bring the light closer, and he heard a voice that, hoarse and faint as it was, gave orders, coherently and in no hesitant terms, into Jago's recorder. And when that flow of words stopped, Jase thumbed the recorder off. The man seemed unconscious. Perhaps even dead.

But the eyes opened slightly, seemed to move in his direction. "Cameron?"

"Yes, sir. It is."

"Damned mess," Ramirez said then, and eyes drifted shut again. "Should have shot him."

"Tamun?"

"Not a bad first choice," Ramirez said. Then: "Jase."

"Yes, sir."

"Closer."

Jase leaned over; and Ramirez's fist had seized Jase's coat, and held it.

"You succeed," Ramirez said, hoarsely, and let Jase go. "You're appointed, fourth seat. Hear me. Hear me, you! — Is that still Kaplan?"

"Yes, sir." Kaplan moved closer.

"You take Graham's orders."

"Yes, sir," Kaplan said faintly. "We're all here. Andresson; Polano, the lot of us. Got to the rifles, couldn't get the rigs. We're armed. There's a bunch of atevi on the station."

God help us, Bren thought. The monitoring.

"Resources," Bren said loudly. Harshly. "About which we won't speak."

Ramirez reached for the side of the bed, tried to put a foot off it, and didn't. "Damn," he said, "damn!"

"Don't get up," Jase said. "Leave it to us, sir. Hear me? *Leave it to us.*"

"Get it done!" Ramirez said, in pain, and Jase pulled away, drawing Kaplan with him toward Bren; and there was no choice but to take the light with them, out to the hall where they gathered to plan their next move.

"What are we going to do?" Kroger caught his arm. "What *can* we do? You're talking about getting a communications panel to work. You want it to reach C1. If they were overhearing us, they already know the captain's here and they don't give a damn . . . you think they're going to listen to orders?"

It was a point. It at least argued they might be free of bugs.

"Then we assume they're not overhearing us," he said, "and we give them a—"

The security door opened, not their doing, a spotlight shone at them.

Bren shoved Jase to the wall and down as Kaplan and Kroger just stood helpless in the light.

Banichi, however, had not ducked, and the light went down, spun like some alien sun about a hall turned chaotic with bursts of electric charge, and Jago moved, and Tano, three shadows of giant size against the light. Bren remembered the gun in his pocket. He snatched it out, stood up and aimed it, heart pounding, but his eyes found no targets, just three atevi, a suddenly lengthened hallway, and a human lying flat in that truncated circle of light, struggling weakly under Banichi's foot.

"Others have escaped," Banichi said. "I advise against pursuit, Bren-ji."

Tamun's supporters might be few, but misinformed crew might number far too many to risk casualties, even in their dire straits; that was his thought about pursuit. But then he saw what the straggler was wearing.

"Is that a security rig? Are they security?"

"One believes this man is," Banichi said. "Watch the corridor," he said to Jago and Tano, and removed his foot from the struggling captive, who scrambled away, but only as far as the wall and an abortive attempt to rise.

Jase and Kaplan together seized on that man and spun him against the wall.

"Bobby," Kaplan said to the man as he struggled to get loose, "Bobby, you hold it, hear! Don't make a fuss. The old man's alive, you hear me? Ramirez is alive. You want to see, or do I beat your head in?"

A wide-eyed stare met the erratic light as Kroger retrieved the intruders' lantern.

"Yeah," the man named Bobby said, "yeah. If that's so, I want to see him."

"We get the rig," Andresson said. "So turn it over. Tamun's gone right out of his head. Shot the old man. Now he's shot Frank for no good reason. We got to get rid of him."

"You say!"

"We all say! These aliens could've diced you for the cycler and didn't, so shut it down and be polite. They're sane. Tamun's crazy. You're alive and the rest are still breathing. Think it through."

The wind seemed to go out of Bobby then, and he let Jase and Kaplan both help him up and haul the rig off him, piece by piece, Kaplan fitting it on as they went.

More light came into the corridor, this time from the chest-lamp of Bobby's equipment as Kaplan turned it on.

"Let Bobby talk to the captain," Jase said, "and then let Bobby go, to tell anybody he wants to. Tamun's *out*. He's damn-all out the air lock when Ramirez gets hold of him."

"What's Ramirez doing with the aliens?"

"Surviving," Jase said. "No thanks to the human sods who won't help him."

"You come with me," Kaplan said, taking Bobby in tow.

"The light is a target," Jago remarked quietly in Mosphei', never taking her eyes from the hall. Her pistol was in her hand. "Dangerous, Gin-nadi."

Ginny Kroger looked disturbed as Banichi took the light from her unresisting hand and killed it.

"A light down the hall," Jago said, once that light was shut down. "Growing brighter."

Bren didn't see one in the direction she was looking, but his eyesight was nothing like hers in dim light. That fitful reflectivity of atevi eyes showed now as Tano glanced his way in the small light Jago held aimed at the floor, and it was more than an ornamental distinction.

"Take cover, nandi," Tano said.

"Someone's coming," Bren said to Kroger and the rest. "They're coming back. Everyone under cover."

The pocket-torch went out immediately. He had the illusion of total blindness, then, but he heard someone coming up near him, from the direction that Bobby and Kaplan had gone, and his ears said two men, at least two, in hallway they controlled.

"I'm with the old man." A stranger's voice somewhat dismayed him. Bobby's, he thought, where he had expected Jase's. "He says go, I go. Let me loose down the hall. I'll spread the word. Don't go shooting at my team."

"Then go," he said. He whispered, more loudly, "Jago,

Tano, Bobby-nadi is coming through. Let him reach his associates."

"There is hazard," Jago said. "Bobby-nadi, speak out to others down the hall. They are attempting stealth."

"You stay put down there!" Bobby yelled out into the dark, and the shout resounded like the trump of doom. "The captain's here, and they got him alive, and Tamun's a bleeding liar! You can talk to 'em, hear?"

There was a silence, a lengthy, anxious silence.

"Prove it's you!"

"Tad," Bobby shouted out, "you remember who broke the water tap and flooded the section! Would I be telling you that if it wasn't me?"

"Bobby?" came a voice out of the dark, from well around the corner. "Bobby? Are you with them?"

"Yeah. And I'm all right, and Leo's here and Frank and his team, and Tamun shot Ramirez with a *bullet*, Tad. Spread *that* on the net. Shot the old man with a *bullet*. You can talk to Leo on the net. He's got my rig on."

"Tad," Kaplan said, into the communications on the body unit. "You hear me? Frank Modan's gotten a bad shock. Blew a hell of a lot of his rig out. There's the lot of us trying to save the captain, but he's in a bad way, shot in the chest. We got a tape, which is him, which I can play for you, if you'll just plug into C1 and pass it on, and keep passing it. You're still live, aren't you? You're hearing me loud and clear."

"They're telling the truth!" Bobby shouted up the corridor by voice. "Tell C1 just the hell *do* it, all right?"

"You got that recorder, sir?" Kaplan asked under his breath.

"I have it," Jase said. "No adapter, just take it in on directional mike."

The small sound of the recorder's play button, the initial whisper of the leader sounded unnaturally loud in the waiting silence.

"Ramirez here." The recorder gave out that thread of a voice. *"Don't believe a thing Pratap Tamun says, don't take his orders for spit. I'm alive now only because Jase got me out. Tamun and his cousins are guilty as sin. Jase Graham to sit fourth. Jase, you get him out, hear?"*

27

"Do you read?" Kaplan asked when the recording played out. "Tad? You hear that loud and clear?"

Kaplan paused a moment, and his expression showed alarm. "There's somebody moving up on them. —*Tad! You get to us, hear! Run!* —Ma'am, mister," this, incongruously, to Banichi and Jago. "They're moving our way, they have to! Don't shoot!"

"I understand, Kaplan-nadi," Jago said, a voice that was calm itself. "Banichi?"

"Cenedi is behind them," Banichi said.

Bren said, very quickly. "Kaplan! They should stop, immediately, and stand still. Our own security is in the corridor. Tell them stand still, offer no threat!"

"You guys stop!" Kaplan said urgently into the mike. "You wait! Stand still, it's atevi security behind you. Don't spook anybody, just don't move. Those guys are hell!"

Then Kaplan acquired a renewed puzzlement. "Yes, ma'am," he said, and: "I'm getting a query from *Phoenix*comm. *Sabin's* up there. *She* heard it."

"What side is *she* on?" Bren asked.

"Shall I ask, sir?"

Incredible, Bren thought, standing in the dark, with security units moving every which way, the dowager left in the dark at dinner, his own security hair-triggered, Ramirez struggling for breath to stay alive, and they had to ask a *Phoenix* captain where she stood on the issues.

"Ask," he said.

"What's the captain want?" Kaplan translated the question, and then relayed the answer. "Sir, C1 says she's looking for Ogun, evidently he's out of touch, and she doesn't want anybody going anywhere."

"He could be dead," Bren said. "Tell C1 what happened to us."

Kaplan began to do that in rapid terms. Meanwhile, light appeared at the intersection, and a handful of men in security rigs walked in their direction.

Then very tall figures bearing lights appeared behind them and came their way, too.

"Tell the captain," Jase said to Kaplan, "I'm acting on Ramirez' orders, fourth seat, by his appointment. Ask her if Tamun's up there with her."

"Yes, sir." Kaplan relayed that. "No, sir," he said when he heard the reply. "Sabin doesn't know where he is, either."

"Tell her I request she find Ogun, don't let Tamun near the buttons, and keep the hatch sealed until we can get word out. Tell C1 to broadcast Ramirez' message. If they didn't copy it, we can play it again. Tell Sabin to get the power on! The captain can't take this."

Kaplan relayed that, too, and said, "Sabin says stand by."

An unexpected siren blast, brief and loud, made the atevi wince; and a second later the lights flared up to noonday brightness and the ventilation fans came on. They had a number of station security uncertainly exposed to view, and Cenedi and half a dozen of his own men were on the far side of the humans.

Ramirez's message suddenly, loudly, recycled through every wall unit.

"Is the captain's message going out?" Banichi asked, to be sure.

"Indeed, Banichi-ji. Advise everyone things are going moderately well."

"Going very well," Banichi said, "since I believe by now Lord Geigi and his men are growing impatient, and will take to the dock."

"Lord Geigi is *here?*" Bren asked in shock. "Himself?" He realized no one had ever told him to the contrary, and he had assumed, since they said Geigi's men, that they were a loan. The roundish, sometimes outrageous lord of the coast . . . indeed, Lord Geigi *would* come out on a wild venture like this, especially in 'Sidi-ji's wake.

The dowager never, ever traveled without resources.

And on the docks . . . Bren thought, with the shuttle exposed to danger, and, my God, the *ship,* that Holy Grail of all human activity. The ship they had seen on approach, not far from the shuttle dock . . .

"The ship, Jase. The access is there, isn't it? Same dock as the shuttle?"

"Adjacent," Jase said. "Same area. If Sabin holds the hatch, they can't get in, but if she thought human lives were threatened . . ."

"We've got to get down there. Up there. We can't have Geigi threatening *Phoenix,* whatever else. The crew will think the worst."

"His objective is the dockside," Banichi said calmly. "And the safety of the shuttle."

"Misunderstanding is all too possible in this situation. Banichi, they mustn't go yet. Get word to them to hold."

"We have no reliable contact with them," Banichi said, "except by *Phoenix* itself, and we should not, Bren-ji, advise them Geigi is there. We cannot betray Lord Geigi. We will cost atevi lives and endanger the aishidi'tat."

"We have to get up there," Bren said. "We have to stop this before it blows up."

Banichi offered no argument to that. "Cenedi. A potential associate holds the ship, Sabin-aiji; Ogun-aiji cannot be found. Ramirez-aiji is here, wounded and weak. Geigi, if he moves, will possibly create confusion of forces up on the dock."

"Three quarters of an hour until Geigi moves, unless these humans move against the shuttle."

"Ten minutes by lift for us to get up there," Jase said. "Nadiin-ji, we must go, we must go *now,* to hold the docks open and prevent misunderstanding." Negotiations were going on among Bobby's group and Kaplan's, in jargon and shorthand, a desperate, profane babble of argument. "Kaplan is in contact with Sabin. Shall we advise her we're coming?"

"Tell her *we're* coming, so she expects atevi." Bren made the critical judgment, a commitment they had to take.

"Don't say a thing about atevi already up there. Don't mention Lord Geigi. —Ginny. You're going to have half a dozen security and a few of the atevi in your section, with Ben and Kate to translate. They'll keep you safe. We're going upstairs to try to defuse this before it blows."

"I don't like this," Kroger said. "I don't like this in the least. Let *me* talk to Sabin."

"Do, if you can get through. Advise her to just keep that hatch shut. We're trying to sort it out."

"*You* will not go, Bren-ji," Jago said. "Make no such plans."

"Someone has to negotiate between the dowager and Sabin," he said. One grew accustomed to gunfire, and lights going on and off, even to the notion of power cut to the whole station. He experienced no fear of those things; but of the random misunderstanding that could kill the whole enterprise and start another war . . . of that he was mortally afraid; and it was in his lap.

The dowager, God help them, and Lord Geigi.

And Sabin.

He attached himself to Banichi and Jago, with Jase tagging after him. "Let us go, nadiin-ji. We have no time to debate this."

"Go," Banichi said; Kaplan also joined them, with all but two of the others in security gear, Tad having surrendered his to Andresson and others to Pressman and Johnson. Cenedi detailed ten men from his own force to remain on guard, communicating with them as they were moving out. Ten minutes just for the lift, Jase had said, and Bren walked fast, broke into a jog to keep up with Banichi's long strides in the lead, and then the rest of the company began to hurry as fast as they could, down to the main corridor, to the lifts.

The buttons of the lift panel proved dead. There were no lights there. Banichi hesitated not the blink of an eye before starting to take the panel apart.

"Sabin's going to clear it," Kaplan said, and Bren put out a hand to prevent further disassembly.

The panel lights flashed on; the door responded tamely to a button-push as the car arrived.

"All of us?" Jago asked.

"Best we arrive with force," Banichi said. "Suggest, nadi, that C1 contact the shuttle crew and advise them that I am attempting to contact them."

It seemed a very good idea. Bren relayed it to Kaplan, who called C1 on his suit-com. Meanwhile they crammed inside the car, wedging as tightly as they could.

The car started to move. Jase was looking up at the indicators when Bren looked his way, and they both stood as very short humans amid a crush of very tall, bullet-proofed atevi. Bren drew in his breath, having time now to be scared out of his mind, time to review the choices that had put them here, and all the hazards of their position. The car seemed to move more slowly than before, or his mind was racing faster. They committed themselves increasingly to Sabin and a set of switches all under her control, vulnerable to freezing cold, absolute dark, and a bad, bad situation for them if someone stalled the car in the system.

That Tamun might have access to those switches was not something he wanted to contemplate.

The car thumped, gathering speed. They were packed so tightly the eventual shifts of attitude did little to dislodge anyone, only that their whole mass increasingly acquired buoyancy.

Please God they got there, Bren thought, thinking of Tamun, and buttons. He watched the flashing lights change on the panel, counting. It was so crowded he couldn't move his arm to draw the gun in his pocket, so crowded he fell into breathing in unison with Jago, whose deep breaths otherwise pressed at wrong times.

Three levels to go.

Two. They had no more gravity.

The car drifted to a stop, everyone floating as the door opened to a cold so intense it gave the illusion of vacuum.

Pellets hit and sparked around them, atevi spilled out of the car left and right, shoving to get clear and sailing off in the lack of gravity. Bren fended for himself, shoved off Tano, who was behind him, and flew free, trying to do what Jago had done and catch the edge of the door to stop herself and reach cover.

He tried. But a hit convulsed his leg with shock and

prevented his grip on the door edge. A coruscation of impacts flared and crackled on the metal surfaces near him.

A human voice, Jase's, shouted, "Ramirez! Ramirez is alive! Tamun's done!"

He tumbled, instinct telling him doubling up would relieve the pain, intellect telling him it was a way to get killed. He tried for a handhold as he drifted by a pipe.

"Bren-ji!" A hand snagged him, pulled him toward safety.

A second electrical shock blew him aside: he tumbled high above the lift exit handlines, grabbed the icy cold surface of a hose with a bare hand and swung to a stop, or at least a change of view.

He saw Jago drifting loose trying to reach him in this illusion of dizzying height. And he saw a human in concealment with a gun, aiming up at her.

He fired without thinking, jolted himself loose from his grip and hit another solid surface hard. He rebounded, flying free from that, and tumbled, trying to get a view of Jago. He couldn't see the man he'd fired at. He couldn't hear anything but the fading echoes of fire.

He caught an elbow about a pipe, this time high above the shuttle exit. He couldn't see Jago, but he saw that hatch open. He saw a number of atevi exiting on the handlines, all armed, all prepared for trouble, all capable of creating it.

"Lord Geigi!" he called out, twice, and on the second shout, a man paused on the line and looked up, or its apparent equivalent.

"Bren-ji!" Jago called him from somewhere distant. He knew he'd made a target of himself, shouting out; he knew his security disapproved.

"He's up there!" he heard Jase shout.

It had become altogether embarrassing. His whole company was looking for him. He pocketed the gun, fearful of losing it, the final shame; and tried to hand his way along the pipe to whatever route down he could find. It was as if he hung in scaffolding three and four stories above the docking area, in a cavernous, cold place crossed with conduits and free-drifting hoses, where the physics of gunfire had sent him . . . predictable for anyone who thought twice. He didn't know whether the shooting was over; he didn't know whether those trying to retrieve him were placing themselves in danger.

He had no communications except shouting, and he had made enough racket. He began using the tail of his coat to insulate his hands from his grip on the pipes, and finally his rattled brain informed him that, yes, physics had gotten him up here and physics could get him down far faster than hand-over-handing down frozen pipes. He screwed up his courage, ignored the perspective and simply shoved off, flying free, down and down until he could tumble toward a low-impact landing.

He had come in reach of Jago's outstretched hand . . . she snagged him by the sleeve and drew him aside to a safe, warm side. Banichi was there, waiting. Cenedi, too. He was thoroughly embarrassed.

"We shall have to give you a Guild license," Banichi said. "It was Tamun you shot."

"Did I shoot him?" He was appalled, utterly dismayed, his personal impartiality in disputes somehow affected. "Is he dead?"

"No," Jago said, to his very odd relief, "but Jasi-ji has *arrested* him. I believe this is the correct word."

They hovered, a small floating knot of what, after the far cold reaches of the girders, seemed friendly warmth. Jase was coming over to them, drifting along a handline, amid many more atevi than there had been.

Conspicuous among them, a very stout ateva in a thick winter seaman's coat sailed along far too fast for safety, free of the handline.

"Lord Geigi," Bren said. He was shivering too badly to effect the needed rescue, but Cenedi interposed a hand and brought the lord of the seacoast to a gentle halt.

"This is *remarkable*, nadiin," Lord Geigi said, his gold eyes shining, and an uncommon flush to his ebon face. "This is quite remarkable. Have we won? And what are we fighting about?"

"One trusts so," Bren began to say, and then saw three of the human workers drifting toward him.

With them came a human also in the garish orange of the dock workers, a man with a dark, completely familiar face, a man who was armed, Bren very much suspected;

but there was no brandishing of threat, no hesitation in approaching them: this was a man who considered the place *his*.

"Captain Ogun," Bren hailed the newcomer, and there was a quiet, tense meeting, Ogun with him.

"Captain Ogun," Jase said. "Captain Ramirez has set me in the fourth seat. His authority. I'm taking third, until he's back on line to say otherwise. Tamun's under guard. Dresh will be, when he comes out."

Ogun never changed expression. "You have the codes?"

"Since I was with the old man in the tunnels. I can key in," Jase said with no friendliness in his voice. *"Trust* me that I can. I'm not proposing to keep the seat. Only to keep it warm."

"Good sense," Ogun said, as if words were gold, and scarce. "Tamun is out. Dresh is out. You have that third seat. You'll have it until the Council meets. Then we'll discuss it."

"I'll step down at that time," Jase said. "Damned fast. I've no desire to sit on Council, let alone hold a chair."

"First qualification for the job," Ogun said. "Is Tamun alive?"

"Alive," Jase said. "He's become a Council problem."

"A *hell* of a council problem," Ogun said, and touched a metal collar beneath the gaudy orange suit. "Sabe. We've caught Tamun. Jase is third man, Ramirez's appointment. And mine. We've got more atevi aboard, another important one, looks to be. They were waiting . . . to see what we'd do, apparently. Yes. We gave them a hell of a show, didn't we? Now we've got to find beds for the lot. Sabe, pull all crew onto the ship. Council is going to meet. We need to patch what's ripped. We need it very badly."

Sabin must have answered him then.

"Done. You're clear," Ogun said, looking out into the vacant recesses of the dock. "Hold where you are. There's no need for you to come out until this is absolutely stable."

Then he diverted that flat stare to Bren. "Well, Mr. Cameron."

"Well, sir. I'm very glad you escaped. I feared you hadn't. They hit us on the way out of your office."

"Frank?"

"Could use a hospital. He's with Dr. Kroger."

Ogun stared at him a moment with a wry, misgiving expression. "Agreements stand. You'll have what resources you need. Turn over all prisoners, all casualties to us. Systems you've damaged, Mr. Cameron, ultimately, you fix."

"Those within our reach," Bren said. "Fortunately not as long a tab as might have been." His hands were beyond feeling. The leg still hurt and had cramped from the shock, his heart still tending to skip and flutter. He wanted nothing so much as to find a place with air, warmth, and the simple, blessed illusion of gravity and things staying put.

But instead of doubling up to indulge the pain, he had to translate the amenities, the meeting of a Lord of the Association, Lord Geigi, who insisted on trading pleasantries with the acting senior captain of the Pilots' Guild . . . very slow, very formal pleasantries, in which, toward the end, his teeth were chattering. Jase was doing no better.

"Tea," Geigi declared at last. "Do we float about up here like fish? I confess I could do with a hot pot of tea, indeed I could, and maybe a dose of something besides. I trust the dowager has established some sort of comfort. Has she not?"

"Beyond any doubt," Cenedi said, while Bren found it enough simply to drift unmoving until Jago drew him back toward the lift, and a far less crowded descent.

Banichi provided his coat, warm from his body, and Jago another, for Jase, who was in worse case, and feeling the strain on bruised ribs. Kaplan and his friends had come down. Geigi rode with them, and Geigi's personal guard had come. Cenedi, however, had stayed above, with Tano, to assure no misunderstandings broke forth.

Tano had suggested they send for Ben Feldman, and Bren thought it a very good idea. Ben would take to the moment he'd waited for all his long education, his one chance to deal with the interface when it meant the most, and Bren reminded himself that he had to talk to Kroger, advise her, get Ramirez to the best care they could find. And Frank. Frank, too. Everyone they could gather up who'd had the worst of this clash of old suspicions and new ambitions. He relayed that to Kaplan, who relayed it all to C1, and presumably to Sabin and Ogun.

Jase was going down for his own coat, and was going up again when he'd rested. Ramirez had saddled him with responsibilities Jase didn't particularly want, but wouldn't shirk. He'd become an acting captain, in Tamun's place, and didn't want that, either, but someone had to do it.

And he had to tell his mother he was still alive, against all likelihood to the contrary.

Tea seemed a very good idea, too, meanwhile, a bed even more so, and Bren hoped for both not far from where the lift let them out. Jase had picked the level and the area as they got in. Their feet met the floor more and more firmly and the very air seemed to grow warmer and warmer . . . perhaps it was illusion, but he felt it finally gave him enough oxygen by the time they reached their destination and exited into the corridors.

But they were not deserted corridors. Crew were gathering up baggage, leaving rooms . . . just that fast, the order had come down to them to vacate the station, to take up residence again on the ship.

To mend things, Ogun had said, to heal what was ripped up by conflict.

Not to stay walled in their metal shell while the whole station was rebuilt, Bren was resolved in his own heart. They should not do that. They would mend the interface, supply Kaplan and his friends with enough fruit-sugars to keep them sleepless, teach the wanderers the value of planets, the ultimate, luxurious and rare beauty of the world.

Meanwhile he just wanted to get through the corridors without getting shot by one of Tamun's resentful cousins. Narani and Bindanda were advised; the dowager was advised. They might arrive with an untidy amount of curiosity at their heels, but the doors would open, their own refuge would swallow them up . . . they'd get that pot of tea, the hot bath, the bed he was sure Bindanda had ready for him.

An old man, an innocuous old man, stood ahead of them, staring a moment at what had arrived in his vicinity and overturned his orderly if extraordinary life. Many of the crew were old. A few were not. More individuals came out of various rooms along the route, setting baggage out to return to cramped quarters on the ship.

Then a farther section opened, giving up a handful of

young people, both male and female, who stood at a distance: curiosity had become a crowd.

"Walk easily, nandiin-ji," Banichi said calmly in Ragi. "Think of a village, in which the inhabitants have come out to inquire of their lords, and to discover whether the danger is yet past."

"They say the old lady's coming," Kaplan said, being tapped into C1 through his earpiece. "They want to see her. The crew's heard about the old lady coming out. They want to see you. They want to see her."

"They wish to see the aiji dowager," Banichi repeated, as if to be sure he had heard that right.

"The gran," Kaplan said. "The lady."

And indeed, from the intersection, from their own section, in fact, a small party had opened the doors: a party of atevi, black-clad and glittering with silver of their Guild, had set out toward them, a smallish ateva in the center of it all, walking with her cane.

"That's her, isn't it?" Andresson said. "That's the old woman with them."

"They intend no disrespect," Jase said quickly. "It's like saying, *the aiji.* The old woman. The grandmother. Tabini sending *her* . . . that's the ultimate negotiator. The old women don't get into anything until it's over."

It was what Jase had always told him. Women were the peacemakers, the ones immune from quarrels, the ones who didn't fight.

They'd never in their lives met Tabini's grandmother.

But somehow he thought 'Sidi-ji would take a very smug delight in the respects of humans.

Among atevi, too, it was the aijiin who came out to gather up the pieces, the survivors, and paste an association back together by their mere presence. When they were there, the fighting had stopped.

It wasn't necessary they speak the same language, when the results were acceptable on both sides.

28

I *had a message from Tabini,* his mother had written him, amid a surreal stack of messages, some of which advertised skiing vacations on Mt. Thomas and investments in real estate.

> *He's quite worried about you. I assured him you were fine.*
> *Barb is awake and asking about you. I told her you were on the space station and she told me not to make jokes like that, but then I told her it isn't a joke, unfortunately.*
> *The guards are everywhere. They won't let me in the lounge to watch television so I get no news at all, but they did drive me home, which is the first sleep I've gotten with all that's going on, and I cleaned your room. I found one of your cufflinks. I think it's probably an expensive one. I'll keep it for you.*
> *I still haven't had a call from Toby but I did get a card from the kids, which, would you believe, your security people had to give to me? They're going through my mail. I don't know but what Toby's called and they won't let him talk to me. I think it's completely unnecessary. What do they think? That my sons are the problem?*
> *Barb says you should hurry and get back. Paul hasn't even come to see her. She's talking about a divorce, finally, which I think is a good idea and long overdue.*

It was the first of three letters, all similar. The dam had broken. C1 had sent him all the backed-up mail.

He had numerous communications from various committee members and members of the hasdrawad and the tashrid awaiting his attention . . . one official letter, too, from the Mospheiran State Deparment, saying in essence that various personal matters were secured. That was a relief. There was no reasonable threat aimed at his family.

And there was a message from Toby, that said, shortly and simply,

> *From somewhere off the coast. Curious to think you're floating over our heads while we're floating down here. We lie on the deck and watch the clouds and we remind ourselves the world is pretty special.*
> *So are you, brother. We both think so.*

Gratifying. A relief to know they were safe. A little bit of jealousy to know they were enjoying themselves. He could see them. In this place of machine-fabricated corridors, he could see that blue sky and feel the pitch of the waves under him.

He and his mission weren't coming home when the shuttle came down again. Neither, to his slight dismay, was the dowager, who had, in fact, invited up the Astronomer Emeritus, who expected to see stars and nebulae for his pains.

That viewing had to be arranged.

The whole damned court was clamoring to have a view of the heavens . . . and of their station, while Mospheira was completely wound up in the released archive, and suing one another over broadcast rights.

He let Bindanda slip his coat onto his arms, shrugged it into place and shut down the computer before he fussed with the lace. He missed that cufflink, half of his favorite set, that didn't muss the pressed lace getting it in.

Formal tea with the dowager, with the paidhiin collectively, *and* their families, which necessarily involved an acting captain.

He had extreme reservations about this event, but hoped for the best.

C.J. CHERRYH

Classic Series in New Omnibus Editions!

☐ THE DREAMING TREE

Journey to a transitional time in the world, as the dawn of mortal man brings about the downfall of elven magic. But there remains one final place untouched by human hands—the small forest of Ealdwood, in which dwells Arafel the Sidhe. *Contains the complete duology* The Dreamstone *and* The Tree of Swords and Jewels.

0-888677-782-8 $6.99

☐ THE FADED SUN TRILOGY

They were the mri—tall, secretive mercenary soldiers of almost unimaginable ability. But now, in the aftermath of war, the mri face extinction. It will be up to three individuals to retrace their galaxy-wide path back through the millennia to reclaim the ancient world that gave them life . . . *Contains the complete novels* Kesrith, Shon'jir, *and* Kutath.

0-88677-836-0 $6.99

☐ THE MORGAINE SAGA

Scattered through the galaxy are the time/space Gates of a vanished alien race. They must be found and destroyed in order to preserve the integrity of the universe. This is the task of the mysterious traveler Morgaine . . . but will she have the power to follow her quest to its conclusion—to the Ultimate Gate or the end of time itself? *Contains the complete* Gate of Ivrel, Well of Shiuan, *and* Fires of Azeroth.

0-88677-877-8 $6.99

Prices slightly higher in Canada   **DAW: 121**

Payable in U.S. funds only. No cash/COD accepted. Postage & handling: U.S./CAN. $2.75 for one book, $1.00 for each additional, not to exceed $6.75; Int'l $5.00 for one book, $1.00 each additional. We accept Visa, Amex, MC ($10.00 min.), checks ($15.00 fee for returned checks) and money orders. Call 800-788-6262 or 201-933-9292, fax 201-896-8569; refer to ad #121.

Penguin Putnam Inc.	**Bill my:** ☐Visa ☐MasterCard ☐Amex_____(expires)
P.O. Box 12289, Dept. B	Card#_____
Newark, NJ 07101-5289	

Please allow 4-6 weeks for delivery.   Signature_____
Foreign and Canadian delivery 6-8 weeks.

Bill to:

Name_____

Address_____City_____

State/ZIP_____

Daytime Phone #_____

Ship to:

Name_____	Book Total	$_____
Address_____	Applicable Sales Tax	$_____
City_____	Postage & Handling	$_____
State/Zip_____	Total Amount Due	$_____

This offer subject to change without notice.

JULIE E. CZERNEDA

"One of the fastest-rising stars of the new millennium"—Robert J. Sawyer

The Trade Pact Universe
☐ **A THOUSAND WORDS FOR STRANGER (Book #1)**
0-88677-769-0—$5.99

☐ **TIES OF POWER (Book #2)**   0-88677-850-6—$6.99
Sira, the most powerful member of the alien Clan, has dared to challenge the will of her people—by allying herself with a human. But they are determined to reclaim her genetic heritage . . . at any cost!

Alos available:
☐ **BEHOLDER'S EYE**   0-88677-818-2—$5.99
They are the last survivors of their shapeshifting race, in mortal danger of extinction, for the Enemy who has long searched for them may finally discover their location. . . .

Jane S. Fancher

The Dance of the Rings

RING OF DESTINY
(Book Three)

Three telepathically linked brothers, heirs to the Rhomandi dynasty, must unite their powers to face a crisis that could destroy them all. With the Ring cities at war, can these brothers regain the power which is their birthright? The magic behind the rings which power their cities of their world may be their only hope—in an epic struggle of love and war, intrigue and magic . . .

☐ 0-88677-870-0—$6.99

and don't miss:

☐ **RING OF LIGHTNING (Book One)** 0-88677-653-8—$6.99
☐ **RING OF INTRIGUE (Book Two)** 0-88677-719-4—$6.99

TANYA HUFF
VALOR'S CHOICE

"Readers who enjoy military SF will love Tanya Huff's
VALOR'S CHOICE. Howlingly funny and very
suspenseful. I enjoyed every word."
—*scifi.com*

Staff Sergeant Torin Kerr was a battle-hardened professional.
So when she and those in her platoon who'd survived the last
deadly encounter with the Others were yanked from a well-
deserved leave for what was supposed to be "easy" duty as
the honor guard for a diplomatic mission to the non-Confedera-
tion world of the Silsviss, she was ready for anything. Sure,
there'd been rumors of the Others being spotted in this sector
of space. But there were always rumors. Everything seemed
to be going perfectly. Maybe too perfectly. . . .

0-88677-896-4 $6.99

OTHERLAND

TAD WILLIAMS

In many ways it is humankind's most stunning achievement. This most exclusive of places is also one of the world's best kept secrets, created and controlled by The Grail Brotherhood, a private cartel made up of the world's most powerful and ruthless individuals. Surrounded by secrecy, it is home to the wildest of dreams and darkest of nightmares. Incredible amounts of money have been lavished on it. The best minds of two generations have labored to build it. And somehow, bit by bit, it is claming the Earth's most valuable resource— its children.

☐ **VOLUME ONE: CITY OF GOLDEN SHADOW**   UE2763—$7.99
☐ **VOLUME TWO: RIVER OF BLUE FIRE**   UE2777—$7.50
☐ **VOLUME THREE: MOUNTAIN OF BLACK GLASS**

UE2849—$24.95